D1203886

BLOOD DEBTS

A NATE TEMPLE SUPERNATURAL THRILLER BOOK 2

SHAYNE SILVERS

ARGENTO PUBLISHING, LLC

Shayne Silvers

Blood Debts

A Nate Temple Supernatural Thriller Book 2

ISBN: 978-0-9980854-2-5

© 2015, Shayne Silvers / Argento Publishing, LLC

info@shaynesilvers.com

～

For updates on new releases, promotions, and updates, please sign up for my mailing list by clicking the '*Get My Free Book!*' Button at *www.shaynesilvers.com*.

CHAPTER 1

*T*he gnarled oak desk quivered as a subsonic blast shook the entire room. I flinched involuntarily, my drink tinkling lightly between my long fingertips as the lights flickered. I blinked eyelids that suddenly seemed to weigh a ton. *What the hell was that?* Had I been asleep? I couldn't seem to remember the last few moments. Perhaps I had been drinking more than I thought. Indie must have already abandoned me for bed by now, because she wasn't here beside me. And where was Dean? Or Mallory, for that matter? Surely, they had heard the sound. *Felt* the sound. The hair on my arms was sticking straight up in response to my sudden adrenaline spike.

Then I heard the scream. Like someone was being skinned alive.

I bolted from the leather chair in my father's old office – now *my* office – at Chateau Falco. Another distant blast shook the foundation of the house as I darted out the door and onto the landing that overlooked the first floor. Before I could move any further, a fiery comet came screaming through the second-floor stained glass window, barely missing my skull before it crashed through the banister beside me and blazed on into an adjacent room. The furniture inside instantly caught fire with a hungry *whoomp*. Dust and debris filled the air as I looked up in time to see the remnants of the window crash down to the marble floor, shattering into a billion pieces that looked like a detonation of Fruity Pebbles. The cloying stench of smoke instantly filled my ancestral home as it began to burn.

Fast.

More screams and shouts raged through the night amidst a barrage of gunfire and explosions as I crouched, trying to ascertain from where the sounds originated. After all, it was a huge fucking house. Seventeen thousand square feet was a lot of space to search. The single scream I had first heard didn't give me any time to check on Indie, Dean, or Mallory. Someone was dying, right now, his or her screams full of tortured anguish. My home was under assault, by what sounded to be the combined efforts of the Four Horsemen of the Apocalypse.

Unforgivable.

I briefly entertained what I would do to the prick that dared attack my ancestral home. Then I was running, formulating plans and discarding them just as fast, drawing the magical energy that constantly filled the air around me into a protective cloak. The energy that most people didn't believe existed.

But I was a wizard. Special. A *Freak*, as some called us.

I could *see* magical energy. Feel it. Taste it. Hold it.

And *use* it…

To dish out all sorts of hell when I felt so inclined.

And *oh*, did I feel so inclined right about now.

As I raced past empty room after empty room, aged paintings seemed to grimace in distaste at my lack of protection… as if I was the ultimate embodiment of failure for a once-powerful family. I grunted, shrugging off the pain of those looks. It was just my imagination. They weren't really disappointed in me. They weren't even *real*. After all, I had instantly reacted to the attack, right? *Or were you dozing through obvious signs of intrusion, awoken only by the sound of their victory in kidnapping one of your friends…*

My Freudian Id is not a pleasant person. I ignored the smug son of a bitch.

I heard the scream again, and determined that it was coming from outside… along with the incessant gunfire. What the hell was going on out there? I sprinted down more hallways, zigzagging back and forth in an effort to get outside faster. Who was screaming? The voice was either in so much pain or so much rage that I couldn't even determine if it was male or female, let alone human.

2

I finally reached the front entryway, grabbed the massive handle to the front door, and heaved hard enough to tear it from the frame as a surge of magic fueled my strength. I tossed it into the foyer behind me and launched myself into a scene straight from Hell. The icy wind struck my face like a finely woven blanket of cold steel, sobering me instantly.

I practically shit myself with my eyes wide open.

The night was chaos incarnate.

Dragons the size of utility vans stormed the skies, blasting fireballs at my home from every direction. The ancestral home of the Temples was on fire, and the centuries old construction wasn't faring well. The porte-cochere above me leaned drunkenly, one of the supports abruptly cracking in half. I immediately dove to safety before the roof collapsed, nearly dying before I even had time to fully comprehend the situation. I rolled onto the balls of my feet, scanning the darkness amidst the dust, explosions, shout-ing, and dying. The fountain in the center of the drive was now a pile of useless rubble, and bodies decorated the once elegantly-stained concrete. But now it was stained an altogether different color.

The color of fresh blood.

A dozen of my security guards lay in smoking... *pieces* throughout the manicured lawn – bodies still steaming, per my magically-enhanced vision. Energy quested hungrily through the air, the waves of power coursing like gossamer threads of colored smoke. Power was *everywhere...* I grinned darkly. I could use that to my advantage. I saw a dragon or two also littering the lawn, betraying the fact that my security hadn't been caught entirely off-guard, even if their Master had been dozing in his office over a glass of whisky. I shook the guilt from my head. Despite the truth of it, I didn't have the time to feel sorrow. My guards knew the risks in defending my home.

Right? Had *I* even expected an attack of this magnitude?

I shivered as the guilt of their deaths threatened to overpower me. I shoved it down harder. Later. Instead, I sprinted towards a small pocket of humans battling each other near the old horse stable – that my family had upgraded to a car garage – a hundred feet away. I didn't know friend from foe, but I was heartened to discover that at least *some* of my men had survived. Reality seemed to abruptly shift, my vision rippling for a second like I had seen a mirage in the desert. I shook my head, frantically searching for the attacker who was messing with my perception.

But there was no one nearby, and the group of humans was too busy fighting each other to bother with little old me. No dragons either. I was temporarily alone, so who was messing with me?

After a few tense seconds, I took off towards the fighting again, dodging a small, jeweled box lying discarded in the grass. Thievery? A horde of dragons seemed like overkill for a robbery. I growled to myself. I would figure out the *reason* for the attack later. Now was time for *action*. I instinctively made a choice, and launched a crested wave of ice at the most unsavory looking group of men. Some collapsed under the onslaught while others remained upright – now frozen solid – but all as dead as a doornail. The survivors rounded on me with a triumphant hiss.

Shit. Wrong group.

They launched themselves at me with a unified roar of bloodlust, casting battle magic at my face like I had just slapped their grandmother at a holiday dinner party.

Dragons *and* Wizards?

I managed to dodge the majority of the numerous elemental attacks, feeling only a single blast of fire sear my forearm, but I ignored that pain. I shattered a stray arm at the elbow as I came within physical reach, too close for all but the most skilled wizard to use his birthright. It was my only chance against so many foes. I quickly realized I needed backup. A smile tugged at my weathered cheeks.

I bellowed out a single name into the darkness, never ceasing the lethal swings of my arms as they both physically and magically pounded my enemies. A deafening peal of thunder shook the heavens, followed immediately by a crackling bolt of black lightning, which spliced an unlucky dragon neatly in half, causing reptilian blood to rain down upon me. In its wake, a lamenting neighing sound filled the air with a very noticeable physical vibration.

Grimm – a seemingly Demonic black-and-red-feathered unicorn the size of a Clydesdale – entered the fray. The single pearlescent, gnarled, and thorned horn protruding from his skull instantly gored one of my attackers through the heart. I might have hesitated for a second as I saw the unicorn catch a quick swipe of blood with a hungry tongue. I might have also shuddered with unease.

Might.

But despite Grimm's insatiable penchant for violence, I was glad the Minotaur had introduced me to him. He had helped me battle dragons once before… to their detriment. I hoped we would do it again tonight. Flaming, orange eyes met mine in a brief, appreciative greeting before we both refocused on our enemies. I called out familiar whips of fire and ice, utilizing them like Indiana Jones on crystal meth to eliminate the crowd of wizards attacking me. I spun in circles of crackling volcanic and arctic fury, lashing a leg here and a face there, feeding off their dying screams as I lost myself in the mayhem.

A ribbon dance of death.

What could have been an hour later, I realized that all of them were dead. Grimm was staring at me with wide, concerned eyes. I was covered in gore, blood, and ash. And I realized that I was grinning maniacally.

Before I could prove to the unicorn that I hadn't lost my mind, a familiar cry split the night. *"NATE!"* The agonized scream grabbed and shattered my mind into a million tormented fragments.

My breathing came in ragged grunts as I slowly turned, recognizing the voice.

The dragons had Indie. My girlfriend. The love of my life.

My Kryptonite. My Achilles Heel.

I spotted her standing atop the garage, a giant golden dragon gripping her in his talons.

Alaric Slate, the leader of the dragon nation.

My mind went fuzzy for a moment, my vision again rippling like a desert mirage. But… *wasn't he dead?* No. He *couldn't* be dead. He was right in front of me. Holding the woman of my dreams in his razor-sharp claws. A swarm of dragons I hadn't noticed until now unfurled just above our heads, simultaneously striking Grimm from behind. The mythical creature was obliterated in a millisecond, shredded into organic matter like he had fallen into a pool of piranhas. I screamed with vengeful fury at the death of such a magnificent beast – my friend – and cast my power at the earth around me in a fifty-foot radius. The dirt and rock exploded skyward, dropping the dragons into a ten-foot deep hole. A second later, I slammed the earth back over them like a heavy quilt, burying them alive. Tucking the monsters in for bedtime.

Permanently.

An amused chuckle filled the night air. I could hear Indie struggling, but I knew it was futile. I slowly turned to face Alaric, my vision throbbing with rage. He stood like an angry god – half shifted into his dragon form – a single golden talon pressing into Indie's soft skin like a hot knife resting on a plate of butter. "Hand me the box, Temple," he growled greedily.

I... blinked.

Because I had absolutely no clue what he was talking about. If I did, I would have given it to him. Hell, I would have given him *anything* to save Indie. Even my own life.

Indie screamed. "Don't do it, Nate!"

He silenced her by shoving his talon straight through her gut, causing her to grunt in utter shock, and then agony. I realized that I was suddenly closer, having instinctively raced towards him with murderous intent. He held up a claw in warning and I froze with one foot still in the air. His other talon was still embedded inside my girlfriend's stomach. I was stunned, in shock, unable to think straight, but I slowly lowered my foot to the cold earth. How had it escalated so quickly? He'd barely warned me. I glanced down at my feet, trying to control my rapid breathing while frantically assessing the situation for a way – *any* way – to save Indie's life. Her wound was fatal, not superficial. Alaric was a hunter. He knew my plight. He knew my skills. He had effectively commanded my obedience. He knew I would do anything to save Indie. Give up anything.

"Please!" I begged. "Take whatever you want, just release her!"

He nodded. "Of course. The box. Bring it here. Now. She doesn't have long without medical attention." Several new dragons were suddenly pumping their vast wings above me, hovering hungrily, as an added threat. I followed his gaze and glanced to my side, only to see the same box from earlier sitting in the bloody, frosted grass. *Wait... that can't be right. I saw that near the fountain...*

In a confused daze, I reached down, my fingers numb, discarding the stray thought.

"Easy, Temple. No surprises. Bring it here." I hesitated, not with any rebellious intent, but with simple confusion about how the box could have appeared beside me when I had seen it a dozen feet away only minutes ago. Alaric shook his head with a sad smile, abruptly twisting his talon inside Indie with a violent, final jerk.

"Nate..." she whispered between tortured gasps.

My senses instantly shut down. I was suddenly numb with disbelief and impotent fury. My body began to quiver, rattling the forgotten jeweled box that I still held in my now numb hands. The lid began to pry loose from the box. I looked down curiously. *Yes, do it. Do it now...* a strange voice cooed in my ear. I listened to it, not even caring about its origin, and began to open the box, knowing that Indie was already dead. A part of me was now dead, too. Only ashes remained of my heart. The world could burn, and thank me for it.

I no longer cared.

"No!" Alaric's voice boomed as he tore his claw entirely through the love of my life, effectively slicing her in half. I felt the mass of dragons dive for me as one cohesive unit, a pack of claw and fang. As if in slow motion, I realized that my death would be a painful one, and I also realized that I was fresh out of fucks to give. I deserved it. I had inadvertently allowed this to happen. Allowed them to kill the woman I loved.

So, I opened the box.

A wail of despair from the very pits of Hell filled the night before my vision turned an amber-tinted urine color, tunneling out to a single point. Indie.

The dragons' claws tore into me, trying to prevent me from opening the box. But they were too late. The world ended in a climactic symphony of pain and sound as I embraced death.

I *became* death.

Then, nothingness.

CHAPTER 2

I jolted awake, shattering a glass of liquor that was clutched tightly in my fist.

The other patrons of the bar sprang back from their stools with a shout. The man beside me was the only one to remain in his seat, casually raising a drink to his lips. I was panting heavily – as if I had just finished a marathon. Adrenaline coursed through my veins, my eyes darting back and forth, trying to make sense of my change in surroundings, desperately searching for Indie and the dragons. But I wasn't at Chateau Falco.

I was in a seedy bar.

What the hell?

Then it hit me. It had been another of the night terrors – now turned day terrors – that had plagued me since the aftermath of the dragon invasion a few months ago. They were happening more often, now. Escalating in their brutality. But I was getting used to them.

Kind of…

I began my usual mental process of rationally stating the facts in order to calm my racing heart. *The dragons are no longer a threat. Indie is safe. I'm not at Chateau Falco…* After a few repetitions and deep breaths, I began to calm down, and reality slowly began to emerge from the depths of my fractured mind. I glanced at my watch and scowled. *I'm in a seedy bar waiting for some-*

one. The man who called me with information on my parents' murder. I had dozed off. Again. By sluggish increments, my breathing returned to normal.

I had lost track of the numerous variations of my terrors, but the mysterious box was always center-stage, and the vision only ended when I opened it. But while in the dream, I knew nothing of the box on first sighting. It was always a random prop, like any other piece of furniture. But some time later, I would realize I needed to open it to escape the dream, the monster, the demon, the pain, the torture – whatever flavor of torment my dream chose that night. So, I would open it…

Then, nothing but pain.

I waved at the bartender who was watching me skeptically – likely wondering if it was past time he asked me to leave since I had obviously fallen asleep while drinking, even breaking one of his glasses in the process of waking. "I'll sport a round for the bar. Sorry, guys," I apologized. "Long couple of days." The bartender eyed me warily, no doubt wondering what would happen if he told me to leave. After all, I was the infamous *wizard* and local billionaire, Master Nate Temple – the *Archangel* – as some had taken to calling me. But I preferred the self-appointed moniker, the Notorious N.A.T.

Biggie Smalls had nothing on me.

"I'm fine. Really. Let me make it up to everyone. And get me another one while you're at it," I muttered, plucking a few pieces of glass out of my now bleeding palm. I squeezed a napkin in my fist to staunch the blood flow. After a few moments, the bartender finally conceded. Several of the other patrons shook their heads and decided to drink elsewhere. I couldn't blame them. The calm man next to me still hadn't moved.

The bartender placed a new glass of cheap, gasoline-spiked whisky onto the warped, sticky, wooden counter. I scanned the room with a frown – of both anger and disgust. It had been many years since I had been in a *Kill* – a bar where violence was commonplace, even encouraged, and the hygiene equally dangerous – and was eager to pay my tab and get the hell out. But only *after* I got the supposed information about my parents' murder from the cryptic caller who had asked me to meet him here. If not for that fucking caller being late, I could have been home already.

I sighed. No use. I was already here. Might as well wait a bit longer. My notoriety was apparent, judging from the hateful glares cast my way from various men filling the bar. Which might say something about me. After all,

9

a Kill was where only the most nefarious of supernaturals – or Freaks, as we were discreetly named – hung out. My reputation had really jumped after the Solar Eclipse Expo a few months back, when a harem of were-dragons had decided St. Louis was the ideal place to host a ritual spell that would ignite the rebirth of the ultimate god of all dragons, as well as being a convenient locale to announce to the world that magic was, in fact, very real.

I hadn't agreed.

And they hadn't survived.

Now, even the locals were apparently terrified of me. And when I say *locals*, I'm referring to the *magical* locals. *My* people. Where I arrived, death and destruction was now expected to follow. That dragon event was what led me here tonight to *Achilles Heel* – the deadliest bar in town – waiting to meet a stranger who might know something about my parents.

I swiveled a bit on the squeaky wooden stool, scouting the seedy bar in a way that I hoped seemed nonchalant, doing my best to look inconspicuously lethal...

And my clumsy, bleeding fist knocked the drink plum out of the hand that belonged to the older gentleman sitting beside me. Some of the liquor splashed onto my open wound, causing me to hiss in pain. I instinctively called on my gift, filling myself with magic in order to defend myself from the octogenarian, doing my best to ignore my stinging palm.

Sure, he might *look* like a frail old man, but you never knew in a Kill. Plus, he hadn't freaked the fuck out when I had my conniption a few minutes ago. He had steel nerves. Which usually resulted from having a severe case of badass-itis.

The man smiled amiably at me, waving me off with a forgiving motion of his hand. "It happens. No worries." His eyes twinkled like arctic ice, seeming to glow. The silence stretched as I waited for him to make his move. His smile grew wider. "You can release your power now. It was just a drink." I let loose the breath I hadn't known I'd been holding, and then, slowly, my magic.

This was when he would attack. I knew it. *Wait for it...* I was ready for anything. I would never let my epitaph say: *The dragon slayer that was slain by a nursing home patient.*

He shook his head as if amused at a child's antics, and turned back to the bar, for all intents and purposes, seeming to dismiss my lack of trust. I finally swiveled back in my stool, still tense as a spring. *What the hell? Courtesy?* Ever so slowly, I began to relax. "Huh. Paint my lips and call me Suzie. You meant it."

The man turned his mercurial gaze my way, and I briefly noticed purple flecks in his icy blue eyes. "Why would I call you Suzie? You're Nathin Laurent Temple, of course. Kind of a big deal." He seemed amused at that. "And why would I say something and act otherwise? Is this a riddle? Or one of those New Age ideas that don't seem to make a lick of sense? Are you a… Hipster?"

The word sounded unfamiliar on his lips, but I could see that he was proud to have used it, as if it was one less thing pulling him from the grave, a last clutch at his youth. But as I appraised him, I began to wonder if he was really as old as I had originally thought. He had a youthful… vibrancy to him. I managed to stammer a response. "No, never mind. I thought… you know… this *is* a *Kill*," I finally grumbled, as if he were the one being strange. He shrugged and promptly ignored me as he studied the bottles of liquor behind the bar, apparently deciding on his next drink.

Which was extremely odd. See, my reaction was an important stance in a place like this. I compared a Kill to an African watering hole – where you went to do your business, grab a drink of water, and then efficiently retreat to your hidey hole – all the while watching your back for any threats. The place wasn't full – big surprise, with it being cold as balls outside and a weeknight to boot – but enough patrons lingered here and there to justify the sultry guitarist idly strumming cover band music in the corner. Because it was vitally important to keep this crowd entertained.

For they were primarily Freaks, as the *Regular* folk called them, or supernaturals.

Even though my new glass was a few inches from my hand, a distinct chime overrode the guitarist in the corner, as if I had tapped my glass with a fork. "Get him a replacement, please," I mumbled to the bartender, and then reached out to down my drink. "Me, too. But not this swill. Get me a decent whisky." The grizzled barkeep grunted, and I received a new glass of Johnnie Walker.

I lightly sipped the new drink in an effort to fuel my lidded eyes from drooping further. *Mustn't fall asleep again.* I visibly shook myself, noticing a pair of men down the bar whispering to themselves and pointedly glancing at me. I shrugged to myself. "I have enough friends," I muttered under my breath. I wasn't in the market for new ones.

The older gentleman rapped idly on the gnarled wooden counter with a bony hand as he spoke out of the side of his mouth for my ears only. "You can never have enough friends. *Never*. Also, this doesn't seem like an ideal place for sleeping." No one else had heard him. I was sure of it. "I'll take a *Death in the Afternoon*, Barkeep," he requested in a louder voice to the bartender, who seemed to be respectfully waiting for the man's order. *Absinthe and champagne*, I mused, immediately interested, and a little alarmed at what quality of champagne they might have behind the bar. If any at all.

"Nice choice," I mumbled, suddenly aware that this might be my contact. The man had been here before I arrived. Had he been quietly assessing me before deciding to follow through with passing on his information? I was suddenly glad I hadn't stormed out.

The man glanced over at me, his unique frosty blue eyes twinkling in amusement. He was gaunt, skeletal even, but wiry with a resilient strength underneath, and he sported long, straw-colored blonde hair in a man-bun. He was dressed sharply; formal even, and seemed to fairly reek of money, looking like Don Draper from *Mad Men*. I concluded that he definitely wasn't as old as I had originally thought. Just frail. He plucked a cigarette from an ornate silver case, casting me a curious brow as if asking my permission. "Coffin nail?" He offered me one. With a Herculean effort, I managed to decline, waving him to go ahead. He lit up, speaking softly between pulls. "I became infatuated with the drink many years ago. It's the color, I think. Silly reason, but there it is."

I nodded distractedly, trying to catch a whiff of the second-hand smoke. I had recently quit, but still craved a drag. "It's an inspiring drink." I dredged through my exhausted eidetic memory. *"Anything capable of arousing passion in its favor will surely raise as much passion against it."*

The man grunted in recognition. "Hemingway was a great man, even though bull-fighting is slightly antiquated." He appraised me with a side-ways glance. "Shouldn't you be attending some high society function or ritzy ball rather than entertaining a barfly in a Kill?" he asked with a refined degree of politeness, as if only making idle conversation.

"The public has always expected me to be a playboy, and a decent chap never lets his public down." I winked, trying to flummox him with a different quote.

"Not many have read Errol Flynn. Learn that at one of your fancy dinner parties?" he drawled, unimpressed.

I leaned back, momentarily surprised at his literary knowledge. I finally nodded. "Sociability is just a big smile, and a big smile is nothing but teeth. I didn't feel like entertaining the crowd again tonight." I decided, for simplicity's sake, to refer to this stranger as *Hemingway*, after his drink of choice.

Before I could ask if he was my contact, I felt a forceful finger jab my shoulder, sending a jolt of power all the way down to my toes. Hemingway chuckled in amusement at the stranger looming behind me. I lifted my gaze to the bartender and realized he was not moving.

At all. Not even to blink. Then I realized that *no one* else in the bar was moving. No one but Hemingway, the stranger, and myself. In the blink of an eye, my sense of alarm reached a crescendo.

The sizzle of power still tingled in my feet from the stranger's touch. This person was juiced up to a level I hadn't seen in a while. And he had apparently gone to the trouble of stopping the flow of time in order to speak with the notorious N.A.T.

Knowing my luck, the night was about to get... *interesting*. And I had allowed myself to become distracted by Hemingway.

Who apparently *wasn't* my contact.

CHAPTER 3

I lazily swiveled on my creaky stool to face the man. Time seemed to move slowly to me as well, whether a result of the stranger's power or my sleep deprivation, I wasn't sure. Delicious tobacco smoke drifted through the air in lazy tendrils, now motionless. Every surface of the room was wooden, splinter-laden, and filthy – coated with decades of blood, smoke, and various assortments of dried booze – an arsonist's wet dream. When fistfights and worse were frequent, why spend the money to spruce things up? Especially when the owner was Achilles, the legendary Greek Myrmidon, and sacker of Troy. No one dared challenge his aesthetic vision. Or lack thereof. Unless they liked having pointy things shoved through their jugular.

The man before me stood out as if the Queen of England had entered the Kill. He was dressed too nicely. And when I say *nicely*, I mean nicely as in formal wear a few hundred years or more out of date. He had a pompous air about him, as if about to check his shoes for filth. He sniffed idly, as if smelling something that personally offended him. He scowled at Hemingway's polite grin with equally polite disdain before returning his fiery eyes to mine. His long, black hair was pulled back into wavy order like a Prince. "This is a courtesy call. I apologize for my tardiness, but your methods of travel are unreliable." His gaze assessed me as I pondered his odd statement.

"Stop digging into the murder. Nothing good can come of it. Accept that fact like the rest of them have."

My rage spiked at his tone alone, not even taking the time to get angry at his message. "Them?" I asked in a snarl, surprised that this person was my contact.

"Yes. The humans. Do try to keep up," he answered, sounding annoyed.

I didn't dare risk asking him what he was, in an effort to not appear ignorant, but I noticed a faint glow around the man, something that would be visible only to wizards. Odd, because he was definitely not a wizard. I just didn't know exactly *what* he was. He was wearing a bulky 1980's era trench coat that clashed with the practically archaic dress clothes underneath, and he was much taller than me. He sported a clean-shaven, baby face, and moved with the grace of an underwear model. My wizard senses picked up the smell of frost and burning gravel. Which was an odd combination... I had never seen anyone quite like him. And the fact that he didn't know how to dress to fit in with the modern-day humans was unnerving. It meant he didn't belong here. On Earth. No doubt a smart person to avoid.

But the cheap liquor and his unexpected warning had me wanting to vent off some steam.

"Am I to understand that you arranged a meeting with me – to which you arrived abhorrently late – in order to tell me to stop meeting people with information about my parents' murder?" He nodded. "Our phone call would have sufficed. Otherwise, I might be inclined to think that you were *deliberately* wasting my time. And very few people would consider doing that to me." The man shrugged, unperturbed. "What if I keep digging?" I pressed, idly assessing my surroundings for collateral damage, shivering as I remembered that everyone was frozen and unable to escape. That changed things. Hemingway took a sip of his drink, watching the exchange with undisguised interest. Why was *he* not immobilized like everyone else?

My contact assessed me up and down, not with overt disrespect, but merely as if wondering what form of creature sat before him. "This is a Heavenly affair, not your... jurisdiction. But it's your funeral." Hemingway immediately burst out laughing. I frowned at him. Was he drunk? My appointment was obviously powerful, and Hemingway looked as if a strong wind would blow him away like a kite. Something the man had said drew me back away from the frozen patrons of the bar. The man had casually said *Heavenly*. Was he being literal?

"This is none of your concern," the man hissed at Hemingway, causing my drinking partner's grin to stretch even wider, revealing dazzlingly white teeth.

Him threatening my brand-new drinking buddy pissed me right the fuck off for some reason. "Are you," I began, giving the stranger a mocking head-to-toe appraisal, "threatening me?" The man... blinked, as if seeing a kitten suddenly sprout horns. It fueled my anger even more. I mean, I wasn't the scariest kid on the block, but I was formidable.

Wasn't I?

"I don't need to threaten a man hunting for death." The stranger shared his glare with Hemingway and gave a faint grunt. "Just a polite warning." He began to turn away, his business obviously concluded.

But I wasn't finished. Not at all. He needed a lesson in manners. Since Hemingway seemed content to merely watch, and the other patrons of the bar were immobilized, that left me as the tutor.

I pulled the ever-present energy that filled the room deep into my soul in a cocoon of raw power. Enough that my vision began to twinkle with black flecks, and then I let loose a wallop of pure power straight into the stranger's stomach, before he had finished turning away. It punched him about as hard as a Mack Truck, and he went sailing out the front door, taking half of the frame with him. I grunted, nodding in satisfaction. Hemingway's eyes shot wide open in stunned disbelief.

And then alarm.

I was instantly surrounded by shiny, pointy things, all resting at my throat. I hadn't even seen anyone move. Wasn't everyone in the bar frozen? I swallowed. Carefully. Apparently, I had misread the situation.

I very cautiously glanced at one of my assailants, my gaze cool despite the uneasiness squirming in my belly. "I don't take kindly to pointless meetings, pointy things at my throat, or threats."

"Don't speak, mortal, or I will carve out your jugular," the pompous ass threatened.

I shrugged slowly, trying to appear unconcerned as I studied the gang of swords. They were professional. Not a single wrist quivered, and eyes of cold, merciless justice met mine. And they each wielded Crusade Era swords. The creature I had sucker-punched strode back into the bar a minute later, shaking off dust and debris from his trench coat, his face a thunderhead. For the amount of force I had dished out, he looked perfectly... unaffected. "Did you need some fresh air?" I sneered.

He halted before me, and his gang slowly lowered their weapons. "Do you have any inkling of what you just did, and who you did it to?"

"Man, if I had a nickel for every time I heard that line," I muttered.

"Don't be coy, wizard. You just struck an Agent of Heaven. I have every right to carve out your eyes."

"But then that would make me the holey one, and I was under the impression that was your shtick."

The man scowled at me with disgust, not amused by my blasphemy. I could take any number of insults, but *disgust*? That was just... confusing. Who had the balls to feel disgust for wizards? I mean, we were some pretty heavy hitters in the supernatural community.

He stared me dead in the eyes as I somehow managed to formulate a parting threat in retaliation to his disgusted look. "Words have consequences. You should be careful how you speak to one such as me."

He met my gaze, shaking his head with arrogant disdain. "One such as you..." he repeated with amusement, as if at a child. My anger was only growing stronger at the lack of respect he was showing my kind. He didn't acknowledge my threat, but sniffed the air curiously. "You stink like Demons. This whole town does." He leaned closer, taking in a big whiff of all the glory that is my aroma. "But you practically *reek* of it," he added. His mob of thugs inched closer as if to protect him, despite the fact that I had just laid him out with my best punch, and he had merely shrugged it off.

I blinked at the change of topic, uncomfortable with a strange man smelling me so deliberately. "Do dragons count as Demons?" I asked, feeling the weight of the new bracelet against my forearm. The bracelet that held the late Dragon Lord's teeth.

The stranger cocked his head. "It's not your trophy. It's *you*. Have you been consorting with Demons in your search for the murderer?" he accused, somehow seeming to gain a few inches of both height and width. His thugs grew tense, swords slowly rising again, ready to stab on command.

"No," I answered honestly, too surprised to take offense. "Listen, you probably shouldn't hulk out here. Achilles wouldn't like it. He's territorial like that." My mouth just wouldn't stay closed. Chalk it up to sleep deprivation, or whatever floats your boat.

He grunted, slowly returning back to his normal size. "It would behoove you to wash the smell away, lest it offend your betters. We believe that your parents' murder was directly caused by Demons, which you stink of. We have people on the case, but these people..." he said with a proud smile, holding out a hand to his gang of backup dancers, "are the kind to stab and exorcise first, saving questions for later. We wouldn't want any damage of the... *collateral* nature now, would we?"

"Okay. If you want me out of it, that's fine. But I demand progress reports."

The man blinked. "Only *One* commands us, and you are not *H*—"

"Daily," I continued, as if he hadn't spoken. "Yes. Daily progress reports should suffice."

The man actually let out a stutter of disbelief, followed by a momentous silence. I managed to control the urge to fidget. Barely. Then he finally spoke. "I would be cautious if I were you, mortal. Everyone has limits. Everyone should know their place in the world."

"Hmm. I'll take that as a *No* on the progress reports then. If that's the case, I won't be able to drop my investigation." I leaned forward. "I need answers to this. There's more at stake than my own grief. Although that's reason enough." I leaned back into the bar, reaching out for my drink. I took a sip as I considered my next words. *Why not poke the bear a bit more?* the insane Id of mine whispered. I – very stupidly – listened. "I'm sure you know what it's like to lose a father figure without explanation." I had time to smile before I was suddenly slammed up against the bar. Although the man hadn't moved, he was fairly tingling with blue power, and his shoulders were quivering as if threatening to bust out of his trench coat. Was he sporting a pair of wings under there?

Hemingway sputtered out his drink, but the hulk of a man dropped me immediately, holding up his hands, placating... to Hemingway.

Huh.

"Peace!" the man commanded. Still, his tone was nothing but threatening. "Be careful to whom you blaspheme. My Brothers are not so tolerant. And my sons have no compunctions against violence in *His* name. That is their purpose, after all." His smile was ice. "You've been warned. Consider yourself lucky."

I let out a nervous breath. "And you've been given your answer as to my next move, pigeon." I was playing a wild card, assuming by his words that he was an Angel, but the drinks had me feeling irrationally courageous. And I was pissed that he had slammed me into the bar without even a reaction on my part. A heavy hitter, for sure. I'd need to be on my A game if I wanted to tussle against him and his brothers. I was sure that Angels couldn't simply *off* someone. Which was why he had immediately backed off when Hemingway reacted. Hemingway knew what he was, and knew that he had crossed a line. Apparently, there were rules. There were always rules. There had to be rules…

I hoped there were rules…

"Out of respect for what you are going through, I will let this minor annoyance slide, with a warning. If you ever strike a Knight of Heaven again, you won't even have time to apologize. We will smite you out of existence. If our nephews and nieces – the Nephilim, here – don't find you first. They have less scrutiny about their daily duties than we Angels." With that, he turned on a proud heel, nodded to his gang of warriors, and they all left the bar. His shoulders fluttered anxiously underneath his coat, as if alive. Then he was gone, ducking slightly through the broken door.

I sat down, breathing heavily.

I had sucker-punched an Angel, and I was still kicking.

I noticed that a man down the bar was appraising me thoughtfully. Somehow, he also hadn't been affected by the Angel's manipulation of time. He didn't look impressed at my bravery.

Or maybe stupidity.

Time jolted, and everyone in the bar seemed suddenly surprised at his or her abrupt locomotion, as if wondering whether or not anything odd had happened or if they had simply drunk too much. Even the Freaks hadn't sensed the Angel's ability to stop time. I heard the bartender begin shouting about the broken door. His eyes quickly flicked towards me but I was still at the bar, obviously nowhere near the damage. His brow furrowed in thought, no doubt wondering how I had done it. Hemingway finally belted out, "Balls! You've got a titanic pair of balls. Or you have a death wish," he exclaimed between bouts of laughter.

"Shut up and drink, Hemingway."

Hemingway smiled at my nickname, lifted his glass in salute, and downed his drink, shaking his head as he continued to mutter to himself.

What had I gotten myself into?

CHAPTER 4

I continued to stare at the broken doorway with a frown of
concentration, noticing that the chill air from outside was
sucking out a good portion of the bar's heat. Thanks to me. People began
putting on their coats, but remained inside.

I was too tired to connect the dots. I needed to clear my head. I stood
and strolled outside, hoping to catch a glimpse of the Angel again. I checked
up and down the street but saw no sign of him or his thugs. Just the typical
Mardi Gras revelers.

I scratched my jaw thoughtfully.

Apparently, someone sent from *upstairs* wanted me to stay out of my
parents' murder investigation. I just wanted justice. Nothing more. But
someone was watching me. Did that mean I was close to the answer? Why
were freaking Angels investigating their murder? And to top it all off, I
reeked of Demons? But… *why*?

I had no idea. Shivering, I stormed back inside, ready to pay my tab and
leave.

Sauntering over to the bar, the TV caught my attention. Someone had
turned up the volume. As the words reached my ears, I groaned inwardly.
Hemingway seemed to be listening with rapt attention. It was the now
familiar news rehash about me from the last few months.

"Master Temple is still refusing to comment, so the world is full of speculation.

*As everyone is aware, a few months ago, our beloved benefactor, Nate Temple –
recently nicknamed the* Archangel *– and heir of Temple Industries after his
parents' murder, was allegedly involved as a person-of-interest in a murder spree
the likes of which St. Louis has never seen before. At this time, he is not considered a
suspect."* Her tone said otherwise. *"Alaric Slate – Master Temple's business
partner in a so-called coalition of* supernaturals *– is apparently missing, so no
interviews with him are expected."* The news reporter then went on to declare
that the high-speed car chase over the Eads Bridge involving a *Demon* was
no doubt a monstrous hoax. A woman *had* been found at the bottom of the
river, but it was determined that she was most likely just an innocent crash
victim. They had yet to determine her identity. I scowled. She hadn't been
an innocent bystander. She had been a silver-scaled dragon intent on muti-
lating me. My best friend – werewolf, and now *ex*-FBI agent – Gunnar
Randulf had barely helped me out of that one. Literally. Silver and werewolves were not cuddle-buddies.

I idly fingered the bracelet of misshapen teeth on my wrist. Dragon
teeth. Acquired from the late Dragon Lord, Alaric Slate. I had killed him,
and used his dental palate to make a fashionable bracelet. It had made me
feel marginally better. When Alaric's ritual had backfired, thanks to yours
truly, the spell had then transferred the power and designation of *Obsidian
Son* to his offspring, Raego, making him the new de-facto leader of the
dragon nation.

A two-fer if I ever heard one.

Raego, always savvy, chose to break the morbid news to his fellow
dragons by making my bracelet an award, like a goddamned Purple Heart,
declaring me a friend of dragons everywhere. One phrase in particular
stuck out in my eidetic memory. *"He is the ultimate death for us. Our very own
Grim Reaper for those who wish to act terrible to humans... or those who disappoint
me."* I fingered the bracelet angrily. "I won't be Raego's fucking hit man," I
growled.

I felt Hemingway turn to study me acutely. "What?" I snapped, nervous
at both the attention the news story might have caused in the bar, and his
reaction to my last comment.

But he didn't acknowledge my statement. "I'll rephrase. *Grandma, what
great big balls you have!"* he chimed in a falsetto voice, grinning widely.

I grunted, which only made him laugh. I pondered my recent encounter.

"You really think so? He didn't look too tough. Although he walked off my sucker-punch pretty well," I added, thinking back on the strange man.

"Well, does it take more guts to twice traverse a staircase in a burning building or to make a one-time leap into a volcano? Damned if I know, Kemosabe. All I know is when you're making those kinds of calls, you're up in the high country."

I chuckled. "Never heard that before."

Hemingway nodded. "One of the Greats. S. H. Graynamore. Interesting character." He took a deep pull from his drink. "I hate those amoral ass-hats."

I choked a bit on my drink, biting back a laugh. "Pardon?"

"That was Eae, the Demon thwarter. But he's nothing compared to the Archangels." He looked me up and down. "The *real* Archangels..." His eyes twinkled, referring to the nickname the media had granted me.

I felt an icy shiver crawl down my spine. "That really *was* an Angel? I thought he might have just been a temp employee. *Eae?* For an Angel, that name's pretty... lame."

Hemingway simply stared at me. Like, *really* stared at me. I began to fidget after what felt like a full minute of silence.

"Okay. It's a badass name. Terrifying. The Demon thwarter... interesting job description." He continued to stare. I decided to change the topic to deter his gaze. "Why didn't you stop me from pissing him off? He could have smote me... smited me... no, that's not right either..." I mumbled, having no idea how to conjugate the word. "Anyway, I could have used a warning."

Hemingway's intense scrutiny finally broke with another amused grin. "You handled yourself well. Except for launching him into the street. You shouldn't make that a habit. You wouldn't look good as a pillar of salt. Then you called him a *pigeon!* In front of the *Nephilim!*" He roared in laughter. "*Pigeon...*" he muttered again before taking another sip. "He was right, you know," he added, almost as an afterthought.

"About what?" I grumbled, still trying to wrap my head around the fact that I had just sucker-punched a freaking Angel. And then mocked him. And in front of his crew no less. I pondered his thugs. Nephilim – the offspring of Angels and humans. Supposedly powerful soldiers of Heaven, although I had never crossed swords with any of them before tonight. I hadn't even believed they were actually real.

Boy, was I damned.

Hemingway scouted the bar carefully. Having already scoped the place out myself several times – keeping track of the people who had entered and exited – I again noticed the other man who hadn't been affected by the Angel's time manipulation. He was several chairs away from us at the bar, and was currently glaring pure frustration at Hemingway. I briefly turned back to Hemingway and watched him nod amiably at the scarred man. The Irish-looking man just continued to scowl back, but finally gave a dismissive nod in return, swiveling to instead watch a pair of particularly cute vampires playing pool. I assumed the man was one of Achilles' generals. Playing bouncer 2,000 years later must suck after such a glorious feat as starring in *The Iliad*. Hemingway didn't seem concerned with the stranger, so I let it go. Well, put it on the back burner, anyway.

Maybe I was reading too much into things. I mean, it's not often that an Angel arrives in a bar to politely tell you to *cut it out*. How many other Angels were in the bar? Or Nephilim? Jesus. I had never considered tussling with an Angel. I hadn't even known they were real, let alone on our plane of existence. Thankfully, no one was close enough to overhear us as Hemingway took a long pull from a fresh cigarette.

My nervous fingers ached to reach out for the cancer stick, but I managed to compose myself. I had successfully remained smoke-free for a few days now, and was proud of my discipline. But I had just survived a smiting. Perhaps I deserved one. Just one. I shook my head defiantly. *No.* "So, what was the Angel right about?" I asked instead.

"You smell like Brimstone. It's a pungent odor, and it could get you dead quick if some of his more blade-happy brethren caught you unprotected." I sniffed myself, picking up the light sulfuric smell, surprised that I hadn't noticed it earlier.

"I don't know why I smell like that. I haven't summoned any Demons. Lately." Hemingway blinked at me with those eyes that seemed able to weigh my soul and judge my guilt. Was he an Angel too? Eae *had* seemed nervous of him. "Honestly," I said, holding up my hands.

Hemingway shook his head. "I believe you. But regardless, this town reeks of it. *You*, specifically. The rumor mill does hint at Demons being involved in your parents' murder." I blinked, suddenly pissed. This mysterious stranger, among several others, seemed to know more information about my parents' murder than I did. Hemingway continued, unaware of my frustration. "Get rid of the odor as soon as possible. It will only attract the wrong kinds of attention, as you just noticed. Angels don't make a habit of appearing to mortals, but when they do..." his voice and gaze grew distant. "Nothing good comes of it," he finally finished in a soft voice.

He studied me for a moment before deciding to continue. "I once heard a story from a down-and-out farmer about Angels and Demons. It might put things into perspective for you, as it did me. Especially since you're not bright enough to leave well enough alone." He winked. "It shook me to my core. But I was a different man, then. A virgin to the true ways of the world. Perhaps wiser. Perhaps less." His eyes grew far away.

He shook his head after a moment. "Anyway, the man was distraught, filled with grief. And despite offering him a ride the following morning, I never heard from him again. He fled in the middle of the night. I've thought of him often as the years have passed me by, curiosity getting the best of me. Perhaps he was telling me *his* story." Hemingway winked again, face mischievous. "Alas, I never discovered his identity..." He took a sip of his drink, gathering his thoughts. I nodded for him to continue and hunkered down, ready to listen. I would stay a little longer to hear this. Because I knew next to squat about Angels.

His words enveloped me like a warm blanket. Stories from an experienced raconteur could do that. "I'll tell it to you like it was told to me." I nodded. He cleared his throat again, his voice changing slightly as he began to tell me a tale.

An exhausted local farmer was on his way home from selling his wheat at the market a day's ride away. It was drizzling, but a true rain would fall soon. He knew these kinds of things after farming for so many years. He didn't know how he knew, but he was right more often than not. He was eager to get home and see his family after a long day, eager to share his success, and eager to revel in the more important joys life had to offer... family. He wasn't an established farmer, with vast fields and many clients. No. He worked only for himself and his family.

A prideful, peaceful, god-fearing man.

He trotted beside his horse and cart up the final hill to his home... only to discover his son's broken body on the lawn that led to the front porch. The farmer froze, unable to even blink. His boy was not even ten years old. His beautiful, daring, carefree son had been left to suffer, the long smear of blood trailing from the porch and down the freshly painted steps to the lawn was a statement of his tenacity to escape. But escape from what? What could so terrify his bold, courageous son in such a way? Especially while mortally wounded? The farmer could not even begin to fathom, let alone truly accept the death before him.

His heart was a hollow shell of ice, liable to shatter at the slightest breeze. The wind began to howl, heralding the approaching storm, but it was a distant, solemn sound in his ears. He carelessly dropped the reins to the horse and crouched over his son's broken body. He brushed the boy's icy-blue eyes closed with shaking fingers, too pained to do more for his fallen, innocent offspring. But what he would see next would make him realize that his son had been the lucky one. The farmer managed to stand, stumbling only slightly against the growling, suddenly fierce wind, and entered the small, humble foyer of his home. Like so many times before, his wife immediately greeted him, although those past circumstances were never as abhorrent as this.

His wife had been tied down to face the open doorway. Her dress lay in tatters beside her nude, marble-like form. There were many empty wine bottles on the ground, and several piles of ash from tobacco pipes. Enough ash to signify that several men had bided their time in this room while he had been away at market, bartering higher prices for his wheat. The house reeked of tobacco. And he wasn't a smoker. He subconsciously knew that his future path would now lead him to darker places than he could ever imagine. His life would be forever changed.

I shivered, feeling the dark story touch a part of me that I had to fight to squash down. I had enough frightening memories to fuel my recent night terrors. I didn't need another. But I knew Hemingway would tell this story only once. Also, this story would be my only knowledge about Angels and Demons outside of the Bible. If Angels were watching my movements, I needed the information. I waited for him to continue, signaling the bartender to refill Hemingway's glass. The storyteller nodded in appreciation.

Upon seeing that his dearly beloved wife had been brutally tortured and then murdered, the farmer crashed to his knees, the forgotten purse of money that was clutched in his fist dropping to the floor like... a sack of wheat. The coins spilled across the gnarled wooden planks, one coin rolling toward the tear-filled, terror-laden gaze of his wife, before briefly brushing her long lashes and settling flat against the floor in a rattle that seemed to echo for eternity. That and the desperate panting of the farmer's breath were the only sounds in the haunted house. But they were enough to fill it completely. He had been anxious to see the look of joy in her eyes at his successful accumulation of coins.

The sensation of pride from her had meant everything to him. It lent him his own pride. Instead, he received this glassy, empty stare that would forever haunt his dreams. The woman who had made his life worth living, the woman who had saved him from his own darkness, the mother of his beautiful son, the woman who had made the endless hours of toil in the fields worth it... now lay before him, filling his vision like a never-ending scream that tore at the very fabric of reality. Thunder rumbled outside as if an extension of his grief. He would never be able to look at a coin again without remembering this scene. He had been proud to come home. Proud of his success at market. Proud of what the money would mean to his family. The prideful, peaceful, god-fearing farmer felt a scalding tear sear his weathered cheeks.

He distantly realized that he was no longer a prideful man.

A cold, amused voice emanated from the shadows. "Do you seek justice, farmer?"

The farmer jolted, hands shaking with fear... and something else. A feeling he had not experienced in many years. White-hot rage. He stared into the shadows, only able to see a hazy silhouette, wondering if it was one of his wife's rapists mocking him. If it was, so be it.

Everything that mattered in his life lay dead before him. He would welcome the cold, merciless slumber of death in order to escape this haunting grief. Or he would avenge his grief on this wretched soul. It was a long time before the farmer answered, knowing that farming held no interest to him anymore. Nothing *held any interest for him anymore. Well, one thing did...*

Vengeance. The sight of their *blood on his weathered knuckles, the scent of* their *fear filling his nostrils, the feel of* their *dying struggle under his blade. The sound of* their *endless, tortured screams was the only sensation that would appease this once prideful, peaceful, god-fearing man.*

"I do." *The farmer rasped, realizing he was no longer a peaceful man.*

Lightning flashed, the thunderous crack instantaneous, rattling the open windowpanes, and billowing the curtains. With it came the downpour of rain that had been biding its time in the dark skies above. A new voice entered the conversation from another shadowed corner of the room.

"Together, then. We must each give him a gift. To represent both worlds. He must agree to neutrality. To live in a world of grays, as the final arbiter of truth." *This voice was deeper, more authoritative, and obviously hesitant at the situation, judging by his tone. The voice addressed the farmer again.* "After your vengeance is complete, do you agree to forget this past life, and embrace your new vocation? I cannot tell you what it might entail, but you shall never be able to deviate once the choice is made. I can promise that you will not be alone. You will have Brothers to aid you in your cause."

The farmer nodded. "If I can obtain justice first, I agree. I have nothing else left to me."

The first voice grunted his agreement with a puff of stale sulfur that the farmer could taste even from across the foyer. What could only be described as a Demon slowly uncoiled into the light, red eyes blazing with anticipation, his leathery, scaly skin covering an almost human-like frame. The horned, shadowy creature, pulsing with physical shadows of molten fire and ash, handed the farmer a gift, placing it over the man's face, which instantly illuminated the approaching darkness into a hazy green glow, the shadows evaporating under his newfound night-vision. The Demon stepped back, appraising the man before him with satisfaction and uncertainty... even fear, before waving a hand in the direction of the other voice. The farmer turned to assess the second creature, eyes no longer able to show surprise. The man-like being that stood before him crackled with blue power, like lightning given form. An Angel. Wings of smoking ice and burning embers arced out from the creature's back, sparks drifting lazily down to the wooden floor, dying away before contact. The Angel extended a marble hand, offering up a gleaming silver gift. The farmer took it, the item familiar in his hands.

The two creatures spoke as one. "Gifts given. Contract made. He shall be the first. Now, ride forth into your new life. You shall find a new horse befitting your station waiting outside." *Twin peals of thunder cracked the night, and the once peaceful, prideful, god-fearing farmer was alone again.*

The farmer stood in the empty house, and realized he was no longer a god-fearing man.

Over the coming year, he found every last culprit in the crime that had destroyed his life. Their screams unsuccessfully attempted to fill the empty void in his soul, and he reveled in every sensation he created from their broken, mangled, twisted bodies. Immensely. But it was never enough. Then he faded from this world, to fulfill his new responsibilities, forever regretful of his decision to accept those cursed gifts.

CHAPTER 5

I blinked at Hemingway. I could sense that he needed a moment to collect himself, so I downed my drink, waving at the bartender to fill us back up. I tried to comprehend the dark tale, leaning forward over the bar. "Wow. That was... dark. Really, *really* dark. Have you heard of Christopher Nolan?"

Hemingway glanced my way, ignoring my last question. "Most true stories are. I didn't do it justice. The pain in this man's voice was something... something I'd never experienced before. Or since." His eyes were lost to his past for a silent moment. "Desperation can lead men to do stupid, but necessary things. Or at least it might seem necessary at the time. I don't know what became of the farmer, but be cautious of folly, lest you face the same choice as he."

I pondered that in silence, considering how to respond. "You couldn't have done anything. I know what it's like to lose someone dear to me. If a survivor wants to disappear for a while, he'll disappear for a while. Solitude is sometimes the only true solace available for that level of grief. Perhaps this guy knew the farmer. A relative or something. Had too much to drink and shared his story. Felt guilty in the middle of the night, then left."

It sounded hollow even to me. "Perhaps," Hemingway muttered. "All that to say that Angels are bad news. Demons are bad news. Both together are worse than bad news. Advice given."

"So... the moral is not to make deals with Angels and Demons?"

"No. The moral is not to deal in any way whatsoever, with Angels or Demons."

I leaned back, considering. "What did they give him?"

He shrugged. "I told you the story as I heard it. The best stories are mysteries."

"I guess," I answered.

He made a dismissive gesture with his hands. "So, what really brings you here?" he asked, seeming eager to change the subject.

My mouth began moving without thinking, and I was suddenly telling him my story. I told him everything. I felt like the man who had shared that dark story with Hemingway so many years ago. Something about his presence pulled out the darkest part of my life like a moth to a flame. Perhaps he had an empathic ability to draw out the poison in one's soul. I finished speaking and felt about as limp as the damp rag near the bartender. But the invisible weight around my shoulders also felt lighter. More manageable.

"I've heard the tales regarding your parents," he finally said, lifting his glass. "To Pillars of Society." We drank deeply. "They truly were great people. Don't ever let anyone tell you differently."

I blinked. "Did you know them?"

"I met them once." He studied my face. "One time, and one time only. They made a distinct... impression on me. Between black and white is not a gray area, but a quicksilver, honey shade; a shiny, enticing, and altogether beautiful dividing line. If employed correctly, that is. That was your parents. Take the *pigeon*. His kind are as white as white can be. Now, there are varying degrees of white, yet for the most part, they're *White*. Capital W. Then there are their brothers. The Fallen. Now, they're considered as black as black can be, and for the most part, they are. But they didn't start out that way. They just wanted more of a father figure. God upped and favored humans over them, and it rightly pissed them off. Now, end of story, right?" I shrugged uncertainly; curious of how this strange man was using the present tense to describe something that had supposedly happened thousands of years ago. "Then there are the *Others*. The Policemen. The ones with horses, if you know what I mean..." I visibly started in understanding, eyes widening.

"The Riders? Are you talking about the Horsemen? Of the *Apocalypse*?" I stammered.

SHAYNE SILVERS

Hemingway darted a cautious look about the bar, shushing me before finally nodding. "Them bastards have faces like justice. One look in their eyes, and you'll shit yourself with your mouth wide open. Trust me. You ever did anything wrong, they *know* it," he said, meeting my eyes. "However, they don't rightly *care*. You're just a speck of dust to them. Literally. Their concerns are the Angels and the Fallen. Light and Dark. Black and White. They're the policemen of your very existence, the Universe's Supreme Court. They are the Judge, Jury, and Executioner. And they take their jobs *very* fucking seriously."

I waited a moment, and then spoke. Softly. "Our." Hemingway's brows furrowed. "Policemen of *our* very existence," I clarified.

Hemingway frowned, and then downed his drink. "Yes, that's what I meant. *Our* very existence. Are you the grammar police or something?" he muttered something in an ancient middle-eastern language, but I knew enough to catch his gist. *It's hard getting grammar correct when you learned to speak a now-dead language.*

I agreed with him. In roughly the same language. I think. Either that or it was drunken gobbledygook. Same thing to my ears.

Hemingway started, slowly turning to face me with hawkish interest. "Well, I'll be goddamned." He began to laugh, a deep belly sound. The numerous drinks caused me to play a very dangerous hunch as Hemingway leaned over the bar.

"Aren't you already?" Time literally halted as I was slammed up against a warped wooden pillar for the second time tonight, my head smashing against the splintered surface with a resounding *crack*, hard enough for me to see stars. Again, my magic had been useless. Everyone around me stood still as statues, not even blinking, as if they had all been encased in Jell-O. Just like with the Angel, Eae.

Hemingway spoke with a gravelly voice. "No. I. Am. Not." I gulped, holding up my hands in surrender. I was way too drunk for this right now. "Easy, Wizard. Let's not cross that line. It's not nice to accuse a stranger of being one of the Fallen." Hemingway was crackling with a vibrant green energy, different than Eae, like a fairy in a cartoon. He stared into my eyes for a few intense moments before finally stepping back. "If I was one of them, do you think that Pigeon would have just walked away?" I slowly shook my head. "I've had enough to drink. Need another drinking partner sometime, here's my calling card. I might be bored enough to... *assist* you."

He tossed a large, heavy card on the bar before scooping up a small set of motorcycle keys near his drink. Odd. He didn't look like a motorcycle kind of guy. The keys had a miniature, curved blade of some sort as a small adornment. I picked up the card through blurry, alcohol-filled eyes, but my drunken state just made the colors swim wildly, so I stuffed it into my back pocket.

When I looked back up, he was gone. The world snapped back into focus at normal speed, and everyone had a slightly confused look on their faces for a second, as if they again sensed something wrong. But they dismissed it just as quickly – as if they had briefly suffered another drunken spin moment – before carrying on. They were having a rough night, what with Eae and Hemingway distorting the flow of time twice in less than an hour. I shambled out of the bar again, but saw no sign of the man. I spotted several Mounted Patrol Units trotting down the street, scowling at the drunks exiting the bar, but I ignored them as I stood on my toes, searching the street for Hemingway, but I could only see more drunks parading around for their *pre-Mardi Gras* shenanigans. I drifted back inside to finish my drink and text my ride. It was fucking cold outside.

As I waited, I decided to do a little mental decluttering of recent events in order to see if I was missing something glaringly obvious. It had been that kind of night.

My parents had been murdered a few months ago, by an unknown assailant.

At the same time, someone else had broken into their company, stealing a debatably magical music box from a secret stash of dangerous items they allegedly kept under lock and key. The lock and key I had yet to penetrate. Their Pandora Protocol. Said thief had been one of my closest childhood friends, Peter, tempted into working for the group of dragons that had recently plagued my city in exchange for power. I had taken care of the thief, and discovered that he had coincidentally had nothing to do with my parents' murder.

I had hunted down, maimed, and murdered all known related dragons. With a little help from my friends. But I still had the bit in my mouth. I wanted the full story. Why had they been killed? Who had killed them? Why had Peter stolen the supposedly magical music box from my parents, who had looked upon him as a surrogate son? What *was* the music box, really? Was it maybe worth a pile of money? It sure wasn't magical, as I could attest to, after having experimented with it in every way imaginable. I sighed. One thing I did know was that it was nothing like the box from my dreams. It was just a plain, fucking music box.

It only takes one loose yarn to unravel a blanket, and I was searching high and low for that loose thread as if my life depended on it. And I had apparently found the right yarn, considering Eae's entrance into my life.

I rubbed my wounded palm idly, making sure no glass shards were embedded in my skin, and realized I was growing angrier and angrier.

You see, justice was important to me. It truly infuriated me that someone, somewhere, somehow had gotten away with murder, for some unknown purpose. I had even broken into Peter's office in order to find clues. Again, nothing relating to the murder. I *had* found an item I had created many years ago, that magically cloaked the owner, most likely used by Peter to sneak into the Armory – their mysterious *Pandora Protocol* project – but no other clues.

And now, apparently, Angels were investigating the murder and wanted me to back off.

No pun intended, but *what the hell?*

I decided that it was definitely time to go home and get some sleep. This wizard was tuckered out. Maybe Indie and I could go on a last-minute vacation to escape the madness.

Yep. I was booking a ticket out of town. Let the Angels do their digging. If they came up with nothing, I would pick back up where they left off when I got back. No harm, no foul. I had enough on my plate already.

CHAPTER 6

Feeling better with a plan to escape to some secluded, hot, sandy beach with Indie, I let my mind wander. I had met two super-strong people today, neither of which was a flavor of supernatural I recognized. Knowing one was most likely an Angel, I considered that a lucky thing. What would Regular folk think if they discovered that not only was magic real, but actual Angels walked among us? Or maybe I was just special. Maybe he had made his visit specifically to tell me to stop digging. It didn't seem likely. It didn't seem worthy of calling a soldier down to earth all the way from Heaven. That meant they were here, walking among us day-to-day. Perhaps my trash guy was an Angel. It made me a tad bit anxious. That was a lot of pressure to be good at all times – a skill I didn't have. Yep. Beaches, here I come.

Waiting for my ride, I scanned the bar, watching the various Freaks in their natural habitat. The belief of most of the world was that magic didn't exist. We didn't necessarily want to correct them on that grievous assumption. It was easier to stay in the shadows. It had never ended well when we with ability made our presence known to the world at large. Think of the Salem Witch Trials. Every culture had purges of a sort where they tried to banish, maim, or outright murder the Freaks that stood out for their unique abilities. Although the world had progressed since those times, it was still a tough nut to swallow, and we liked it that way. We preferred it, actually.

SHAYNE SILVERS

However, recent events had blatantly smeared my name across the evening news as not only the well-known, corrupt, billionaire playboy, but also a dangerous wizard. Most took it in stride, assuming the media had been desperate to sell copy that day, coming up with outlandish stories to garner viewers, but many more wanted explanations. Explanations I wouldn't provide. I wasn't about to confirm their allegations. Do I look crazy to you?

I turned back to my drink – exhaustion threatening to overwhelm me as I took another sip – hoping the excessive amount of alcohol would help keep me awake. Any time I closed my eyes for more than a few seconds, it was even odds that I would be sucked into another of my night terrors. Maybe it was post-traumatic stress disorder from the dragon ordeal. I had never before experienced such a prolonged malady, and was starting to show signs of wear as a result. I shook my head clear of the twisted memories of my most recent nightmare, knowing Hemingway's story would find a nice, comfy spot in my subconscious for later nightmares.

Yippee.

The tumbler of whisky abruptly shattered in my fist, causing the blood to flow freely again from my previous wound. I hissed, sticking my palm to my mouth in irritation. I was systematically destroying all the glasses the bar had to offer. Before I consciously thought about it, I had slapped a crisp, new hundred-dollar bill – the kind that looked like monopoly money – on the warped bar, prepaying for a new round of drinks. It spent the same as the old bill, although I was willing to bet the bartender had never seen one before. Sometimes I forgot how others viewed money. I had been born into it, and couldn't fathom having to work my body to the bone in order to achieve it. My parents had created a multibillion-dollar company, Temple Industries, specializing in all forms of technology. I was no stranger to making money of my own, but I was a stranger to living on the line, never knowing how the next bill would be paid.

It was a humbling thought. What was I without my money?

Several patrons scowled at me. The bartender grunted as he poured me a fresh glass. "Try not to break this one," he grumbled. I nodded, pressing a fresh napkin into my palm before taking a sip of the fiery liquor. I didn't want any trouble, but I wanted everyone in the room to know that I wasn't an easy target. Trouble in a Kill ended in just that – Death.

I quickly realized that I was unashamedly hammered after talking to the mysterious Hemingway for so long. I hadn't realized how much I had been drinking. I had been so enamored by the man's story, and the man in his own right, that I hadn't minded my liquor. I realized this most obviously, as is most often the case, when I attempted to stand up, and consequently bumped the beer out of the hands of the man behind me. *Come on! Twice in one night?* The man's hackles rose. Great, a werewolf. I spotted the same scarred knuckled man from earlier chuckling down the bar, turning his stool to watch as he gripped his mug like he was watching the last two minutes of a good football game. The werewolf bucked up, slamming his empty can on a nearby table. "Pay attention, wizard! Master Temple or not. You're just another drunk here." He realized he had the crowd's attention. "Not safe without your pet guard dog, I see. Maybe I should show you what a real Alpha can do."

I looked at him, trying to duplicate the intensity of Hemingway's gaze, but most likely looking like a roaring drunk.

Which was truer.

"Okay." I peered past his shoulder, scanning the room. "And where is this elusive bitch you cower from?" Before I could react, the man literally growled as he violently grabbed me by the collar, lifting me high enough to catch a glance over his shoulder. Which is when I saw her.

A beautiful, tiny woman stood in the broken doorway, limned by the light outside. She was wearing a cute polka dot dress and giant red heels under a little fur coat. Stiletto-saurus Rex. Her eyes shone like lightning bolts as she spotted the man holding me up. Tory Marlin.

And she suddenly looked hungry. I nodded before glancing down at the large werewolf holding me up in the air. "Oh, goody. Girl fight!" I sneered. He squeezed tighter in white-hot rage, frowning momentarily at my comment, but no doubt still angry about my *bitch* reference. I struggled to draw in another breath before all hell broke loose.

"Release him now, *Bitch*," Tory hissed. I instinctively laughed while choking for air.

"Yip, yip, yip," I managed between gasps. The man continued to glare at me, ignoring Tory. Which wasn't smart. I could taste the Budweiser on his breath as he dropped me back to the ground. My bracelet of dragon teeth got caught on his sleeve and snapped, scattering dragon teeth across the floor. He took an aggressive step towards me. But Tory was suddenly in the way. The man reacted instinctively, shoving Tory hard in an effort to get back to me. She stumbled slightly, and her heel broke.

She looked down at the six-inch heel now dangling from her shoe. I whistled as I leaned down to swipe up a handful of the scattered teeth and the cord from my broken bracelet on the dirty floor. "You just fucked up your whole night, pal," I chuckled.

"Go back to your tea party, little girl. The adults have business to discuss," he growled dismissively.

Tory decided to show her displeasure at his words by unleashing unrequited hell.

She let loose an uppercut that slammed the man into the ceiling fan above our heads. It splintered amidst a crackling shower of sparks before crashing to the ground near Tory. On the werewolf's way down, Tory then unleashed a right cross to his angular, hairy jaw in order to politely break his fall. He flew across the bar, and struck the pool table with a *thud* that I felt in my boots. Tory was kind of a badass, way stronger than any three men I knew combined.

The werewolf didn't get up. The music had stopped and the crowd stared at Tory in disbelief.

"*My bitch bad,*" I sang familiar rap lyrics into the stunned silence.

The crowd reacted like a fart had gone off in church, and an epic bar fight ensued.

Someone began to take a sucker-punch swing, and a sickly-looking man seemed to be in the wrong place at the wrong time. The swing wasn't intended for the fellow, but he was about to be laid out. I cold-cocked the attacker with the force only a drunken sailor could wield, sending the assailant clear over the bar, shattering all seventeen dollars' worth of quality liquor stored there. The sickly man looked up at me and chuckled with a dry raspy sound, but nodded appreciatively before moseying down the bar, carefree. The fight was suddenly everywhere. I realized that the scar-knuckled Irish guy from down the bar was not taking part, and no one was bothering him. The guy I had just saved from the Hail Mary was right back in the middle of the fray, but was also not being bothered. Huh. He must be one of the ancient Greek warriors with a free pass from Achilles. I hadn't seen the famous Greek warrior tonight, but hadn't been looking for him either. Good chance this fight would bring him out, and I needed to make sure Tory and I were gone before that happened.

The vampires at the pool table were beating the bejeezus out of two more werewolves with their pool cues. A couple of trolls were ganging up on a pair of fairy men that looked like Abercrombie models. It was mayhem. I realized I was cackling maniacally.

I felt someone forcefully pick me up so I took another drunken swing, connecting solidly with a triumphant shout. I heard a grunt. "Damn it, Nate. It's *me*," Tory snapped before lugging me out of the bar, not trusting me enough to let me go. I saw that the bar fight was escalating rapidly, but the Alpha werewolf was still incapacitated. Poor lil' guy. Moments later, the frigid night air hit me like a bucket of cold water. Tory carried me a good dozen paces away from the bar. She wasn't even breathing hard, but the uneven steps of her carrying me on a single heel didn't feel great, like I was riding in a broken elevator that went *up, down, up, down*, incessantly.

I spotted Gunnar perched inside an idling Mini Cooper, reminding me of a gorilla in a golf cart, looking angry, as per usual. Tory set me down and I stumbled, the world spinning wildly for a few seconds. I almost decided to throw up, but the feeling slowly passed. The passenger window rolled down. "You cause that?" he asked, pointing to the sounds of insanity pouring out the broken door of the bar. I shrugged, stumbling slightly again. "You're hammered!" he declared.

I scowled, leaning on the car's frame for support. "And you're a party pooper." That earned an amused chuckle from Tory. "Give me a straight line to walk! I'll show you that I'm as sober as a priest!" I bellowed. One of the St. Louis Mounted Patrol Units was watching my meltdown with mild curiosity, glancing from me to the loud bar fight, but wisely remaining on his horse. "You!" I pointed in his direction, kind of. He sighed, and then trotted over to us. Gunnar almost had an apoplectic seizure.

"Nate, this is a bad idea," he warned, his fingers momentarily transforming into inch-long, claws. Werewolf claws. They retracted after a glare from Tory. It was her car after all.

"How may I help you?" the dark-skinned officer asked, guardedly. "Did you cause that?" He pointed at the bar fight. I shook my head. "Are you harassing these two? Ma'am?" He turned to Tory.

She shook her head with a laugh. "We're his ride."

"Sorry to hear that," the officer stated in a neutral tone from his high horse.

"Oy! I'm right here."

The cop nodded at me. "So you are. What did you need? Xavier doesn't give pony rides. Especially to drunks," he stated blandly.

"Draw a line," I snapped.

"Excuse me?"

Gunnar groaned. I held up a righteous, wavering finger. "I want to show them my ability to walk a straight line."

"I don't have time for this. You have a ride. Get in. or I'll bust you for disturbing the peace." Ignoring him, I chose a long, straight crack in the sidewalk in front of a dark alley. And walked the shit out of it. Then backwards. The cop blinked. "Now, that *is* impressive, given your state of inebriation," he said, looking flabbergasted. He leaned closer to me. "Want to see if your luck extends to a Breathalyzer?" he asked with a wry grin.

"No. Everyone knows that test is rigged. I think I made my point. Thanks. Sorry your rider is a smartass, Xavier," I said empathetically to the horse. The beast neighed loudly in what I took for agreement. My head began to spin again so I leaned against the wall near the alley. The officer studied me thoughtfully, possibly recognizing me from the news, but finally turned back to Tory and Gunnar to verify that everything was all right, and that they were, in fact, taking me home.

No one saw the claw-like hands grab me by the short hairs of my soul, and yank me back into the shadows of the alley. The claws – although invisible – whisked me into oblivion like a cosmic toilet being flushed, and I was shat out into the very bowels of space.

It wasn't pleasant.

CHAPTER 7

*J*re-materialized in a dusty, murky building. The sounds of the city were completely gone. Then I promptly threw up. On my captor's shoes. He danced back with a hiss, letting me go with a shove that threw me into a wall. I bounced off said wall, dizzy, banged my shins against a metal beam of some kind, and collapsed to my knees with a shout of blinding pain. My head was spinning crazily, and my body felt tingly from the apparent teleportation. And shin bumps were the worst form of torture.

When my vision steadied a bit, and I had recovered from the blunt force trauma to my shins, the first thing I saw was shoes.

A fuck-load of shoes, no doubt belonging to an equal fuck-load of assailants.

"Okay. Now you've done it. I hope you're all prepared for an ass-whooping. But first, throw-up shoes needs to tell me how to apparate."

I tried to stand, and was promptly kicked in the ribs by a steel-toed boot. I grunted in pain, the breath knocked out of me, ribs bruised but not broken, and remained on the ground. For reconnaissance purposes, only. I swear. After a minute, I managed to find my voice, walling away the fire in my ribs and shins. "Fine. I'll…" I gathered my breath. "I'll just have to beat it out of you," I wheezed.

I tried to stand and the boot reared back to kick me again. I feigned clumsiness, hoping I was agile enough to catch the boot before a commanding voice shouted, "Stop!" The boot listened. My vision was only just now able to distinguish that bodies belonged to the boots. I looked up and saw silver masks staring down at me. My heart stopped. Each mask was a depiction of a different human emotion, and continued past the jaw like a silver cloth to rest on their chests. This wasn't good. At all. "I see you recognize us, but given your state of intoxication, I'll speak as if to a small child. We are the Justices. The police of the Wizard Academy. And you have been found guilty of criminal actions on multiple counts. Your sentence is cooperation or annihilation. Which do you choose?"

I stared back; ready to unleash a snarky comment, but the retort abruptly froze on my tongue. I blinked. "I figured it out," I said, more to myself than to them.

His voice dripped sarcasm. "How very clever of you. You deciphered the riddle of who we are from the complicated words I used."

I scowled. "No, daft-wit. I figured out how to apparate. And I didn't even go to Hogwarts!"

And I *had* figured it out.

I didn't know how, but it was as if the very experience of teleporting had shown me exactly how to do it. Perhaps my subconscious had been paying more attention than my drunken conscious mind, but I had never learned something that fast before. Ever. Especially not while roaring drunk. It didn't make any sense. But I was confident I knew how to freaking teleport, now, thanks to these ass-hats kidnapping me.

"What is this *apparate* word you keep saying? And what is Hogwarts?" the leader asked, genuinely confused.

"Only the finest school of Witchcraft and Wizardry in the world," I mumbled, shambling to my feet. I swayed slightly, assessing my kidnappers.

"I've never heard of it. It must not be *that* great," someone spoke with a rough tone.

I ignored him. Anyone who couldn't get a Harry Potter reference was beyond help. "So, couldn't take the time to schedule an appointment with me over a cup of tea? Had to snatch me up while I'm hammered drunk? And what are these crimes I'm apparently guilty of, because they're news to me. I never even got a ticket!" I grumbled, discreetly counting my assailants.

The eight thugs didn't find it funny. Or maybe they did. It was hard to tell behind their masks. Paying closer attention, I saw the differences in each mask. There were smiles, frowns, scowls, tears, screams, and several other variations of human emotion. It made me think of Snow White and the Seven Dwarves. I turned to the leader again, the only man not wearing a mask. "That makes you Snow White."

"Jesus, he's *sloshed!*" one of them chuckled.

"And I still kicked your ass," I snapped back.

"Throwing up on my shoes hardly counts as kicking my ass. You only just managed to pick yourself up off the floor."

"Oh, that's right. The ass-kicking comes in thirty seconds. Sorry, my mistake." I took an aggressive step forward for a surprise attack I knew they would never see coming. Another masked man swiped my foot out from under me like a ninja. I crashed into a table, and then my nose hit a nearby chair, causing an orange explosion of light behind my eyelids.

Sweet darkness took hold of me, read me a bedtime story, fucked me gloriously, and tucked me in for a nice long nap.

What felt like an eternity – or a second – later, an icy bucket of water struck me in the face, ice cubes stinging my cheeks like a swarm of frozen bumblebees. I gasped, yelping as I leapt to my feet. My nose was on fire, and I tasted icy, bloody water pouring down my face. I swung my fists wildly in all directions. A pair of strong arms grasped me around the shoulders. "Easy, champ. We're only here to talk."

"The hell we are, Gavin. This man is a criminal. You forget your place," the leader growled.

"Of course, *Snow White*," the man holding me muttered so that only I could hear. I smiled. I had won at least one of them over to my side. Maybe.

"What was that, Gavin?" the leader demanded.

"Nothing, Jafar." A pause. "Sir," he added as an afterthought. So, I had a name. Snow White, AKA Jafar.

"I thought so. Now, where were we before we were almost overwhelmed by Master Temple's daring attack against the chair? Ah, yes. His crimes," Jafar grinned.

I knew this wasn't going to be good. The nameless leader had told me they were Justices of the Wizard Academy. That was a very politically-correct term for them. The honest description of their vocation was *legal hit men*. They snuffed out rogue wizards and other supernatural criminals like candles. They were notorious, the grim reapers of our world. Which also meant they were badasses, and they didn't typically show up *just to talk*.

Usually the sentence had already been given, and they merely showed up to enforce the Academy's will.

The silence grew brittle. My face was on fire, but my chest and ears were shivering from the ice water. I turned from face to face. "Anyone going to elaborate for me, or am I supposed to guess?"

Snow White finally spoke. "We received your report on the events in your city a few months back," he began. I stared back, hiding an insolent smile. Smartass comments would do me no favors here. I needed to tread carefully. But I did despise authority, and this guy reeked of it. He also reeked of loyalty and duty, one of those men who follows orders first, then thinks later, if at all. Not the type to question his betters, even when necessary. "Care to elaborate?" he demanded.

"Well, I assume that you mean that you didn't just *receive* it, but that you also *read* it, or were the contents above your pay grade?" The man kept his face a cool mask, devoid of any emotion, not rising to my bait. But I could tell that inside he was practically ready to stomp his feet and throw a tantrum.

He nodded. "Obviously, I *read* it. Sarcasm is the lowest form of humor, by the way, but if I was facing my impending doom as you are, I might be flippant as well."

I shrugged. "Nothing else to say, then. As entertaining as this has been, I'm glad we got this all sorted out in a professional matter without me having to lay waste to your seven dwarves. So, can you be a good man and return me to the bar? I'm thirsty." I smiled.

He arched a brow at me in disbelief. "Only the guilty or disrespectful would refuse to elaborate on the report that you emailed us from the free email account *hotmale17@hotmail.com*."

I kept my face deadpan. "The other numbers were taken so I used seventeen. I had security issues, so set up the free account to get word to you and no one else. Seemed legit. My other choice was *naughtywizarddragonslayer@hotmail.com*."

Jafar quivered slightly. "We thought it was a prank until we saw the other reports. You should have come to explain yourself. For example, you didn't mention that black magic had been used on an acquaintance of yours. Peter. An old friend, if our intelligence is correct. Using dark magic on Peter to shut down his brain for a night is a crime punishable by death. That wasn't in your report. But I'm sure if you could produce Peter to tell us his side of the story, we could at least clear up *that* charge from your growing list of crimes. We have been unable to do so on our own. Almost as if he disappeared. Permanently. Which would also be a crime."

I hid a nervous gulp. How had they found *that* out? Worse, did they know it was me who had used the dark magic on Peter? "I never found out who did that, or else it would have been in my report."

Jafar studied me for a moment, a look of resignation on his face. "Anything else you forgot to mention?"

"No," I answered too quickly.

"Hmm. What of the bar fight tonight?"

Damn it. They had obviously been tailing me. "I didn't start it... on purpose. I spilled someone's drink. Then everyone freaked out. But it's okay. I *finished* it," I added with a dark grin. "Since when do bar fights concern the Academy?"

"Since it involved Nate Temple. The rumored author of the coalition of supernaturals here in St. Louis. Imagine our shock upon hearing that. One of our own was not only outing magic, but was forming a fan club with a renegade weredragon. At a national convention." I scratched my pathetic scruff of a beard.

"Well, that wasn't really my idea. I got bamboozled into it. I never said a word about it. To anyone. Check the records. I was declared an author of it, but nowhere will you find me talking about it to anyone. It was the Dragon Father's idea of putting me in a corner. And nobody puts baby in a corner." I glanced around the room waiting for a laugh. At least a chuckle. The mindless thugs stared back with their stupid silver masks. "Seriously? Nothing? Have you guys even heard of movies? Philistines!" I turned my back on them to face Jafar. "Regardless, it didn't work out too well for Alaric Slate."

"Yes. I'm glad you brought that up. We seem to have a new Dragon Father. A Black Dragon to be precise. A messiah of some kind to them. The Obsidian Son. And again, you were directly involved."

I shrugged. "St. Louis is a happening place."

"Enough. We have been requesting your debriefing about that whole ordeal for quite some time. Unsuccessfully. We demand an explanation of a great many things from you, young man." He paused, wrinkling his nose, suddenly distracted. Then his gaze locked onto me like a bird of prey spotting a field mouse. "What. Is. That. Smell?" I froze, not knowing what he was talking about, but all too aware that he literally had the authority to end me, right here, right now.

"Brimstone, Sir," another wizard hissed in surprise.

"What have you been up to, Master Temple?" Jafar asked, seeming cautious for the first time.

"Damn it! You're the second person to say that. Do they make Demon Febreze?" No one moved. "I was told that the whole city reeks of it, but that I smell the strongest of it. Test the truth of my words. I don't know why I smell like Brimstone. I swear it on my power."

The man studied me, finally nodding. I had sworn it on my power, so I literally couldn't lie about it. That was good... but it didn't mean I was safe. The smell wasn't why I had been kidnapped.

"Listen, I think we got off on the wrong foot. I don't even know this list of alleged crimes against me. My city went to hell a few months ago, and it was either stand and fight it by myself or let a group of weredragons run amok, murdering civilians. I never once saw the Academy show up to help." The thug who had kind of bonded with me shifted from one foot to another.

"Did you have something to add, Gavin?" The leader asked with menace.

The thug turned to his boss. "He's got a point. How can he be guilty if he was the only one here to fight the threat? Condemning a man for being a vigilante when it was the only course available to him isn't justice."

The leader watched his man for a few tense moments. "It seems Gavin's resolve is weak. Sympathy is not becoming in a Justice."

"Maybe it should be," he answered defiantly. I hid my smile. A partner in crime! I held out my hand for a fist bump. He ignored me, still staring at his boss. I scowled at the side of his head, lowering my hand.

The leader blinked. "We will discuss this later." He shot Gavin a scowl that brooked no further discussion. "Like Gavin already said, my name is Jafar, and I'm the Captain of the Academy Justices. Let's move our discussion to a topic of much interest to the Academy. The Armory your parents supposedly stashed away. The cache of supernatural weapons. This was the reason the dragons were here in the first place, correct?" I felt my faint glimmer of hope sizzle out and die like a bug colliding with a bug zapper. He seemed to enjoy the look of shock on my face, enjoying my mental backpedaling. "No need to deny it. We've all heard the stories of how they stole artifacts from other families over the years, robbing graves, or outright buying items that should have been handed over to us for safekeeping. Until now, we had presumed them to be rumors, but your actions, and those of the thieving dragons, prove otherwise. Now, you are going to hand it over to us, as should have happened in the first place. Where is it?"

I hesitated. Dare I hand it over to them? Especially since it was... mine? But was it? *Really*? Had my parents stolen the rumored items that filled this elusive Armory? I hadn't yet been able to prove that it was even real, despite everyone else seeming to know so much about it. But, assuming it was everything that everyone feared, did I have any right to hoard it? Did the Academy have any right to *take* it? Thinking of their wrinkly, power-hungry hands caressing those items hidden away by my parents made me cringe deep down inside... like a dragon hoarding his gold. These men hadn't been in St. Louis to help me with the dragons, but as soon as they heard about the booty to be gained, all of a sudden I was a liability, and they wasted no time in visiting my city to take the prize. But they hadn't given a damn about the lives that could have been taken if I hadn't stood up to fight back. And now they dared call the actions of my noble friends and myself a crime. Did the world need men like that with such potential weapons at their disposal? I decided right then that they didn't.

Jafar continued. "I can see your dilemma. Do you die a martyr in a vain effort to thwart me out of some ill-conceived notion of honor for your parents' murder? Get the last word in, so to speak? Or do you play it smart, and bow to your betters? The men who play the longer game. The Academy. The ones who make sure you can tuck your loved ones in at night?" His eyes twinkled as he watched me.

I looked from face to face, gathering strength, judging the Justices. Their silver faces were supposed to embody human emotion in an effort to prove their empathy for the greater good. But they weren't good. They were just another breed of political animals. "Do you sleep well at night?" I asked softly into the still silence of the room.

"Pardon?" Jafar asked.

"Do you sleep well at night? You know, when you climb into your jammies, drink a glass of warm milk in your impregnable castle that's guarded by hundreds of other wizards. Before you close your eyes, because you are tired from a long day of paperwork. Do you think about the people who were murdered in my city a few months back before sleep takes you? The ones who had no idea what was happening, what they were dying for, the ones who were brutally murdered by creatures out of a nightmare, creatures that even I didn't know existed. The innocents who lost their lives while you were safe in your ivory tower. The ones who died while you delayed coming to my aid. While you were playing the *long game*, as you put it, people were dying. You seemed to have no problem coming to St. Louis as soon as you heard about the Armory. So, where were you when my people needed someone to 'tuck them in safely,' someone to keep them safe from the monsters of the night?"

The other Justices fidgeted uncomfortably. Jafar sensed it. "That was your own doing. Without the Armory, your city would have been safe. If your parents had handed it over, as was their responsibility, none need have died. Which is why we're here, now. To prevent further bloodshed."

"Tell that to the slain. I didn't know about the Armory. How could the Regulars have known? Regardless, people died, and it had nothing to do with the Armory. The dragons were after a book, not the Armory. And you can sit there with a straight face and tell me that my parents *caused* the mayhem? No one even knew why they were being attacked. Two of our own, my parents, were *murdered*, and yet you did *nothing*. Who was left to prove a point to, when they were already dead? After that, you should have been here to help. That is your fucking *job*. To protect the innocent. Yet you failed. And now you kidnap me, accuse me of being a criminal for saving innocent lives, and dare have the audacity to critique *how* I saved those lives? Go sip your warm milk and get bent, Jafar. My city has no need for cowardly thugs."

Jafar's face purpled. "You dare speak to—"

"You're still talking," I said smoothly, tapping into the innate confidence of the Master Temple, as my father had taught me. "What part of *get bent* did you not understand? I've never seen this Armory. I don't know a thing about it, despite spending months trying to find the truth of it. But even if I did, I wouldn't hand it over to the schoolyard bully."

The Justices loomed around me. Some looked confused, not knowing whether to attack me, arrest me, or cheer in agreement. Jafar snarled back, "Your parents were criminals to deprive the Academy of these stolen items. We don't tolerate vigilantes, especially ones who hoard stolen power. These things belong in the care of wiser, older wizards – those who've been appointed as a collective think tank to keep us all safe. Your parents had no right to take this into their own hands through thievery. The Hubris! Especially not to pass on these stolen goods to an irresponsible wizard like you. Does this have anything to do with the Brimstone smell permeating your business? Have you perhaps already made a deal with a Demon to bring your sweet parents back in exchange for the Armory?"

Power exploded out of me. An explosion of pure force buffeted the Justices off their feet. One managed to cross his arms in some kind of warding spell and was merely knocked into a table rather than over it, but the rest were blown back into the wall none too peacefully. My outburst had been purely instinctual. "Say that again and I'll have your head spiked to my front gate. Consequences be damned," I hissed as Jafar struggled back to his feet. Several other Justices were also scrambling to their feet, gathering power to subdue me. "Enough!" I commanded, slashing all power from the room and tying it into a neat knot within a foot of my chest. I didn't exactly know *how* I did that, but no one was able to touch their power without getting into my bubble. They stared at me in what appeared to be blank shock, several masks having fallen askew. "That was in no way an intentional attack. Think how you would have responded to be accused of Demoncraft when your parents are not even six months in the grave," I spoke softly, genuinely, letting them know I was not a loose cannon. "Your boss has a big fucking mouth to dare speak to me so callously, and he deserved much worse than getting his clothes a bit dusty from a fall. I mean no harm to anyone here." With that, I released my hold on the loose energy of the room. I wasn't sure I should have been able to do that, but it had apparently been effective.

"You will pay for that, Temple," Jafar began.

"Shut it, old man. I've had enough of your wobbling dentures. They're giving me a headache."

Everyone stiffened at that. I had just mocked their boss. Probably not smart. But after surviving an Angel and a gang of Nephilim tonight, his title didn't impress me much. One of the Justices spoke up, a female. "If what you say is true, how did you just manage to stall eight wizards while so obviously drunk? That is not... usual. Despite your rumored strength, we are all battle trained and you just swatted us down like insects. How do you think that looks to us?" she asked politely.

"Probably like I'm a big fat liar." I shrugged guiltily. She nodded, holding out a hand to show her point. "But I'm not. I noticed my power surge after my parents' deaths. Are you implying that it's not normal for parents to gift their strength to their offspring, upon death?"

"That... isn't even *possible*," the woman spluttered, turning to face Jafar with a curious brow. He nodded in agreement with her.

"Then I truly don't know," I answered honestly. "Now, if you are demanding I turn over the Armory, go ahead and arrest me. I don't know how to give you something I don't have. Next, you are the second person to mention Brimstone. I was led to believe that the whole city reeks of it, but that I specifically smell of it. What would cause this? I've had absolutely no contact with Demons. To be honest, it never even crossed my mind. I never thought to seek out a Demon for an answer when no Demon was involved with my parents or the dragons. If you have any answers, please give them now. Otherwise, I cannot help you." No one spoke for a long moment.

"Well, of course you would lie about consorting with Demons. It's against the law."

My gaze froze his scowl. "You said I already broke a gazillion laws. If that's true, what's one more crime when you make it sound like I torture kittens in my spare time? And I already swore on my power that I didn't consort with Demons." He merely glared back angrily. I could sense that I hadn't turned the tables. I was still the enemy, and they were eight. I had merely shuffled the deck a bit on a few points. It was a start. "Now, all I've been doing is investigating the same rumors you've apparently heard. I've never seen this Armory. I've just been following any leads I could dig up. As you well know, my parents were murdered the same night that a thief broke into Temple Industries. The thief was not the murderer. There was a third party. I saw the video of the attack. That's all I know. I'm simply investigating the why, how, and who. Like any responsible CEO and son would do."

"Let's assume you're telling the truth," Jafar began. "It is now time for you to hand over any information you have amassed on this Armory, and come with us to the Academy to answer for your crimes. You are in our crosshairs, Temple. You have repeatedly risked our secret to the Regulars. You never requested our assistance with the weredragons, you allegedly used black magic – even if in self-defense, and a long list of others crimes." *So, they* did *know it was me that had used black magic*, I cringed inwardly. "Your parents' actions were also unsanctioned, and therefore must be reviewed by us. Pass on this information and it will go a long way into removing you from closer... scrutiny. Hand over your knowledge of the Armory."

"I can't do that. I don't have anything to hand over. But even if I did, I'm not sure I disagree with my parents. You haven't exactly shown much discretion or restraint in this encounter. Imagine if you had nuclear launch codes and I accidentally bumped into you. You threatened me after I told the truth a few seconds ago. How can you say this alleged Armory is safe in your hands?"

"How about we just sniff around for the source of the Brimstone, then?" he asked with a hungry sneer.

"Please. Be my guests. I'm just as curious about it as you are. I'll set up an appointment."

Jafar smiled a dark smile. "No need for the appointment. Do you not recognize where we are?" His smile stretched wider.

I blinked, finally scanning the room we were in. It was a warehouse. No, a laboratory. Several orbs of light filled the room as one of the Justices cast them against the far walls to stick like giant lightning bugs. Then I saw the symbol on the wall. We were at Temple Industries.

Shit.

"We have sensed Demoncraft all over St. Louis, and think it might have something to do with you or possibly this Armory. The fact that you smell so strongly like Demons after admitting to researching this endeavor seals the deal. Now, show us the entrance to prove you are not consorting with Demons."

"I can't," I answered softly.

"Can't, or won't?" Jafar asked with a disgusted snarl. Before I could reply, he continued. "No problem. We will just follow the scent of Brimstone."

Huh. I hadn't thought of that. But then again, I also hadn't sensed the Brimstone before tonight. If it seemed to be centralized here, it made sense why I stunk of it so strongly. I had been here almost every day trying to get into the Armory. But why did my company smell like Demons? Were there Demons imprisoned in the Armory? I shivered. That was a sobering thought.

I had no choice but to follow them. The female Justice who had spoken earlier drifted out of the laboratory and down the hall like a dog on scent. Going straight for the door I had seen in the video footage. Could they be on to something? After a few minutes, we found ourselves in the fated hallway, staring at a blank wall. I bit back a smile. None of us could see anything unique about this section of hallway, as the room had apparently been spelled invisible by my parents. The first time I had realized anything was here was when I had seen the video footage of the attack, as the camera had shown through all magical energies, revealing the door behind the spell. The wizard waved a hand and a blast of hazy heat seared the protective spell from the air, revealing the giant *Omega* symbol above a worn, ancient door that hadn't been there a moment ago.

She smiled back at my surprise, and then placed a dainty hand on the door handle. After a deep breath, she yanked the door open, and instantly let out a yelp of surprise as a broom handle struck her in the mask where her eyebrow would be. I laughed. I couldn't help it.

Jafar strode forward, peering into the closet angrily. "This doesn't make any sense. This is where the Brimstone smell is the strongest. A mighty being manifested near here, and spent a great deal of time on this spot. Repeatedly, in order to be this pungent. This must have to do with the Armory." I laughed even harder.

"I don't know what you're talking about. I mean, that mop is kind of dangerous, but I doubt it's been spelled. You can have it for ten bucks." Even though we were standing directly in front of the alleged Armory's entrance, it was nothing but a broom closet. I didn't know whether to laugh or cry. I had, of course, already tried this. The broom must have been spelled because I had been armed for bear and had still been hit in the eye. I didn't know how it was possible, but the room was guarded somehow. It hadn't been when Peter had broken in, but perhaps the spells had been ignited upon my parents' murder. Without warning, Jafar slammed me up against the wall. "Give me the Key to the Armory. It belongs to *us*."

"I will tell you one time to let me go. Exactly once. Then I will knock those fucking dentures out of your ancient mouth," I warned in a soft tone. His grip tightened. "Don't think I can't. I've already shown you my strength. Do you really want to look a fool in front of your crew? If so, I'm your Huckleberry."

Jafar's arm quivered. He was strong for an old man, but he finally let go. He turned away and took a few deep breaths to calm down. Then he turned back to face me. "Hand over the Key to the Armory." I had no idea what he meant by a *Key*. He must have noticed this from my blank stare. "Magical crossroads like the one required to keep something like this secret for so long require a Key. You must have it. Your power is double what it should be, what it was last time you and your parents stood before the Academy on your Name Day." That brought back the terrifying memory of meeting the Academy for my first time. The Name Day was an initiation day for young inherent wizards to be accepted for training. I hadn't gone to their school as the majority of wizards did, having instead been 'home schooled' by my parents. They hadn't been too big of fans of the Academy, or the politics that were indelibly imprinted on her students.

"Give us your information on the Armory, and we will help you. Refuse, and we will take it by force. It belongs in our hands – where it is safe – not with one family. Until you see the errors of your ways, we are assigning you a caseworker. One of our best detectives. He will shadow you at all times. Gavin?" The Justice who had seemed to agree with me stepped forward. I merely stared at him, refusing to give them what they wanted. Jafar nodded after a few seconds. "You leave me no choice then. Akira?" I flinched, having anticipated an attack from Jafar or Gavin. They didn't move. Instead, I suddenly found myself set upon by the entire ring of wizards, simultaneously. I struggled for a moment, but they were too quick for my drunken reflexes. A warm blanket of energy began to settle over my shoulders, and then it turned to a tingling, icy pain as it was yanked away. I roared, feeling as if the skin was being torn from my bones. Darkness and a swirl of sparks filled my vision as I crashed to my knees.

When I came to, I was still on the floor, heaving through a raspy throat. Jafar's face appeared before me. "You brought this on yourself. You've been cursed. From this day forward, your power will no longer restore itself. As you use it up, it is gone... *permanently*. This curse will remain in place until you choose to comply. You have three days. Then I will come back to hear your answer. I'm interested to see what happens if you use up all your power between now and then. Logic leads me to believe that if you use up your magic, it will be gone for good, even if we remove the curse, but we've yet to test it out. Regardless, the longer the curse rests on your shoulders, the higher the risk that the power loss will be permanent. This is fitting, as the extra magic you briefly wielded was not truly yours, and could have only been granted through black magic or Demoncraft." His smile mocked my fear. Was this really happening? What was I without my magic? Who was I if not a wizard?

I was about to find out.

51

"The only way we will remove the spell is if you comply. Or beg Gavin's aid. It most likely won't replace what was already taken, but will halt the continuous deterioration of your magic. Again, all we demand is your compliance – your pledge to serve the Academy – and access to the Armory. It's past time for renegade wizards to do as they pleased, unchecked. I think we are done here, unless you have something to add?" he asked with a leering grin. The other Justices looked troubled, but resolute. This was all they knew. They didn't know me. They knew their indoctrination into the Academy, and wholeheartedly believed the creed enforced upon them from such a young age. This was why my parents hadn't let me train at the Academy. At least Gavin looked uncomfortable. That was a plus, right?

One fear plagued my thoughts. "How am I supposed to rid my city of Demons if my power is waning and you aren't helping? You told me I should have asked you for help a few months ago, well, now I'm asking."

Jafar looked at me with the cold eyes of a bureaucrat. "Of course… right after you give us what does not belong to you. Or when you come crawling back to us in three days, powerless. It's up to you. In the meantime, Gavin will be there to make sure you break no further laws. Despite his insolence earlier, he's a firm believer in order and justice. He's a tough task master."

I cursed under my breath. "I'll figure it out on my own, then. Like I usually do. You know, this is the kind of action that makes wizards rebel." The words hit me as doubly true after my conversation with Hemingway at the bar. He sympathized with the Fallen Angels… sort of.

With a rustle of fabric, everyone disappeared except Gavin and I. "So, this blows," I muttered. Gavin stared at me through the mask that resembled a frowning face, offering nothing. "Are you not allowed to talk to the criminal?" I asked him.

He cocked his head slightly, and then tore his mask away. It disappeared in a puff of vapor. Huh. Fairy make? "My job is to make sure you don't break the law. We aren't friends. I'm not here to *help* you, but to *watch* you. To make sure you don't cross any more lines. I'm not saying that I agree with the Captain, but I also don't believe that what you did was right." I simply stared at him, curious. Silence brought on the best answers, I had found, so I waited. "Order is important. Laws are in place to keep the greater good safe," he said, vehemently.

"I guess the greater good doesn't include Regulars, then," I said softly, watching his face. He looked torn.

"Apparently not," he answered with a sigh. "Look. The current system is broken. I agree, but without a system we are animals. Something is better than nothing. What can we do?" he asked with a helpless frown. "You want to find your parents' murderer. I understand. I won't stop you. But let's get one thing clear. I won't let you hurt anyone in your effort to do so. Jafar was right. You caused a lot of trouble with the dragons. The Academy should have helped you. But even though they didn't, it didn't give you the right to take the law into your own hands. If all it takes is an ideal and the power to enforce it, how is a vigilante any different than a criminal?" he asked me with all the passion of youth. I sighed.

"Fine. Stay out of my way, and we won't come to blows." His shoulders stiffened. "Easy, kid. That wasn't me picking a fight. You can tell by the fact that there isn't a Gavin-shaped dent in the drywall over there." I waved at the wall with a wry grin that seemed to diffuse the situation. I tried to ease the tension. "About that curse... Was he literal? If I use up my power between now and my trial date, will I become a Regular?"

He studied me for a few moments, judging how much to say. "Jafar doesn't joke. Or exaggerate. He's old school. Very old school. When he says something, he means it. But he was also right when he said he's interested in finding out what would happen. Theoretically, the effects would be permanent. It was either cast the spell or arrest you. He did give you an option, if you recall. Now he can justify his actions to his superiors on the Academy Council. He's a thug, but an efficient and necessary one. He genuinely believes everything spouted to him from on high. And he's in charge of the Justices, so they believe as he does. Most of them, anyway..." he offered with a shrug. "Enough to matter."

I nodded, turning back to the door. One problem at a time. I'd figure out the magic thing later. Perhaps I wouldn't need magic to fend off Demons and Angels while I tried to hunt down my parents' murderer. Yeah, right. I tried the handle and got bopped in the head with the damned broom, just like Akira. I bit back a curse as I heard Gavin muffle a chuckle. I turned abruptly, casting out a hand behind him as if we were suddenly under attack. He bought it, turning with his own hand cast out defensively.

That's when I gathered my power around me – like a cloak in a corny opera – cackling for good measure as I prepared to apparate back to the bar, using my memory of how the Justices had kidnapped me.

"Muah-ha-ha!" I pulled the room around me like a blanket, reaching for the darkness hidden in the air at all times, and grasped it like my life depended on it, all the while firmly imagining myself back outside the bar from earlier. I hoped I had gotten it right. I heard Gavin curse as he realized my ploy. Perhaps it was my evil magician stage laugh that gave me away.

The spell wrapped around me before I thought about how much magic it might use. What if it used up all my strength? But it was too late. I was hurtling through space at an alarming rate like a plate of Jell-O on a roller coaster.

CHAPTER 8

*M*y feet landed firmly on the concrete just outside the alley where I had been whisked away from not too long ago. Confident that I wasn't about to throw up again, I cheered. "Boo-ya!" I fist bumped the air in triumph. It had worked!

The chill hit me fast after the warmth of the warehouse at Temple Industries. I took a deep breath of the frigid air, trying to sober up a bit. The street was quiet. I scowled in the general direction of where Tory's Mini Cooper had been parked, but they were gone. Since Gunnar and Tory had rabbited, I would just have to call her back and ask her to pick me up. Again. Hopefully there wouldn't be any more bar fights. I dared not go back inside. Even though it was warmer. I was sure Achilles wouldn't be pleased to see me.

The alcohol sloshed uncomfortably in my belly as I began to walk, but I let out a deep laugh. It took me a few seconds to truly comprehend the fact that I had just teleported. How freaking cool was that? But I was too scared to try it again until I got a better grasp of the curse that had been placed on me. What if I burned myself out? I shivered, nothing to do with the cold this time. Right. Dwell later. Get home now. With the important decisions made, I reached into my pocket and whipped out my cell phone.

And saw that it was dead.

I blinked at it. Had I not charged it? I had been forgetting more and more of these simple tasks as my sleep deprivation increased, which probably wasn't a good sign for my mental well-being in the long haul. Like an elevator button, I pressed the power button repeatedly, confident that persistence would pay off. But, like the elevator, it didn't.

I looked up, judging how far I would need to walk to catch a cab. I wasn't necessarily in a spot many cabbies visited of their own choice. That was fine. Perhaps a walk among the *Mardi Gras* patrons would help sober me up a bit. Give me time to plan my vacation with Indie. Then I hesitated. But I couldn't go on a vacation now, not with this curse. I scowled at nothing in particular. Damn Jafar.

I began hoofing it, striding drunkenly along with angry stomps of my feet. Jafar would pay for that, but for now, I had to get home. And to do that, all I had to do was make it to a main thoroughfare. Simple. I quickly realized that there weren't many people on the street, but I could still hear them off in the distance. They had most likely congregated to a more *happening* place. A place with more bare breasts than Achilles Heel. After all, starving college girls needed beads for food, right? Someone had to provide for them. I realized I was idly searching my pocket for beads, which brought my thoughts back to Indie. She was no doubt at Chateau Falco, wondering why I wasn't back home yet. I wondered if Gunnar or Tory had called her, terrifying her with my abrupt disappearance. If so, I was in for a rough night.

I spotted a mounted patrol officer near a streetlight a hundred feet ahead of me and began to walk faster. He probably hadn't seen me clearly yet. After all, I was standing in a vast pool of darkness between the dim glows of the aged lights. Neighborhoods like this one didn't have too serious of a relationship with the city's maintenance crew. More like infrequent one-night-stands. I smiled as I sashayed in a mostly straight line towards him. I wasn't in that rough of a neighborhood if a mounted police officer was standing watch.

That's when I smelled it.

Brimstone.

The little hairs on the back of my neck jumped to attention as my eyes squinted, trying to retain any night vision I could. How had I missed the odor? Especially after being told repeatedly that I was doused in it. But this time it wasn't me. This was fresh. I shook the thought away as a dry, raspy voice seemed to whisper directly into my ear. "Does the Master Temple need a ride?"

I jumped, twisting like a cat in midair, swinging my arms wildly in a carefully orchestrated defensive maneuver. Lucky for him, I missed entirely. But I knew it had to have scared him a little. It was a ferocious display of the pure essence of manliness incarnate.

"Was that a seizure?" his voice crackled drily, pretending not to be terrified.

I didn't speak as I continued to stare in the general direction of the voice, hoping to get a solid glimpse of what I was up against. In the darkness, a shape materialized out of nothing, as if un-shedding the very night from his shoulders. A Demon. He looked similar to a man, but was covered in gravel-like skin. Rough and rigid. Not scales, but like hardened, hundred-year-old, weathered lava that had cooled off sometime before the ice age. Other than that, he was a beautiful specimen of the health benefits in Hell. I scowled. "No need to act tough. I know I scared you."

"Yes. Very frightening, mortal. Almost made me lose my appetite." With a puff of ash, he was gone. I took a step back, questing the darkness, and flinched as his voice whispered in my ear again. Behind me. "Almost..." he drawled. I whirled, trying to keep him in my sights, wondering how he had moved so stealthily. He chuckled, a sound like snakes slithering through dead leaves in the fall.

Fall. Fallen, my subconscious repeated, remembering my encounter at the bar.

I shook my head and briefly wondered exactly what Demons were. *Were they all Fallen Angels? Or were some just damned souls?* I raised my hand. The Demon coalesced again, cocking his head before nodding for me to proceed. "What exactly is a Demon? Are you just some poor bastard who made bad life decisions, or are you a Fallen Angel?"

He snarled in fury like a doused cat. "Do *not* blaspheme against my master. You are not worth the breath the Fallen take."

"You guys breathe?" I asked in disbelief. The Demon merely stared at me. "I mean, I guess I just thought that it was kind of hot and ashy down in hell, and that there wouldn't be much oxygen. I'm not much of a geography guy, so don't take offense. I honestly don't know what's down there. I've heard it's... less than ideal though, you know? But what about *you?* You've *been* there!" I slowly began walking as I talked, hoping to get closer to the cop I had seen a moment ago. The officer seemed to be watching me curiously, or at least squinting in my general direction, but I knew that if the Demon saw his attention, the man was as good as dead. "So, what's your opinion on hell? Good, bad, need a bit of a renovation? You obviously find it more desirable up here, or else you wouldn't be here." Another step. "Are you even allowed up here without a hall pass?" Another step. I was now only a few feet away from the edge of the streetlight's glow. "Or would a summoner do the trick? Yeah. That could work. Someone calls you up here, you answer. No harm in that, right?"

"Everything alright over here?" a deep baritone called out. "Who are you talking to?" It was the same cop from outside the bar earlier. "Master *Temple?*" the officer barked in disbelief, finally recognizing me. Tory or Gunnar must have told him who I was after my disappearance. "What happened to your face? And where did you run off to earlier? Were you mugged?" He began to reach for his radio to call in backup.

The Demon hissed in annoyance, having realized too late that he had missed his chance to take me out with ease. Then the Demon slowly relaxed. "This could have been so easy. I just wanted to introduce you to my master. But you had to involve the constabulary. Now I'll have to paint the sidewalk with his blood. Loose lips sink ships. Give me a moment. I'll be right back so we can continue our chat." He grinned, gravel crackling off his skin as he exploded into motion. That's when the cop finally saw what I had been talking to. Before then, the Demon had stayed in the shadows.

To the cop's credit, he reacted pretty fucking fast. He moved his hand from the radio to his holster like Clint Eastwood. His gun coughed four times in less than a few seconds as the Demon hurtled towards him and his horse, Xavier. The majority of his shots rang true, judging from the puffs of gravel exploding from the Demon's torso. The horse dodged the first swipe of the Demon by sheer luck, but the creature rebounded immediately, tackling the officer from the horse's back like an NFL linebacker going toe-to-toe against a high school freshman team. I was on top of the Demon in a blink, not sure how I had moved so fast, grabbing him by the throat with one hand, my magic flooding through my arm for strength as I slammed his body into the streetlight twice in quick succession. Things inside of him cracked at the impact, but he wasn't down for the count. Then the horse reared up, planting an iron hoof in the Demon's chest and sending him clear across the street to slam through a glass window in a tinkling shower of broken shards. The building trembled. "Alley-oop!" I crowed. "Good assist, Xavier!"

He snorted a nervous breath, eyes wide, but didn't bolt. The cop was out cold, but was breathing steadily. I had no time, and didn't want to risk duking it out with the Demon when I didn't know how much power I would need to use to win, and with a cop who could possibly wake up at any second. Only to be brutally murdered the moment the demon recovered.

I did the only logical thing my fuzzy brain could think of. I... *invisibled* him. I cast a weak illusion spell over the cop's body, hiding all trace that he was lying in the grass unconscious, and then I grabbed Xavier's reins. I mounted the horse as I heard the Demon cursing from deep inside the building with feral roars of anger. Then we were galloping away into the night towards the masses of humanity celebrating *Mardi Gras*.

The wind in my hair felt good, even if it was cold. Freedom and escape always tasted great. A few minutes later, we were far away from the Demon, and people were everywhere, many pointing up at me – a man who was definitely not a police officer riding what was definitely a police officer's horse. That sobered me up a bit. What if a cop saw me? It wasn't grand theft auto, but it was most definitely a crime. I couldn't just leave Xavier to wander around on his own, though. Some drunken idiot would no doubt find the courage to mount the horse, and then cause some mayhem...

Heh.

Pot. Kettle. Black. Yeah, I get there eventually.

The only way forward was to take the horse to Chateau Falco and find a way to discreetly return him in the morning. I didn't have time to debate with myself. I had fire in my belly, an unconscious cop hidden a quarter mile behind me, a fine steed between my legs, and a Demon on my heels. I leaned over to a group of gawking sorority co-eds. "Beads, please." A pretty redhead flashed me. "No, you've got it backwards," I said with a grin. I flashed her my chest instead.

"Oh, *right*," she giggled, obviously hammered, before handing me a fistful of beads.

"You're Master Temple!" one of her drunken friends chimed in loudly. I nodded with a smile. Her group of friends froze in awe. Then they all flashed me for good measure. I laughed like a maniac, tossing half the beads back before spurring Xavier on. Time to go talk to Indie.

CHAPTER 9

$\mathcal{I}$t took me a while, but it was a pleasant way to sober up, after growing accustomed to the rhythmic gyration of the horse's stride. And even better, I hadn't been spotted. Well, I hadn't been *stopped*. Plenty of people spotted me on my way home, which only added to the thrill.

I wished I could have snapped a picture of my Butler's face when I pulled up to the gated drive of Chateau Falco atop Xavier. It was priceless. Of course, I didn't offer an explanation, and Dean never asked for one. Despite this being a first, he was too proper to question the Master Temple. He merely asked if either of us needed refreshment. I patted Xavier's head. "Horsey want an apple?" The horse snorted. I guessed that was a *yes*.

I tied Xavier off to one of the cars left outside the garage, near a patch of withered grass. A silver bowl of sliced apples had been placed on the doorstep. I grinned, picking it up and heading back to Xavier. I fed him a few slices, and then walked him inside the garage to stay warm, as it was climate controlled inside, and definitely *not* climate controlled outside. I placed the bowl beneath him, but left the saddle on, unsure how to take it off successfully. I would have to see about returning him tomorrow. How the hell that could be accomplished discreetly, I didn't know. I put it on my mental to-do list for tomorrow.

Return Xavier to the police. Secretly.

Find parents' murderer.

Avoid Angels and Demons.

Take a bath to wash off the sulfur smell.

Find a way to remove Academy's curse.

Gain access to the Armory.

Maybe get some milk.

That settled, I stumbled in through the front door of my mansion, locking up behind me before wandering through the house in search of Indie. I tried to be quiet in case she was asleep. I knew it was late, but with my phone dead, I wasn't quite sure of the exact time. I very disturbingly recalled the day-terror I had experienced at the bar – Indie being gutted in front of me. Familiar with the sensation, I managed to shake it off, but my brain felt like it was swimming in a little pool of alcohol.

I reached the stairs, and was immediately assaulted.

I was struck in the face by what felt like a hot iron shoved to the hilt up my nostril, right on the spot that had kissed the wooden chair at Temple Industries. Light flared as my mind shattered into a million blinding shards. I was knocked into a nearby vase, shattering the priceless clay. I lurched to my feet, letting loose an explosion of raw force at a nearby fluttering curtain. It shattered the window, which immediately set off the alarm. The sonic wail could be felt on a molecular level. I clasped my hands over my ears, eyes watering freely as I scanned my proximity for my attacker. And I found it.

My assailant was an overnight bag that had rebounded off my face and into the curtain. Of all the dumb luck. I had apparently overreacted. Fresh blood poured down my face and into my mouth, which was becoming a familiar taste. I clutched my head, awaiting the pool of sympathy in which I would soon be swimming.

Someone was about to feel downright guilty for launching luggage at my face from up the stairs.

Indie and Dean both appeared on the landing in a flurry of stomping feet. "I'm so sorry, Dean!" Indie was yelling over the blaring alarm. Dean was on the phone. I couldn't hear him over the screeching alarm, which was making my vision practically wobble. A few seconds later, the alarm shut off, and a buzzing whining sound filled my ears in the absence.

"Thank you, that will be all," Dean said into the phone before hanging up.

My ears continued ringing and my face throbbed. Indie was halfway down the stairs, crying hard. Here was my sympathy parade. Soft words, a soothing icepack, and a smoking hot Indie to tuck Nate into bed after a long day, but not before a full minute of apologies for injuring her boyfriend. "Nate! Are you okay? What *happened?*"

I braced for the attack. Her hug hit me like a train. I, being all that is man, survived it. But only just. "Shh... It's okay, Indie. It's just a window. No big deal. Don't cry," I said with an amused smile that she luckily couldn't see as she sobbed into my shoulder.

"It's not the window, Nate. It's... Wait, your face is covered in blood! From the bag?" I decided to let her think she had caused it. Easier than explaining my kidnapping. "And why do you smell like a farm?" she asked. My hopes for sympathy began to flicker and die. Surely any minute now...

"Is the horse taken care of? Did he appreciate his supper?" Dean asked wryly.

I nodded, impatient for the world to bow down to my desires for a nice bed with my feet propped up. "Horse?" Indie asked. "What is he talking about? You bought me a horse? What in the world would I do with a horse? I mean, the gesture is very sweet, and I appreciate it, but I don't know a thing about horses. And isn't it a bit late to buy a horse? I thought you were meeting up with a lead at the bar? I'm confused." She looked horrible. Don't get me wrong. Indie was a goddess. Beautiful on a level that was astounding, but she didn't cry well. The pretty ones never do.

"I had to borrow the horse to get home. Gunnar and Tory rabbited."

"Borrowed from the St. Louis Mounted Patrol Unit," Dean offered helpfully.

"The *police?*" Indie burst out. I glared at Dean. He was ruining my chances.

"I can explain. And I'm fine. The bag just caught me off guard." They stared at me blankly. I cleared my throat. "But first, please don't worry about the window. It's really not a big deal." Dean harrumphed, implying that to him it *was* a big deal, as he would be the one to arrange for it to be fixed.

Indie finally stepped back, mascara pouring down her face. "It's not the window—"

"I'm fine. I already told you." She shook her head. My hopes for sympathy began to die by crucifixion, now. I sighed. This just wasn't my night. "The vase then. We can always find another vase."

"*Ahem.* We most certainly can't. That was one of a kind. As are most of the furnishings of the home. Macedonian, if I recall correctly," he added, nudging a piece of clay with his foot.

"Nate, it's not the vase either. It's—"

"Jesus. I'm an idiot. I didn't even think about it. Tory and Gunnar probably scared you half to death with their phone call. It's fine. It was just a bar fight. Then someone…" I decided to play it safe, "wanted to talk to me about something. They were pretty mysterious and kidnapped me right from under Gunnar's nose, which is saying something. But I got it all squared away. I—" Indie placed a finger on my lips.

"Bar fight?" she asked with a frown. I began to backpedal furiously, knowing I might need to resort to my beach vacation idea in order to escape unscathed.

"Well, yeah. Kind of. But Tory broke it up. Or broke *him* up. You should have seen it. She laid him out flat. No problem. *Wham, bam*, no more werewolf." I chuckled. "But really, it's nothing to be concerned about. My phone died so I couldn't call you. I'm sorry I caused you to worry. I have an idea though. I—"

"Nate. Shut up for a second. Gunnar never called. Neither did Tory." She didn't sound pleased about that little detail. "It's… my mother. She fell and hit her head. She's in the hospital. I need to go see her. "

"Oh. Is she okay? We can leave right now. I'll pack a bag. I… crap. Can I erase the last few minutes from your memory and go back to before I mentioned my night?"

"No." She was tapping her foot angrily. If she had been a cat, her tail would have been twitching like mad.

"Right," I muttered. So, no sympathy and no vacation.

"Bar fight. Kidnapped. Stole a mounted patrol horse. Why don't you flesh that out while I finish packing?" I sighed as she turned on a heel and headed back upstairs. Dean coughed into a polite fist as he sauntered off into the house, leaving me to my fate. My life.

It took us a few minutes to get to our room where Indie had been packing. I threw myself onto the bed, careful of jarring my face. I fidgeted for a few moments, trying to get comfortable as Indie bent over one of the suitcases. I finally gave up on comfort.

"What is the point of this?" I fumed angrily, holding up a torturous, sparkly throw pillow. I was lying on the bed, my head propped up against another of the expensive decorative pillows that sported even more tassels and sequins. No matter how I shifted, they bore into my neck like needles.

"They look nice."

"Pillows are supposed to *feel* nice. These feel like torture devices. Do you think Martha Stewart designed them while in jail? Out of spite?"

She shook her head idly as she continued packing. "They aren't supposed to be used. Just to look nice."

I grunted, rearranging the death-shard pillow. "So, your mom... What happened?"

Indie shivered a bit. "I'm not sure. She doesn't remember, but it looks like she fell and couldn't get back up. Luckily, a friend came over when she didn't appear for their weekly book reading club. They took her to the hospital where she's undergoing tests to make sure she didn't injure her brain. She broke her hip after banging her head on the kitchen counter." The Life Alert commercial that many found humorous on a dark, sadistic level very briefly replayed in my mind, but I wisely kept it to myself, even though I thought that it might have actually been helpful in this instance. This comment, I was sure, wouldn't help me. "I need to go to her. She's confused, not remembering exactly what happened." Indie's eyes were far away, as if recalling the event clearly in her mind. I wondered if she was telling me the full story or not. But I wasn't about to press her on the details. Because I wasn't *entirely* stupid.

"I understand. Do you need money? Want me to arrange the jet to take you there?" I asked, feeling helpless to make her feel better.

"No. Dean already booked me a commercial flight. It leaves in a few hours. He's driving me to the airport." She wasn't looking at me, and began stuffing a few more shirts into her suitcase in a distracted manner. I knew how she felt, having recently lost my own parents. It was numbing to realize that the ones who raised you were, in fact, mortal. Frail.

"He didn't book two tickets?" I asked softly. She hesitated, still not turning to face me. I propped myself to see her better, suddenly understanding. "You... don't want me to go with you..."

She threw her hands up in frustration. "It's not that I don't want you to. It's... complicated. You have enough on your plate right now. You haven't slept in how many days now? You look like death, and I don't think I want death looking over my mom in the hospital." Well, that was harsh. "Plus, I saw the news today..." Her tone was suddenly icy, shifting as adroitly as a figure skater performing a... well, whatever type of move figure skaters performed. All that mattered was that anger replaced her concern in the blink of an eye.

"Oh?" I answered dumbly, hoping she wasn't referring to the blurb I had seen at the bar about my involvement with the dragon attack on the Eads Bridge a few months ago.

But hope abandoned me with a sadistic chuckle.

Indie slowly stood, leaning against the closet door as she began to tap her foot. This wasn't good. "I distinctly remember bathing your injuries around the time of that attack. You never mentioned it."

"Oh, you know how the news is. Always jiving for a story..." I answered lamely.

"No, I don't. You apparently didn't trust me. You didn't tell me you fought that dragon on the bridge."

I shrugged. "Allegedly. They never found the body, and the city thinks it was a hoax. They also think I killed a cop at Artemis' Garter. Or that Gunnar did. Everyone is fighting for their ten seconds of fame."

Her eyes weighed my soul. "Did. You. Fight. A. Dragon?"

I shifted uneasily, finally giving in. "Yes," I admitted.

She looked hurt, and I suddenly felt like crap all over again. But her next response surprised me.

"Thank you, Nate." I tensed, waiting for the trap to close. But nothing happened. I finally looked up at her. She looked pleased. "That wasn't so hard now, was it?" she asked softly. I felt my shoulders loosening. She was right. It felt good. Almost as if I was the one who had placed so much pressure on the topic in the first place. Which was true. I had wanted to keep her safe, away from the truth so that she couldn't become collateral damage later, but my answer hadn't scared her at all. She seemed happy, relieved. I let out a deep breath.

"It's dangerous to tell you these things—" I began.

"You could tell the truth, you know, to the media. Prove yourself," she answered, interrupting me.

"Yeah. I could." Her smile stretched, slowly, surprised that she had gotten through to me so quickly. Before she could pounce, I continued. "And confirm Alaric's very public speech about me being a wizard and starting a coalition of Freaks? No thanks. That would bring back another, more violent, remake of the Salem Witch Trials. Not even considering what the Academy would have done tonight if they had believed that the coalition talk was legitimate."

Indie watched me intently, no longer tapping her foot. "Tell me about this Academy."

I hesitated. "I really shouldn't." Her foot began tapping all over again, making up for lost time. "Indie, they're dangerous. There were a lot of them tonight. They're like the Russian secret police from back before the Iron Curtain fell. Immunity from almost anything they feel justified about. It was only quick thinking that got me out of their version of jail tonight." I didn't need to tell her about the curse they had put on me. Indie had enough to worry about. Then again, perhaps their curse would drain me of magic. I would become a Regular and none of this would matter anymore. No more secrets from Indie. I shivered at that. But what was I, if not a wizard? Then I shook my head. Who was I kidding? The Academy would never let me walk free with everything I knew. Even if I was a Regular.

"Fine. If you're not going to tell me, I need to leave."

"Indie…" I began, holding up an imploring hand. "These guys are heavy hitters. You don't understand. They have all the sympathy the Nazis showed the Jews." She began to shove things into her bag with more force than was necessary. "I just can't, Indie. Not right now. It's too dangerous. You don't know what you're asking me. It's an unnecessary danger."

"You don't think I can take care of myself? Is this how it's going to be? You keeping secrets from me? That's a great foundation for a relationship, Nate," she snapped.

I frowned, growing angry. How did she not understand that I was only trying to keep her *safe*? "There are things that I can't talk about, Indie. It's got nothing to do with me wanting to tell you or not. I just can't." *Without putting you in grave danger*, I didn't add.

She was silent for a few seconds, shoving and rearranging items into her luggage. She finally spoke, and I wished she hadn't, "I think you need a bit of time to yourself. To clear your head." She turned to look at me, mascara still running down her cheeks. I wanted to hold her, comfort her, but I knew that was the last thing she wanted. We were going to be in for a long debate tonight. She never dropped things. Especially this topic.

Which was why I was surprised when she spoke. "You need to get some sleep. I'm worried about you. All you do is hit up the bars or tinker at your company, when you really need sleep. Uninterrupted peace. By the way, any news from the bar about what your parents were hiding? Or who killed them?" she asked, somehow able to bury the topic from a few seconds ago. I shook my head in answer to her question about my parents.

She sighed sadly, as if having hoped I had finally found something to help soothe my grief. "Nate. I'm beyond pissed at you. But I know you have a lot on your plate, and it's not your choice to be in the situation you're in. I know you would drop everything to come with me, but it's not what *you* need. Despite your brave look, I can see that you are close to a meltdown. You're always working at the office, picking fights at shady bars, and you never sleep..."

I sighed. She was too good for me. The night terrors *had* forced me to dive headfirst into work, digging for information on my parents' murder, the Armory, and my growing magical boundaries. Well, they *had* been growing, up until tonight. Now I was on the opposite end of the spectrum. I was on borrowed power. How long would it last? What were the long-term effects of the curse? I shivered, not wanting to consider them. But I knew I would find myself back in the lab in the small hours of the morning, tinkering, building, making things... anything to keep my mind away from the night terrors. I would deal with it later.

All I'd wanted to do was to take Indie on a vacation, to get away from everything for a while. To smell the roses, so to speak. Indie was watching me sadly. "Nate... Maybe if you got some sleep you could look at it from a fresher perspective."

I sighed. "I'll try."

She smiled sadly. "We started dating during one of the most stressful times of your life, and that stress hasn't left. In fact, I think it's only grown more intense. Not that I blame you, but I don't think you gave yourself the time you needed to clear your head. I don't want our relationship to suffer because you were repressing what happened with your parents. Despite Raego trying to help by keeping the dragons in line after the murders, you're still far from the answers you thought you'd have by now. It's eating you alive. We barely talk. You wake in cold sweats, murmuring, fidgeting, and even shouting, during the little sleep you *do* get." That was news to me. "Perhaps you need to talk about it with someone. Maybe you're experiencing a wizard's version of post-traumatic stress disorder." Which was exactly what I had been wondering earlier. It wasn't every day you went up against a harem of weredragons and survived. "You keep me sheltered, and that's not okay. I hate to say it, but maybe this break is just what we need. I'll go take care of my mom for a few days, and you can focus on yourself for a bit."

I punched the pillow, scattering sequins over the bed. White-hot anger burned through my veins. Anger at myself. And... guilt. Damn it. She was right. I hadn't been there for her. She was great. Perfect for me, but I had been an ass. Between the night terrors, dealing with the new mantle of CEO of Temple Industries, and spending every waking minute – which had been a lot – trying to find the truth behind my parents' murder had put a large strain on Indie and myself. I needed to get some perspective. I was also still concerned about her... Regular-ness. How could I bring her into my life of danger? Werewolves, the Academy, dragons, magic, and now Angels and Demons. It wasn't fair for her. She had once told me that danger wouldn't keep her away, but I had. I had kept blinders on her, not allowing her to get closer than necessary to my oh-so-dangerous life. To keep her locked up in an ivory tower, not providing her the necessary training she would need to defend herself. And it had inadvertently hurt our relationship.

Indie looked pained as she watched my frustration. She climbed up onto the bed and placed a comforting palm on my thigh. "Nate, I'm not *too* angry with you, or disappointed in you, or even mad about everything, really. I understand. What you went through... Well, no one should have to go through that. In my eagerness to be near you, I might have done you harm. I should have given you space, but I wanted so badly to be with you that I let my emotions get ahead of me. You needed space to figure things out, and I didn't give you that. I blame myself. Now, you keep things from me. You don't talk to me about anything meaningful. You're scared. Scared to let me get close to the *real* you. Well, I think it's time for you to put your big boy pants on. You've got three days to figure out what you want."

Her timeframe momentarily chilled my blood. The same timeframe as the Academy's curse.

"If you want me, then you'll remove the walls you've built around your-self, or... we will probably never see each other again." My heart stopped as I stared at her in disbelief, which started her tears again. "I'm not sure that I could go back to being a mere friend after knowing what we have, *could* have, together. So, while I'm in Colorado with my mom, you need to really think about what you want. When I get back you need to tell me what that is. If you want me, you will tell me... everything. No secrets. I deserve that."

"Indie..." I warned, ready to tell her how bad of an ultimatum that was, how dangerous.

"Can it. I've been training with Tory and Misha. They've been teaching me how to take care of myself. Like you should have done." That stung. "You'd be surprised what I'm capable of. Regardless, this is just something you'll have to accept... or not. It's all or nothing, Nate." She smiled sadly at me. "Just know that if you choose wrong, I will be using everything Tory and Misha have taught me to hunt you down and teach you the error of your ways. Your magic won't save you from my wrath. They say hell hath no fury like a woman scorned. Well, you don't have to scorn me to see my wrath, just piss me off." Her pearly white teeth shone in the dim room.

I placed a hand on hers, nodding with a faint smile at her threat.

"And now, Dean is going to take me to Plato's Cave to get some sleep. You're still drunk, and after your shenanigans tonight, you don't deserve to see Nurse Indie." She winked darkly. I groaned. "Shush. You brought this on yourself. Bar fights earn no sexy time. And you have a lot to think about while I'm gone. You can start tonight. Absence makes the heart grow fonder, right?"

"You're a cruel, cruel woman, Indie. I know I've been keeping you at a distance, and you know why I do, right or wrong is irrelevant at the moment. But maybe I can work on my communication skills with you while you're gone. Would that break your rules?"

She assessed me for a minute. "Perhaps I should use this tactic more often. Look how malleable my Master Temple has become. I tell you I'm leaving for a few days and you're already asking if we can talk on the phone. You're a teenaged girl," she teased, pinching my leg. My face turned beet red as I began to blurt out an argument, but her laughter overwhelmed my arguments. She tapped her lips playfully, enjoying this way too much. "I would like that." She leaned forward and kissed my brow for a long second, careful of my nose, and granting me an expansive view of her cleavage, which she definitely knew she was doing. She was sneaky like that. "Good night, Nate. Sweet dreams..."

Her hair tickled my neck as she trailed a kiss down to my ear, breathing huskily before she gave me a playful nip. My pants constricted as my subconscious threatened to take control and pin her to the mattress and sequined pillows. She placed a constraining hand on my chest, shaking her head as if she could read my thoughts. I closed my eyes, the alcohol dragging them closed as mercilessly as if she had spelled me. I sensed the lights flick off from behind my closed eyelids, and then she was gone, dragging her suitcase out of my room.

I was peaceful for perhaps ten minutes, rehashing everything she had said to me, realizing that she was right about it all. Then sleep dragged me under like a sack of potatoes, and the haunting night terrors waited anxiously to welcome me back to their domain like an old friend.

CHAPTER 10

$\mathcal{I}$ stood alone in a field of fresh wheat beneath a purple sky. Humid air pressed down on me like a thick, wet blanket. I was physically sore. Exhausted even. Wisps of clouds scudded low in the sky, hovering over distant peaks like campfire smoke, and the air tasted like damp earth. I sniffed the air idly, catching a faint hint of wood smoke. It wasn't overpowering, and somehow made me feel relaxed. I spotted a house on a hill, a quaint, primitive place one might find in ancient Greece, mostly stone, and surrounded on all sides by more fields.

A farmer lives there.

Something tugged at my memory, but the thought was gone just as fast. My memory seemed to do that a lot of late. Why worry about the house, when I was merely out on an evening stroll in such a peaceful place? I decided to approach the house. Perhaps I would make a friend so that the next time I walked here I wouldn't be lonely.

Loneliness. The word tingled up my spine like the fingers of death. Now why had I thought that? I wasn't lonely. I had everything I needed. I had a woman, a steady life of farming, and a strong boy to teach my trade to. I shook my head as I began to walk back to my house.

My house... that wasn't right, was it? Then I was smiling as I imagined my wife greeting me at the front door, my son rushing out from between her legs to tackle me to the yard where we frequently wrestled. I dropped the reins to the horse behind me, as well as the tools I used to cut the wheat as I began to trot up the hill. The house loomed before me, both larger and smaller than it could be in real life, but this *was* real life, wasn't it?

"Hello?" I bellowed as I reached the front door. "Papa's home!"

Papa? I would never use that phrase. I was a *Dad* kind of guy, wasn't I?

No one answered me.

Then I smelled it. A sulfurous stink tinged with frozen stone – a cold, hard smell with a... coppery after-taste. That was odd. I had smelled that coppery flavor before, back when my horse had injured herself in a fall. Why would it smell like horse up here? No, not horse... blood. I looked back in confusion, expecting to see my horse injured. But I was utterly alone in the field. I blinked. *Hadn't I just left the horse behind me?* I shrugged after a moment. I must have worked harder than I remembered. Nothing that a good wine wouldn't resolve.

I stepped up the creaky wooden steps only to hear voices.

A jeweled box stood in the open doorway, all by itself. Beyond the box, my wife lay motionless on the floor. My son sat on his heels, rocking back and forth. "*Open the box, open the box, open thebox, open thebox, thebox, box, box...*" he muttered to himself over and over again, his eyes wild like a stray dog.

"Son, what's happened?" I demanded. He didn't seem to hear me, brushing his mother's hair out of her eyes as he continued his chant. I couldn't understand. All I had wanted to do was to sit down beside my wife with my son on my knees as we played a game and ate dinner together. I didn't want any violence, any problems, I had no enemies. I only wanted to be a good farmer. That was all.

I looked further on and saw a man standing between two creatures, speaking quietly. Now that I was inside the house, I noticed that it was storming outside. But... *hadn't it just been pleasant outside?* I was so confused.

I couldn't hear the words, but I saw my son look up at me, with a sharp rictus of a smile. "*You mustn't listen to them. Open the box, open the box, the box, box, box...*" he muttered over and over and over, his voice sounding like nails on a chalkboard. I cringed, tuning out the almost demonic chanting. Something about this seemed all too familiar, but I couldn't understand why. One of the creatures handed the man something and the world exploded in a green hue. My son screamed louder. "The box!" His words had a physical sensation to them now, like my very eardrum was the chalkboard. I grabbed my ears in pain, glancing up in time to see the other creature handing a tall tool to the man. The tip gleamed silver in the incessant flashing of lightning raging outside. The world seemed to be tearing itself apart – the house imploding in an explosion of sound, wind, and distant screams from the blackest pits of hell. My son huddled over his mother as if protecting her from the insanity. I glanced over at his frantically pointing hand to see that despite the strength of the wind, which was pushing even me back from the door, the box lay unmoving as if bolted down. I clawed my body closer to it, dodging flying planks of wood from the destroyed windowsills I had made last year. The box glittered encouragingly. I heard the snap as of great wings lifting a bird to flight, and a *crack* of sound as if the world itself had opened up. Not daring to look, I dove for the box, my son screaming over and over again. *"The box, box, box, box!"* my fingertips touched the box in a flash of scalding skin and I managed to flick the lid open with my thumbnail.

The world went white and I heard my son scream as my mind liquefied.

CHAPTER 11

I woke up panting hoarsely. Another night terror. Had I screamed out loud again and woken Dean? Then I remembered that he was either dropping Indie off at Plato's Cave or taking her to the airport, depending on how long I had slept. Then he was out of town for a few days as well. I was entirely alone. Even Mallory was getting some sand in his hair and sun on his face for the next week. Pure bachelorhood. I growled, squashing my puny pity with my mighty willpower. I would be fine. I didn't need anyone to watch over me. I was a grown-ass man.

"Yeah. You're a grown-ass man," I cheered myself on with pure testicular fortitude. I tried to smile, but the constriction of my face muscles almost made me cry out like a small child. My nose sure felt like it was broken. I touched it gingerly and winced, realizing my hands were raw with several hundred thousand tiny cuts from the broken whisky glasses at the bar. Oh, well. Nothing for it. I glanced at my phone – which I had somehow remembered to plug in before I fell into a coma – through sandy eyes. Six in the morning. I had slept for several hours, despite having felt like I had only just closed my eyes. It might have been the longest I'd slept in weeks. Even catching some much-needed horizontal, I had the familiar sensation of being hung over. I groaned at the headache behind my eyelids as I rolled onto my back.

What the hell had my night terror been about? I realized after a few moments of deep breathing that I had dreamt about Hemingway's story from the bar... kind of. It was as if I had been the subject of the story, but also an outsider. Then there had been the cursed box. Always the box. Every night terror I had revolved around me opening a box. The boxes changed in appearance, but they were always there, and despite the chaos of the dream, the only way to escape was to open it. Which was always terrifying, and hurt like hell. I wondered idly, as I had a hundred times before, if the box was a subconscious replacement for the music box Peter had stolen from my parents' Armory during his brief sojourn inside. But I didn't understand how that could be true. I had tested the box. Again. And again. And again, to no avail. There was absolutely nothing special about the box. At all.

So why did I keep dreaming about it? Was it because it was all the evidence I had about the Armory?

And did I dream about Hemingway's story simply because the grim tale had been on my mind? Or was there some deeper meaning? I shook my head, kicking my shoes off the covers – which I had slept on top of – to place my feet on the ground. Of course, it had nothing to do with a deeper meaning. It was a dark fucking story, and I had heard it a few hours before passing out. And my dreams had incorporated it into their mad funhouse of horrors. That was just how lucky I was.

I was simply over-stressed. At some point in the past week, I had deduced another possible reason for dreaming about a box. My dad had once used a different phrase to refer to the Armory... Pandora Protocol. It was how I had heard about the Armory in the first place. One drunken night when he had said it a few times under his breath. He had been speaking about a secret project at the family company, Temple Industries.

I later found out that his Pandora Protocol had actually come to fruition. His goal of using extreme measures to hide dangerous items of power. An Armory. It was real. Real enough for the Justices of the Academy to hunt me down to take it. My father had called his project the Pandora Protocol as a subtle nod to the 'secrets' hidden away from mankind inside Pandora's Box. Thinking on it now, I was merely glad that no one else had heard his pet name for the project. If the Academy had heard Pandora Protocol, they would have no doubt killed me on the spot tonight for thinking it was literal, when my father had simply been grandiose with names.

I decided to go to the kitchen and scrounge up some food. Maybe snort a line of Tylenol for both my headache and what felt like a broken nose, even though the mirror showed me it wasn't. I prodded it gently and winced at the insomniac panda staring back at me. The day was starting off well.

I needed to run over to Temple Industries to catch up on some work before Ashley and Gunnar left for Bora Bora. That brought a smile to my face. Gunnar was going to propose to Ashley in a few days.

Silver lining.

Thirty minutes later, my phone began blaring from the nightstand while I was halfway through my pushup routine. I jumped to my feet, ignoring the pounding headache, and snatched up the device. "Gunnar," I answered, breathing heavily.

"Nate! What the hell happened last night? We tried calling you for an hour. The cop thought it was one of your drunk tricks and wouldn't take us seriously."

"Yeah. I talked to him about it after," I mumbled. If saving his ass from a Demon counted for 'talking about it,' we were golden. "I was picked up by some Academy... detectives." Gunnar was an ex-FBI agent. He could relate to the term *detectives*. Not so much, *Assassin squad*. "They wanted a debriefing on the debacle a few months back."

"Didn't you send them a report already?" he asked, voice tight, as if doubting I had ever sent said report.

"Of course. It was all done up official and everything... via email." Gunnar sighed. I continued before he could butt in. "They wanted a face-to-face. I gave it to them and told them where to stick any further inquiries."

Gunnar was silent for a moment. "Which means they didn't take it very well."

"Relax. They understand the picture now."

"That's odd. Because I don't even understand the picture." He didn't sound happy. "Anyway, I'm glad you're alright. I didn't want to call Indie without solid news, and I heard her mother is in a bad way. I didn't want to add to it. Neither did Tory, or Ashley." His tone grew more responsible. "You put us in a tough situation last night. You continue to keep things from her, which makes the rest of us keep things from her, which makes a big fucking wall in the trust department. I would appreciate it if you would fix that. Pronto."

I rolled my eyes. "On it. We talked last night. She's going to Colorado to take care of her mom. She basically told me to get my shit together while she's gone so we can square up for round two. At least I'm still in the fight at the moment."

He sighed on the other end of the line. "Nate... I'm not the king of relationships or anything, but perhaps your love life would be simpler if you wouldn't relate your talks to boxing matches. If anything, they could be related to tag-team wrestling matches. You're supposed to be on the same side, not squaring off against each other."

"I know," I admitted. "But—"

"She's a Regular. Yeah, you told me. It's becoming less and less of an issue. Look at Ashley. She's doing fine, and she's dating a werewolf. You're just some schmuck wizard. Really not even in the same league." I could sense his shit-eating grin over the phone.

"Bad puppy. No treats for you."

He grunted. "Ashley and I are flying out at 2 pm. Need anything from her before we are incommunicado for a week?"

"Nervous?" I asked seriously.

"Fucking terrified. Square me off against a silver dragon any day, but this... man, it's a lot of pressure on a guy. What if she says *No*, or waffles about timing? Now I know why you stayed single for so long. This commitment thing has a lot of pitfalls."

I laughed. "Yeah. But this kind of opportunity comes along once in a lifetime. You have to grab it and assert your dominance. Hump the hell out of that leg, know what I mean?"

The line was silent for a few moments. "Nate. I'm a werewolf, not a schnauzer. I don't always think like a dog, nor do I need references made to relate human interactions to their animal equivalent to understand basic concepts."

"*Who's a smart puppy? Gunnie! Oh yes, Gunnie is.*"

"Nate, you need to stop talking. Right now."

"Oh? You're packing for the most terrifying moment of your life. Proposing to Ashley on a romantic vacation. We won't see each other for at least a wee—"

The door to my room suddenly imploded in a shower of splinters as a fucking mountain of white fur tackled me to the floor, jaws snapping amidst a flurry of drool and ivory canines. The phone flew out of my hands to slam into the wall behind me. We tumbled into the nightstand, and I barely remembered my curse as my instincts threatened to take over and incinerate the threat with magic. Instead, I rolled with my attacker and used my feet to launch him behind me into the dresser. The white-haired werewolf sailed into the mirror, shattering it with a heavy crunch before bouncing off the dresser and rolling to his feet. He sat down on his haunches with a panting doggy grin.

"Goddamn it, Gunnar!" I snapped, panting heavily as I tried to calm my racing heart and ease my pounding headache. I didn't know how I had restrained myself from using magic. It had been a near miss. But the fear of the curse being permanent had flown into my mind at the last second. Then I had noticed the white fur. Before I had consciously made a decision, I had used simple grappling techniques to toss him from my personal space, but if it had been a real threat, I wasn't sure I would have been so lucky.

He shifted from his hairy werewolf form to his usual self – a chiseled, blonde-haired, mountain of a man. His long blonde hair hung around his bearded face, framing his pearly white grin. And he was completely naked. I averted my eyes, which made him chuckle. "I warned you to watch your mouth," he said, glancing at the shredded fabric dotting the floor. His werewolf form didn't tolerate human-sized clothes very well.

"How the fuck did you get in here?" I answered, pointing at my wardrobe so he could nab a change of clothes.

He nodded in appreciation, opening the dresser as he answered. "Dean gave me a key a while back. To keep an eye on you and Indie. He didn't know who or what might come looking for you two after the Dragon ordeal." He cocked his head for a second. "Hey, why didn't you Hogwarts my ass like you usually do? I mean, to be honest, you kind of just got your ass kicked. Like a little man bitc—"

Before I thought about it, I vaporized like I had learned last night, vanishing from Gunnar's view to appear directly behind him. Part of my shirt tugged at me, and I saw a piece flutter to the ground where I had been standing a moment before, having been caught in the void of the teleportation spell and not making the trip along with my body. I used the momentum of teleporting – as it felt like riding a rollercoaster – to cold-cock my best friend in the jaw. The resounding *crack* was satisfying as his head snapped to the side and into the dresser before he crumpled to the ground. It only took him a second to shamble to his feet, eyes wide as he blinked up at where I now stood and where I had stood only a second ago. He rubbed his jaw, stunned.

"Okay... give me a minute... that was pretty... I mean, *wow*. What the hell just happened?" he finally asked in genuine awe.

I grinned back at his astonishment, slowly walking back over to pick up the piece of fabric that had been left behind, hiding my fear of both using my limited power for no real reason, and what might have happened if that little piece had been a more permanent part of me. "I just *Hogwarts'd* your ass," I said drily.

He blinked at me. "Is that one of the things you've been tinkering with in your psychotic research experiments? I've never seen you do that before."

"Kind of." I shrugged. "Learned it from the Academy thugs last night. Apparently, it's a secret of theirs. They weren't pleased I picked it up so fast... or at all. And hangovers give me a short fuse. Sorry. You all right?"

He shook his head as if to clear it. "Yeah. Just didn't see it coming. How far can you do it? Just in close quarters like you did here?" he asked, curious.

"No. I teleported from Temple Industries to the Bar after my talk with the Academy last night. But that took considerably more power than what I just did," I said more to myself, realizing that it had barely cost me any of my dwindling magic to clock Gunnar.

"Wow. Well, consider myself all apologized. I was just giving you a hard time. I don't think you pulled that punch at all, did you? Rage issues much?" he teased. Werewolves could take a lot of pain and keep on ticking. Anyone else would have been out cold from my punch. But Gunnar was one tough son of a bitch, and I was glad to have him on my side.

I ignored the comment as he began to throw on a pair of slacks and a tee from the dresser. I kept clothes in his size throughout the house for events such as this when he needed to replace a destroyed wardrobe. "By the way, why did you send Tory into the bar last night instead of coming in yourself?" I asked.

"It was a powder keg in there, Nate. I can't believe you could stand it, what with how much loose energy was dancing around in there. I could even sense it from outside. I thought things like that messed with wizards."

"It does," I said, nodding, although I hadn't particularly noticed it last night. "I've just been so tired lately that it must have slipped my mind. I'm kind of off my game. I've been somewhat... reckless lately," I admitted.

Gunnar grunted. "That's why I sent Tory in there. My presence would have just instigated a territorial fight from the wolves. Also, Tory isn't necessarily an enemy of any of the creatures in the bar. She's just a woman with extraordinary strength. A supernatural Switzerland to the creatures inside the Kill." I was just glad it had all worked out. "Which leads me to wonder why you were in a Kill in the first place. You. Stupid. Bastard." He enunciated each word with tightly bottled frustration.

"Easy, swear-wolf. Virgin ears here."

Gunnar merely stared harder, if that was possible. "Looking for answers again," I finally explained, plucking my phone up from the carpet. The screen featured a spider web of cracks, eliciting a grumble of displeasure from my throat as I held it up to Gunnar, hoping to change the topic.

He shrugged. "You're good for it."

I pressed a button and saw that I could more or less still make out important details. I tossed it in my pocket as Gunnar continued. "Now, back to the important stuff. I thought you gave up searching for information after you were booted from several bars. For life."

"Nah. Can't sleep, so I hunt."

There was a long silence. "You're still having the nightmares?" I nodded slowly. He shook his head in disbelief, part concerned, part angry that he couldn't do anything to help. "Well? Did you discover anything helpful?"

I hesitated. Did I want to bring him into this? Angels were in a league of their own. I knew I could trust my friends, but I didn't want them in over their heads. I had no choice, but they did. "Nah," I lied. "But I've heard a lot of stories about my parents lately. Apparently, an impressive number of people considered them scoundrels. Not as many as praised them, but still... enough to make me reconsider."

"What do you mean? Why would they say anything bad about your parents? They were saints," Gunnar growled, instantly defensive and territorial. I smiled to myself, turning away.

Because my parents had helped Gunnar, and many, many others, with various magical maladies. Gunnar was no longer a slave to the cycles of the moon, thanks to them. They had given him a rune tattoo that allowed him to shift into a werewolf at will. Most other werewolves couldn't do such a thing. Unless they were super powerful or super old. Regardless of shifting at will or not, almost all werewolves had to shift during the full moon. But Gunnar didn't. All because my parents knew of an odd rune that allowed him to master his inner wolf.

Now that I thought about it, how the hell had they known how to do such a thing? If it were common knowledge to wizards, I would have heard of it at least a few times. Wizards would have sold that to trusted werewolves for a high price. Or maybe in exchange for an alliance. But I had *never* heard of a wizard doing a spell like that for a werewolf. Odd. Where had my parents learned it? And that wasn't the only uniquely magical cure my parents had given back to the community. In fact, it was one of *many* magical cures they had given out. Almost as if they had access to knowledge most wizards didn't. A shiver ran down my spine as the obvious answer came to me. The Pandora Protocol. The Armory.

I spoke over my shoulder. "They allegedly stole some things a time or two, always from old families. Random things. I've heard them described as heirlooms, paintings, and even ancient knick-knacks with no known nature or origin. Every story is different. But then other people denied those same accusations, admitting the items had been fairly purchased. Regardless, these stories are a decade old. Nothing useful to me, now. Still, it's an odd thing to hear. I think these informants all assumed that if they told me something juicy I could owe them a favor. I quickly discouraged that line of thought, which got me kicked out of the other bars. Everyone's just scared after Alaric's speech at the Eclipse Expo about outing magical creatures. They fear that if I give in, like Alaric told everyone I would, they would all be outed as Freaks, too. The world is crazy lately," I said, raking a hand through my hair.

It was almost as if the deeper I dug, the more I realized that I hadn't known my parents at all. They were public tech-tycoons during the day and devoted parents at night. All while being full-time wizards with secret agendas at their own company. And now I hear they were part-time thieves? But why? Had they amassed an armory of random weapons and artifacts in their Pandora Protocol? And what was the Titan warning on the video feed I had seen?

I could sense Gunnar still staring at me with concerned eyes. It ticked me off. I didn't ask my friends to look after me. I was fine. "Anyway. Enough psychoanalysis. How are you?"

"Great. Nervous about this whole proposal situation, though." I smiled, but he changed topics back to me. "It's probably a good time to get out of town, Nate. *Mardi Gras* is nuts in St. Louis. Maybe a vacation is what you need, too." I know what he really wanted was for me to stop digging into the darkness that was plaguing me lately. Maybe he was right. It would have been nice to get away, as I didn't want to get mixed up in Angel business. Or Demon business. But the Academy had put a stop to that with their curse.

I was being forced into a lonely stay-cation.

Gunnar continued. "Our new gig as black ops wizards – or supernaturals – could get dicey, so I'm taking a vacation while I can." He and Ashley weren't wizards, but since the world at large considered any Freak to be a wizard, our team's nickname had worked for me, although I wasn't betting on any government contracts in the near future, if ever. More just neighborhood vigilante jobs.

"I'm happy for you two." I was doubly glad I hadn't mentioned the Angel in the bar, or the Brimstone stench. If I told him what had happened in the bar, he would no doubt cancel his plans. And Ashley would agree. They were the best kind of friends. But I couldn't do that to them. I could handle this on my own.

Which reminded me...

"You have time to drop me off at Temple Industries before you leave, right? Dean is taking Indie to the airport, and then he's hopping on his own flight out of St. Louis. He hasn't left the Chateau in a while, so I gave him some time off. Mallory also left to get some sun and sand, so I don't have a ride. Plus, my headache will probably impair my vehicular control. I'd hate to start off the day with an accident."

"Yeah. Lately, with your temper and lack of sleep, an accident could easily turn into vehicular manslaughter." He paused, studying me. "You could always take your new horse," he added with a scowl of disapproval.

I blushed. "My horse?" I asked innocently.

"Yes. Xavier, if I remember correctly." He was tapping his foot. "That's a federal crime, you know. I don't even want to ask how it happened. Plausible deniability." He folded his arms.

I threw my hands up. "I didn't have a choice. I'll say this, though. My actions saved two lives. So, I'll take the consequences any day. But I'll have Dean return him as soon as possible."

Gunnar grunted for good measure. "Fine. I'm already packed and Ashley is at the company wrapping up a few loose ends. Workaholic," he said, rolling his eyes. "This actually saves me time. We can leave for the airport from there."

"Good. I have one more pit stop to make on the way."

He studied me skeptically. "Okay... where?" he asked warily.

"The church on the way to Temple Industries has a fountain outside, right?" Gunnar blinked before slowly nodding. "Good. Take me there. I fancy a dip. Care to partake in the morning's debauchery?"

He cocked his head. "Nate. You do know its seventeen degrees outside, right? I think I'll take a rain check."

"Seventeen…" That was the exact number of minutes Peter had been inside the Armory. "Of course," I mumbled to myself. "I'll be quick," I added hastily before he could question my comment.

Gunnar shook his head. "It's your funeral."

I smiled, preparing myself for the chill. "Not my funeral today, Gunnie."

This was one thing on my to-do list I could cross off… "How's the rest of the gang?" I asked idly, finishing up my pushup routine as he dressed.

"Raego is leaving for Europe to strengthen his rule. Tory and Misha are going with him to help, or maybe just so Misha can show Tory her home-land. It's cute. You should see Tory wrestle with Misha's… *dragonlings.*" We hadn't known what else to call them. "Disturbing, but cute." He smiled. "I can't blame them." His gaze grew thoughtful. "With us all out of your hair, maybe you'll get time to clear your head. Get some real sleep." He assessed me like only a long-time friend could. "Or just get roaring drunk in a dangerous bar. I think they're both the same to you, lately."

I wrapped up my workout, feeling marginally better, grunting agreement with his comments. As I got dressed for the day, I found myself hoping that I wouldn't be attacked by one of my most recent enemies before lunch.

CHAPTER 12

*G*reta smiled smugly. "You look like a raccoon," my secretary said, pointing at my rapidly forming black eyes. Then her eyes roamed with distaste down to the puddle at my feet, and continued back along the trail of wet boot prints I had left from the entrance. "A drowned raccoon. Or a slug."

I very carefully stifled my anger, not rising to the bait. "Don't change the subject, Greta. For the last time, I find it highly doubtful that this found its way to my mail cubby via regular mail. There's no stamp on it. This is junk mail. Or a solicitation, which is against company policy…" I warned.

"Well, if you consider your eternal soul to be junk, then you're technically correct," she answered drily. After a short silence, her eyes grew softer, motherly. "Just read it. You might learn a thing or two." With infinite tolerance, I pocketed the religious tract and didn't crumple it up to throw in her face. She meant well. Really. I just didn't take it well when people told me in a roundabout way that I wasn't a good person. The title read *Jesus and You, Your Only True Friend*. Gunnar very wisely kept a straight face.

We walked past Greta's desk and into my office. I instantly froze as my eyes settled on the room. A giant cross was nailed to the wall behind my desk, at least six feet tall and extravagantly detailed. On my desk sat a fresh cup of coffee inside a mug I had never seen before. A depiction of Christ adorned the coffee mug handle. "Greta?" I called out warningly.

She shuffled into the room on arthritic hips with a curious look on her face, not appearing to see anything amiss. "Yes, Master Temple?"

"It seems someone took the liberty to find me the actual cross that Jesus was crucified on, and then decided to hang it on my wall. And I seem to have a new coffee mug."

"Oh, goodness. I thought perhaps you had purchased the mug after reading the various pamphlets you had received. I don't know how the Cross got up there, but perhaps reflecting on his sacrifice might ease your stress. Touching Jesus daily might help also," she offered, pointing at my mug.

I stared at her in disbelief, then the handle of the coffee mug. "I'm sure palming his crotch would be a religious experience for some, but to me it's merely distasteful."

She prickled up indignantly. "Well, if I were in your shoes, I would take into consideration that someone must care for you very deeply, and I would cherish these gifts for that reason alone. Someone obviously holds a great deal of concern for your soul, despite your constant mockery of their faith." Her face was red, ready for me to command that the no-doubt expensive artifact be torn down and tossed in the trash. Religion was everything to her, and it seemed her sole purpose in life was to 'Save' all the lost souls around her. Namely, me. It was sweet... and annoying. Plus, I was sure she had expensed the extravagant purchase to Temple Industries, meaning I had paid for it myself.

I wanted to lash out on the old woman, but knew it would do no good. I sighed. She was right. It was done with the best of intentions. "That will be all, Greta," I answered in defeat. "Why don't you take the rest of the day off? Didn't you mention a charity event you were planning to attend after work? Why don't you go there early and help them set up? You deserve it," I said with a forced smile on my face.

Her beady eyes assessed me with distrust for a few seconds before slowly morphing in humble victory. She very wisely didn't press her luck, and instead turned to grab her purse and leave for the day. She called over a shoulder. "One of the interns found a broom closet he swears was not there last week. I set him straight, but you should look into it. He said it had an odd symbol carved above the door. Interns should be seen and not heard," she grumbled more to herself. My shoulders stiffened slightly, but she didn't notice.

"I'll check it out. Have a great rest of the day." She grunted back, not looking at me. Then she was off. As soon as she was out of sight, I instinctively reached to my magic to tear the cross down from the wall, but an icy chill of warning stopped me at the very last second. I couldn't waste my magic like that right now.

Instead, I called out to one of the minions in a nearby cubicle. "You." I pointed. It was the same man that I had terrified a few months ago, when I had first met Greta. The kid was as unconfident as I had ever seen. I needed to help him grow a backbone, but working for someone like Greta seemed to make that impossible. "Take down this monstrosity immediately. Then place it behind Greta's desk."

The kid stared at me, dumbfounded, before finally stammering an answer. "Um... you're my boss, but... she will literally kill me if I step foot into her Jesus-Zone. Then she will kill me again when she sees that I put the cross she gave you behind her chair. It's bigger than she is," he added nervously.

"Does she really call her workspace the Jesus-Zone?" I asked in disbelief. Surely, he was exaggerating. But he nodded, a sober look of fear on his pale face. "Tell her that you caught me trying to remove it and before I could throw it away you decided to put it in the only safe place on the floor – the Jesus-Zone." I winked at him. "This is a lesson in politics. Finding a way to work with conflicting orders to your best advantage. It's very useful information to know." The kid shivered, doubting his future as soon as I was not there to protect him from the saintly secretary.

"Gunnar, let's go find Ashley." He nodded, chuckling under his breath as we headed to her office. "Can it. It's really not that funny. It's not like I'm a horrible person or anything. Where does she get off passively telling me that I'm such a wreck that I need an intervention?"

"It's very... touching," he answered, his laughter fading. Great, he was siding with her. This was ridiculous. Why was everything turning against me lately? I didn't need to worry about religion when I had literal Angels scouting my trail. I was probably closer to Heavenly scrutiny then Greta would ever be... I pondered that for a few steps. Maybe she had a point.

Nah. I was probably fine.

I was here to study the Armory if I could find a way inside. That was all. Then I could be on my way. Wherever that was. I still shivered a bit from the dip I had taken in the fountain on the way here, but it gave me peace of mind to know that perhaps one problem was now gone. However, my damp clothes didn't feel very pleasant at the moment.

I began pondering the Armory as we walked in silence. I had spent practically all my time at Temple Industries trying to find some solid information on the secrets that were allegedly buried inside. But I had come up with nothing. Oh, sure, I had clarified a few points, but that was all.

Point one – Peter had broken inside the Armory the same night my parents were killed. The security camera that seemed omnipotent – able to detect the magical abilities and identities of almost everyone in town – hadn't known what to make of Peter, as he had been shrouded in living shadows, belying the fact that he had used something to trick the camera and disguise himself. I had found proof of this after sneakily raiding his office once things had calmed down a bit. He had stolen a ring from my desk that helped one become forgettable, a spell of sorts I had been tinkering around with at one point in my life. It must have sat in my desk for years at Plato's Cave before Peter swiped it. After seeing the video, and after the chaos had died down, I realized that the distortion in the video had paralleled the forgotten spelled ring I had once made. I must have mentioned it to Peter at some point, as he had made it a priority to steal it from under my trusting nose.

So, Peter had broken into the Armory and returned with an apparently useless music box.

Point two – some unknown person had simultaneously broken into Temple Industries to kill my parents. I now knew that neither party had been affiliated with the dragons. That had merely been a coincidence that the late Alaric Slate, then leader of the dragon nation, had capitalized on. Peter had immediately tried to sell his music box to Alaric in exchange for the gift of magical power. It hadn't worked out for anyone, and I had gotten the music box back.

So, now I knew that some third party had been after either my parents or the Armory. Immediately after Peter's intrusion, my father had locked down the room and then been killed by said third party, leaving behind a cryptic message on the security feed for my eyes only. Which made no sense to me. Even now. Then the word *Titan* had popped up on the feed, and the video ended. No one had been able to enter since, even after we removed the security door my father had activated. But if the additional security was now gone, and it was the same as it had been when Peter so easily opened the door, how could I not enter? It was baffling. Even more concerning was that now, thanks to the Justices, the illusion hiding the door was gone, leaving it visible to anyone.

Ashley appeared from around a corner, carrying a pile of paperwork in a manila folder. She smiled hungrily at seeing her beau, Gunnar, and then more professionally at me. Then she froze. "Jesus! Your face!" she blurted.

"Better not let Greta hear you talk like that or you'll get an avalanche of these on your desk." I tossed her the religious tract.

She caught it easily and then glanced around my shoulder, as if verifying Greta wasn't here, before deftly adding it to her manila folder. "Been trying to save you again, eh?" she smirked. I nodded. "So, did she hit you in the face with a Gutenberg or something?"

Gunnar lost it, his laughter filling the hallway. I scowled at the two of them. "It's not that funny, but yes, you could say Religion punched me in the nose."

She frowned at my choice of words, but let it go. "What brings you two rogues here?"

"Easy, you two," I muttered before Gunnar could say anything gooey and romantic. He didn't look pleased at my efficient slaughter of the mood.

"Why are your clothes wet?" Ashley was frowning at the trail of wet footprints I had left behind me. I had used a quick effortless spell to squeeze out the majority of the water from my wardrobe, but some still remained. Any stronger a spell than that would have used too much power.

Gunnar piped up in response to Ashley. "Don't ask. He's completely mental. Howard Hughes mental. He went for a swim in a holy fountain, but wouldn't tell me why."

They both turned to me, hoping I would elaborate. But I didn't feel like doing that. It would only bring about more questions.

I began walking down the hall, calling over my shoulder. "Shall we?"

Ashley and Gunnar shared a look before following me. I guided us to the door that had started it all. I was both excited and terrified to gain entrance to the Armory. I wanted, *needed*, to know what was inside, but wasn't sure if I was ready to handle it. *Anything* could be in there. It could in fact be the equivalent of nuclear warheads, as the Academy feared. What would I do if that were the case? I wanted to ask myself what my parents would do, but that was obvious. They had hidden it away, after all. I shook my head, noticing Gunnar and Ashley watching me discreetly as we meandered the halls.

Did the room have something to do with my night terrors, and their recent evolution into daymares? They had started immediately after the dragon attack. Was it some form of lingering effect of the dragons' mind-magic? But no, Raego had informed me that it wasn't. Unless... he was in on it. I shivered. If I couldn't trust my friends, whom could I turn to? I had even begun to look into the myth lore of Pandora – stretching for leads a bit since my father had named the project Pandora Protocol – but I had run into nothing substantial. Pandora had died, or disappeared, and no one had heard of her or the box – or urn as most stories elaborated – since. Maybe it was just an allegory – an example – of powers left best untouched that my father found fitting as a title for his secret project. A project that involved dangerous powers he wanted out of the hands of the community. What better name than Pandora? I had even pondered going to talk to Asterion – the Minotaur – to see if he knew anything about the myth. I mean, he would have been around during her origin. If anyone knew her story, he would.

Gunnar broke the silence. "So, made any new gadgets lately?" he asked me curiously.

I looked over at him, then away. I didn't feel like talking about it, as Indie's harsh words about me ignoring her for my 'tinkering' were still fresh in my mind. "No."

Which was a lie.

It was all I had been doing since the dragon attack. Every time I tried to sleep, the night terrors were there to welcome me. So, I tinkered. And I had managed to create some truly incredible things. It was as if my sleeplessness had awoken the Leonardo da Vinci hiding inside me.

Raego had provided me with a literal truckload of silver scales from the dragon I had killed over the Eads Bridge, and despite not knowing what I wanted to – or could – do with them, I had used them to create quite a few useful tools. The magical boost in power I had received after my parents' murder had fueled me to new heights of creativity I was sure no one had anticipated, but I needed to be careful with those secrets. If anyone found out what I had been making, they could use my friends against me to divulge those secrets. Very dangerous secrets. Secrets that might become necessary if my powers failed me and another Angel or Demon knocked on my door.

We entered the hallway that housed the now visible door to the Armory. A crude *Omega* symbol was etched into the stone over the frame, causing me to shiver. That symbol translated to *the end*. We were just down the hall from where I had been abducted by the Academy less than 12 hours ago.

"Um. Why is it out in the open like this?" Ashley asked nervously.

"I removed the spell hiding it, obviously," I muttered. Gunnar eyed me doubtfully, remembering my mention of the visit from the Academy Justices last night.

But, like a good minion, at least Ashley accepted my answer. "We still don't know how to enter, but your parents might have hidden their trail. They must have had some kind of key," she offered cautiously.

"The Academy goons mentioned something about a key, also. They seemed to think I had it on me, but I have no idea what or where it could be."

Ashley raised a brow. "Academy? As in, the secret wizard police?" she asked with growing alarm.

I nodded. Gunnar looked more concerned by the second.

"Maybe we need to stay in town for a while to help you, Nate," Ashley said, ever the corporate soldier. Gunnar's gaze crashed and burned with both the resigned weight of responsibility to a friend and the dying dreams of his impending proposal. I couldn't let that happen.

"No. You two need a break. They're just fact-finding at the moment. They want to know what happened here. And they took their sweet time coming to ask. I don't think they're in much of a rush or they would have come knocking on my door sooner. I think they're just trying to tie up loose ends for documentation purposes. They didn't really seem that concerned."

Gunnar's eyes weighed heavily on mine, but I could tell that as much as he wanted to stay and help me, he wanted to propose to this amazing woman even more. I couldn't blame him. He had spent his whole life looking for the perfect woman, never sleazing around, but merely waiting. This could literally be his once-in-a-lifetime chance at claiming true love. If I told them anything about the curse the Academy had placed on me, or my new parole officer, Gavin, I would never get rid of my friends, and Gunnar would never propose to Ashley. There are times when my life just really sucks. I could definitely use their help, but *my* problem did not constitute *their* problem.

Thinking of Gavin out there somewhere in my city, scouting me unseen, made me nervous all over again. Maybe he was using an Academy trick to watch me even now... I shrugged that one off as a bit excessive. They wouldn't have needed to confront me if they could do that. I hadn't noticed anyone trailing me on the way here with Gunnar, but *lack* of proof of being tailed was not proof that I *wasn't* being tailed. It's only paranoia when you're wrong.

I quickly realized that having asked to see Ashley might actually destroy Gunnar's big plan. I had to get rid of them. Now. I would have to figure this out on my own.

"Listen, guys. I'll be fine for a few days. Indie's out of town with her mother since the accident, and I could really use the *me*-time to clear my head. I know I've been impossible to be around lately, and to be honest, I'm not sure I dealt with my parents' murder the healthiest way."

"I don't know. Slaying a harem of weredragons felt very therapeutic to me." Gunnar grinned.

I smiled back weakly, nodding. "True, but I've got a lot of Demons, you know?" *No pun intended*, I thought to myself. "And I need to find a way to banish them before it costs me my friends, the company, or... Indie." Ashley's eyes glistened sympathetically as she laid a hand on my shoulder for support. I was definitely speaking literally *and* figuratively, but they didn't need to know that.

"Don't worry, Nate. You'll figure it out. You always do. Maybe you're right. No distractions for a few days. Clear your head. Tinker around a bit, and we'll be back to clean up the mess in no time." I scowled back and she smiled mischievously through still damp eyes. "You will barely even know we're gone." *Right*, I thought darkly. I would be too preoccupied with Angels, Demons, and the Academy to realize that my only allies were thousands of miles away, getting engaged. "If it wasn't for Gunnar winning those airline tickets online, we might not ever have decided to go. Admitted workaholics." She smiled, winking at Gunnar. I noticed Gunnar's gaze shifting to mild concern as he studied my face, reconsidering based on something he saw deep inside my eyes. I couldn't have that.

"Well, I'm glad he won the tickets," I said. "You guys really drag me down sometimes. An eagle needs to stretch his wings or else he becomes a chicken." Gunnar growled at that. I smirked back darkly. "Really, I'll be fine. Besides, I do have other friends, you know." A thought sparked at the words, but I kept my face straight. I hoped I sounded genuine. Gunnar was an ex-FBI Agent who could smell a lie a mile away, not even accounting for his werewolf sense of smell.

Gunnar's concern disappeared as Ashley reached up to caress the long scar on my jaw that had been caused by Alaric Slate's death throes. She hesitated near my nose, for which I was thankful. "No repeats of last time. We need you in tip-top shape." She spoke with concern.

Gunnar grunted. "Well played, Nate. I think we need to get out of here before he convinces you he's a decent guy," he warned Ashley, chuckling at my resulting sneer. Ashley punched him playfully on the arm, immediately flexing her fingers in discomfort afterwards. It wasn't fun to punch a werewolf. Gunnar kissed her knuckles sweetly before they waved a final time and left me alone in front of the door. I shot Gunnar a last second thumbs up out of Ashley's view. He scowled back with a shake of his head.

Great. I had gotten rid of any potential casualties.

Now what?

CHAPTER 13

I hung up my cell phone with a marginal twinkle in my eyes. Perhaps I would actually get some help without risking anyone's life after all. It felt good to possibly be ahead of the bad guys for once.

With nothing else to do, I stepped closer to the mysterious door – or broom closet, as it now appeared to be – that led to the Armory. And I knocked.

Politely.

Hey, you never know when something is going to knock back, and it costs nothing to be polite. I felt more than a little ridiculous knocking on a broom closet door, but magic was funny like that. When I opened the door without permission, it was a broom closet, but if I knocked… things might be entirely different. I waited.

And waited.

And continued waiting a few moments longer.

But nothing happened.

I pounded the door with my fist. Nothing. So, I slapped it in a fit of rage with my open palm, immediately breaking open the wound caused by the broken bar glasses last night. I saw the hot blood splatter onto the door before the sting of pain registered. "Motherf—"

But I bit my tongue as the door began to suddenly open with a long, eerie creak, like the middle of every bad horror movie. A warm wind buffeted past me, ruffling my coat. Huh. It wasn't a *Key* after all. Maybe the password to open the door was an expletive. That sounded like just the kind of humor my father might use.

Then a chill went down my spine as I applied a sliver of brainpower to the situation. It wasn't a curse word. It had been my *blood*. My veins suddenly felt like lava as the long-term consequences of *that* thought entered my mind. That meant that whoever had my blood had the Armory.

I was the Key.

All one had to do was catch me, and they could use me whenever they wanted to open the door. That didn't sound good.

Not at all.

This made me a free agent for any baddie out there.

If anyone ever discovered my secret.

A lilting, feminine laugh drifted from beyond the now open doorway, chilling in its innocence. "It's about time, Nathin, my host." I shivered, trying to peer through the darkness without stepping a foot inside. Should I do this? Or should I wait for backup? But... I didn't *have* any backup. Everyone was gone. I guessed I could call that intern who was tearing down the crucifix in my office. *He would make good cannon fodder,* I thought idly. Then I blinked, surprised at my callousness. That wasn't a good sign. I had subconsciously decided to let the lowly intern risk his life in order to protect mine. Granted, it *was* part of the job description of interns everywhere – *five percent other duties as instructed...* but still, that wasn't like me to be so cold. Was it caused by my lack of sleep? Was I losing my empathy? I didn't have time for that train of thought, so I shrugged it off.

So.

Was I scared? That might sound like a dumb question. Of course I was scared, but that didn't usually slow me down. I always confronted my fears. But I always made sure I had backup somewhere or an ace up my sleeve, in case things got dicey. Now, I didn't have backup. I was entirely alone, and my magical reservoir was capped off. I would have to play this game differently than I was used to. Normally, I blew things up that scared me. Now I would have to think first, blow shit up later. If at all. To conserve my power.

"I didn't know men these days were so shy," the voice teased from the shadows.

I decided to answer back. "You're not a Demon, are you?"

The cute voice that answered had an entirely different tone this time. It now barely restrained eons of experience at fatal threats. "Never."

"Oh, okay. Well that's a start. Are you going to eat me if I come in there?" I asked, not knowing exactly what was on the other side of the door. That hiss could have been a monster. It sure didn't sound human.

"I am no beast. I'm a petite, curvaceous dream woman. No blades, fangs, or sticks. I swear. But I *detest* Demons," the voice called, sounding more human again, and slightly… amused.

"Um. Alright. I'm coming in now." I took a step and waited for the gates of hell to grab me by the short hairs. I realized my body was rigid, ready to flee at the drop of a hat. Listen, she *might* be a little girl, but she *also* might be a giant, dreadlock-clad, flying, gorilla-vampire hybrid. One never knew. Sensing no inhuman presence ready to gobble me up, I took another cautious step into the darkness. The door slammed shut behind me, bumping me forward a few inches. My butt cheeks were clenched tight enough to crack a walnut, not wanting to get pinched by a four-hundred-pound door.

In a blink, I realized the darkness was entirely gone, replaced by gold, crimson, and orange hues reflecting off thousands of metallic objects. Elaborate clothing, armor, and classic artwork from eras long extinct decorated the wall between literal piles of weapons and artifacts. The room I stood in had an open balcony with sturdy marble railings that ran right up to a sky that seemed afire from a vibrant sunset. A wide, long hallway stretched from the opposite end of the room, leading away for what seemed like forever.

And this was one room.

I could see dozens more openings spaced along the hallway.

The enticing voice floated to my ears from the balcony as I spotted a silky, lavender colored fabric fluttering in the wind. "Come out, come out, wherever you are," she teased.

I blinked. She was facing the opposite direction, but her thick auburn hair flowed in the breeze like a shampoo commercial's wet dream. She could be hiding razor-sharp Katanas in front of her, or she could have a gorilla-vampire hybrid's face after all. I had to be careful here. I didn't know the rules, but this obviously was not Temple Industries. I was somewhere else. It wasn't sunset in St. Louis, and it wasn't even remotely warm there. Here, it was almost toasty, as if I had stepped into a beach town near the equator. I didn't even know whether this place was real or a mental construct… or maybe even another daymare. My eyes suddenly darted back and forth eagerly, searching for a box, but I found nothing. Then again… I wouldn't even know to look for a box if this was a daymare, which meant that this *must* be real.

"Please turn to face me, if you don't mind," I called politely. Her amused laughter caused a pleasant tingle over my skin. It was captivating – the perfect mixture of amusement and darker, adult undertones. She turned to face me and my breath froze. Large almond eyes greeted me. Her face was oval and naturally tanned, with a sharp jaw and large, luscious lips, which were smiling up at me to reveal large, brilliantly white teeth. She was short, but a genuine goddess. And yes, she was definitely *curvaceous*. Was that my parents' secret? They had kidnapped a goddess? "You look… normal," I said bluntly.

She cocked her head curiously. *"Normal?* Well, you sure know how to woo a girl. I'm curious, were you *really* expecting a gorilla-vampire hybrid?" she asked, mischievously.

I blinked. *How the hell did she know that?* I opened my mouth after a few seconds of silent gawking. "If you knew my life, you might not think that so odd. Can you—"

She interrupted me. "Yes. I can read minds. Most of the time. It's my duty," she answered softly, curtsying like a princess out of a fairy tale. "I am at your service, if you will have me."

"I don't think I need any servicing." I realized how that sounded and instantly went on defense. "I mean, I'm all set in the servicing department. I've got this girl I really like, and she really likes me, too. She services me just f—"

Her laughter cut me off, and my teeth clicked sharply as my face flared beet red. "Not *that* kind of servicing. I guess you could say that I *work* for you. Perhaps that is a more modern phrase."

I nodded, relieved. "Oh. Yeah. Of course. That makes more sense." I studied her curiously, the silence stretching as she met my gaze with infinite patience. "Why do you work for me again?"

"You could call me a librarian. Of sorts. I was created to be the ward of this place." Her eyes twinkled with excitement as she spread her dainty hands to encompass the room. "Here. Let me show you a few of my favorite things." She was suddenly directly in front of me, seemingly not having crossed the space between us. I didn't even have time to flinch before she eagerly grabbed my arm to lead me deeper into the room. I didn't have time to stop her, and I was caught up with her infectious glee at finally having someone to talk to about her toys. And I was damned curious about that, after having spent so long trying to gain entrance to this place.

We rapidly moved from pile to pile, weapon to weapon, rug to painting, all the while with her name-dropping ancient items of power that made my skin begin to crawl. I was flabbergasted as we darted from one astonishment to the next. Gems, jewels, art, weapons, maps, and hundreds of other things filled the vast room in every direction, and this was only one of many, many rooms. She had already pointed out a lamp with a genuine genie trapped inside, the Nemean Lion's skin that had adorned Hercules, and even a few journals written by the Brothers Grimm – the sociopathic hitmen of the supernatural world.

The artwork alone was worth millions of dollars, not even considering the jewelry.

But it wasn't just weapons. I spotted a collection of boxed action figures, signed baseballs, expensive antiques, and even vinyl records. It was a hoarder's paradise.

And it was all…

Mine.

It was slightly humbling. With only a handful of these items I would be practically unstoppable, and wouldn't need to worry about my curse at all.

A small part of me felt like Smaug hoarding his treasure, but another small part of me began to grow concerned. Was I worthy of being the Armory's caretaker? *Power corrupts, and absolute power corrupts… absolutely.* Lord Acton was right on that old phrase.

"You're like a playboy bunny version of Jiminy Cricket," I blurted after a time, perhaps too honestly. "The conscience for this place, like Jiminy was for Pinocchio." She smiled at my compliment, and released my hand. "Did my parents command you to keep watch over the Armory? Did they *create* you?" I studied her more carefully. I had felt her hand, so I knew she was a physical being, but where did she get her nourishment? Was she merely a construct created by my parents and this was all happening in my head?

"No. They didn't create me, and yes, I'm real." Her eyes threatened to suck me into their depths, so I quickly turned away. She laughed, patting me on the arm innocently. "This is but one of the world's armories. Albeit the most notorious. Your parents have transformed it into the greatest of all of them. But perhaps I say that only because I am here to help." I nodded politely, not knowing what to say. She eyed me up and down appraisingly. Then she took a slow step closer, brushing the scar on my face with a gentle touch. "How did you acquire... oh, a dragon." She had read my thoughts again. "You are a warrior then, a dragon slayer? Yes. I see it now. You're wearing war paint to terrorize your enemies." She pointed at my black eyes. "I like it. Who are we destroying today?" she said it with the tone and excitement a small child might use to declare we were about to play tea-party princesses. I shivered. "We have many weapons here if you so desire. You will never have to risk a scar again." I took a polite step back and cleared my throat. She smiled, respecting my distance without offense. "Your parents didn't tell me that they actually succeeded in granting you the power of a Maker, though."

She stared at me, waiting for me to speak. "A Maker?" I asked curiously, and with a small amount of alarm. She nodded, but her excitement slowly began to fade as she realized I had no idea what she was talking about.

"Have you noticed an increase in your power?" she asked instead. I nodded with excitement. Finally! Answers. "But they didn't warn you? They never explained why?" she asked with disbelief.

"They never had the chance. They were murdered," I answered softly, my hopes for answers crumbling to ashes.

She seemed to shrink a bit at the shoulders. "I know. I'm sorry. I didn't mean to bring that up. What I meant was that they took something from this place in order to give you a... parting gift, as it were. A workshop for your new gift to flourish."

I stared back at her blankly, a little mollified that my parents had experimented on me without my knowledge. "Gift?"

"You are the first Maker to walk the earth in hundreds of years."

I pondered her words. "Maker... That sounds kinda... silly," I finally answered.

She giggled. "It is in no way *silly*. It is how wizards came to be in the first place. It means that you can literally create new forms of magic the world has never before seen. Other wizards stick with the old tried and true spells, replicating what they have seen done before. They do not have the power to push the boundaries and create *new* magic. As a Maker, you can quite literally do whatever you can imagine. Whatever you dare attempt. Magic that your enemies could not counter, since they never would have experienced it before. It is a gift from the gods. Your parents wanted you to be strong enough to defend this place... and yourself."

Create magic? Unbelievable. My parents were pulling strings even from beyond the grave. "Well, it seems their hard work has only painted a bulls-eye on my back. The Academy wasn't too pleased to notice my jump in power."

She nodded sadly. "The world's thugs never are. They don't like things they cannot explain." She straightened her shoulders. "Well, I hope you made a right mess of those vipers at the Academy. You are, after all, limited only by your creativity and imagination."

"Well, I didn't make a *right mess* of them. They actually cursed me. My power is now fading, and will be gone in three days if I don't comply with their demands to give them the Armory. It will fade faster if I use my magic up before their deadline."

She locked eyes with me. "Then I must help you eliminate this wretched spell." She closed her eyes and lifted her arms to point in my general direction. I tensed, but nothing happened. After a few moments, she opened her eyes with a low growl. "Impossible! I can't even *touch* the curse. It repels my power like oil on water." She studied me for another second. "Even with your new abilities, it is too strong for you to remove on your own. They must have used a circle of wizards."

I nodded with frustration. "Eight of them, to be precise."

She growled. "Cowards!" I liked her already. The enemy of my enemy is my friend, after all. "It seems that the only solution is for you to find more power."

I blinked at her, not hiding my mounting frustration very well. "You and Asterion, both. Simple, but efficient with your fortune cookie answers."

She visibly started. "The Minotaur *lives?*"

I hesitated, not knowing if I had accidentally given up a State Secret. "Um. Yeah. We're kinda' bros." She watched me, uncomprehendingly. "Friends," I amended.

She continued to stare at me in silence, thoughts I couldn't even fathom churning behind those magical eyes of hers.

"Anyway," I continued, feeling uncomfortable. "How exactly do I find more power?"

She arched a brow, relaxing as she fought a growing smile. Finally, she sighed and lifted her arms at the Armory around us. I slapped my forehead in embarrassment, remembering at the last second to be gentle for my injured nose. Of course. Armory. Power. Duh.

"This is all *yours*. You can borrow items from here to aid you in your investigation. It's fitting, really. Use your parents' tools to discover their murderer. It wouldn't be the first time some of these items have reentered the world. After all, you've already been transformed into a Maker." I looked around, feeling slightly thick that I hadn't considered the idea immediately. But like earlier, my thoughts grew concerned. These things had been locked away for a reason. Surely, they shouldn't be wielded outside of the Armory. But… wasn't I already contradicting that statement? My parents had already done just that to transform me into a Maker. Supposedly. Did I trust this woman? Could she be lying about their gift? Then I thought about it for a few seconds.

I *had* made some remarkable discoveries lately. Tinkering had become a fiery passion where before it had been merely an interesting diversion. And I had learned to Apparate rather quickly, in a way that I had never learned anything before. Maybe she was right. It would explain the power spike that had so surprised the Justices.

I decided to change the subject, allow my mind to warm up to the idea slowly. "Why does everything I see remind me of the Greeks?" I asked curiously.

"Because they were brilliant marketers, of course. We have totems from practically every culture here. You just don't recognize them."

"You said there are more places like this in the world?"

"Yes, but they pale in comparison. Your parents quite outdid themselves bringing additional items of power here." She studied me as I scanned the room, fighting the selfish urge to arm myself for World War III. I could be all but invincible with even a handful of these items. I could take out the Justices, swat away the Angels, and banish the Demons with ease. No one could stand in my way.

But… and there was always a *but*.

My parents had locked them away for a reason. Power had a tendency to change a guy. And I liked myself the way I was. The urge was still persistent, but I squashed it. "Do as you will, but you are not without options," she said softly, reading my thoughts. "You are a Maker and must not give the Academy access to this storehouse," she warned.

"Is this Maker gift how I was able to learn how to teleport just by experiencing it one time?"

"Teleport? I don't know this word," she answered with a frown.

"You know. Moving from one place to another really fast."

"You learned how to run?" she teased with a grin.

I scowled. Of course she was a smartass. Why not? "Over great distances in the blink of an eye."

Her eyes sparkled. "Oh. You mean Shadow Walking." She tapped a lip, watching my pensive frown. "You mean this is not common knowledge among wizards?"

I stared at her for a few seconds before shaking my head. "No. Apparently, it's only known to a select few." I regarded her thoughtfully. This ability was nothing new to her, even though she had never heard the modern word *teleport*. Interesting. *Shadow Walking*. I wondered where I had been when between locations. An alternate reality? Was it dangerous? Most likely it was, or it would be common knowledge. Another fact hit me. The Academy was guilty of doing exactly what they accused me of – hiding power. Which instantly confirmed that I shouldn't trust them. They wanted the power for themselves. Not for the good of the supernatural community. They wanted control, weapons, and power. But why?

She had frowned in disapproval at mention of the Academy hiding knowledge like this from other wizards. She finally shrugged in answer to my original question. "Makers learn quickly. Their subconscious runs on overdrive. Always watching, cataloguing, learning." Her eyes were thoughtful as she watched the uncertainty on my face. She was obviously finished with that conversation because she moved to another topic after glancing at a nearby sundial. "Your situation could be worse..."

I blinked. "Losing my power? I'm helpless with this curse. It won't go away until I give them access to the Armory. To *you*. If even then."

"Then you must die, Maker." She didn't even look ashamed at the comment. Seeing my reaction, her eyes grew softer. "Some men aren't meant to find peace or happiness. They are meant to challenge Death. Fight Wars. They are meant to be *great*."

"Well, my death will put a damper on just about all of those things."

She shrugged, changing the topic again. "Now that you are my new master, how do you wish me to aid you?"

I could sense that she wanted me to formally acknowledge her assistance, but I was a tad nervous about what that might obligate me to do. My father had always taught me that there was no free lunch. "I just want to understand what this place is and why it was locked away."

She laughed. "Come now. Of course, your parents told you of this place," she said. I shook my head and she considered me, face slowly morphing to awe. "They never told you about this fortress? About... *me?*" I shook my head again, blushing slightly at her offended tone.

"Uh... nope."

"Well, I am here to serve... you, if you will have me. I keep record of the items of power stored here. What exactly do you wish to know?" Disappointment was clear in her voice.

"Just answers, I guess. I don't want to force you to tell me anything you don't want to tell," I said conversationally, looking over her shoulder at the vast array of items. As was typical for me, my gaze rested on a set of books that sat neatly on a table. I found myself wondering what their story was. Their spines were elaborately decorated, but they held not a speck of dust.

Her tone grew cold in the blink of an eye, arctic. Literally. Frost instantly coated the table and books. "But... you will if you must. Already you resort to threats. Against a slave, no less."

My mouth clicked shut, realization dawning too late. "No. No, that's not what I meant. That wasn't a threat. That was just a statement. I merely meant that I don't know the rules here. I am not like those you may have served before."

She chuckled sadly and the frost on the table simply disappeared, which was entirely creepy. Shouldn't it have melted rather than just disappear? "Never heard *that* before. I thought you might be different."

"Look, is there anything I can do to prove that I'm not here to hurt you? I didn't even know you existed ten minutes ago." Did this mean that my parents had abused her? Was that why she was so jaded?

She watched me curiously. "We shall see," was all she said. I was surprised that she hadn't asked me to free her, to beg for my help. I didn't think I would have said yes, but I wasn't sure. Perhaps I would have. Everyone deserved freedom. But I didn't know her story or the Armory's history. Not yet. I needed to be sure she wasn't dangerous first.

So, I let her assume what she would. Cold, but effective. I guarded my thoughts with a sudden wall of impenetrable power so that she couldn't read me. She squinted back, noticing my defense, and not seeming to be pleased.

Confident my thoughts were safe, I thought for a moment. It was obvious why my parents had been killed. Someone wanted access to this place. "But *who* killed them? Why am I having night terrors? Why does the door back there," I pointed behind me, "smell like Brimstone?"

Her sudden silence caused me to look up, realizing I had spoken aloud. Her eyes had changed to a milky lavender shade, gaze distant as if she could no longer see me. The difference in her voice caused the hair on the back of my neck to rise, as it was totally different from when she had spoken before – older, wiser, and more lethal – like a completely different person. Like... an entity of knowledge *should* sound. "The doorway to death can truly be a hallway of opportunities. To tread the sharp edge of a sword – to run on smooth-frozen ice, one needs no footsteps to follow. Walk over the cliffs with hands free. Death will provide answers to thee." Then she blinked as if just waking up, unsure what had just transpired.

"Are you telling me that the only answers I can find will be through *death*?"

"Only the *ultimate* answer can be found through death," she answered distantly, her eyes slowly returning back to normal as she caught a hand on the table for balance. What the hell? Then she chuckled, as if amused at her own words.

"Very punny," I growled. "Now, what the hell did you mean, and what just happened? You almost fell over. And your eyes changed colors."

"I'm sorry, I don't know where the words came from... it happens sometimes. I'm not sure if it's the items here or something to do with me." Her eyes darted back to the sundial and widened in alarm. "Quickly. We haven't much time." I blinked at that, but she was already rushing to grab my hand and lead me around the room. I had all the time in the world to give her. She was the only one willing to give me answers. But I allowed her to drag me to a new room, smiling at her excitement to point out various items only read about in stories. A cold chill ran down my neck at some of them. Excalibur. Armor designed by literal Gods. Vials of mysterious liquids and raw energy that she silently avoided. A blue phone booth... *no*, that couldn't be the *Tardis*... could it?

She finally looked content, having shown me some of the more dangerous items. Knowing this was one room of dozens – if not hundreds –

I found myself again wary of my new hideout. "The Armory is a cache of magical items deemed too dangerous to fall into the wrong hands. Most things in here are deadly, but lethality is in the eye of the beholder. To the caveman, fire was dangerous, but one just needed to learn how to control it." She paused, no doubt reading the question on the tip of my tongue with her creepy mind-reading ability. "I don't know why you smelled Brimstone outside. Perhaps the thief from a few months ago resorted to using Demons in order to gain entrance. I don't know how that could be possible, but he ultimately failed. Knowing what he desired, and how powerful it was, I tricked him."

I felt myself lean forward eagerly. *Peter.* "What did he want?" This was it. An answer.

Finally.

She appraised me wordlessly, judging me as surely as if I had been weighed to the ounce. "Power. He seemed fixated on the bathwater of Baby Achilles." She idly waved a hand at the array of vials we had bypassed.

"Well, as power goes, that seems kind of a poor choice." She arched a brow.

"That would be the water from the River Styx, which granted him his immortality on all but his ankle." I shuddered in comprehension.

"Oh. Well... thanks for not giving it to him then." She nodded. "It was as your parents would have wanted. Besides, why would I let him have what he wanted if he wasn't able to grant my freedom?" My mind worked furiously. So, she *did* want something.

"You could have asked him to take you with him in exchange for the water."

She frowned. "Don't think I hadn't thought about it... or tried it in the past. Only the custodian may grant my freedom."

She began studying the nearby weathered sundial nervously. "How can I find the man or Demons responsible for my parents' murder?" I asked, remembering her odd comment about limited time. She laughed, as if the question was too simple to waste her time on.

"That's easy." She immediately shimmered with power before casting a crimson haze of fog at a map of Eastern Europe on the wall beside us. "*Seek,*" she whispered. The fog condensed to several locations on the map, glowing faintly. "That shows current locations of Demonic presence."

The freaky part about it was that I knew I could replicate it, but it would cost me a ton of magic. "Um. With my curse, that spell would drain me really fast. I would have to use a lot of power, which would leave me useless to confront the Demons I had oh so cleverly discovered."

She nodded mumbling to herself as if reading a mental catalog of the items stored here, and then dove into a pile of items on the edge of a desk. After discarding several priceless artifacts, she held up a carved bone the size of a bird's egg. "Here. Take this. It works the same way, only doesn't require your own magic. It's instilled with the power itself. Merely think about what you want to find, say *Seek*, and hold it near a map." She handed me the bone egg and I grunted in surprise at its weight. It was so dense that it felt like a lump of pure lead. It was completely covered in continuous runes, not a single millimeter empty. I idly wondered what could have been sharp enough to carve it. It felt... ancient. Upon my touch, soothing whispers abruptly filled my ears, murmuring seductively, introducing themselves by the hundreds. The voices sounded seductive, and... grateful. Almost as if they were eager to partner with a new wizard after eons of silence. I quickly pocketed the totem and the whispers ceased. I managed not to flinch in fear, and the girl nodded in approval.

"Thanks," I finally said, glad for the silence, and not knowing quite what to make of the voices. I felt conflicted about borrowing anything from this place, but what choice did I really have?

She nodded matter-of-factly.

"I guess now I understand why it took you so long to answer my call. Your parents never told you about me. I thought you would have to develop insomnia before you realized I was reaching out to you."

That got me right in the stomach. The night terrors. "That was *you?*" I hissed, seething with sudden rage.

She began to chuckle, but her brow creased in confused alarm, not understanding my threatening tone. "Yes. I try to give all my hosts pleasant dreams," she finally answered, looking uncertain.

"Is this some kind of sick *joke?*" I bellowed, taking an aggressive step towards her. She squeaked, darting back a good dozen feet to the balcony. Then I took another step. Soon I was racing towards her, fury fueling my muscles.

She was as good as dead.

I *knew* this had sounded too good to be true, that she had *looked* too good to be true. She was the source of all my recent pain. Having visions of my loved ones being tortured and killed again and again and *again*. Some might say I was slightly unhinged.

"I think there might have been a misunderstanding," she spoke softly, suddenly standing just before me. I was panting with unspent energy, my muscles quivering to reach her dainty throat, but I was no longer running. I couldn't move a single muscle below my neck, so I snarled hungrily, ready to bite her throat if that was my only path. But I couldn't even turn my head. Her delicate hands reached up to touch my face, her soft fingertips gently caressing my scar and temples in a very doctor-like evaluation. I was ready to burst with rage, but my body wouldn't respond, and even my magic was tantalizingly out of reach. *What was happening?*

She flinched back with a gasp. "Oh. That makes much more sense. Someone has been tampering with your mind. Altering my sendings." She scrunched her face in thought, poking her tongue out the side of her full lips, Michael Jordan style, and stepped back up to me, grasping my skull more forcefully this time. I still couldn't move. I opened my mouth to threaten her to step back and stop, but even my voice wouldn't work. She was using some kind of magic to overwhelm me. Then, what felt like a bucket of warm oil slowly poured over my head, coaxing my neck, shoulders, and back into the equivalent of warm jelly. It was as if I had just stepped out of a hot bath after an exhausting spa day.

… Not that I had ever *partaken* in such a day. I could just imagine what it would have been like if I had.

My body shivered at the sudden release of tension I hadn't realized I'd been carrying, and the girl stepped back with a curious frown on her face. I collapsed to my knees, muscles too useless to support my weight. The slip of a girl stumbled up to a heavy table and sat down, turning to face me, looking physically drained and… concerned.

"Someone has been in your head," she spoke thoughtfully, lifting a shaky hand to tap her lips in thought.

"And you only just admitted to doing that very thing," I snapped, slowly regaining the use of my limbs.

She nodded distractedly. "My dreams were sent to tap into your subconscious mind and remind you of my presence. Your parents named this Armory their Pandora Protocol. A quotidian name for a place, but it fits." I frowned at her. Noticing this, she elaborated. "Your father was quite the one for elaborate names. He deemed the items in this location to be too dangerous for the Academy and other wizards to get their hands on. So, he named it after Pandora's Box – the legend that housed the world's worst horrors." She looked amused.

"But in the bottom of Pandora's Box was Hope," I said softly. She flinched, looking into my eyes with newfound respect. Her gaze was like a field of lavender on fire.

"That is true. Not many know that part of the story," she spoke softly.

I shrugged, relaxing. "Learning of their name for this place, I did a lot of research into the topic."

"My sending was to place a box into your dreams, reminding you of their pet name for the Armory. Opening it would cause you pleasure."

"Yeah, sure. If pleasure feels like your skin is melting."

Her eyes fairly smoldered. "That was not I. I wouldn't, and couldn't, do that to my host," she hissed. She sounded sincere. What the hell did *that* mean? Who else was in my head?

Instead of jumping down *that* rabbit hole, I looked around the room as my muscles slowly began to awaken, noticing a vast array of armor against one wall. One item in particular caught my attention. Between two shields was an aged section of sheepskin. *Golden* sheepskin. "Is that…?" I asked, my mouth wide open with disbelief.

She glanced behind her at the skin, but shook her head in reply. "No, but Jason's Golden Fleece is here. That is merely a replica your father liked, not realizing the authentic one was already here, she answered as if pointing out a can of tomato soup in a grocery store. I blinked in astonishment. The Golden Fleece! Able to repel any attack. What the hell? I had a brief daydream of me blazing into battle against a horde of Angels and Demons wearing the Fleece, stomping ass and taking names. She interrupted my reverie. "What I'm more concerned about is your dreams. Someone has been melding his or her will into my own projections. Locked away in this vault, it is very difficult for me to project dreams, but it is not impossible. The fact that someone was able to mutate my sending is alarming. It means someone is after you specifically, and trying to do you harm without letting you know who he or she is. Have your dreams been… particularly horrifying?" she asked in a very clinical way, not at all concerned with how much harm they had, in fact, caused me.

"You could say that," I said drily. "The city burning, my friends tortured and murdered, me helpless, but through it all was a box. The only way to escape the carnage was to open a box."

She nodded distractedly. "That part was mine. Just the box. It was agreed upon by your father and I that I would entice you with these visions of opening a box. He said anything more forceful than that would cause you to ignore the call. He called you a bit stubborn, to tell you the truth. At least that part of the dream was pleasant," she said softly.

I scowled back. "Opening the box caused me more pain than I've ever imagined. And each dream caused a new *type* of pain. Burning, freezing, being skinned, and even buried alive."

She looked crestfallen, and then... furious. "Opening the box was supposed to cause you pleasure, to lead you to me. Why would I cause you pain in order to lead you here? Like I said, your father mentioned you had an issue with authority, so these sendings were to encourage you to come *to* me, not scare you *away*."

"True. But who could possibly know about your projections, and how the hell would they tap into them? Were they trying to discover something inside my head? Could it be a Demon?"

"That is a very good question," she answered slowly. "Why do you repeatedly fixate on Demons?"

"Because I was paid a visit by some... people, and they had the distinct impression that I and that door smelled like a severe whiff of Brimstone."

"I would never allow a Demon to enter this place. And you do not smell of Demons." So, my dip in the fountain of holy water *had* worked! "This is my sanctuary. My home."

Her tone sent a shiver down my spine. Even as small and young as she looked, she was obviously very, very powerful. I had been helpless in her hands. And her words had sounded like a queen talking about her castle. "Who are you, anyway?"

"I could answer that if you accepted my servitude. I could be of great help to you in the future, but you must allow me to serve you." Her tone sounded hopeful, desperate, almost.

And it sounded eerily like an unbreakable bond. And she had expressed her interest at freedom. "How about just a name for now." I could see the frustration in her eyes. I felt an uncomfortable twinge begin in my shoulders that was all the more noticeable after her therapeutic touch. *Get out, get out, get out...*

The girl continued, unaware of my predicament. "Fine. I was a wayward soul. One who wasted her life on earth, trying to help those who couldn't help themselves. One you would refer to as a witch. I was killed by my own people for what I was, and cast here to serve as a Guardian of sorts. You may call me—"

"Well, this has been great and all, but I really must be leaving," I interrupted. I was suddenly on my feet and striding purposefully back to the door. "See you soon, Hope." I don't know where the name came from, but it seemed to fit from the story I had shared with her about Pandora's Box.

The door back to Temple Industries opened before me and I stepped out. Before it closed again I heard Hope's voice. "Damn that spell!"

The door shut with a solid boom and the uncomfortable sensation evaporated. Why had I left? I turned on my heel, pounding on the door to be let back inside. Nothing happened. I reopened my wound and pressed it against the wood. Still nothing. *What the hell? I have more questions!* But it was useless. The room was closed again.

Then it hit me. I remembered the odd fact about the room. When my parents had entered – and then again when Peter had entered – they had been gone exactly seventeen minutes. I looked down at my watch. Huh.

Right on time.

Hope had mentioned a spell. That must be it. Perhaps Peter had hit the spell's time limit, and simply grabbed whatever he could before leaving, since Hope had been unwilling to assist him. Then he had 'sold' it to Alaric Slate, sealing his fate. I sighed. What a waste. He had been my friend for years, but I didn't tolerate betrayal.

So, this spell limited time allowed inside the vault. I wondered if there was a way around it. My parents had also been limited to the same window of opportunity – seventeen minutes.

Thinking of my parents made me recall the last time I had seen my father alive. On the video recording taken from directly outside this door. I looked down at my feet. Almost exactly where I currently stood. I might or might not have shivered at that thought. I remembered his last message to me, when he had mouthed his dying words to the security camera that was currently blinking at me. Luckily, I knew how to lip read. I had only been able to see the video a single time before it had been deleted, but I recalled his message perfectly. It made me angry, but some of it began to inch toward an inkling of sense after meeting Hope.

I let it go, thinking about the door. I heard footsteps coming down the hall, but they stopped, no doubt someone picking up papers from a printer before running back to their lab. I ignored the sound, pondering the Omega symbol over the door. Why that symbol? I could think of no real reason other than to scare someone. Then there was the door itself, and my blood was the Key. If anyone ever discovered that, I would become everyone's best friend. I couldn't ever let anyone figure that out or I would be locked in a cell forever to be used as a tool whenever necessary. "I am no one's tool," I promised myself.

A withered old voice responded from the hallway behind me. "You obviously didn't read the pamphlets I left you, for we are all God's tools." I sighed in frustration. Greta.

"I thought you left already," I grumbled. I heard no response, so turned around. No one was there. I instantly tensed. No footsteps. I cocked my head, listening. After a few moments, I relaxed. I was alone. Then I began to wonder if it really had been Greta or if someone *else* had been lurking behind me, using her voice. Or had I imagined it? How tired was I?

That's it. My paranoia was at an all-time high.

I scoured the hallways, searching for anyone, but found nothing. Not a soul. I gave it up as my imagination caused by sleep deprivation. After spending another hour at the door, trying everything in my power to open the Armory, I gave it up as fruitless and decided to leave. I was on borrowed time, with Demons hunting me down for the Key to the Armory. And the Academy's deadline was only two days away now. After that I would be a magic-less wizard. I couldn't stand still for too long.

I had things to kill and problems to solve.

CHAPTER 14

I stormed out of Temple Industries, too distracted to be concerned with the brisk winter weather. It was the first time I had felt entirely relaxed in months, thanks to whatever Hope had done to quell my daymares. I was marginally dry from my brief stint in the Armory, and was ecstatic that I no longer sported the Demon's version of *Eau de Toilette.* I was also overjoyed that I'd finally be able to go get some real, uninterrupted sleep. Sure, I knew I needed to stop the Demons, but I suddenly felt practically comatose. I required sleep or I was likely to make mistakes. Also, thanks to Hope, I wasn't even sure I could make it home before falling asleep. I was that tired.

Indie was most likely already with her mom. I considered calling her when I got home. If I wasn't drooling and stumbling by the time I made it there. I was on borrowed time and I needed to figure out a way to appease the Academy while finding my parents' murderer before the curse ran its course. But... I deserved a quick nap before I faced any Biblical threats, especially after months of practical insomnia.

I dug in my pockets, searching for the keys to the emergency car I left here in the parking lot. I had learned pretty quickly that I usually found myself here after a few too many drinks, or being dropped off here by Mallory or one of my other friends, and rather than constantly waiting for someone to pick me up, I had set up a car to be left in the parking lot. It wasn't as flashy as my other cars, but it was really just a driver anyway.

I finally found the set of keys in my pocket and hit the remote start. The Xenon lights on the Vilner customized Mercedes G-Wagon pierced the night as the engine roared to life across the parking lot. I stood there for a few seconds, admiring her beauty.

As if the sound of her glorious purr had been a signal, a team of black SUVs suddenly swarmed into the parking lot on screeching tires, flashing lights in red, white, and blue. I froze. Was this a joke? The police? Then I frowned. Was this a ruse? Maybe some of the Demons had managed to possess a posse of officers to catch me off-guard. I waited as the cars skidded to a halt in a loose circle around me, closing off any chance of escape for the big, bad, scary wizard. I smiled at the unintended compliment.

The men – all wearing identical blue coats – launched themselves out of their cars in near perfect synchronization. "I smell Kosage," I sneered to the closest man, who was unashamedly pointing a gun at my face.

His was the only voice to answer, so I assumed he was in charge. "FBI! Freeze!"

I blinked. FBI? My concern began to escalate considerably. "I'm pretty sure my balls resemble two ice cubes at the moment, so I think we're set."

"Don't move!" the leader clarified, his cinderblock head swiveling on slabs of beef that remotely resembled human shoulders. He had no neck. As I scanned the men before me, I thought I saw a few familiar faces from the St. Louis Police Department mixed in amongst the unknown agents. What the hell had I done to get these two departments to join forces against me?

"Despite it looking like I'm moving really fast, I'm actually standing still. I know. Trippy, right?" I muttered. My exhaustion was making me angry.

He glared back. "Don't be a smartass. On the ground!" A few of the other men chuckled, but they didn't lower their weapons. I heard several murmurings about my face and the obvious black eyes. I scowled in their general direction until they grew silent.

"I'm actually quite content to stand until I hear a reason for this detainment, and I also require you to show me some identification." The man blinked. "You know, those flippy leather wallets you carry with a driver's license and your shield? The one with the agent number on it that I will memorize in order to ruin your career for eternity, if you don't provide a *damned* good reason for postponing my nap." I smiled through my teeth. This was it. If they didn't provide proof that they were in fact agents or police, I was Shadow Walking my happy ass out of here, consequences be damned.

Two other agents stepped forward with their shields out. I pretended to look at their badges, but studied their faces instead, clutching the artifact in my pocket. The one Hope had given me. If they were Demons, surely, I would sense some change in it. I should also smell Brimstone. I sniffed, and then blinked, which caused the officers to cock their heads in confusion. No Brimstone. No reaction from the stone.

Huh. I honestly didn't know what to do next. I'd been so prepared for supernatural problems that I hadn't considered what to do about the Regular old FBI or police.

That might say something about me.

"So, um... you're official. What can I help you with?"

"You're under arrest."

"For wh—" I began, but I unsuccessfully failed at suppressing a sudden massive, jaw-cracking yawn. I could have literally fallen asleep standing up. The agents pounced on my moment of weakness like a pride of lions on a gazelle. They violently tackled me to the ground, handcuffed me, and forcefully picked me up to press me against a nearby car door. I was so exhausted that I let them. I wasn't about to attack a squad of FBI Agents. They were supposed to be the good guys.

"What exactly am I being arrested for?" I wheezed, my anger beginning to wake me up a bit as the cuffs ground into my wrists.

"You're wanted as a person of interest in an ongoing investigation. Missing person. Alaric Slate. Among other things."

"Like?" I asked, barely restraining myself from unleashing my power on them. But it would do no good, and I needed my power for the Demons. Best to go along with them. For now.

He held up his phone, which showed a perfect image of me cold-cocking the stranger from the bar last night. Then he smirked as he studied my face. "Looks like it didn't end well for you."

"Goddamn it. How many people were keeping tabs on me last night?" I snapped, more to myself. "And for the record, I totally kicked some ass at that bar fight." I pointed to my face with pride. "This was from the fight afterwards with a totally different group of people, where I also kicked some major ass." He looked doubtful. "But I digress. Since when are bar fights part of your jurisdiction?"

The bulldog agent stared me down. "We're on a joint task force with the local police. This picture just gave us a chance to bring you in. We also have you on corruption of a fellow Agent, Gunnar Randulf. Your assets have been temporarily frozen until we get to the bottom of it all. Last time the police brought you in, you threatened to buy off a politician to make sure Kosage lost his badge. He took that personally. I mean... *professionally*," he corrected with a sadistic grin, shrugging his massive shoulders. His coat was barely able to contain his massive frame.

"Is that a s-medium sized coat? You know, the size between a medium and a small that some people use to feel manlier? You must pop your collar on your days off, too. Real studly."

His face began to grow a pleasant shade of purple as his fists flexed at his sides. Then my phone began to ring. The man held out a hand. One of his subordinates handed him my phone from my pocket, chuckling at the cracked screen. "Nice," he mocked me before answering the call on speaker. The other agents began patting me down. "*Master* Temple's phone," he answered in a polite drawl.

"Who is this?" Indie demanded. "Let me speak to Nate."

"This is the FBI, Miss. Master Temple is currently wanted for questioning and isn't able to answer the phone. Can I give him a message?"

There was an abrupt pause, then, "You can go fuck yourself, thank you very much. Give Nate his phone. This is an invasion of his privacy."

The Agent's face morphed back to that satisfying purple shade, but he kept his voice neutral. "I'm sorry. I can't do that. You should have just left a message. He won't be calling anyone for quite some time. Unless he uses you as his one free call. Good day." He hung up with more force than was necessary.

"Give me my goddamned phone you self-righteous, no-necked, son of a bitch. I've broken no laws. You can't arrest me." He merely glared back smugly. I took a calming breath. "I'm trying to work on my communication skills. At least let me put her at ease. Then I'm all yours for questions. After which, I will be leaving your tender loving care."

"Uh-huh. You can talk to her..." I nodded thankfully, glancing at my phone. "As soon as you *communicate* with *us*. It will be good practice. Put me at ease on a few topics. Like bribery of a fellow Agent, for starters." He winked darkly. The other agents finished taking everything from my pockets, turning off my car when they found my keys, and grunting in surprise at the weight of the bone artifact Hope had given me. Then I was shoved into one of the SUVs.

One of the agents jangled the remnants of the dragon tooth bracelet that had been broken in the bar fight last night. "Cute. Did you get this from Panama City Beach during Spring Break or something? One of those cheap souvenir shops? Billionaire wearing cheap shit like this? Must be facing hard time."

"*Times*, you ignorant hick," I growled.

As if expecting this, he grinned wider. "Nah. *Hard Time*, as in, that is what you're facing right now."

I sneered back, not daring to use my magic to scare him. I used something else. "Those are the teeth of the Demon I killed on the Eads Bridge a few months ago. You guys must be very brave. I hear they even have footage of me killing it on YouTube. They call me something… what was it again…? Oh, that's it. *Archangel*. I knew it was something catchy…" I leaned forward with a grin that showed my teeth. "And true."

His smile evaporated as he turned back to the front of the car. A small victory worked for me. Still, I was fuming by the time we made it to the interrogation room of the local police precinct. Agent No-Neck had uncuffed me and brought me to his superior, Special Agent in Charge Wilson, who sat in silent stoicism, watching me with raptor-like eyes. I idly wondered if anyone knew about the horse I had stolen, but no one had mentioned it yet.

I didn't have to wait long before a familiar face entered the room. I laughed. Hard. For a good, long while. Tears were actually wetting my cheeks before I calmed down. "If it isn't my favorite hundred-pound hero." Wilson made a sound like a muffled cough, but his face remained stoic. Kosage merely stared at me, embodying a cold rage that was only mildly warmed with the satisfaction of having me under arrest and at his mercy. "*Confusion now hath made his masterpiece.*" I winked at Wilson, and not so discreetly pointed a finger at Kosage. The Agent managed to keep his face neutral, but I saw his eyes sparkle with amusement, recognizing Shakespeare's quote and seeming to silently agree. Then I turned to face the little firecracker himself. "Still toadying, Kosage?"

He scowled in response, his face slightly reddening, but kept his mouth shut.

"Go ahead, Kosage. I know you have something you would like to say to me. I'll even let you vent a bit before I put you back in your place. Like last time." I smiled, crossing my legs as I held out a hand for him to proceed. His red face grew darker.

Someone knocked on the door. Kosage and Wilson turned with a frown before the agent barked out a terse, "Enter."

Agent Jeffries, the human lie detector I had met a few months ago, stuck his head in, and I grinned. I wasn't sure what was about to happen, but he was a friendly. He nodded respectfully to his boss, ignoring Kosage entirely. "This hasn't been approved by the appropriate channels, Sir."

"Back off, Agent Jeffries. This is above your pay-grade. You're on my turf," Kosage snarled.

Jeffries didn't even acknowledge the vermin. I almost wished I had popcorn as I watched Kosage's fury practically steam out of his ears at being so blatantly ignored. "Permission to speak freely, Sir?" Jeffries asked his superior. Wilson nodded with carefully hidden amusement, so as not to further offend the already furious Kosage.

Jeffries slowly turned to address Detective Kosage, his eyes resting about a foot above his head – at the height most heads would reside. He gave a start, and then lowered his gaze to Kosage's much lower eye-level with a look of genuine surprise. I almost lost it. It was a total dick move to pick on a little guy's height. I liked it. He cleared his throat. "You're telling me that this is *above* a Federal Agent of the FBI's pay-grade, but still meets the pay-grade of a *lowly* curb-kicker on the St. Louis P.D.? You guys must have one hell of a benefits package. Perhaps you didn't spend a whole lot of time on criminal law over at the Police Academy. It's understandable. It's a *big* book. Lots of pages. I, on the other hand, being a *lowly* minion for the great cog that is the FBI, studied it quite profusely. I'll summarize for you. You can't arrest someone without probable cause. Even if you really don't like them. Even if – hypothetically, of course – they made you look like the *tiniest* little douche-bag idiot ever promoted to Detective that St. Louis has ever seen... Hypothetically." Kosage was quivering with each enunciated word referencing height or size. I was quivering, too... with barely restrained laughter. "Without solid evidence, detaining anyone – especially the wealthiest person in St. Louis – is enough to make said curb-kicker look like nothing more than a *little* Napoleon. *Over compensating*, even. Know what I mean?"

Kosage sputtered in wordless sentences, unable to speak through his anger, but I noticed that Agent Wilson was fighting a grin. "You should probably leave, Agent Jeffries." My only chance at a legitimate escape nodded before turning to me with a shrug as if to say, *Sorry*. Then he was gone.

Wilson spoke. "He's got a point, Kosage. Just ask your questions, and we'll move on from there." He turned to me, face composed again. "We do have surveillance of you at that bar last night. That should be enough for Kosage to hold you for 24 hours if he really wants to." The translation was obvious: *if we don't like your answers to our questions.*

Then Kosage laid into it, taking out his impotent aggression on me. Questioning me on everything that coincided with the dragon attack a few months ago – from the cow-tipping charge to the bribery of Gunnar. The alleged 'Demon' attack on the bridge. The cop killed at Artemis' Garter. Alaric Slate's disappearance. Then the *coup-de-gras*, "It seems that an officer lost his mount outside the bar you were caught fighting in last night. Know anything about that?"

I blinked, keeping my face neutral. I was so tired by this point that it was not that difficult. "You mean Xavier?" I asked with a frown.

Kosage leaned forward anxiously, slapping the table with a dainty palm as he finally heard something he liked. "How do you know the horse's name if you didn't kidnap him?" He accused triumphantly, turning to Agent Wilson with a victorious grin. Wilson was watching me, not acknowledging Kosage.

"Horsenap," I mumbled after yawning.

"Pardon?" Kosage breathed anxiously.

"I think you'd call it horsenapping. Calling it kidnapping seems disrespectful and... weird. If a horse is stolen, I think it's called horsenapping." I kept my face straight, speaking as I would at an academic debate, or to a small child.

"Fine. *Horsenapping* is against the law—"

I swiveled to Agent Wilson, not hiding my sudden excitement. "*Please* tell me you got that on the record. Me being accused of... horsenapping?" Wilson's eyes creased with an inner struggle not to laugh, but he nodded. "Great. That will be *excellent* in the courtroom later."

Kosage lunged at me, but Wilson barred his advance with a solid arm. Kosage knocked it away aggressively. I shrugged at Wilson. "Toddlers, right? You just can't win."

"Xavier is a mounted patrol officer for the City of St Louis. *That's* a felony. Where did you take him?" Kosage roared in retaliation.

I shrugged patiently. "I met him when I left the bar. His handler was a bit of a smartass, at first, but he ended up being cool in the end. He introduced me to his mount. Then I left. I was pretty drunk at the time, but I remember that much. Then I went home. He's probably eating an apple somewhere. I hear horses like apples."

Kosage scowled. "If you went home after that, why did the officer report some kind of attack less than an hour later by some sort of animal?"

I realized Kosage was actually waiting for me to answer that. "Perhaps it's because... *he was attacked less than an hour later by some sort of animal?*" I offered with a puzzled brow. I could tell it was infuriating Kosage, but I was loving it.

"The officer reported that someone else was involved."

I shrugged. "And? It's *Mardi Gras*. People are flooding the streets this time of year. This citizen must have helped him or your officer wouldn't have had a report to give you." I hoped, feeling slightly guilty, that the confusion of the attack might have allowed the officer to forget my presence. Fog of war. "What kind of animal attack?" I asked curiously.

Kosage drummed his fingers on the tabletop, realizing that he hadn't tripped me up at all. "He didn't know. I do find it curious that you were there less than an hour before he was attacked and his horse was stolen. You have a reputation for... unique events trailing you."

"Just my good fortune, I guess. Can I go now? Oh, I'll also need you to unfreeze my assets. I see no warrantable information to have done so, and I will definitely be speaking to the Mayor about this injustice. And about horsenapping," I shook my head, letting out a chuckle.

Kosage flashed me a sadistic smile. "Well, Nate. I'm so sorry to be the one to tell you, but you will be staying the night after all. Don't worry. I made a reservation under your name, on the house, of course, since you can't touch your money. I'll have more questions for you in the morning." I turned to Wilson. The man sighed, and then shrugged. "Resisting arrest. Verbal threats. Also, the missing horse is curious. You might have been the last one to see him. We'll need an alibi."

"Your no-neck detective hung up on my alibi when he arrested me. Call her back. Indiana Rippley."

The man nodded, writing down the name. "Kosage also has video footage of you tossing the cuffs back at him in the interrogation room a few months back. Then you left without being processed. He could make it stick. Tied to all the murders, it puts you in a funny spot. He just needed a little more mayhem from you to get a judge's permission. Last night was it." Wilson shrugged helplessly. He wasn't pleased with the situation, but also saw no way out of it. I nodded, actually coming to appreciate that the guy was just doing his job.

"Fine. I'll make sure you keep your job, but I predict that Kosage will be making balloon puppets for children's birthday parties next week." Kosage stood, snarled, and then stormed from the room.

They processed me, and placed me in a concrete cell. I passed out instantly, despite fearing the Demons finding me while I slept. I literally couldn't stay awake. Hell, I was lucky I hadn't nodded off during the interrogation.

Sleep found me on the rickety bench, and sent me into the equivalent of a mild coma. I was smiling as I drifted off.

CHAPTER 15

I awoke as a drip of water struck me on the nose. It was warm. I blinked at my surroundings, trying to remember where I was. Nothing looked familiar. I was in a cold concrete room lying on a rusty bench that was bolted to the wall. Was this a night terror? Then I remembered. I was in the police station. Another thought hit me.

I had *slept*. And had no horrifying nightmare! I wanted to shout for joy. Hope's gift had helped me sleep in peace, after all!

Another drop of warm water struck my forehead this time, startling me from my reverie. I reached up to wipe it off, fearing what kind of diseased water was leaking through the pipes. When my fingers touched the water, they came back slippery. Like oil. Or blood.

I jumped up, glancing at my fingertips in the filtered light from the other room. The fluid was clear. My spine tightened in sudden alarm, but I managed to maintain my composure.

It was drool. I slowly arched my head to look at the ceiling, recognizing a smell for the first time.

Sulfur.

I had a cellmate.

"No one told me I would be sharing this cell," I muttered.

"The situation of sharing the cell is only temporary. It's about to be vacant again shortly, man-ling. Don't fret," a feminine reptilian voice hissed back in a low tone.

I let out a breath. "Well that's good. I was about to call dibs on the bench." I stared back at the Demon as she unpeeled from the ceiling like a lizard. She was naked and her body was covered in scales, but cloaked in shadows of some kind. She landed on huge, webbed talons like a dragon. But she wasn't a dragon. She was worse. The creature unfurled from her crouch, appraising me darkly, a shadowed cape billowing around her as if alive.

"We have something to discuss," she hissed.

"Really? Because I can think of absolutely *nothing* I want to talk to you about. I mean, literally nothing. In fact, it would be best if you just left. I was having a really raunchy dream about exorcising this scaly, ugly son of a bitch." I hesitated, appraising my cellmate more closely. "In fact, she looked a hell of a lot like you. Isn't that weird?" I shifted my stance in order to better react to any attack. The Demon blinked. Then she laughed.

"Exorcise? Me? You really are as arrogant as they say." She shook her head, wiping a jagged claw across her face as if to wipe away a tear. "They didn't tell me about your sense of humor! *Exorcise!* Ha!" She slapped her knees, laughing, the shadows swarming around as if alive. She was creepy, deadly, and I was scared out of my mind, but I briefly thought it would be pretty cool to have a coat that looked and acted like a shadow. I felt whispers in the corner of my mind, hypothesizing, analyzing, and mentally discarding ways to achieve just that.

It was as if I suddenly had a team of mad scientists in my brain working overtime for my subconscious. My thoughts briefly snagged on a way to possibly make a cloak of shadows and I froze for a second. "Well, shit. That wouldn't actually be that hard. How come no one else has figured that out?" I asked aloud. I was pretty sure I could make one. I had a mental image of my subconscious scientist doppelganger sporting horn-rimmed glasses and a comb-over as he fist-bumped me with a successful screech at figuring out the shadow cloak.

I hesitated, wondering again if this was another one of those dreams. The Demon was watching me as if doubting my sanity. "What in the bloody Heavens are you talking about, wizard?"

I shrugged. "I dig your threads," I said, pointing at the wavering shadows. One of the tendrils reeled back and hissed at me in the shape of a cobra.

I jumped back in surprise. Well, maybe I hadn't figured it *all* out yet.

"Enough. I'm here to talk of my brother. You had a horse kick him. Through a building. That wasn't nice. He just wanted to take something from you. The Key. I'm here to accept your apology."

She waited.

I waited.

"Well, this is awkward. What did your brother look like again? I've taken out quite a few Demons lately."

She watched me. "Apologize, and I won't strip the flesh from your bones... as slowly as I originally intended. If you give me the Key now, I'll even grant you a clean death."

My muscles tightened. The Key again. What was with these guys? What could they want from the Armory, and how could I give them a Key that didn't exist? I knew I was in for a scrap, and without using magic, I would simply *become* a scrap... of discarded flesh and bone. I decided to stall as I set my mental team of mad scientists to finding a way for me to beat this Demon without magic. Which probably wasn't likely, but worth a shot. I would no doubt have to resort to tapping into my power or become a puddle of goo for the morning janitor. At least Kosage would enjoy my ending. In my head, I knew that any solution even remotely tied to me being a Maker would no doubt require a shitload of magic, which I couldn't afford to do, even though I wanted to see what kind of things I could actually accomplish. I silently encouraged my minions to go old school.

"What exactly do you want the Key for? I don't think Demons would last long in the Armory," I said honestly, remembering Hope's hatred of them.

"True. But the answer will not aid you."

"The Angels really don't want me talking to you."

"You've spoken with them?" she hissed in surprise. I nodded, hoping this would scare her off. "Ah, but the Angels can't really *do* anything in this realm, can they? There are rules, after all."

"Rules?" I asked, feeling slightly better... and worse. If the Angels couldn't directly act on this plane, then I might have a chance to survive being turned into a pillar of salt. It also meant that I would be killed sooner, like right about now.

The Demon smiled, revealing rotted, blackened, razor-sharp fangs. "Angels cannot act on earth. It would ignite Armageddon. If they acted overtly, the Demons could also act overtly. Which would start World War A." I blinked.

"World War A?"

"Yes. As in *Armageddon*." The Demon grinned wide, lips peeling back with excitement. "Everything must be in balance. If an Angel acts discreetly, a Demon can do something discreetly. This is why we use cat's paws."

I stared at her. "You mean possessions. Summonings." It wasn't a question.

The Demon nodded.

"Then how do Angels act? With the Nephilim?"

The Demon flinched at the word, watching me with renewed interest. But she didn't answer. "Enough. I'm bored. Time to give up the Key." I shook my head, trying to come up with a way to fight this soldier from Hell. "So be it. Say *hello* to your parents for me." She smiled.

Then she moved.

I juked to the side, causing her talons to dig into the concrete for a better purchase. I grasped the bench, and with a tiny boost of magic directed at the bolts securing it to the wall, I tore it away and swung it at her head. She raised an arm to block. It crumpled over her arm and shoulders, leaving a Demon shaped dent that she shrugged off after a moment. Then she began to laugh. I pointed at her hand.

"But I did break your nail. I bet a manicure for something like that isn't cheap. Do you use bolt-cutters or something?"

She looked down at her claw, and then used her fangs to forcefully rip the talon from her finger before she spat it out onto the floor. Drops of blood dripped freely from the wound, sizzling on the concrete floor like sulfuric acid.

She appraised me with a cocked head. "My turn." My mind went a million miles an hour, trying to find a way to fight her without draining my power. But there was nothing else in the room to use as a weapon or distraction. It was magic or death. Even with magic, it would be like...

Well, a prison brawl.

Demons were tough. After all, I had just hit a home run on her arm with an aluminum bench and it had only broken her nail. She darted at me, her shadow cloak whipping back and forth erratically so that I couldn't really see exactly where she was. The only way to kill a Demon was to hack them to pieces or exorcise them. Exorcising was out of the question because I had been stripped of any items that could possibly help me do so, and I didn't dare risk wasting the power necessary to do it without those items.

Then I had an idea. I waited, stock still, knowing it was reckless, but that it might be my only chance. I let her hit me, her claws latching onto my chest. Her talons began sinking into my flesh, and... I Shadow Walked. Kind of.

I teleported us a few feet away, releasing the hold on my magic almost the same instant we started to shift. I heard a gasp from her snarling fangs as they lunged closer, ready to eat my face. I twisted my head back to dodge the fangs and look where we had stood only a moment ago. The bottom half of her body had been cut off as I let go of the magic, essentially slicing her neatly in half. I had gotten the idea from the tiny piece of fabric I had seen when I cold-cocked Gunnar earlier today. It had been a piece of my shirt. Luckily, I had found out about the dangers of Shadow Walking on my tee, but it had come in handy just now. I shoved off the sudden weight of her upper body, careful not to get any of her blood on me. Her claws hadn't sunk in deep, but my chest still burned as I extracted them from my torso. She blinked up at me, stunned. "The Key isn't up for grabs. Tell your boss I said so." Blood pooled on the floor, hissing as it scorched the concrete. I sat in the corner of the room and hugged my knees, watching the life fade from her eyes.

I didn't have time for this. I could always Shadow Walk out of here, and hope that it didn't use up too much energy. But that would only freak out every cop in the building and put me on the most wanted list. And I knew the cops would have to release me tomorrow. They didn't have any solid evidence to hold me. And I *did* need the sleep. But apparently, I wasn't even safe in jail. They were taking great risks to get the Key to the Armory.

Time.

I didn't have any of it to waste. I needed to find a way to remove the curse from the Academy. It was going to get me killed if I was always hesitating. Maybe I could talk Gavin into releasing me. Yeah, right. The Demon's body disintegrated into a pile of ash with a puff, but the blood remained. That was odd. I watched as it slowly ate away at the concrete, edging closer and closer to me. I doubted it would actually reach me. It was already slowing down.

My thoughts went to Indie. I hoped she was okay, and that her mother was feeling better. I knew she had to be terrified after that son of a bitch officer had answered my phone. They had conveniently forgotten to grant me a phone call yet. My thoughts drifted to the cops and FBI. They had frozen my assets. I was essentially penniless. I had no idea how legal that was, but with someone as rich as myself, perhaps they had different rules. I could, after all, buy my way out of almost anything. Maybe they considered that a flight risk. Kind of like a weapon. Huh. I hadn't ever thought of it like that, but it was pretty smart on their part.

This was the second Demon to attack me in less than a day, and they had both wanted the Key. The Key that was actually my blood. They hadn't seemed too concerned about killing me, which let me know they had no idea how valuable I was. Which was good. If they killed me, they would never be able to get into the Armory. Hoorah! Temple wins by default! I remembered Hope's idle comment about answers being found through death. And I shivered.

I understood how Demons were able to interact on earth, but how did Angels sneak around? I mean, I had been directly manhandled in the bar by one of the feathery saints and his crew of Nephilim. How was that kosher? Did that mean that even now, a Demon had been granted the opportunity to act overtly? Had Eae's assault allowed the first Demon to appear only an hour later and attack me? Was that why the Nephilim had been with him?

Jesus. Had the Angel caused the war by coming to talk to me? I sensed the air with my powers, knowing that it didn't actually use any of my magic to do so. Everything felt more or less the same. The world didn't feel Armageddon-y. I shook my head. Regardless, I needed to find out how Angels were *supposed* to interact on earth – most likely through the Nephilim – lest I be surprised by a third party over the next few days. I couldn't afford a surprise attack. And I really didn't know how I felt about killing a soldier from Heaven. Even though the only Angel I had met so far had been kind of a dick, he was just doing his job. He saw me as a threat for some reason. Still, I thought there might have been a better way for him to handle it. Like with a group prayer or something. I sighed, frustrated. So far, I had managed to piss off an Angel, two Demons, three cops, a gaggle of Nephilim, and eight Academy members. Each of these groups had given me contradictory demands. Abiding by one set of commands made me *persona non-grata* for the other groups. Catch-22 to the third power. Even worse, I had limited power to fix the situation, and no friends to help me out. I felt my anger growing as I tried to think about what I could do to get out of this shit show.

Then the lights in the room abruptly winked out.

I scanned the darkness as I lurched to my feet, fearing another Demon was about to appear and jump me. I found my way to the bars and tried to peer outside my cell. I was pretty sure that the power to the entire building had just gone out. Emergency lights flickered to life, bathing me in a faint red glow. I began to get real nervous as I heard feet pounding down the stairs. I slowly backed up, ready to unleash hell. I had no idea who was here, but I had no doubt they were coming for me, and the only people coming for me were the biggest of the big hitters. Angels. Demons. Academy Justices. If I was lucky, they might create a joint task force to take me out together, like a dark Justice League. My thoughts ran with that as I heard a door finally open and the footsteps quickly approach my cell.

I raised my hands, ready to vaporize the intruder. I spotted my foe across the room, slowly creeping closer and closer as if on all fours. A green glow emanated at its hip, which made me think of Hell. Then a *face* from Hell materialized as it crept closer. Horns, and war paint covering the upper half of its head. Then it sparkled in the green glow. I blinked. Glitter? Bedazzled Demons?

"Pharos?" I heard a familiar voice call out quietly.

My fear was instantly replaced by confusion and… hope. I raced back to the bars. "Othello?" I hissed in disbelief.

"The one and only." She said, sliding back her *Le Carnevale* mask to reveal her familiar face. I could have cried. She stepped up to the bars to touch my fingers. Pretty girls make graves, and Othello was breathtaking. Shorter than some, but stacked more than most, she sported a thick, wavy pony tail, and she had a small oval-shaped face, with plump cheeks just perfect for squeezing. I glanced at her *Le Carnevale* mask, shaking my head. "Like my disguise? I have one for you also," she cooed. "It's *Mardi Gras*, after all," she said with a grin.

"What are you *doing* here?"

"You didn't answer your phone." I blinked. "I guess you could call me clingy." She winked. I scowled back, shaking my head at her grin. "When you didn't answer your phone, I traced the embedded GPS and saw, to my surprise, your phone was here in this government building. Of course, I decided a face-to-face was necessary. Nobody takes my Pharos. Especially not the government."

I smiled. Othello *hated* the government. Any of them. That was why she was one of the world's most renowned cyber criminals. And they didn't even know who she really was. She was *good*. For her to risk breaking into a federal building to save me had put her at great risk, and it showed me how much she cared for me. Even after all this time. I wasn't quite sure how she spent her time outside of cyber stuff, but I had reason to believe that it wasn't *all* computer stuff. She had made several hints about having unsavory contacts in her debt.

Her glow stick illuminated my cell – revealing the Demon-shaped bench and the blood all over the floor. "Why is there... blood on the floor? Did they hurt you?" She looked suddenly murderous.

"I had a visitor. From my side of the park," I added, emphasizing that it hadn't been a human. "She wouldn't leave when I asked her to." Othello finally nodded after a moment.

"Good riddance," she muttered. "Now, stand back," she warned. Then she began fidgeting with the barred door. I did, still wondering how the hell she was here, what the hell she was doing, and how the hell we were going to get out. This was the freaking police station. For St. Louis. Not really a Barney Fife-type operation with only a single cop napping outside. These police had military grade weapons and a SWAT team for crying out loud. It seemed I was going to need to tap into my magic pretty soon.

I was kind of pissed about this. Here I was, about to be broken out of jail, which would only put me further in the cross-hairs of the police. When it was very likely they were going to release me tomorrow.

"Othello," I warned. "This is crazy. They're going to release me tomorrow. I don't have time to add *America's Most Wanted* to my resume. Just wait. I'll find you as soon as they release me so we can talk. But right now, you need to go. Please. They'll be here any second."

She halted, looking up at me. "No. They won't," she replied in a very cold tone.

My skin pebbled at that. She said it with such finality, as if there was no way the cops were going to come down here. As if... they were no longer a danger. At all. Or ever again.

"Othello... what do you mean? What did you do to them? They were only doing their jobs."

She blinked at me, and then laughed. "I didn't *kill* them. Jesus, Nate. They're *cops*. I called in a threat to empty the majority of the precinct." Her voice jumped an octave, sounding terrified as she mimicked a phone call. "Oh, my gawd! There's a bomb at Queenie's, the gay bar downtown. They're threatening to blow the place up to cleanse the way for God's Children! They said they would only surrender to a man named Kosage. I just came out here to dance, and now everyone's running and screaming! I already see a news crew setting up a block away! I have to go!" She flashed me a self-satisfied grin.

"You're telling me that you set up a bomb at a gay club to... bust me out of jail? I assume it's not going to explode in a shower of glitter and rainbows? You could hurt people!" I needed to get her out of here. And go save the people at the bar.

"There's no bomb, Nate. Although that glitter idea would have been great. When the cops arrive, they're going to see a poster-sized picture of your friend Kosage on a float wearing a pink unitard, with the song *'I'm coming out, I want the world to know...'* blaring on three sets of independently-wired speakers. I informed the patrons at the bar that a famous detective would be arriving tonight to come out of the closet and to support the gay community in St. Louis for *Mardi Gras*. His fellow officers were gathering to support him, with flashing lights for a celebration. The news was also in on it, so they needn't be alarmed." I blinked at her, my mouth opening wordlessly several times. And then I burst out laughing. "The float is titled *Napoleon comes Out*," she added softly. Apparently, Othello had been working on this for some time. There was no way she could have arranged this since my call to her earlier this afternoon.

"This wasn't a spur of the moment thing, was it? How did you Photoshop a picture of Kosage in a unitard, and... why?" I asked in genuine amazement.

She began to laugh, doubling over as she placed the last gadget on the cell door. "That's the best part." She enunciated the next words concisely. "*It. Wasn't. Photoshopped.* I'd intended to use the picture and the float at the Parade, but with what he did to you, the timing couldn't have been more perfect. It serves him right. I used sleeping gas to knock out the rest of the officers upstairs, so me and my team could bust in. I didn't *kill* anyone, Nate. But..." Her face grew troubled. "They aren't planning to release you tomorrow. I hacked into their phones. You weren't going anywhere. That's why I'm here. To bust you out. Something big is going down in St. Louis. And I think it has to do with your investigation into your parents' murder." She watched my face. "We'll talk about that later. Now, I need to get you out of here. Step back. I don't know exactly what's going to happen when I push this button."

"Then maybe you shouldn't—"

She pressed something and the metal at the door disintegrated in seconds, amidst a whining, grinding, and electrical sound like a thousand termites in fast-forward. It stopped after two seconds. The door let out a final groan before it fell into my cell with a resounding crash, barely missing my toes.

"Wow," she said, sounding surprised.

I blinked. I hadn't sensed any magic, and didn't smell any chemicals. And it hadn't been explosive, either. I stepped closer to her, staying on my side of the door, careful not to touch the gate that had fallen into the cell. "What in the hell was *that?*"

"Nano-bots." She grinned at the look on my face, and then shrugged. "Put this on." She handed me a *Le Carnevale* mask and a flannel shirt. I put them on. She adjusted it so that it was crooked, as if forced on me. "Good. I already grabbed your stuff from lockup, since the things you carry are usually dangerous to the uninitiated Regular. Now, come on." She grabbed my hand. Her fingers were feverish as we rushed out of the holding area. She hesitated at the last door, peering through the window. I could see several bodies slumbering on the floor, and several spent canisters lying here and there like discarded beer cans at a party. She nodded to herself, rearranging my mask again slightly. "Okay. I need you to follow me. Act like you're being kidnapped and that you're drugged from the gas. That way they can't suspect you in what happened, and what happens next." She grinned at that. "Don't speak. Building is wired. Just follow me like a victim. A scared puppy."

I began to protest when she suddenly kicked the door open and jerked me forward. I stumbled, playing the part she had requested, but inside I was fuming. What did she have planned that was any worse than what she'd already done? The mask scratched at my face, and ruined my peripheral vision, but I continued on, following her lead obediently, sluggishly.

Instead of heading for the front doors, or even a back door, we headed into the office area for the detectives. This couldn't be good.

Othello reached into her backpack and tossed an official looking folder on a nearby table.

She tossed another, different looking folder on a separate desk, then she jabbed me in the stomach, pulling her punch at the last second. I had instinctively tensed up for the hit, but quickly realized she was acting for the camera in the corner ceiling. She was good. I doubled over before allowing her to yank me the opposite direction. I followed on her heels, shuffling my feet as she led me out to a back alley where I discovered a limo idling for us.

"Here's our ride. Let's go." I followed her into the backseat and slammed into the leather as the driver floored the gas. With that, we were roaring through the city. Othello tore off her mask and hooted out the open sunroof.

I looked at her in amazement. "Wow. You're kind of awesome," I said after a few moments.

She grinned back, grabbing my hand. "You have no idea."

She continued holding my hand. After a few seconds, I politely pulled away and took off my mask.

"Your *face!*" she hissed.

"Not exactly one for bedside manner, are you?" I scowled. She smiled guiltily, shaking her head. "What exactly did you put on that desk?" I could see a calculating look in her eyes at both my black eyes and the fact that I hadn't resumed our handholding. But now wasn't the time to tell her about Indie. *Hey, thanks for risking your life to bust me out of jail, but I've got this kick-ass girlfriend. You two should meet. Maybe go shopping or something! It would be so much fun!*

Yeah, right.

Her smile came back in an instant. "More pictures of our friend, Kosage."

"What kind of pictures?" I asked carefully.

"BDSM." She caught my gaze. "Again, *not* Photoshopped."

I blinked at her. Then I hooted out the sunroof. Despite what happened next, Kosage's life had just gotten a whole lot shittier. Thanks to my little friend, Othello, cyber-criminal extraordinaire.

Life was good.

"I also included some photos of Kosage involved in some questionable extracurricular activities."

I shook my head, grinning. "Oh?"

Her eyes twinkled. "I didn't like how he treated you a few months back so I made a file for him. Currently, he's known to frequent Craigslist for Dominatrixes. The file has some pictures of him in some compromising gear. Pink gear. He will shortly be on the news for an altogether different reason." She didn't elaborate, but I could hardly wait. "I don't like people causing my Pharos trouble."

Picking up on her not-so-subtle words, I changed topics. "Who's driving us?" The divider was up, so I couldn't tell.

"Someone who owed me a favor. He repaid it with the extraction and the sleeping canisters. I think I about used up all my favors with this job. He's taking us to a safe-house since I assumed yours was not usable anymore." She leaned forward eagerly, squeezing my hand. "The other file I left was a ransom note for one Nathin Temple, by the way. Perfect cover for you. You can't be suspected in your own kidnapping!" She looked triumphant.

I shook my head, smiling at her. Oh well, I was technically broke, now, so I could use the money. If anyone paid. It wasn't like I could pay my own ransom. I mean, all my funds were frozen. Things were getting interesting. But she was right. At least I'd managed to escape without being an accomplice. "I guess we're about to find out how much the city likes me."

Othello grinned. "They can't afford you. I set it at One Hundred Million."

"Oh, well…" At least I was free for now. I would just have to make sure that the FBI didn't spot me in the next few days. Maybe I could call Jeffries to help me out. I didn't want to ruin his career though, so I would only do so as a last resort. I knew if I spoke with Jeffries, whether I told him the truth or not, he would *know*. It was his gift. He could sense lies. Talking to him at all would basically get him involved on a level that could ruin his career. I couldn't do that to a friend. Like I had with Gunnar.

And the party of one became two.

CHAPTER 16

*A*fter several minutes of small talk, Othello reached into her bag and handed me my stuff from lockup. I eagerly turned on my cell phone and began shifting through the rest of my belongings as I waited for the phone to power up. Othello turned to watch the streets for signs of pursuit, but so far so good. I looked out my side of the car, wondering where Othello's safe house was as the number of graffiti-scarred ancient buildings began to increase. We were miles from the police station by now, and I felt my tension slowly evaporating with each passing block. The lights grew fewer and farther between as we headed through a more desolate section of the city. The air was cold, and the darkness of night reigned supreme, but at least we were police-free. I turned back to my goodies, pocketing some of them until only the most relevant items still sat in my hands. There was the Demon-sensing stone Hope had given me, my wallet with a little bit of cash in it – which would come in handy now that my accounts were frozen – and a few other magical knick-knacks. I texted Indie the moment the phone turned on. *Sorry about the confusion earlier with the FBI. Available to talk whenever you are. I didn't want to wake you up in case you were sleeping. Miss you!*

As I set my phone down, the Demon-sensing stone began to vibrate in my lap. I picked it up and stared at it for a few seconds, confused. I hadn't said anything to it, and I couldn't hear the creepy voices speaking to me.

I could feel Othello's tension rising as she watched out of the corner of her eye. "Why is it doing th—"

An incredible force suddenly slammed into the side of the limo, knocking us into a nearby building with a squeal of tires and crunching metal. The side of my head rebounded off the door, making my injured nose flare with heat, and my skull ring like a Looney Tunes character. Broken safety glass showered the inside of the car and brick dust clouded the windshield, eliminating our chances of seeing outside the car to discern what had caused the wreck. I grasped the door handle to try and get us out, but it was pointless. I was wedged up against the wall of the building.

Before I could speak, more glass exploded into the driver's seat as a giant claw entered the car, latched onto the driver's skull, and simply... extracted it like a berry from a bush. Blood splattered the windshield, front seats, and dashboard, even the glass divider that protected the driver from his passengers, painting everything a gooey, viscous red. As the blood and gore began to drip down the glass, something heavy landed on the hood with a *thunk*.

Through the blood and dust, I saw that it was the driver's head; eyes still wide with shock, staring at us in confusion. I hadn't even known his name.

Othello began to scream, lunging towards me as another clawed fist shattered the back window and latched onto her leg. I grabbed onto her hands and we were both promptly jerked from the car, my side slicing open as I was jerked over the remaining safety glass and through the tiny opening in the window. Othello's continued screams filled the night, but so did a malevolent, ancient laughter. Still attached to each other like the children's toy, *Barrel of Monkeys*, we were then unceremoniously tossed into the brick building. My head cracked against the brick hard enough for stars to explode across my vision.

Lucky for Othello, I had hit the wall first, so my body significantly cushioned her impact against the ancient brick, which didn't feel great for me in general, but especially didn't feel great over my freshly scraped sides. We hit the ground heavily, my head ringing from the two impacts in less than a minute. I felt like Humpty Dumpty. I heard Othello groan as I quickly assessed my injuries. She wasn't cut out for this, and she had stepped into a game against forces she couldn't even fathom, let alone survive.

I stumbled to my feet, still clutching the bone artifact in my fist. My phone lay in the center of the street by the smoking limo.

Directly in front of a towering Demon.

He was at least nine feet tall and covered in knotted dreadlocks with broken teeth and bones woven throughout his coarse body hair like a sinisterly-decorated Christmas tree. "They have people who do corn-rows in Hell?" I mumbled under my breath.

The Demon snarled back at me from beneath the wild mane of hair around his ginormous head, brushing the bones on his fur with a purring noise. There were enough bones woven into his hair that they might have even doubled as an armor, of sorts. Giant scarred fists flexed at his side as he let out another leonine roar, drool dripping off his fangs as he flexed his entire body, bulging with energy-filled muscle. A lot of it. "It speaks," the Demon growled.

"And *it* is about to whoop the living fuck out of you, Thundercat," I took a step forward and felt a warning wave of heat strike me like an oven door had just opened. The Demon's eyes flared like the burning embers at the center of a fire, halting my advance. There was no way in hell I was putting up with this right now. There was also no way we were surviving if I didn't dig deep into my magical reserves. I could sense the energy pouring out of this monster like a furnace. There was no running. Only fighting. I was fine with that. I was done pussyfooting around, even if it would drain a big chunk of my power. I held up my fist, and the offensive heat diverged around me. I held my fist out as I began to stride forward again.

My phone began to ring. It was pretty close to his foot. "Hold on, pal. I need to take this really quick." I began jogging towards the Demon, holding up a finger for patience.

The Demon stared at me in disbelief, and then lifted a giant clawed foot, ready to bring it smashing down onto my phone. "You won't be conversing with your metal Familiar."

My metal Familiar? He didn't know what a phone was? Rather than pondering that too long, I unleashed a hissing whip of purple darkness, the new power a result of the energy-manipulating experiments I had been tinkering on for months. It consisted of the coldest substance I had ever heard of, and once it grabbed onto something, it didn't let go until I commanded it, literally causing the worse freezer-burn ever. I lassoed the Demon's foot, the power of the substance burning straight to the bone in a second and a half, causing the stench of burnt hair to fill the street. The Demon roared in true pain. Then I swung the whip wide, hurtling the Demon straight into a lamppost across the street.

It bent into a ninety-degree angle.

The Demon crumpled to the street. I didn't even wait to see if he got up. That *had* to hurt him. At least a little bit. I needed to answer my phone or Indie was going to kill me.

I quickly snatched it up, answering the face-time call through the cracked screen. Indie's face filled the screen and I smiled at her. "Indie!" I shouted in relief. "Listen. I'm kind of tied up at the mom—"

"You don't listen very well, wizard." A fist grabbed me around the neck, lifting me high into the air and holding me there as I futilely kicked my feet. The air was slowly being choked from me and I couldn't even speak. The Demon warily plucked the phone from my fist, glancing down at the cracked screen with slight anxiety, as if nervous of the floating face that was cursing at him. Then he pointed it away from his face in apparent fear.

Indie's shriek filled the deserted street. "Nate? What *was* that? What's going on? Are you okay? I got your text. *Nate?* Say something. Stop breathing into the phone like a creep!" She sounded exhausted, and frustrated, like she had been up all night crying.

"I am a Greater Demon. On the pathway to becoming a true Knight of Hell after this brief sojourn. And I am about to skin your lover. Your assistance will not save him, Familiar," the lion Demon growled back at the phone, still fearful of directly facing the screen, despite his brave threat. He was on track to become a true Knight of Hell? What did that even mean? Was he, like, a recruit for Sir Lucifer's Knights of the Crooked Table or something? A sword-bearer for the Prince of Darkness? I mentally upgraded him from Thundercat to Hell's version of Lancelot. Sir Dreadsa-lot. Then he shattered the phone on the ground, stomped on it several times for good measure, and hooted in triumph. As I dangled there helplessly, my vision dwindling to a single point, I realized that this Demon honestly thought he had vanquished a great foe – my phone. He looked back up at me as if surprised to still see me dangling, choking to death in his fist. Then he tossed me over the limo, back into the brick building where I struck a bit harder than the first time, and then I landed on top of Othello in a heap of elbows and knees. It seemed to wake her up because she swung an elbow and clocked me in the ridge above my eye in self-defense. I gasped in pain as my nose flared with sudden heat. I blinked several times through the pounding headache. My breath came in through raw gasps. It felt like I had torn some important muscle or ligament in my throat, my breath making slight whistling noises. I could feel the bloody scratches from his claws on my neck burning slightly, frighteningly close to my femoral artery, or was it carotid artery? Regardless, it was one of my body's important blood tubes, but the wounds weren't deep.

I climbed to my feet and stumbled around the limo, noticing that the Demon eyed me more warily than before, the skin of his leg still smoking from my first attack. "Now I'm going to have to kick your ass, because she is going to kick mine for that."

"I destroyed your metal Familiar. It is no more." He pointed at the shattered device, quivering with a proud chuckle.

I blinked at him. Was he really that ignorant to the ways of the world? That was both a good thing and a bad thing. If he was really that ignorant, it meant that he hadn't spent much time on earth, which meant that he hadn't possessed anyone yet or else he would have had their knowledge at his disposal. Which meant that maybe he wasn't exaggerating when he said he was a Greater Demon. Which meant that he was *really* dangerous, and *really* old.

Goddamn it. I didn't even know if I had the juice to take on a run-of-the-mill possession, let alone a literal Demon that had been summoned here in the flesh.

Then I blinked as that dawned on me. The *only* way a real Demon was here on earth in the flesh was if someone had *summoned* him. That meant someone else was calling the shots. Someone I didn't know about. Before I could say anything brilliant, the Demon spoke, taking an aggressive step forward.

"You killed one of my daughters this night. I shall have my retribution by flossing my teeth with your flesh and adding your bones to my armor."

"Well that's uber-gross. But that's not how this is going to play out, Sir Dreadsalot."

The Demon chuckled. "You think you can defeat *me*? A Greater Demon?"

"We'll get to that in a minute. First of all, I have a question. Being a Greater Demon, how is it possible for you to be here? Is it because Eae interacted with me at the bar last night? I don't think even the baddest of wizards could summon a Greater Demon. Not without a whole bunch of people, and even then, there are rules. Certain times of the year, rituals, relics, certain number of people, and tons of other particular things that I really don't believe could have occurred."

The Demon blinked. "You know more than you should about the rules of Heaven and Hell. How?" he asked me, genuinely appearing threatened by my knowledge. Shit. I had stumbled across something I wasn't supposed to know.

"Your daughter told me," I answered.

His muscles bunched together, increasing his size. "She wouldn't."

I shrugged. "How else would I know? It's not like I summon many Demons. You should know the truth of that."

The Demon's eyes appraised me, and suddenly looked more than slightly afraid beneath all of that life-threatening muscle, teeth and claws. I was pretty sure that I had just been upgraded to a liability.

"Enough. I do not suffer liars. You attacked my son, and killed my daughter. For that, you shall die. You will give me the Key, and then I will let you and your plaything die."

"You see, Sir Dreadsalot, I don't think your boss would like that. You know, the wizard who summoned you," I clarified, not wanting him to take it as me talking about God, or Lucifer, or someone from his neighborhood. I really needed to brush up on my hierarchy of Angelic and Demonic beings. I honestly didn't know who worked for whom, and in what order, or if maybe some of them were free agents. "He wants the Key, which means that you have to *get* the Key. I can honestly tell you that killing me would get you nothing, and I know a bit about what powers a summoner would hold over a Demon they call to earth if said Demon fails. They take a bit of your power for themselves. I don't think you want that, do you?"

The Demon scowled back.

"Now, if you want me to help you, I need to know the who, what, and why of your situation. This is the third time I've been attacked by your kind about this Key, so it's obvious your boss wants it, and made it a condition to allow you to run free. I've been attacked by my own kind for this Key, and even the Angels have threatened me about it. I want—"

"The Angels have been in contact with you? How dare they interfere!"

"Yeah. Pot. Kettle. Black," I said. I didn't let on that I saw Othello creeping around a second parked car. She was holding something. Not good. If she entered the fight, there was no way I could protect her. "So, answers?" I demanded, attempting to distract him.

137

The Demon watched me thoughtfully. Then he pulled a freaking sword out of the Ether, straight from Hell. "We will do this my way." Then he charged me. I backed up against the limo, and felt blood wetting my back from the driver's corpse. It pissed me off. I held out my arms and cast a cloud of steam straight at the Demon's head. It instantly melted the flesh from his face, and he shrieked in agony, diving away from the cloud and swatting his face with a meaty paw. I began to feel good. Like I maybe had a chance at survival. "Bad kitty," I snarled.

The sword missed me by a millimeter, sinking into the limo by my shoulder like it was made of paper. I blinked. I hadn't even seen him move. He had freaking hurled it at me. Then he was charging me again, on all fours this time. I could see his skull through the dying skin on his face as it peeled back at the force of his speed. I jumped to the left just as he swiped at me, and unleashed a blast of white-hot fire directly onto his back. He roared in pain and swatted me onto the ground where I bounced, once, twice, and then struck another nearby parked car. I lay there, suddenly noticing the power I had been throwing around. It was a lot. As I delved into my reservoir, I noticed that it was significantly lower. I gulped. That wasn't good. I touched my head, noticed I was bleeding, and looked up to see the Demon slowly walking towards me. Then he hesitated, a new thought crossing his ugly melted face as he studied me on the ground.

"As much pleasure as I would get from skinning you, I believe I could cause you more agony by doing something else. I sense that your power is dwindling, but that you would use it all against me if necessary. Instead, I will allow you to live, and to keep what remains of your draining power. You will need it to choose who lives and who dies."

I blinked at him, confused. "Pardon?"

The Demon smiled through his scalded face. "Every day you delay in giving my brethren what they seek, I shall murder one of your fellow wizard-lings."

I stared at him. Wizard-lings. That was ancient terminology. It didn't mean wizards, it meant any number of magical creatures: wizards, were-wolves, fairies, witches, and vampires. "What do you mean?"

"Every day you delay in giving me or my offspring the Key, I will arrange for one of your fellow supernaturals to be murdered in a very public way. I've enjoyed my jaunt into your realm, but I tire of servitude. Give me the

Key and we both walk away happy, with less death on your shoulders, and less annoyance on mine."

I knew this was a tricky situation. Even if I wanted to save their lives, I couldn't give up the Key to the Armory... my blood. I *literally* couldn't. Then who would stand up to the summoner? No one would even find out who he was if I was dead. If I survived, others would think that I simply gave up the Key like a coward. The Angels would be after me. The Academy would be after me. Or if I were already dead, my friends would pay. They would shun my name to the entire magical world, and I would become the most hated being ever to walk the earth, depending on who wanted the Key and what they were intending to do with it. My guess was that if the summoner was using Demons to get it he didn't have noble intentions.

"Give me the Key to the Armory so I can give it to my master and be done with my servitude. I'll even let you live, wizard. No one needs die, and I will cast my Demons back to Hell. Win, win."

His offer chilled me. But I just couldn't give him the Key. Even if I wanted to. I was kind of... attached to it. I briefly remembered Hope's warning about Death being the ultimate answer and shivered. After a deep breath, I nodded, feeling something in my pocket that I had stashed away earlier. "On one condition. You tell me who murdered my parents."

The Demon watched me, considering. Then, a dark smile crept over his face. "Deal." I pulled the small object out of my pocket, looked at it once in defeat, and then tossed it to him. His eyes gleamed as he snatched it from the air. He began to examine the music box that Peter had stolen from the Armory. I had tried everything, testing it every way I could think, but had yet to find anything dangerous or powerful about it. It was simply a music box.

But the Demon didn't know that, and he seemed particularly aloof to the ways of my world, not even knowing what a cell phone was.

"*I* killed your parents."

Time seemed to slow, then stop entirely.

My vision turned red and my blood instantly boiled, making me feel like an inferno of fire, as if someone had just lit a fuse deep in my soul. My parents' murderer stood before me, and I was ready to burn away the last of my remaining strength to incinerate him so ultimately that even his cell-mates in Hell would never recognize him.

He watched my impotent rage with an amused smile. "They stood between me and the Armory. Of course, back then there was no Key. But I knew they would prevent me from entering so I eliminated them. Then that thief snuck in while I was entertaining your parents, locking the entrance from me. Since then the room has been guarded by a Key. It all could have been so simple if it wasn't for him." He growled with minor frustration. Then he smiled at me. "But you know that already. If not for him, your parents may still be alive. Shame. He was your best friend after all. If that's what you do to your friends, I'd love to see what you do to your enemies." His fangs glittered in the moonlight. I could only see red. This was my parents' murderer. Right here. In front of me.

And I couldn't do a goddamned thing. I was tapped, magically speaking. If I fought this Demon here I wouldn't have enough juice for the summoner, and he was the real problem.

He watched me, enjoying my pain. "Easy, wizard. You might use up the last of your strength. Then who would save your friends? Now that I have the Key, we will depart this plane." He fidgeted with the box, and then frowned at it. He held it up to his ear. Scowling, he opened it to the effect of a tinny version of "You are my sunshine," filling the street. He roared in anger, throwing it on the ground. "What trickery is this? You thought you could fool me?"

I smiled. "Well, technically I *did* just fool you. Don't be offended. I do it to everyone."

The Demon moved. And when I say moved, I mean faster than even I could clearly see. He raised his arm, a nebulous dark ball of energy coursing around his fist. Then it came screaming at me. I raised my trembling arms to block it, but it bypassed my defenses easily, and a burning sensation struck me in the forehead like he had thrown a well-aimed, scalding rock. It instantly seared my skin like a brand. I found myself on the ground, staring up at the starry night. It had begun to snow, looking like the very stars were falling all around me.

Like Fallen Angels cast down from Heaven.

I didn't know how long I lay there, but it must have been only seconds, as I heard the Demon step up to me with a curious respect in his eyes.

"You shouldn't have tried to trick me. You have now been marked. The Angels will see you as an Agent of Hell. Even their sons will hunt you, and the Armory will be lost to everyone, for they will raze it, and possibly your entire city, to the ground. Also, my previous offer of your brethren dying upon each denied offer of the Key still stands. Each night you delay, we will murder a member of a different supernatural caste. Since you seem to care for the werewolves so much, we will begin with them. One will die before sunrise, unless you give me what I seek."

I briefly wondered how many of his brethren were enjoying their stay in my city. How many I needed to fight to protect my people. Sir Dreadsalot took a step closer, leaning so that I could see his scarred, melted face clearly. "I do applaud you on your trickery, and that lucky strike, though. Never seen anything like it. Do you make a habit of discovering new spells? Most wizards repeat the same old same old. Boring. But you, you're... *fun*." He seemed genuinely appreciative. "Don't waste it here. Save it for our next encounter. I love anticipation. Foreplay. Mmmm... Just imagine how much fun the werewolf will have tonight."

My soul hurt. I was basically condemning an innocent werewolf to die. For some reason, all I could imagine was someone killing a puppy. No matter how badass the werewolf was, I'd just had my ass handed to me by this thing. No way a werewolf would fare any better. I shook my head. I couldn't pass the Key over to them. If I did, the Academy would kill me. Literally. If I didn't, the wolf would die. I had to find a way out of this before things got too out of hand. I was suddenly very happy my friends were all out of town. There was no way they could defend themselves from this thing.

The Demon smiled. "Thank you for the dinner. I love me some... *puppy chow*. Is that the right phrase?" he asked, grinning. "When you come to your senses and realize the forces against you, and are ready to discuss terms, ignite the Thirteenth Major Arcana in a confessional booth." My breath momentarily caught at his comment, but he continued. "Or when you are entirely out of options and tired of being hunted by the Nephilim. They exist to destroy agents of Hell, which you now appear to be." My blood chilled. The Fallen Angels had their minions – the Demons, whereas the Angels also had theirs – the Nephilim, the offspring of Angels and humans. Practically superheroes, if the rumors I had heard were correct. But I had yet to meet a person who had actually encountered one. I was almost 100% sure I had met an entire gang of them in the bar with Eae and Hemingway. "Both sides will now be hunting you. It's delicious, really. *Check*, as they say Master Temple. Your move." He turned to go, but slowed. "Unless, of course, you are ready to make a deal now... I specialize in these transactions, and a deal from one with your reputation would benefit both of us... I could eliminate your curse and give you new powers to make up for what you already lost..."

"Not a chance in Hell, Sir Dreadsalot."

He shook his head in disappointment. "Don't be so sure, mortal." I fumed, stumbling back to my feet. My legs wobbled and I fell back against the car. The Demon watched me pitilessly. "I would love to destroy you myself, but in your weakened state, it would feel like a cheap victory. Perhaps some other time, when you have full use of your power. I honestly don't see why you fight me so. Your own people have injured you, made you impotent. You continue to fight out of some mistaken creed. On the side of those who have shunned you. Even Demons have honor. Some of us, anyway. More than your allies, at least." He turned to walk away.

"What did my parents discover that warranted their deaths?"

He turned to face me. "That is none of your – or my – concern. Like I said, if not for Peter..." He winked.

Forget Peter. I knew the Demon would have killed them regardless of the horrible timing on Peter's part. The summoner. He was the *real* problem. I had to get to him. Also, I now had to watch out for the Angels' minions, the Nephilim...

He noticed my growing anger. "Easy, wizard. You might use up the last of your strength. Then who would save your friends? Who would save your friend over there?" He grinned, glancing over my shoulder at the limo. Then he noticed Othello wasn't there and began to frown.

"Hey, pussycat!" Othello called from across the street behind a trashcan. The Demon whirled, directly into an attack that even I hadn't expected. She shot something at the Demon, which he lifted his meaty paw to block. But whatever she shot at him stuck fast to his elbow. She shrugged. "That will have to do." I heard a click, and the next thing I knew, the Demon was on the ground, screaming as a thousand Nano-bots destroyed his arm from the elbow down, eating absolutely everything before falling to the ground, lifeless. His roar shook the windows, shattering several, before he disappeared in a cloud of smoke and ash.

I stared at Othello. "That was... incredible." She smiled weakly. "But you just made a very big, bad enemy. What were you *thinking?*" I demanded.

"You're either a meal or a monster in this world. I prefer to be a monster, or to at least have others think I am. It's safer." She helped me up, supporting my shoulder, glancing pointedly at my forehead before brushing my hair to cover it up with a shiver. I didn't care at the moment. I would check it in the mirror later. I had more pressing concerns at the moment. We glanced at the limo and stopped, staring sadly at the remains of its lone occupant. I studied our surroundings, shocked to realize that none of the fighting had attracted any attention. We were in a commercial district of some kind, but apparently, none of the businesses operated after traditional work hours. Lucky for us. I was, after all, a ransom victim.

"What the hell was he talking about at the end? Ignite the Thirteenth Major something. That sounds… ominous." I nodded, but didn't explain.

She studied me, waiting, but realizing I wasn't going to explain, she chose a different question. "What about the Nephilim? What are they? You looked concerned."

"Let's get somewhere safe, first. I'll tell you all about it."

CHAPTER 17

We continued to assess the car in respectful silence, Othello nodding her head in agreement that it was time to leave. The driver was obviously dead. The side that wasn't slammed up against the building was covered in a mix of both a little of my blood and a lot of the driver's blood. Then, of course, there was his headless corpse in the seat, and his severed head on the hood. I shivered, glad that it wasn't facing me. I glanced down at my side, noticing a few shallow, but bloody gashes down my ribs. I had forgotten about them while being slammed into walls and such by the Demon. They weren't fatal.

"He might be on the surveillance footage with me, breaking you out of jail. This car will definitely be spotted. It's a burner anyway, but it could hold trace evidence. If they link this to you, it won't go well. Burn it all. No trace. He knew what he was getting himself into. He volunteered after hearing about you and the weredragons a few months ago. As did the others."

"Others?" I asked softly.

"I have some friends waiting for us at the safe-house. They have a few tools for us, but then their contract is up. Unless you have another twenty-thousand to pay them."

I blinked, not turning away from the dead man. I didn't realize I was such a celebrity with the supernatural mercenaries. "You paid them that

144

much… to help *me?*" I asked softly, feeling both guilty and… appreciative. She nodded. "Using them over the next few days might not be a bad idea. I'll write them a check."

"Cash only," she answered.

That made sense. "Oh. Okay. That shouldn't be a prob—" Then I remembered that all my bank accounts were frozen. I scowled at life in general. "I guess we're on our own, then." She shrugged. Knowing my power was dwindling, I agreed with her assessment of the evidence. I felt cold, deep inside my soul. This stranger – who had helped me escape – was dead. The money Othello had paid him wouldn't ever be utilized. I didn't even know the man's name. I decided to honor the dead man by calling on the old Boatman. At least last respects would be granted.

I summoned up a storm of fire and incinerated the vehicle without a single movement. Othello jumped back in surprise. "It still gets me when you do things like that. You didn't even say anything. Or move. You used to have to do things like that to use your power." I looked at her thoughtfully. She was right. I normally had to perform some kind of physical action to use some of my larger spells. But with the power spike from my parents' deaths – transforming me into a Maker, as I now understood – I didn't need any assistance for spells that used to be difficult for me. Of course, none of that would matter in three days when my power disappeared entirely. I called Charon with a mental whisper.

The boatman hesitated when he saw me, sniffing the air. I frowned. The Boatman had never done that before. Maybe my Demon cologne wasn't entirely gone. Or maybe Sir Dreadsalot's smell filled the street. But the Boatman departed with his usual acceptance of the man's soul and a final wave of gratitude, sailing off into the curtain of falling snow before disappearing.

Othello waved back. I didn't. I turned us away and began to shamble down the street, letting Othello know it was time for us to leave. A voice called out behind me. "That was a crime." I froze. Othello jerked to the right, raising her Nano-bot gun. I slowly turned, and then held out my hand for Othello to stand down. She frowned, but complied. I scowled at Gavin, my parole officer.

"How long have you been watching me? I could have used some damned help."

Gavin watched me, looking angry. "It seems like plenty of *damned* people were here already," he spat. I frowned, and then understood that he was referring to the Demon as a *damned* Angel. A *Fallen* Angel.

"Why didn't you help?" I demanded, voice raspy with barely bottled anger.

"It is not my job to help you. It's my job to *prevent* you from performing any more crimes. Which you just did. Also, you seem to be out of jail, where you rightfully belong. I should deliver you back to them." He looked conflicted. "It would be the right thing to do."

I blinked back at him in disbelief. "*The right thing to do?* Arresting the only person who seems to give a shit about Demons running around my city, slaughtering innocents, and raising hell? That sounds like the *right thing to do?* You're one twisted bastard, you know that?" I spat back in disgust.

Gavin took an aggressive step forward. "Don't tempt me. I could justifiably end you. Right here, right now."

"*Tempt* you?" I snarled, quivering with anger. "I just fought a Demon in the middle of the street and you sat there and watched. Even the *Regular* jumped in to help me. What the hell is *wrong* with you? Are you honestly delusional enough to think you are wearing the White Hat here? The Academy has fallen a long way if that's the case. You guys are completely brainwashed if the right and wrong side of this situation is confusing to you. I used to be proud to be a member of the Academy. But your actions *disgust* me."

Gavin stared at me, trembling with rage and... doubt. In himself? But it didn't last long. He was back to his arrogant self a second later. "There were no innocents here to defend. Only a criminal and his sidekick," he argued.

"Now wait a damned minute. I am no sidekick. I just took out a Demon!" she hissed indignantly.

Othello was pissed. I looked from Gavin to her, and then shrugged. "Well, he has a point. It's kind of what sidekicks do. Save the day when the real superhero is down."

She slowly turned her fiery eyes to me and I took a step back in case she had any more ammunition for her death-eating, minion launcher. I turned back to Gavin. "Regardless, you were a disgrace. After seeing me fight a Demon, I'm pretty sure you can safely deduce that I'm not working with them. I nearly died trying to keep him from getting the Armory. And my power is fading. Fast. What the fuck more do you want from me?"

Gavin rolled his eyes. "The Key." I took an aggressive step forward. "As you were commanded. You were also commanded to end the Demons in St. Louis. I don't see how you believe this to be a noble reaction on your part when you are simply doing as commanded."

I wanted to rip his face off. Slowly. "No one *commands* me, Gavin. Fucking *no one*." I was literally shaking with rage and utter disbelief at his piety. "Especially a bunch of hypocritical little bitches sitting safely on the sidelines. I would rather slit my wrists than be associated with scum like you. You literally sat there and watched as a Demon fought me for your precious Key. Were you waiting for him to end me so that you could run to your boss, and get a promotion for how good a boy you'd been? Pathetic. I'm finished with the Academy. You're a stain to honor, everywhere."

Gavin slammed his fist into his thigh. A pulsing greenish light slammed into the ground and hurtled towards me, knocking me clear on my ass. I jumped to my feet ready to fight, but he still stood in the same spot, and looked... slightly embarrassed. "I'm sorry. I shouldn't have attacked you," he whispered.

I blinked.

He took a deep breath. "I don't appreciate anyone making a mockery of my life's work." He shifted from foot to foot. "However, I understand your frustrations. Working as a Justice hasn't been... exactly as I thought it would. I, too, sense... darkness in our purpose. It used to feel honorable, but now..." His eyes grew distant, confused, frustrated. "I'm not so sure. I see a lot of things happen, a lot of commands given, that I truly don't understand, nor agree with. But... if the good guys don't seem to be acting to the standards I expect; does that mean I am in some way unworthy? That I truly do not know the greater good? I can't seem to accept the fact that they are wrong or have bad intentions. They are the *Academy*, for Christ's sake. If I don't work for the good guys, what does that make me? I just want to do the right thing." He looked genuinely torn.

Huh. Was he really that naïve? Was he so brainwashed that he didn't know how to stand up to his superiors when they seemed to be making bad calls? Maybe that was how they had been trained. To never challenge their betters. In fact, it made sense. They wouldn't want insubordination in a life or death situation. Like the military. But this seemed like a huge chink in their armor. I could clearly see that Gavin truly wanted to be a good guy, but that he didn't know what that meant anymore.

"Gavin, listen to me. What were you commanded to do?" I asked, managing to relax my shoulders into an unthreatening posture. I noticed Othello's eyes darting back and forth between us, ready for anything, knowing me better than most.

"To watch over you and prevent you from making a deal with either party. The Key belongs to the Academy."

My fingers tingled. To make sure I didn't make any deals. Well, that was dicey. How could I use my trickery if I wasn't allowed to play one enemy against another? Making a deal was pretty much the only way I thought I could survive long enough to get to the summoner, which was the only way to end the Demon presence and keep the Armory safe. In fact, it was pretty much a guarantee that I would have to make a deal in order to get a face-to-face with the true enemy.

"And if I were to make a deal, but hadn't actually given over the Key yet, what were you commanded to do?"

He looked up at me with hard, but torn, eyes. "Kill you."

My head sagged. "You do understand that for me to get close enough to the bad guys to end this that I pretty much *have* to make a deal, right?"

He nodded, looking confused.

"Follow that thought to its rational conclusion, and tell me what you see," I said gently.

He did, and I watched his shoulders begin to sag, but he didn't speak.

"So, you realize that you were chosen to, pretty much, be my assassin. I am commanded to go after the Demons and end them, yet your boss bound my power so that I am not strong enough to accomplish the task. Which makes it 100% likely that I will have to use subterfuge and trickery to get close enough to finish this, meaning I would need to at least *pretend* to make a deal. You were hired to watch over me and make sure that I don't break any laws… but even if I *pretended* to make a deal, you were to *kill* me. So, the Academy has taken away my power to fight for myself, meaning I will be killed or lose my magic forever, but if I found another way to usurp them and made a deal, you would be there to kill me… to *end* me." I watched as his shoulders slumped further. "You were hired as a hit man, not a probation officer." I finally said. He wasn't looking at me. "*Look* at me, Gavin. Look at your *victim*. Your *target*. Your *mark*. You know you couldn't take me in a fair fight, so your boss helped you out, made your mark harmless." He flinched at each word, as if I was physically striking him, but he didn't look up. "LOOK AT ME!" I roared. Othello jumped in alarm. Finally, Gavin lifted his gaze. I stared him in the eyes for a long time. "Do you still think your boss is wearing a white hat?"

He finally shook his head. "But if I can't trust them, who can I trust?"

I sighed in resignation, rubbing my hands together for warmth. "Yourself, kid. Always yourself. You might not always be right, but at least you can rationalize all your actions and know why what you do is right or wrong, rather than blindly following some creed. It's never good when you blindly follow some belief system or group of people without consciously deducing whether what they do is right or wrong. The number one test is to wonder what would happen if you openly, but respectfully, questioned your commander's decision when you think it's wrong. If the answer in any way resembles punishment, pain, or ridicule, rather than an explanation, you're probably not working for the good guys."

Gavin nodded his head after a moment. "I want to do the right thing." My shoulders relaxed for a moment. "But I still do not trust you, Temple. You caused so much chaos here with the dragons, and you hold the launch codes to the Armory. I will give you a chance, but that doesn't mean I work for you. I work for myself... and possibly the Academy. I will not let their corruption get in your way, or the way of the innocents, but that does not make us friends. Understood?"

I nodded. "Thanks for hearing me out, Gavin."

"Don't thank me just yet. I won't mention anything to my superiors about what happened here tonight. But I'm still watching you." With a final nod, he Shadow Walked, disappearing with a faint *crack* in the air. The falling snow pulsed away from the void as if repelled, leaving a faint circle of bare street where he had been standing.

Othello watched me in surprise, several fat snowflakes settling on her eyelashes. "So, he's one of the good guys, eh?" I shrugged, letting her guide me in the direction of the safe house. Perhaps Gavin wasn't on my side, but at least I knew he wasn't a zealot for the Academy anymore. My thoughts drifted to the Demon's threats. How would I protect the werewolf? Who was he? Where was he?

At least I knew it wouldn't be Gunnar.

It's the little things that matter.

CHAPTER 18

*S*ince all of my known properties were most likely under surveillance, I trusted Othello's directions. The snow was still falling heavily, making driving less safe, but at least the streets were empty. We were close, so we walked. Apparently, Othello had acquired Raego's old apartment from a few months back – the scarily unhygienic one. I have no idea how. Maybe there was a Craigslist page for dicey Black Ops hideouts. Othello had introduced me to her expensive 'friends,' the ones who had organized my escape. I hadn't been too responsive, focused on the imminent attack on the werewolf community. The men seemed like mercenaries, Tomas Mullingsworth types, but with sneakier spy traits. After several stunted conversational attempts and the stardom of meeting me began to fade, they got back to business, and offered us a whole mess of goodies. Disguises, weapons, fake ID's, and other things that I didn't pay attention to but that Othello seemed to appreciate. I did notice two men excitedly studying the soles of a few pairs of unique hiking boots, and waggled my finger at Othello to add them to the pile. I also made sure we had a whole pile of burner phones. Never knew when those would come in handy. She obeyed with a curious frown. The men finally left.

Othello guided me to the back room and set me down on the bed. "Nate. You need to get some sleep."

I shook my head stubbornly. "Can't. Werewolf's going to die. I need to save him. Or her."

She gripped my shoulders. "Nate. Listen to me. There is no way we could find him in time. You of all people know how big St. Louis is. We don't even know in what part of town to look. He could already be dead. In fact, I'm sure he is. We don't have enough information, and you forget this." She pointed at my head and pulled out a makeup mirror. I stared into it, watching as Othello brushed my hair back. There, burned into the side of my forehead near the hairline was a rune. An ugly, scarred, ancient rune. It emanated bad juju. And it looked like it was weeks old. Despite still hurting like a son of a bitch. "We don't know anything about this. He no doubt wanted you to run out there and try to save the day. This thing could even attract these Nephilim. Or any other number of bad guys ready to take you down. We were lucky Gavin didn't sense it. You're exhausted. We need a plan."

I lifted my tired eyes from the mirror. "We?"

She nodded, determined. "I'm not backing down from this. You're all alone, if you hadn't noticed. You need backup. And I can take care of myself. These guys left me some weapons that work on all sorts of supernaturals. I should be covered. I'm an excellent shot. Even for a *Regular*." She smiled. "There's a lot of talk on your end of the spectrum – with the supernatural community – about St. Louis experiencing a lot of weird events. That's why I came into town in the first place. As soon as I knew your friends had left, I knew you would need my help."

"You're tracking my friends?" I asked in disbelief.

She smiled coyly. "I spy on everyone I care about. And anyone involved in his safety." She licked her lips, not sensing how creepy that sounded. "Speaking of which, I haven't found out much about the Angel, Eae. He is known as the 'Demon thwarter', but other than that he apparently keeps his cards close." I had given her a small list of things to look up when I called her earlier in the day, thinking any additional information couldn't hurt. "Also, your parole officer, Gavin seems clean. Bit of a loner. Not a lot of friends. No social media accounts or email. After meeting him, I can see why. Are they all like that?" Which meant Gavin must have no friends. If Othello couldn't find dirt on someone, it didn't exist. Or he didn't have any kind of social presence, which wasn't out of the question for an Academy Justice. They were a mysterious bunch.

"Yeah. I guess they don't let them use social media. No *twatting* for the

Academy."

Othello let out a cute laugh and shook her head. "I think they call it *tweeting…*"

"Oh. Well, I like *twatting* better. It's catchier," I said.

Othello laughed harder for a few seconds before finally coming back to the facts. "Tell me more about the Tarot card the Demon mentioned, and these Nephilim. What are they?"

I sat there quietly, not having a whole lot to tell her. I did need the help, and she was the only game in town. I couldn't go to Agent Jeffries, as the FBI was no doubt combing the city for me, and I couldn't risk him losing his job, too. "The thirteenth Major Arcana is a Tarot card with a picture of Death on the front. I guess he liked the irony of using it to make a deal." I shrugged. "And the Nephilim are the offspring of Angels and humans. They are the counterpart to Demons in the fact that they're the pawns the Angels are allowed to use to influence the world. Hell – has Demons. Heaven – has Nephilim. Other than that, I don't know much. I've never met one before last night. And I don't think I want to again. They seemed like hired thugs or soldiers. I'd feel bad killing one in self-defense. I don't think God would look kindly on that. Then again, if they're gunning to kill me, what choice do I really have?"

"Maybe they'll listen to reason and know that you aren't really aiding the Demons," Othello offered.

"I'm beginning to realize that *intentions* mean nothing. Not in my world. I'm pretty sure I'm fucked," I sighed, running my hands through my hair, careful to avoid the brand. I needed to find a way to cover it up before I went out into the city. At least it would attract less attention from Regulars. If things got out of hand and we had to fight someone, I didn't want a tell-tale mark of some kind to stick out in people's minds so that they gave the information to the police. Because the police might realize that the branded Freak was none other than the recently-kidnapped Nate Temple. I groaned, exhausted. "You're right, Othello. I need to hit the hay… but I can't. I need to be out there, helping my people. They didn't ask for this. I brought this on them. This is on me."

Othello sighed, nodding in resignation after a long moment. "How?"

I shrugged. "I have no idea. Drive around?" Othello looked disgusted.

"What about that rock?"

I slowly lifted my gaze to her. "Rock?"

"That thing that vibrated before the Demon showed up."

I slapped my forehead in response. A flash of red light struck my brain. Then I was floating in blackness. I woke up, lying on my side, to Othello shaking me in alarm. I batted her hands away after a few seconds. "What happened?" I whispered, my forehead a sheet of flame.

"You hit your head with your hand and immediately passed out. Your eyes rolled back in your head the second you touched it." She looked freaked out.

"It's okay. I'm fine, now. The stone detects Demons. I guess I really am tired. Forgot about the brand on my forehead." My head was pounding with the beginnings of a migraine from the repeated hits against buildings and the accidental slapping of my forehead. I wondered if I had a concussion.

"Maybe I was right," she began. "We should wait until the morning when you're thinking fresh." She looked very doctor-like at the moment. I shook my head and stood on shaky legs, ignoring my throbbing skull. My throat was still hoarse from the Demon choking me out. Then there was my new scar, which pulsed with a steady heat.

And my power was significantly depleted. I had used up a fair amount with the Demon. I realized that I hadn't warned Gavin that the Demon was actually a Greater Demon – not just a run-of-the-mill Demon possession. I was sure that information like that might convince him that the *only* way to stop the Demons was to arrange a deal in order to get the summoner. Next time I saw him I would tell him. Maybe. "Let's go."

Othello watched me doubtfully for a few moments before sighing and standing to her feet. "There's a car outside. What do you need me to do?"

I grinned. "Get a map."

She pulled one off of the nearby table and brought it over. "Now what?"

"You drive while I get my freak on."

She watched me. "Good pickup line. Not creepy at all." Then she walked out the door.

Pickup line? Then I realized the double connotation. I'd just meant that I would do my magic while she played my girl Friday. I sighed. No respect for the finer arts. Ignoring her comment, I pulled out the artifact, rubbing it against my thumb for warmth as Hope had shown me. Then I whispered a word. "Seek," I murmured. The bone began to vibrate. Swirls of inky crimson settled on two points of the map. I chose one at random, hoping it was the right one.

CHAPTER 19

J cringed at the Lincoln Town Car's interior, feeling significantly poorer at being a passenger in such a vehicle. I wasn't snobby. It was just... *come on.* A Lincoln Town Car? Weren't they used exclusively in those old Private Investigator flicks? But since I was broke now, perhaps my taste needed an adjustment.

"You can stop looking so disgusted any minute now. It's not that bad, Daddy Warbucks. Discreet."

"Uh huh," I answered with a doubtful frown. But it wasn't like I could drive one of my flashier cars. I was sure that the FBI had a stack of BOLOs on my fleet of cars back at Chateau Falco. I resigned myself to the poverty of the Lincoln, idly remembering Matthew McConaughey's commercials – and Jim Carrey's SNL mockery of them – with an amused grin.

Othello rolled her eyes as she safely accelerated through the few inches of snow that had accumulated on the street; trying to hurry to the destination I had shown her on the map. We might already be too late. I slapped my cheeks – very carefully – a few times, trying to wake myself up without giving myself a compound concussion. Even with my own people against me, I was risking my life to assist those in need. That had to be worth something. After all, I very easily could have agreed with Othello to catch some sleep first. But I hadn't. I wouldn't have been able to sleep anyway. Maybe pass out, but not sleep. I was used to running on no sleep after living with night terrors for so long. I actually felt better than usual. Refreshed. I had actually managed to get some sleep while in jail. Before the Demon attacked me. Not many would qualify jail as a peaceful experience.

"So, why was it so important to make sure you had a phone? Are you planning on calling in backup?" Othello asked softly. "Am I not enough for you?" I cringed, sensing the words held a much deeper meaning that I definitely didn't want to touch. So, I did what men have done since time immemorial. I ignored it. You see, women spoke on many different levels. Men were snipers, focusing only on the one thing directly in front of us, where women were raging cyclones of a dozen assassins hidden inside a single person. Their conversations sliced and diced an innocent gentleman on several planes of existence... at the same time, and without him being aware of the fatality. I sensed that underneath her words was a plethora of dangers that I wouldn't have wanted to touch with a ten-foot pole. So, I listened to only the *actual* words she had said.

"Of course not. You're a certified badass. You Nano-botted Sir Dreadsalot. A Greater Demon. That will go down as a first in the history books, for sure." She smiled slightly, but I could tell she wasn't content with my answer. I opened my mouth to continue, but she eviscerated my attempt at peace before I could properly defend myself.

"Who called you earlier? When the Demon answered?" Her tone was crisp, professional even. I didn't buy it.

"Indie."

The temperature in the car suddenly felt frosty. "Indie?"

I fidgeted slightly, glancing at the map again to cover my unease. "Take a left here."

She hesitated a second before swerving the car, the vehicle sliding in the snow. Dawn would creep up on us soon, but it was still dark outside. Despite the hour, the snow gave the world a pristine glow. We were entering a low-income area, the kind of place that had recently experienced a jolt of rejuvenation, thanks to the rare tax-credit housing projects that sometimes found their way into major cities. Most of them seemed to occur in rural areas. I knew this because I was an investor in several. I think. I didn't really pay much attention to my various investments. I had a guy for that. I understood enough to verify that I wasn't being leeched, but other than that I was just a silent investor, primarily serving as the personal guarantee for about thirty million dollars' worth of apartment projects. Small potatoes for what I had inherited, but it made me feel good helping out the community. Any personal profits I received were even donated back to the community. I made my profits elsewhere.

"So, Indie?" Othello pressed as we continued driving.

I spoke before thinking, feeling uncomfortable about discussing my current girlfriend with my past collegiate fling, Othello. "She's the manager at my store, Plato's Cave."

Othello seemed to relax. "Oh, *Indiana* Rippley," she said, using her full name. I shrugged in agreement, not understanding why it mattered.

"Yeah."

"The Demon seemed downright terrified of looking at your phone. Is *Indiana* that hideous?" she asked, like a cat flexing her claws, enunciating Indie's full name.

"Um…" I didn't know how to respond to her tone. "No. I think he was unfamiliar with our technology. He seemed to think my phone was a witch's familiar. An entity bound to assist a witch in times of need."

"Oh." Was the air conditioning on? It felt downright frigid in the car.

"Turn right ahead. It should be a half mile away." But Othello continued driving, not heeding my advice. We passed the street. I rubbernecked the missed turn with the same despair as a stranded survivor on a remote island watching a cruise ship sail by without stopping. "Othello. You missed the turn. Take the next right."

She slammed on the brakes instead, sending the car into a complete spin, which didn't seem to concern her in the slightest. The seatbelt saved me from head butting the dash. As the car finally settled, the air inside the vehicle grew thick. "Why was it so important to make sure you had a cell phone from the gear my friends gave us?" she asked tersely.

I slowly turned to face her, but she didn't meet my eyes. Her body was tight, and she was breathing heavily. I didn't have time for whatever this was. "Indie tried to call me and instead she saw a Demon threatening to kill me. I wanted to make sure I allayed her fears, before she freaked out. Her mom's dying. She has enough on her plate without having to deal with whatever is going on here," I snapped. "Now, do you mind if we go save an innocent life?"

"Her mother. In Colorado," she said softly instead.

I blinked. She was keeping tabs on Indie, too? "Yeah," I answered.

"Okay. You just wanted to make sure she wasn't overstressed." I nodded as Othello finally looked into my eyes. What the hell was going on?

"Yep. If you were in her shoes wouldn't you want to know what the hell that was about?"

She nodded distractedly looking down at her lap. "Yes. I would. I couldn't take it if I thought you were in trouble. Especially with my mother's health on the line. Family first."

"Yeah. I just want to make sure she doesn't freak out and call the police or anything. Especially since I'm supposed to be in jail."

"Okay. That makes sense. You should call her. See how her mother is doing." Othello looked on the verge of tears.

"I texted her." Othello nodded, eyes far away and glistening slightly. "But right now, we need to focus on the werewolf that's about to be murdered." Othello's arms tightened on the steering wheel. "You good?" I asked her softly.

It took her a minute, but she finally lifted her gaze again, eyes growing harder as they dried up. "Sorry. Yeah. I'm good. Just… a lot to take in. This might be a normal day for you, but we Regular mortals don't have days like this," she mumbled. "Let's take care of your werewolf." With that, she released the brakes and drove back towards our turn. What the hell had that been about? But I didn't need to ask myself. I was pretty sure I knew *exactly* what it was about.

Othello still cared for me.

And that smug bastard, jealousy, had just made the first of many appearances to come.

Othello and I had frequented many bedroom study sessions back in college, and now… we were back together again. Like Bonnie and Clyde. All alone, taking on the world together. And I had yet to make a pass at her. In the past, even right before Indie and I had evolved, I would have hit on her immediately. I had no reason not to. Othello was beautiful, intelligent, and very… *very* experienced in coital adventures. We had always been casual, never needing more than the sexual foray every now and again, but tonight I was picking up something entirely different. I think Othello's opinion had changed. I think she actually felt possessive of me. I didn't have time for that kind of entanglement right now. I was pretty much up against the ledge on this one. My power was practically gone. I felt like I had been in the ring with Muhammad Ali for three rounds.

I had 99 problems, and – apparently – a girl *was* one.

Gunnar would be beside himself with laughter right now. Lucky for me I hadn't had a chance to call him. I briefly wondered if he had proposed yet. Then Othello slammed on the brakes again, this time a hundred yards away from a small, maybe fifty-unit, apartment complex. "Look," she whispered. Rather than scan the surroundings for danger, I merely stared open-mouthed at the familiar name on the sign out front. *Silver Gardens.*

This was a project I *knew* that I had invested in. It still looked new, especially with the clean snow, but… *rough*. As if the tenants weren't too keen on rules. Which made sense.

Werewolves lived here.

Shaking my head at the coincidence, I finally scanned the street and spotted three silhouettes sniffing the frosty air, patrolling the perimeter around the apartments. They moved on without noticing us, and I let out a breath. If I saw three, there had to be three more I hadn't seen. I glanced down at the bone artifact. It was vibrating violently, practically dancing in my lap. This was it. I opened the car door and jumped out into a snowbank, ready to blast a Demon back to Hell, or to let Othello do it with her arsenal of goodies. I sniffed the air, sensing the familiar faint sulfurous odor of Demonic presence.

Then I heard a lamenting howl from the center of the complex.

A lot of howls answered, causing me to shiver nervously. The three sentries reappeared for a moment, shared a look, and then bolted towards the first howl, still not noticing us.

I raced after them, my feet crunching too loudly in the snow as I ran parallel to their path with a building between us so as not to stumble into a dozen of the beasts by accident. Othello was hot on my heels, successfully keeping a low profile, but making just as much noise. Everything always sounded so much louder when it was snowing, as if the world had been temporarily muted, amplifying the sound of my steps like a Dolby Digital Surround Sound demonstration. I slowed as I neared the corner of the building, ducking behind a bush before peering around it. Othello knelt beside me, catching her breath. Snow was still falling heavily, adding to the several inches that had already accumulated on the ground. How long was this weather supposed to continue?

People were gathered around a single ground floor apartment, where I could hear a lot of agitated arguing from the men, and prayers from the women. It was like someone had kicked an anthill. But no one had noticed us yet. I held up a hand for Othello to stay still. I could see something on the apartment door, like a large wreath or decoration of some kind. Squinting, I saw a gap in the people surrounding the apartment, and I leaned back in surprise. A woman was nailed to the door. Crucified. One beast of a man was utterly silent, kneeling before the door, staring up at the woman he cherished above all others. The other figures fidgeted - both angrily and nervously – as if the man kneeling on the ground was someone important to them.

Then it hit me.

This must be their Alpha. The Demons had taken his mate. The mate of the most important werewolf in the area. I gulped. This wasn't going to end well. I was too late. There was nothing left for us to do, and entering the equation now to express our condolences would not be welcome, and might even be considered suspicious. Suspicion would get both Othello and I killed. I glanced around the complex and noticed several tenants glancing out the windows conspicuously. At first it confused me, but then I understood. Not everyone in this complex was a werewolf. I mean, how likely was it for fifty werewolf families to take over the same complex? That meant there were numerous Regulars living here, amidst a pack of murderous, vengeful werewolves.

Shit.

I turned to Othello and urgently motioned for her to discreetly get back to the car.

She frowned at me, but finally nodded and rose with the silence of a ninja before taking a step back. Right over a Power Wheel truck. She cartwheeled backwards with a crash, the sound echoing loudly. Several pairs of werewolf eyes turned our way but I managed to drop to the ground just in time. Still, these were werewolves. They would investigate. With something we couldn't mask. Smell.

Before I could move, a voice break the peaceful night's silence like a thunderbolt in a clear sky. "Wolves! Tonight, you have faced a great calamity." The wolves forgot us in an instant, turning to locate the voice as they subconsciously formed a protective ring around their Alpha. I pointed for Othello's sake. There, standing on a nearby roof was a silhouette, glowing with white radiance. The wolves bristled with agitation. But part of me wanted to giggle with joy, glad that the voice had conveniently caused a distraction for our escape. Maybe it was Gavin finally giving me some support.

Without it, Othello and I would have most likely been chased back to our car like lame antelope fleeing a pride of starving lions. I motioned for Othello to get back to her feet and flee, before the wolves remembered the noise she had caused.

Karma chose that moment to metaphorically whip me in my family jewels.

"There, between those buildings lies the culprit. I am an Agent of Heaven, hunting a fugitive who has been working with Demons to cause harm to this fine city. *Your* city. Sensing the impending attack, I traveled here to this place only to find myself too late to save her. Yet fortune seems to favor us." I slowly glanced back to see several sets of fiery eyes staring directly at Othello and I. Feral howls filled the night.

So, not Gavin, then.

"Take vengeance on the wizard! He is marked. He currently works as an Agent of Hell, and murdered one of your own on behalf of his new Lords and Masters. Take him down like the animal he is. Hunt the cowardly murderer. Hunt Nathin Temple!"

One voice belted out. "How? He's a wizard. We hold no chance against the gifted."

"As a pack, you are all but invincible," the radiant Angelic voice answered with sublime confidence. The glow surrounding him made it impossible to get a clear look at him.

"Yes," a new, darker, more authoritative voice answered. It was the Alpha. And he sounded... familiar. "We are. Get the women and children inside. Tonight, the men hunt."

Every wolf in the area howled, making the air suddenly seem to vibrate. Every single curtain in the apartment complex slammed shut. No Regular was going to get involved in whatever was going on in the parking lot. Othello stared with utter confusion at the radiant apparition that had condemned us to death. I heard several explosions of fabric as the wolves shifted from their weaker human forms.

"You've gotta be fucking *kidding* me!" I hissed, finally recognizing where I had heard the voice before. It was the same werewolf from the bar the night before. The one Tory and I had made a fool of. "Click your heels, *now*!" Othello nodded in instinctual obedience, eyes wide with fear. I slammed my heels together, too, satisfied at the brief click I felt under my toes. "And now, we *run!*" I shouted. And we did, panting in fear. The sound of dozens of paws crunching through the snow was absolutely terrifying. Because I knew they were coming our way. Fast. We still had a building and numerous cars between us, but werewolves were distance runners. I knew that most of them couldn't shift at will, like Gunnar, but I also knew that they could shift during extremely emotional times. Like the death of their pack leader's mate.

And that was when they were the least rational. During times of war. Even vampires stepped carefully – or fled entirely – when the mangy mutts were working as a single unit.

I knew we had no chance of talking our way out of this. Especially while they were in wolf form. So, we hoofed it. Luckily, we had new scoots on our feet, thanks to Othello's mercenary buddies. I'd overheard two of the men whispering to each other about a unique feature of the hiking boots and, knowing what we were going to be facing tonight, I hadn't ignored serendipity's call. I had pointed at the gear, and Othello had added them to our pile. I still found it awkward to run in them, but they might just come in handy, given our current flight.

We rounded the building and I saw two werewolves scouting out our car. They were in human form, but they were sniffing the vehicle with too much interest. They let out a howl, triangulating our position. I quickly darted around the corner between the bushes and the building, racing towards the adjacent neighborhood. Unfortunately, a stealthy escape wasn't in the cards for us. The snow left a perfectly clear trail of boot prints wher-ever we went. I instinctively flung my hand back towards the car, casting our smell past the vehicle and racing a hundred yards further, not even considering my dwindling power. We would be dead if I didn't use my gift right now. Many of the wolves darted after the faint whiff as they rounded the building.

But many didn't. The Alpha hesitated as he rounded the corner, sniffing the air. He was huge, as black as midnight, and his predatory eyes and long teeth fairly glowed in the moonlight's reflection off the snow. Then two of the nearby wolves barked in our direction, still not seeing us, but sensing our presence. Othello followed my lead, staying low as we continued to run across the street. I launched myself over a backyard's chain link fence. Othello tried to duplicate the move behind me but her clumsy boots caught on the tip of the fence, causing the snow-covered metal to rattle loudly before she crashed into the yard. The wolves howled as they pinpointed our location, and then they loped after us with a fresh burst of speed. I cast balls of fire and ice blindly behind us, catching a few lucky strikes, bowling several groups of wolves over with yelps of pain.

But half-a-dozen more continued after us, unfazed.

Including the Alpha, who had seemed especially motivated after hearing the Angelic being say my name. But he had been the one to start the fight in the bar. Tory and I had merely ended it. More Tory than myself.

We were screwed. The wolves were almost upon us and there was no way we could outrun such a motivated pack. They were out for blood. "Click your heels again!" I hissed at Othello, low enough for only her to hear me. "Just a dozen more feet and then we make our stand." Othello nodded, clicking her heels right after I did. We stopped where I had indicated, breathing heavily and arming ourselves. She drew her gun, armed with silver bullets. I merely turned around, drawing my face into hard, tight lines, the face I wore when I was in a scrap. The wolves quickly surrounded us, but remained a safe distance away, yipping and growling in a rotating circle of claws and fangs. The Alpha approached us with slow, triumphant footsteps. He wasn't in full wolf form, but instead resembled a horrific beast of a man, part wolf and part human. Which was better... and worse. It meant he would be more rational than his pack, but also that he wanted to *rationally* cherish the violence to come.

One of his packmates suddenly shifted to human form, no doubt a lieutenant if he had that kind of control. "Sir, I spotted other paw prints in the area. Big ones."

"It was probably our own. Or a neighbor's dog wandering the streets," the Alpha responded in a growl, drooling as he stared me down, taking a step forward.

"Respectfully, it wasn't either of those," the lieutenant said, bowing his head. The Alpha snarled, backhanding his lieutenant in the face, sending him into the fence we had just jumped. Which was impressive. The lieutenant didn't get up. The growling ceased amongst the pack, suddenly leery of their Alpha's temper.

"Of course it was. Do you see or smell any other werewolves here?" He laughed, an odd, barking noise. The wolves yipped and whined in agreement as the Alpha stepped closer to me.

This was my moment. Use the chaos to my advantage.

In other words, it was time to fuck shit up.

"*Disrespectfully*, they belong to *my* pack," I said, lacing my voice with a heavy tone of authority.

The Alpha froze, cocking his wolf head at me, intelligence brimming behind cruel eyes.

"You are about to be eaten, slowly, by my entire pack." He looked amused. "I'll grant you this last farce."

I obliged him. "I have a pack of spirit wolves. They belong to the many wolves I have killed over the years. Having tasted my victory, they bowed down to my power and chose to follow me from the spirit realm. They are my constant companions." Without moving, I simultaneously cast several spells at once, all relatively small in power, but frighteningly effective nonetheless. No one noticed, which was the point. The spells drifted around the clearing like knives on velvet, patiently awaiting my next command. The snow continued, masking our confrontation from any nearby spectators, which was good. Things might get dicey.

The Alpha waited for a count of two, then he began to laugh. For a full minute. His pack slowly began to mimic him with anticipatory growls, but only after a few seconds of silent wariness. They were still leery. Of my words or their Alpha's instability? "You expect me to believe that you have a pack of spirit wolves protecting you? I've never heard of such a thing. You're just trying to scare my six bravest warriors, but it won't work." He held up a hand for silence. His pack complied.

But a sudden *yip* split the night and I smiled.

"Five," I said softly.

The Alpha turned to see who had caused the noise, then back to me. "What?"

"There seems to be only five of your warriors left."

The Alpha's shoulders tensed as he counted his remaining wolves through the now rapidly falling snow. One was indeed missing. "What is the meaning of this? Did he run away?" he snapped at the remaining wolves. One of them whined, as if fearful of telling his Alpha the truth, but also suddenly terrified of the night.

The Alpha pointed at Othello. "Take her!"

I activated another of the sentinel spells, allowing the whining wolf to scream in agony before my next spell camouflaged his now unconscious body. A gunshot filled the night and another wolf dropped, wounded in the rear leg, yowling pityingly in the falling snow. Everyone froze. Othello was a good shot. She smiled at the Alpha, licking her lips. *"Three* warriors."

He growled, taking a threatening step towards her. "Easy," I spoke soothingly. "You don't want a repeat of the bar last night. I didn't kill your mate. Look me in the eyes and see for yourself. We only just arrived."

The Alpha glared back, his mindless rage threatening to take control. I knew this wasn't about rationality anymore. His mate had been killed.

This was *absolution.*

For a loved one.

I get it. I had resided in that endless, eternal swamp for the past few months now.

"I swear on my power as a wizard that I didn't kill her. I came here to help. Having known it was *your* pack I might not have made the trip." I paused. "If I'm being perfectly honest."

The lieutenant came trotting back towards us from the fence where he had been lying since the Alpha had backhanded him. "Sir. It's true. The wizard only just arrived. I was on lookout at the street. Although having taken three of your wolves, I'd say it's only fair that we kill them anyway," he added with a growl, counting the rest of the pack.

The Alpha was panting heavily. Other than that sound, we stood in a vacuum of silence. I could even hear the snow hitting the ground. "Get out. Before I change my mind," he rasped.

I nodded politely at him, urging Othello to stick close. No sudden movements around bloodthirsty werewolves. "Thank you." Once safely out of the perimeter of wolves I hesitated near the Alpha, watching cautiously as his muscles quivered with impotent fury. Out of respect, I didn't meet his eyes, but I kept my spells handy just in case. "I don't work with Demons. I will find the monster responsible for this and make him pay. It seems no one else is willing to protect this city. Even my own kind." I spat into the snow, and reached out a hand. The Alpha appraised me in silence before finally reaching out a clawed hand. His grip was in no way friendly, but at least it was there.

"This doesn't make us friends, but I'll owe you one if you make him suffer."

I smiled darkly at him. "That's my specialty. Your packmates are alive and well. You'll find them after sunrise." I had set the camouflage and sleeping spells to dissipate at dawn. He nodded at me with unexpected relief and… respect, like a fencer acknowledging a worthy opponent.

Then Othello and I left.

CHAPTER 20

*O*thello shook her head in disbelief as she carefully exited the snow-covered highway. "I thought you were bonkers when you had me add those boots to our gear. They're supposed to be for hiking, in order to deter lurking beasts or hunters from a campsite."

"It wasn't just the boots. The boots in combination with the inexplicable disappearance of their comrades is what did it. You'll find that the best way to survive is to cause doubt or fear in your enemy. If you can instill that emotion, it stays with them in the back of their minds, always ready to be the first answer to the next unexplainable event that goes wrong. People will believe anything if they are afraid that it might be true." *Thank you for that, Terry Goodkind*, I thought to myself with a tip of a mental hat. "You just have to cause the doubt."

"Yeah, but they were only rubber paw prints on the soles of our boots. You'd think a werewolf would know the difference. Or that they could smell the difference."

"That's why I told them they were from spirit wolves. It compounded their fear even more. They didn't know how to disprove it. Would a spirit wolf have a smell? Would spirit wolves steal a body entirely? Who knows? That's why I had us click off the paw print extensions before we stopped. It would have been pretty obvious if the prints ended exactly where we were standing, and then if we moved during the fight they would immediately realize it was a bluff."

She stared at me for a moment. We were at a red light. "You think that far in advance?"

I shrugged. "I guess so. Being a wizard means you have to think on the fly a lot, and make the best of the cards you're dealt. I didn't know the boots would be helpful at all. I heard your guys talking about their unique feature, and unique features can always be exploited." I waved her on as the light turned green. "Also, it's cold as balls outside and my sneakers wouldn't have kept me that warm in the snow, so I opted for us to change to boots."

She chuckled, mumbling to herself as she accelerated again. The car grew silent, the cheer slowly fading. We hadn't actually accomplished anything worth celebration. We had, in fact, failed to stop the Demon, and had in turn been framed by the Angel or whatever that thing had been. Had it been one of the Nephilim? My thoughts drifted as I tried to come up with a new game plan. "So. What happened to the wolves? Did you really kill them?"

I shook my head. "I knocked them out. When they wake up and reappear at dawn, it will make me look even more mysterious. Which is a good thing in my world. Mystery keeps enemies on their toes."

"Okay. That makes me feel better. I didn't want to kill mine either. I mean, I would have, but it didn't feel right. They thought we were murderers. Why would the Angel do that to us? Aren't they supposed to be the good guys?" she asked nervously.

I shrugged helplessly. "I'm beginning to find that there aren't really any good guys in this race. The Angels think I'm consorting with the Demons, so they figured they could get the wolves to take me out and keep their wings clean. The Demons just want the Key, as do my own people. No matter who I look at, everyone is making this harder than it needs to be."

"Well... *you're* a good guy, Nate." I didn't answer. The silence grew. "Right?"

"As good as I can be, I guess," I muttered, wondering exactly what I was. Was the Academy truly deserving of control over the Armory? Was I being petty? Greedy? Were my actions causing the equivalent of a nuclear arms race? Was *I* worthy of being in charge of the Armory? I didn't know. "I'm trying to be, anyway. I won't let anything happen to my people, or the people of my city."

That seemed to satisfy her, but she looked too thoughtful, as if gaining moral fortitude from my words. *Whatever helps her cope*, I thought to myself with a sigh.

We finally parked out back behind the safe house. The snow had finally stopped during our drive, but was still at least a few inches deep. We shambled upstairs and into the shabbier of the two bedrooms – mine – peeling out of our wet clothes before hanging them to dry. We got ready for bed and Othello sat beside me on the dirty old mattress that lay on the floor. "So, what's the plan for tomorrow?"

I had a vague idea, but I was too tired to discuss the Armory with her right now, anticipating the horde of obvious questions that would follow. "Maybe I'll come up with one after some rest. One thing I do know is that we're going to need to use that artifact to hunt down another Demon. Then use him to find the summoner. He's the one calling the shots. Shut him down, and we can shut the rest of the Demons down. Hopefully that will even get rid of this mark on my forehead. Then I kill the Greater Demon who killed my parents. That's all I ever wanted to do in the first place, to find my parents' murderer. The Greater Demon we met might have done the deed, but the summoner put him up to it. It had nothing to do with Peter's theft. I have to take the summoner out. Then I can confront the Academy and try to talk my way out of this curse. And if I can shut the summoner down, perhaps the Angels will realize I'm not a bad guy."

Othello frowned. "Explain that part for me. You've been cursed? By your own people? And that's supposed to encourage you to comply with their demands to give up a gift your parents left you? A gift that cost them their lives? Why would the Academy do that to you? And why would you even consider it?"

I nodded with a shrug. "They're scared. I've got..." I thought about it briefly, "Two more days before my magic is entirely gone. If not sooner. They want the Armory that my parents discovered. They think I'm reckless and a danger to society. So, they cursed me and told me that if I managed to wipe out the Demons and then hand over my parents' Armory, they would remove the curse. I'm not sure if I trust them with it, though. And the Demons want it, too. Well, maybe it's the summoner who wants it. It's why my parents were killed. What started this whole mess. And the Angels just want me to stay out of it entirely."

"Kill them," she growled.

I blinked. "Excuse me?"

"The Academy. Kill them. They deserve it. Taking your power away, and promising to give it back only if you can perform a miracle – taking out Angels and Demons *without* magic – and *then* that you must *also* agree to give them something *else* that's yours. The Armory. That's insanity. That Gavin guy seemed all right, but he's blindly following their orders. Men like that can't be trusted with what your parents discovered. Especially if it's dangerous. You should just kill them. All."

I sighed. "That would only increase my problems. Then I would be a fugitive from the Regular police as well as every other wizard in the world. You don't murder the police. That's what these guys are. That's why Gavin is keeping tabs on me, making sure I don't make a deal with the devil. I have to somehow prove that I'm not a bad guy."

"With your hands tied," she spat.

I nodded tiredly. "It's the only way, now. I wish it were different, too, but... It is what it is. There's no use whining about it. It's either sink or swim. *When you find yourself knee-deep in shit, don't sit there complaining about it. Start walking.*"

She chuckled softly before bending over to kiss my temple, careful of my scar. "We'll figure it out, Nate. Don't worry. I'm not leaving you." She looked torn, but perhaps that was simply because she still cared for me and I hadn't reciprocated her romance. I kept my face stoic, hating the pain it was causing her. I couldn't bring up Indie right now. Othello stood and walked away from the mattress, shutting the door quietly behind her.

"Good night," I said softly, before closing my eyes.

CHAPTER 21

*W*e entered the vast, office complex of Temple Industries. The heat blasted over us like a warm blanket as we walked through the front door. It felt pleasant after the weather outside. The snow hadn't picked back up, but it hadn't melted either, and the mass of humanity swarming St. Louis for *Mardi Gras* had put the snow plows in a bit of a pickle. We had slept the day away, utterly exhausted after fighting almost until dawn. It was afternoon, and I could almost feel the daylight slipping away.

I had wanted to make sure that our visit would be discreet in the event that the police or FBI was keeping tabs on the building. So, I had very sneakily dressed up like an accountant, wearing heavy framed glasses, khakis, and a short-sleeved dress shirt. With a pocket. The coat I wore was too small and only added to the ridiculous nerdy vibe I was putting off. I hated it, plucking at the threads as if they were a straitjacket.

"Stop fidgeting. You look nice." Othello nudged my shoulder with a grin.

"Yeah. As if I had never seen a girl before."

"Innocent. Just the way I like them." She winked suggestively.

"Not how I recall it," I answered instinctively, falling into our old flirtatious habits way too easily. I adjusted my dress shirt and then the glasses to cover up my knee-jerk reaction. Othello noticed with a contented grin. I ignored her. It felt odd walking into the impressive castle that was Temple

Industries, knowing that all my assets were frozen and that I was more cash poor than anyone that currently worked for me. It was...

Humbling.

I had only the small assortment of bills buried in the back of my wallet, the pile of plastic cards utterly useless to me now. Was this what life was like for everyone else?

We encountered a guard who briefly touched his service piece before I took off the glasses and he recognized me. He did a double take, eyes widening in confusion, and then a scowl. I tapped my finger to my lips for silence, hoping he understood my meaning to keep my presence a secret from any outside curiosity – like the police. But his confusion only seemed to increase, as did his scowl. He muttered into his earpiece, no doubt to give a heads-up to the other guards in a hopefully discreet way. I couldn't afford to have the guards on alert. Othello looked highly uncomfortable. The guard nodded curtly and continued on his rounds. That was weird. Had I pissed him off at some point in the past? After a few minutes, we reached Greta's desk outside my office. She scowled at me with a no-nonsense look designed to deter outsiders.

"It's me, Greta," I said, watching her face morph into recognition. "We'll just be a few minutes."

Her eyes grew abruptly judgmental, no doubt assuming that I was cheating on Indie with the svelte woman beside me. "You were kidnapped," she said bluntly. "It's all over the news."

"Yeah. About that..." I began.

"Is this your kidnapper? Are you under duress?"

"Not yet," Othello quipped, to Greta's shock.

I held up a hand. "Everything is fine, Greta. I'm just showing an old friend around the company. She's an avid technology student. I was going to show her our drone program." I belted off the first thing I could think of. Greta appraised me, her arthritic hand on the telephone as if to call for backup. "I promise."

"The FBI froze the corporate accounts. Payroll was halted. You need to fix it. I was supposed to buy groceries tonight. What sinful acts have you committed to attract such attention?"

I blinked at her, ignoring the last question. The guard's scowl suddenly made more sense. No one had been paid. Then I arrive with a smoking hot girl beside me, as if nothing was wrong. And then I silently asked him to do me a favor. I hadn't truly considered the long-term consequences of them freezing my accounts. After all, my home, Chateau Falco, was held in trust, and the earned interest on the investments in that trust paid for any and all maintenance expenses she incurred – like taxes, utilities, food, etc. You know, the things that make a house a home. I'd never thought about what it might mean to my employees. "Um. I don't think the FBI is going to allow me to circumvent their freeze. Especially since I am being *ransomed*."

"You don't look like you're being ransomed," she said, folding her arms with a huff. "You look perfectly fine, although dressed more respectfully than normal. You look like a nice young boy, for once. A nice young boy who shouldn't be entertaining pretty women while you are considered missing, and while your girlfriend is out of town." Othello stiffened. "Should I be concerned? Is the company going to be shut down? Even if you don't need the money, we do. We consider this company a second home. It's how we pay our bills. You know, those pesky things that regular people have to concern themselves with. I wouldn't expect you to understand."

I stared at her. Really? Right now. "Greta. Everything is fine. Just a big misunderstanding. I'm trying to get it resolved as we speak. But I can't remove the freeze on the accounts. I'm supposed to be *missing*."

"Like I said, you look perfectly fine to me. Is your entertaining a pretty young woman more important than the welfare of your employees? Ashley wouldn't allow it if she was here."

"I know. I'm trying to get it fixed. Some bad people are after me, attacking the company to get to me."

"Yet here you stand, completely healthy, with a pretty young girl, walking into your own company, dressed respectfully for once, to show her our... *drone program*," Greta said, distrust obvious in her tone.

I groaned. "Greta..."

"I almost ripped our poor intern to shreds when I saw what he had done with our Savior's Cross. Move it back into your office or I'll call the police right now. Also, I think I'll make today a half day since the owner refuses to take care of his employees. Double pay."

I groaned. This was ridiculous. My own secretary was extorting me, too? But I didn't have time to argue. "Okay." I trotted over to the cross and hoisted it over a shoulder. It was surprisingly light. I heard Othello speaking with her as I set the cross against the wall inside my office.

"I think that's a great idea. How much do you need for groceries? I'm sure Nate will fix the issue as soon as possible, but in the meantime, let me help you."

Othello began to peel off a few hundreds out of her purse. Greta folded her arms in refusal. "I don't need your help. I need my boss to take care of his company."

Othello looked at me, siding with Greta. "She has a point."

I blinked, realizing I was suddenly outnumbered. I had no significant money on me, having spent the majority of my cash at the bar, *Achilles Heel*. Then a thought struck me. "Greta. How much is payroll this week?" She blinked at me before opening a document on her computer, no doubt checking her email for the amount that was denied. Rather than getting involved, I decided to trust her with a bit of responsibility. "Never mind. If I gave you a pile of cash, could you distribute it to everyone? Don't worry about the specific amounts. Just pay everyone three thousand dollars. If it's not enough, I'll take care of it with the FBI once everything has passed. If it's too much, they can consider it a bonus for the delay. Can you send out a mass email to make sure that I have record of it all?"

Greta blinked at me. "You have that kind of cash available? I thought they froze your accounts also?"

I nodded. "Ashley and I keep a rainy-day fund in my safe. No doubt she would have already resolved this, but since she's not here, and I had no idea you guys were impacted, I'm asking you to help me fix it. Immediately."

She folded her arms, leaning back in her chair, judging me. "You would trust me with all that cash? What if I just took it all? It would serve you right."

"I doubt our friend upstairs would think very highly of that." I pointed at the cross I had just moved to my office. Her frown grew steadier, not appreciating my comment. "Of course I trust you with this. There is at least two hundred thousand dollars in our safe. Write receipts for any money given out, since we don't want the IRS to audit us due to this confusion, but tell no one of the details. Deal?"

She finally nodded. I gave her the codes and she snorted as if dirtied by having to handle this duty. But she wrote the code down, and smiled at Othello. "At least he has one other respectable friend. Thanks for talking some sense into him. Honestly, he doesn't listen to anyone. He needs someone to keep him in line." Her matronly tone dropped. "Even if he already has a girlfriend."

"Greta," I warned. "Just take care of this for me. Please. I had no idea they froze the company accounts. I only just found out about my personal accounts being frozen. It's a big misunderstanding, but I'll get it fixed." I had no idea how, but she was right. I needed to take care of my own.

Greta finally nodded. "It will be taken care of. Be quick. If you're supposed to be missing and the FBI comes here asking questions I will have to provide them with anything they ask me for, including video surveillance."

"You wouldn't," I whispered in disbelief.

"I would. Jesus would demand it of me." She smiled back satisfactorily.

Othello saved me. "You're a saint, Greta. We'll be quick. I promise." Greta nodded once and headed into my office to gather the money. I would double check everything later. Make sure too much wasn't missing.

"Thanks for having my back," I muttered to Othello, leading her deeper into the building.

"It's easier to comply than confront women like her. It's a matronly thing."

I continued walking, hating that she was right.

"So, girlfriend, huh?" she asked, deadpan.

I nodded, spotting the hallway with the Armory entrance just ahead. "Yeah. Indie. She and I have been dating for a few months, now. I don't deserve someone as good as her, but she sticks around for some reason. She's been with me through some pretty rough patches. Like the dragons a few months back," I said.

"I see," she answered crisply. "If you recall, I was also *there for you* with the dragons. And busting you out of prison. Kosage's float. The Greater Demon. The werewolves."

"I know that, Othello," I said. I took her resulting silence as an end to the conversation. "We're here," I said, waving at the broom closet before us.

Othello looked at it suspiciously. "A closet? Did you take me here to have seven minutes in Heaven? You have a *girlfriend* now, Nate," she said in a dry tone.

"No. That's not what..." I shook my head as her eyes bore through me. "It's the Armory. My parents' secret project. It's just magically sealed right now. But I want to warn you, I don't fully understand what's behind that door. You might be surprised. I do know that we'll only have seventeen minutes to explore. And please don't ask why," I added before she could voice the obvious question. Her jaws clicked shut.

"Okay. How do we get in?" she asked, touching the door after a nod from me. She grasped the handle and pulled. A mop struck her in the forehead and I felt a moment of satisfaction as I let out a very small, respectable laugh. She scowled back.

"I need to use the Key. Turn around, please."

She looked hurt. "Really? After everything we've been through? You don't trust me?"

Some other emotion also flittered across her eyes, but I didn't have time to delve into it. I had already told her about Indie. I didn't want to poke the bear. "It has nothing to do with trust. Literally no one else knows about the Key, and I want to keep it that way. For *your* safety."

"Not even Indie knows?" I shook my head. She finally nodded, looking satisfied at the fact that I had kept this secret from my girlfriend. Then she turned around.

I pricked my wounded hand and touched the door. It groaned as it began to open, and I whipped my hand behind my back so Othello wouldn't see me bleeding. A wave of warm air rolled over us. "Shall we?" I asked, holding out an elbow like a gentleman at a ball.

She stared past me, dumbfounded, which was satisfying.

"You are back, my host. I feared it would be some time before I saw you again," Hope's familiar voice called from inside the doorway.

Othello gasped, taking an instinctive step back. Then she slowly turned to face me, a lecherous grin growing on her cheeks. "Nate... You *dog*. How many girls do you have tucked away for your pleasure?" She looked down-right pleased to hear I had another woman locked away in a room. Women. I would never understand them.

"It's not like that. You'll see."

She grunted doubtfully, but she did accept my arm before we stepped into the Armory.

What was I getting myself into?

CHAPTER 22

*T*he sandstone walls emanated a soothing heat, like we had entered the tropics. The numerous artifacts lining the shelves, resting on the floor, sitting on tables, and hanging on the walls captivated my attention. I noticed Othello staring openly and smiled. "Beautiful, isn't it?" I asked.

She nodded. "Is that...?" She pointed at the fleece that I had asked Hope about.

"No. But the real one is here." I answered honestly, remembering Hope's answer to my exact same question. We continued on. I was here for one reason. I needed to find the summoner, and I was desperate – fearful even – of borrowing power from this room, but what choice did I have? I had no other friends for backup, and my most constant companion, my magic, had been taken from me, or would be soon enough not to make any difference. I had promised the Alpha werewolf I would make the Demon suffer for his crime, but I wondered if he truly believed in my innocence or not. It was mainly fear of my pack of 'spirit wolves' that had deterred them. The Nephilim were no doubt hunting me, despite not having run into them yet. Unless the creature egging the werewolves on had been one... I honestly didn't know, which was why I was here.

For answers. And possibly a weapon or two.

I wanted Othello here to act as my conscience. Another rational being to hopefully talk me out of doing anything too rash, like taking too much power from this place. But she seemed anything but rational at the moment. Talk of Indie had turned her into an ice queen.

We continued towards the balcony. A vast sunset cast a warm, reddish glow over a beautiful desert. I stopped, scanning the horizon. "Is this place real?" Othello asked beside me.

As if summoned, Hope stepped out of the shadows, looking just as beautiful as the last time I had seen her. "Yes. And no. The entrances are few, but this is a memory palace of a very real place."

Othello took a step back. "You're stunning," she said bluntly. Then she turned to me with a wry grin. "You're telling me Indie is better than *that?*" she asked, pointing a thumb.

Hope dipped her head in appreciation before turning to me with a questioning smile. "Just because she's beautiful doesn't mean she's mine for the taking. She's her own person," I grumbled.

Hope turned to Othello. "I offered him my services, but he told me he is being sufficiently serviced at the moment."

Othello burst out laughing.

"Can it," I muttered. "How are things, Hope? Sense any Demonic presence lately?"

"I adore the pet name you've given me, my host. I have seen no sign of Demonic presence, but..." she appraised me curiously, "I notice your power has drastically dropped since we last met. Because of your curse. Have you come to inherit your birthright? I have power here like the world hasn't seen in thousands of years. All yours now, in exchange for your acceptance of my servitude. Is that why you are here?"

Othello slowly turned to me. "Is she serious?"

I shrugged. "I think she's a very literal person."

"You look sad, downtrodden, defeated," Hope said, sounding concerned.

I could only nod.

"Accept my service."

I stared at her for a good long while, debating. This was my last hand. After all, I didn't *have* to use anything here, but Hope *did* need a guardian. I think. "Okay."

She beamed. "Thank you, my host. Contract made." I felt gossamer threads of power briefly settle over my shoulders as she spoke, and then it faded away as if I had imagined it all. I shivered.

"Now, let me show you something," Hope offered.

"Will it hurt? I haven't decided to take anything from this place. I fear the ramifications. I came here only to speak with you."

She nodded in understanding. "That is your prerogative. I am here only to serve. But allow me to show you something. It will do you no harm."

I finally nodded. She approached me and I realized my shoulders were suddenly rigid, afraid. She was powerful. I had thought she was going to lead me deeper into the Armory, but apparently not. She gently laid a hand on my temple and I was immediately overwhelmed by what I could only call a *vision*.

Sand blasted my face, and the sun threatened to scald any normal person's skin, but I was no normal person. I was a Myrmidon, *the* Myrmidon, and this was *home*... kind of. I glanced down at my hand and realized I was holding a short bronze sword. My other fist held a trio of spears tucked beneath a bronze shield. I was covered from head to toe in bronze armor. *Greek* armor.

I looked up and saw giant city walls before me, lined with archers, all hesitantly aiming their arrows at me. Thirty-foot tall city gates barred my entry, and I was alone.

I turned to look, but saw no one behind me. No Hope, no Othello. *Who are Hope and Othello?* Part of me was aware that this was a vision, but part of me was confused by the sudden thought, wondering if the daymares were back. I squashed my inner dialogue in order to pay attention to the experience.

"HECTOR!" I heard myself roar in a leonine voice that was raw from constant shouting.

Apparently, the man was very responsive, or I had been here for a very long time, shouting for him to come out. Because the gates opened, revealing a lone warrior.

How crazy was I? I stood alone against an entire city, and I was demanding for a man to emerge from the safety of his walls. Then I recognized the setting. More specifically, *where* I was, and *when* I was. *Who* I was, and what I was *doing*.

I was Achilles.

At the gates of Troy.

At the infamous battle with Hector, seeking revenge for my dead cousin,

Patroclus. I felt my rage bloom at the thought. This man, Hector, had killed my most beloved of cousins. And I was about to rectify that grievance.

The man striding towards me looked saddened, defeated, apologetic, but still a formidable adversary. I shook the thought away. It didn't matter. He had wronged me. Rage and absolution ruled my emotions. He finally settled a safe, but approachable, distance away.

"This is *your* war. In war, there are casualties on both sides," he said in a rough voice.

I nodded. "A fact I mean to display to your city today. I will show them the true definition of *casualty*. What hope will your people have left after they see me slay their precious prince before their very gates?" I sneered.

"It was not my intention to kill your cousin. He wore your armor. Fought beside your men. I should have known after such a quick fight that it *couldn't* have been you. The gods did not favor him."

This was the wrong answer. "Are you telling me my cousin fought like a babe? You dare make a mockery of the dead? I will show your city mockery like they have never seen before."

Hector dropped his head in defeat. "That is not what I meant, and you know it. I meant to honor your *prowess*, not to dishonor Patroclus. You see only vengeance before you. It is clouding your vision."

"Honor my prowess by drawing your sword, Princeling. I have other tasks to attend to at camp. I hope you have said goodbye to your loved ones. You will not see them for some time."

Hector's shoulders tightened in resolution. "I have. But there is no guarantee I will not see them again shortly."

"Oh, but there is. Do you not know of my story? I am the son of *Zeus*. I am immortal. You stand no chance. I will deliver you to the gods – my *family* – this afternoon, and drink to your death in an hour," I leered. "Now, draw your spear." I drew mine as well.

The moment Hector complied, I hurled a spear at his face. He hadn't been ready, and only just managed to deflect the deadly throw. That was fine. I didn't want a quick fight. Hector would be the best I had ever fought.

The best I had ever killed, soon enough.

I raced towards him, eagerly launching my other two spears in quick succession before drawing my sword. I was hungry for face-to-face combat, not a killing blow from a dozen yards away. I wanted to taste his last moments from up close. Patroclus deserved it. Hector narrowly avoided

SHAYNE SILVERS

being impaled, and dropped two of his spears, choosing to fight the old way – his spear against my blade. My sword struck the tip of his spear with a *clang* that echoed off the walls before us. I grinned. "You hear my sword? It's *hungry*. For Princeling blood. For my cousin's vengeance. It will be sated soon enough, Trojan."

Then I launched all my skills at him, seeing only the killing blow to come. Hector was well-trained, blocking everything I threw at him, but he was becoming weary from my berserker blows. I – on the other hand – was fueled by the gods, by my rage. Honor was on my side. I wouldn't tire before he lay before me, a rapidly cooling carcass. I wouldn't sleep until his body lay at my feet.

Hector finally began to attack, no longer defending, no doubt realizing that he could not halt or even slow my tirade of attacks. He was good, but not nearly good enough.

It finally ended in a flurry of metal. My sword slashed deeply into his calf, dropping him.

From the ground, he slashed at my ankles wearily and I jumped back in sudden alarm. "Easy. You might scratch my sandals," I spat, kicking his spear away, successfully hiding my anxiety. He had almost struck my heel. I lifted my sword, aiming for his heart, and scowled down at him. "Prepare to meet my uncle, Hades, and atone for your mistake."

This was it. My moment. My retribution. Everything would be well after this blow.

Hector stared into my soul as my sword plunged through his heart.

I stared down at him, satisfied as I watched his life bleed away. The archers on the wall gasped collectively. I waited for the gift of peace to fill me. The peace I deserved in exchange for the justice I had delivered.

But nothing happened.

His body struck the ground, sliding off my sword. Still... nothing. No sense of peace.

I finally screamed in rage. What was wrong? I had served justice. Why didn't I feel better? In a fit of rage, I strode back to my chariot, and bringing back a coil of leather rope, I hastily tied a knot around his ankles. He obviously hadn't been punished enough. The gods demanded more shame from this once great warrior. I could do that. Anything for inner peace.

I climbed into my chariot, blocking a lone arrow that sailed my way by a disgruntled archer. I scowled up at him and shook my head one time.

No more arrows came for me, but lamenting screams filled the air, begging forgiveness.

I raced back to my camp, willing to drag Hector's corpse to the four corners of the earth if that's what it took to honor the gods. For some reason, I couldn't help but feel that even this might not be enough to quell my pain...

What felt like a bucket of ice water abruptly showered my soul, and I snapped back to myself, no longer a part of the vision.

Despite being back in the room, my heart still pulsed with Achilles' anger. It had been infectious. Even now it was hard to release. He had been so *angry*. I could honestly say that I had never been that angry. Achilles had lost it, completely. There was no more hero in him after Patroclus' death. Just grief. Despite attaining his vengeance, it hadn't been enough, and he had then chosen to cross a line of respect that had existed for thousands of years. It was hard to even fathom, let alone believe.

My voice was raspy, and I glanced up to see that Othello's eyes were full of concern. "What... what was that?" I croaked.

Hope watched me. "The price for vengeance. And now it's time for you to leave," she added sadly.

I looked down at my watch, noticing the time and cursed under my breath. Sixteen minutes. Othello looked from me to Hope. "What? We haven't gotten what we came for. We haven't even discussed it with you." A faraway look abruptly replaced her agitation. "Yes, we're late. It's time for us to leave." I nodded, understanding her urgency to leave on a slightly different level than last time I had been booted out. I was semi-aware of not really wanting to leave yet, but I still found myself traipsing out of the mysterious Armory.

"I hope to see you soon, my host," Hope's soft voice carried through the vast hallways in a faint echo. The door slammed shut behind us with a resounding boom.

CHAPTER 23

I t had taken Othello a few minutes to calm down, pounding on the door in a fury. Now, she followed me out of Temple Industries, using a different path than we had used to enter. I didn't feel like running into Greta again, and I also wanted to use a different exit in an effort to thwart anyone who might have tailed us here. She was still grumbling as she followed me. "That was totally pointless. You watched a memory of a great hero. How does that help us? She knew we were on borrowed time. You knew we were on borrowed time. Why did you let her touch you?"

I glanced over my shoulder, just as frustrated as her. "She said she wanted to show me something. How was I supposed to know it would take as long as it did? I thought we would have plenty of time." But now we didn't, and night was rapidly approaching. Which meant that another flavor of supernatural in my city was about to be murdered by the Demons. Since I hadn't turned over the Key to the Armory, I would have to live with another death on my conscience.

And there wasn't a thing I could do about it.

I didn't even have a clue as to where to start. But I knew I could use the artifact Hope had first given me. At least that would let me pinpoint out a few locations, and then I could choose at random, hoping I was correct. It was life or death. If I didn't guess correctly, an innocent died. A gamble.

But the only way out of this mess was even worse. Let the Demons or their summoner – which was most likely worse – have access to potentially unlimited power. We sauntered out of the building via a side exit, which was actually closer to our car. I saw a pale slip of paper flapping in the chill wind and raced for it. It was tucked under her windshield wiper. I unfolded it as Othello shifted nervously from foot to foot.

"Vampire," I cursed.

Othello leaned in, reading the single word. "Subtle, aren't they?"

Instead of answering, I tossed her the keys and opened the passenger door. "I'm going to try to hone in on any Demonic activity in the city, see if we can find an exact location. If we aren't too late, like last time." Othello turned the key and revved the engine. I rubbed the artifact over the map and whispered the word *Seek* under my breath. Scarlet smoke settled on three locations. The mausoleum where my parents' bodies rested, Plato's Cave, and Chateau Falco. I sighed. The Demons were taunting me. First, it had been an apartment complex I had helped finance. Now they were going to murder a vampire – likely in the most gruesome of ways – at another location that led to me. To poke my rage. I recalled the memory of Achilles in a new light, feeling myself being pushed dangerously close to the same ledge he had stood on, where he had jumped off into an inferno of vengeance that ultimately led to his death.

I squinted, trying to think like a Demon. Which location? Othello was tapping the steering wheel, letting out a soft whistle as she saw my options. "Which would hurt more?" I asked myself. My ancestral home, Plato's Cave – my bookstore, my very own creation. Or the final resting place of my every ancestor. It seemed pretty obvious. They had killed my parents. Of course they would mock them in death.

"Bellefontaine Cemetery," I finally growled.

Othello nodded once, placing a calming hand on my thigh, and then shifted into gear, peeling out in the parking lot.

I cracked the window as we drove towards the cemetery, desiring to feel the brisk air in an effort to cool my fury. It didn't help, especially since about a million cars stood between us and the cemetery. I resigned myself to waiting, using the time to try and center myself. The Demons were about to desecrate my one place of peace, and the final place of peace for my parents. It seemed the obvious choice, but I honestly didn't know if I was right. All three places were vitally important to me for different reasons.

What if I was wrong? I pondered this for what seemed like days, but was more likely an hour as we darted through traffic, willing to risk dinging the Lincoln if others didn't get out of our way fast enough. I felt my rage building upon itself as we drove, which wasn't good. I needed to be cool, calm, and collected. I had limited power and was about to go toe-to-toe with a big meanie. I couldn't afford emotions right now.

We finally arrived at the cemetery, and I used my fob to open the gates. Having helped them refinance some renovations, I had been given my own key. Also, so I could visit whenever I felt the need. I jumped out of the car the moment we parked. I could hear Othello's feet racing to keep up with me as I ran to the Temple Mausoleum, dodging headstones and piles of snow. The frosty winter landscape eliminated the need for light as the moon rose higher and the night crept closer.

I scanned the cemetery, searching, questing for Demonic presence as well as the more mundane footsteps in the snow. I smelled nothing, saw nothing, and the night was silent. Frustrated, I began stalking the perimeter of the mausoleum, ignoring the beautiful carvings and statues for once. Othello followed me, eyes scanning the horizon for any sign of danger. I circled the entire building, and then focused on the large locked entrance. No one had been inside. There were no tracks, and there was no way for anyone to bypass such modern technology – especially a Demon. The building was warded against it.

"This doesn't make sense. They should be here. It's the worst place they could kill someone. The cruelest." Othello stayed silent. I pulled out the arti-fact and the map in my pocket, activating its power. There was no Demonic presence at the cemetery. I blinked. Had I just imagined it, or was this some kind of diversion? Or were they already done killing the vampire? I sighed in defeat, knowing that I had to use my power to see if anything had happened here. I calmed my racing thoughts and quested out with magical feelers. Another spell I had developed recently was a way to detect any Freak's presence... and even a way to detect any recently dead presences. My magical feelers scouted the entire cemetery, and I could sense even that small amount of power burning away, being used up, never to return again.

But there was nothing. No recently murdered body. It had been a ruse.

"What are you two doing here?" an authoritative voice asked from only a few feet behind me. I released my feelers and turned to the voice, jumping slightly to the side in case they were about to attack. My spell hadn't picked up on the voice.

As I turned, I saw a familiar face. Gavin.

"I own this building. What the hell are you doing here?" I snapped.

Gavin appraised both of us before answering. "Following you, of course. Why did you come here? Was it because of the Demonic presence a short while ago?"

I continued to stare at him.

"They're long gone. They merely came to scout your family mausoleum, and then left. They did nothing other than look, or I would have exorcised them."

"Here's an idea. Perhaps, if you see Demons, you exorcise first and ask questions later," I snapped.

"Not in my job description," he answered coolly.

"Figures. Don't do anything to aid the guy you've crippled, that way you can look better when things go to hell."

Gavin's eyes lowered at that. "It's not like that."

"It is *exactly* like that. You see a fucking Demon, you exorcise it. It's really not that complicated. Demons are bad news. Help, or get the fuck out of my way." My vision was red. This was ri-god-damned-diculous. Here I was, trying to keep my city free of Demons while my parole officer was basically giving them free rein to do as they pleased, waiting for me to fail when said parole officer could have easily deterred them. But no, they wanted to be able to tell their superiors that I had failed. Not mentioning the small fact that they had taken away the necessary weapons I would need to prove my innocence. I knew *that* fact would never appear in the official report.

"You understand how crazy this is, right, Gavin? You took away my power, then expect me to banish all the Demons, while you sit safely on the sidelines ready to accuse me the moment I fail... the moment I fail as a direct result of you limiting my ability to stop the carnage." Gavin's eyes lowered... slightly. "You have literally set me up to fail. I am still out here risking my life despite the fact that you've taken away my only weapons... or severely limited them. How can you honestly say it's fair that I'm guilty if I fail, when the only reason I might fail is because I don't have the juice to keep fighting?"

"Then give up the Key," he snapped in exasperation, realizing how ridiculous his charge was. I hoped.

"Why would I give up the Key to a group of power-hungry old men, whom are actively allowing chaos to take over my city? You understand how ludicrous that sounds, right? It's called *extortion*."

Gavin stared daggers at me for a few moments before giving up and nodding a single time. "Yes." It sounded like he was pulling his own teeth to say so. "I know it seems ludicrous, but you're harboring a dangerous cache of weapons that belongs to the Academy. The only group able to support and protect mankind from annihilation." It sounded rehearsed, and I could tell he knew it.

"The same group that is allowing innocents to die in order to prove a point, right? The ones who set me up on a suicide mission to prove my innocence. I've even recruited a *Regular* to help me because I'm so desperate. Yet you and Jafar wait for me to fail rather than help. How is that *justice?*"

Gavin's gaze dropped lower, but he didn't voice his agreement. I knew Othello wouldn't take my comment personally. She was just as angry as I was, judging by the fact that she had commanded me to kill them all.

"If you're just going to sit on the sidelines and wait for me to fail, you might as well join me. It won't be long now. My power isn't lasting as long as I would have hoped. I'm spent. But I will press on because there isn't anyone else. Because you, sir, are a fucking coward."

His shoulders hitched, but I turned my back on him.

"Time to leave," I said to Othello. "Let this vulture do as he will. I'll be dead soon, and probably deemed guilty for all of this despite fighting until my last ounce of effort. Even *you* are more of a Knight than this... ignorant child."

I turned to go, Othello following me. But I was suddenly slammed into a headstone shoulder first, and then I flipped over it, landing painfully on the other side. "How *dare* you," Gavin growled. I grinned to myself as I climbed to my feet, rubbing my aching shoulder. I hadn't heard it crack. Othello immediately drew her pistol and fired. I didn't even flinch. I wonder what that says about me.

But then again, neither did Gavin. The bullet stopped a millimeter from his face. He didn't even blink, never moving his glare from the tombstone as I appeared over the side. I showed him my wolfish smile. "Perhaps you aren't as much of a little bitch as I thought, although your string is still showing." I pointed at his crotch. He didn't look, but Othello laughed darkly.

PMS jokes between men were the bestest.

"Now, if you're done being a pawn, it's time for us to go and stop the Demons."

Gavin's icy gaze remained frozen on me for a few moments before he gave me a slow nod. I began walking away, and he followed without flipping me over another tombstone. Baby steps.

Manly baby steps.

I rolled my shoulder discreetly, glad that it was only sore. It would have been super if he would have managed to dislocate it. But the risk had been worth it. Causing him to lose control again helped me prove a point. Hopefully made him doubt his creed just enough to assist me. And it seemed to have worked. Othello opened the door and I flicked my head at the other car that I assumed Gavin had driven since it hadn't been there when we parked. "We'll follow you," I told her. She shot me a calculating gaze as if asking if that was wise. "It's probably not my smartest move, but I need to talk to him on the way and I don't think he will stick around for very long." She nodded once. "To Plato's Cave. At least if I'm wrong I can grab a few things, check up on the place." I could sense Othello wasn't happy with the situation. At all. We'd just been duped by the Demons. Either they had lured me here to give them more time elsewhere, or I had been totally incorrect and the Demon had just coincidentally been scouting out the mausoleum at the same time another Demon was murdering a vampire. I wasn't a big fan of the fact that this was the second murder being committed on soil that would directly link to me. I wondered if there was a reason for that or if they were just trying to drive home a point.

Othello drove away angrily.

Gavin climbed into the driver's seat. It was a Crown Victoria. A typical police car. I grumbled about it as I climbed into the cesspool of mediocrity. "It's not that bad," he stated flatly, not agreeing with my vehicular taste. "And this doesn't mean we're on the same side."

"Hopefully, it means you're intelligent enough to realize that you're on the *wrong* side. Even if it's not my side, I hope you see that your current side is following the opinion of a bunch of fucking imbeciles."

Gavin chuckled, and then abruptly stopped, looking disappointed in himself for doing so. His eyes were lost in thought as he followed Othello through the darkening streets. "Maybe," he finally said.

"The Demons are going to kill a vampire. In a place that directly relates to me," I said, hoping it wouldn't end our current alliance.

He nodded, not exactly with any interest, but accepting of the fact.

I decided to play my card.

"What do you really know about my parents' project? This Armory?"

"Just that it was a cache of objects they deemed too dangerous to fall into the hands of the *all-powerful Academy*. The same Academy that provided them with safety for so many years. I find it hard to agree with your perception of the ruling body of wizards. I know they have room for improvement, but I do not believe the Academy to be evil."

I nodded. "I can understand that. I have to be honest, though. This Armory, as you call it, is news to me. I only recently discovered it. It seems to be the reason my parents were murdered. Coincidentally, the Academy showed up almost immediately, demanding access. You can see my cause for concern, right?"

Gavin nodded in resignation. "Timing. If they could show up when they did, why not sooner?"

I nodded. "Exactly my point. But it does make me wonder what, exactly, my parents were hiding. I understand the draw to power, but what does the Academy expect to find? Something specific? Or just power in general?"

Gavin shrugged. "Mayhap the Academy lost something once, and hope your parents managed to... *acquire* it?"

I shook my head. "I doubt it. My parents were not thieves."

Gavin looked uncomfortable. "May I speak... freely, Master Temple?" I could tell that it pained him to address me by my title. I nodded. "The brief time I met your parents, they seemed to imply that they did... *acquire* some of their objects questionably. I make no accusation. Just speak the truth. I know that they did purchase quite a few objects as well, but when they felt necessary, they did resort to more nefarious methods in order to... protect the masses." I shivered, remembering my father's conversation on my 21st birthday, the only time the Pandora Protocol had been mentioned. I sighed. Perhaps Gavin had a point.

"Maybe. But I'm grateful you offered to help with this small Demonic inconvenience."

"Will it be dangerous?" he asked, glancing at me curiously.

"Consider it your second interview..."

Gavin looked nervous but determined. "Okay."

I needed his help. My power was fading faster than I had thought. I was also a target to the mysterious Nephilim that Hemingway and the Demon had mentioned, of which I luckily hadn't directly tussled with yet. Even if they had tried to throw me to the wolves. I also didn't want to risk Othello. Screw it. Gavin seemed torn on his allegiances. Trial by fire then. I needed to test his mettle. If he wanted to find the good side and ease his conscience, then he needed to earn that trust.

"Do you have a safe word?" I asked him as we continued following Othello. Gavin looked really uncomfortable for a few moments.

"Um, what kind of second interview did you have in mind? Because I didn't mean to give you the wrong impression. I'm not into—"

I chuckled darkly. "Not that kind of safe word. Things might get, not to keep the pun going," I winked, "but... hairy. I was just curious on what kind of tolerance you have for fear." Gavin relaxed instantly.

"Ah. I'm sure I'll be fine. I've sought out plenty of danger in my days. Even met a werewolf once. Filthy beast tried to kill me. Showed him," he said proudly. I smiled guardedly.

"Well, my best friend is a werewolf, so be careful about your prejudices. But that's good to hear. Wouldn't want you freaking out in the middle of a... difficult situation."

"I'll be fine. I know how to subdue any who would do me harm."

"Not sure subduing is an option, but you're more than welcome to try. I'll just say this. With Demons, the rule book goes out the window." Gavin's face tightened, but he nodded.

We pulled up to the front of Plato's Cave, and then drove on by, cruising casually. I noticed a blacked-out Ford Explorer parked near the entrance with two neatly groomed men inside – wide-awake – watching the streets. My place was being observed. Gavin grunted, spotting them. Othello continued on ahead of us, obviously noticing the stakeout as well. We pulled around the block, made a lap to be sure that there were no other spotters, and then parked. My disguise was entirely complete with the fake horn-rim glasses, so I had no fear that they would recognize me. Unless I walked through the front door after regular business hours...

Othello casually exited the car, as if having no relation to Gavin and I, pretending to talk loudly into her phone to a girlfriend. They followed me as I entered through a side door that only the employees knew about, safe from prying eyes. I was ready for anything, not knowing if it would be like the werewolf community, that somehow an entire coven of vampires would be here ready to take me out. But nothing happened. We entered the darkened building... *my* darkened building. And it was empty, the employees long gone.

"It seems clean. No murder," I said, frowning.

Gavin grunted. "Perhaps this is also a false lead."

I looked at him, unable to contain my anger. "There are 1,013,900 words in the English language, and none of them accurately portray how badly I want to hit you over the head with a chair. A heavy Amish chair."

Gavin... blinked. "With all your power, you wish to hit me over the head with a chair? For stating a fact?"

"You took away *all my power*. So, yes. A chair will suffice."

Othello chuckled quietly. "Boys..."

Gavin shook his head, muttering. "A chair..."

"This doesn't make sense," I said after scanning the entire store. I turned for the stairs that led up to my old apartment. Now, it was merely unused living quarters above the shop. But it had once been an old projector room, because the place had been a theater. "Light, please," I said to Gavin. He cast his power out into a bluish dim glow so we could see without turning on the lights and alerting the FBI. They followed me, watching in silence as I gathered a few things and a change of clothes. I was done hiding and using disguises. I snatched up a unique feather stuffed into a jar of pens on my desk – a feather that looked like it had been torn from a Demonic peacock – with a smile on my face. *Grimm.* Might come in handy.

"And what's the escapade behind this?" Othello asked with a leer, pointing at the pair of panties hanging on the desk lamp.

"Indie."

Othello sniffed haughtily. "Classy."

"They did the job," I mumbled under my breath. Gavin watched with curiosity. "Alright, I don't see any other reason to stick around," I said, changing the topic. I hefted the overnight bag over my shoulder. I quickly emptied my pockets to transfer my stuff to my new pants. When I pulled out my wallet, a card dropped to the floor and I truly saw it for the first time since Hemingway had given it to me. "Well I'll be goddamned..."

A large boom at the front door of Plato's Cave shook the building as the door burst into splinters. "I meant *gosh darned*," I snapped. Heavy boots stomped into the entrance below us. "Oh, come on! It was a slip of the tongue!" I bellowed, shoving the card into my pocket.

"Meet your demise, wizard," a cool voice commanded from below.

Gavin merely leaned towards a window to look down at the threat, not actively doing anything to help me. Othello cocked her pistol hungrily.

I quickly darted to the window to see what the hell was going on, hoping my accomplices wouldn't shoot first and ask questions later. I couldn't make out the details, but he looked human.

"Who goes there?" I called.

"The might of Heaven, mortal. Bow down."

"Ice Cube? Really?" I asked. He didn't respond. I held up a hand for my accomplices to hold off, but it seemed Gavin had no intention of assisting.

"I'm not fucking with Heaven," he stated bluntly, and then Shadow Walked his happy ass out of my shop with a resounding *crack*.

I sighed. I had managed to piss off God. And my ally had abandoned me at the first sign of mayhem.

CHAPTER 24

I snarled at the sound, "Hold off on the smiting. I'll be down in just a second!"

Othello followed me closely as I descended the stairs. I really didn't have time for this. I had done nothing wrong. In fact, I believed I was the only one doing anything *right*.

The man hadn't moved from the entrance, but what remained of the door had been propped back in place. He was much younger than I had thought. The youth held a hand on the hilt of his righteous sword, and he looked like he had been plucked straight from the Crusades, decked out in genuine leather armor that was engraved in platinum curlicues and exquisite geometric shapes that made my skin crawl. They were functional, not just for decoration. Spells. And they were so ancient I could only recognize that they *were* spells, but not their purpose.

He was young, appearing twenty-something, but the hard gleam in his eyes let me know he was formidable with wisdom well beyond his years. I settled the bag gently on the ground beside me. "So, what's a nice guy like you doing in a dangerous place like this?" I asked. I kept my hands in a neutral place – for most people anyway, but not that neutral for a wizard – at my sides, hanging freely. He was smart enough to understand they were still a threat, glancing at them with quick, assessing eyes.

The boy watched me coldly. "You are aiding the Demons. I can sense it on you."

I blinked back. He seemed to have no concern for Othello. Apparently, only I was on his list. "If I'm such a naughty boy, explain why I've shut down several Demons in the last twelve hours," I answered coolly.

The boy continued to stare at me, unruffled. "I do not pretend to understand your murky motives, magic mortal."

"Say *that* five times fast."

He blinked like a cat on a fireplace, not amused, refusing to acknowledge my comment. "It is a fact. I know what I see."

"And what you see might be jaded by your righteousness," I quipped.

He quivered with pious judgment. "Do not blaspheme again. I will grow angry." The boy growled. Although he was young, his strength was obvious, and he looked like he had grown up through the school of hard knocks, judging by the faint scars on his face. I guessed battling Demons your entire life left you a little jaded. Or maybe he had been brainwashed at a young age. A lot of that going around lately. "What you do directly affects Heaven, and directly aids Hell," he continued quite calmly. "For that, you must be destroyed."

He drew his huge sword with finality, the whisper of it leaving the sheath a grisly promise of what was to come. Othello didn't waste any time. She lifted her pistol. "I fucking dare you."

The boy seemed to notice her for the first time. "Do not let his words sway you. This man is dangerous."

"Me?" I asked in amazement. "All I've done is fight Demons and my own people the last too many hours. What have I done to piss off *Heaven?*"

"You made a pact with a Greater Demon. I can sense it." He leaned closer, sword out, but not threatening... yet. "I can *see* it." *Then* he moved. He suddenly flicked the sword so fast that he could have taken my head right off. If he had wanted to. It was a warning. The tip rested just above my eye. To the damning mark on my forehead. I could hear the crackling energy of his heavenly power reacting to the rune, feel it tingling against my skull.

"I didn't ask for that. It was forced upon me. I'm not one for brands. Ask her." I pointed at Othello.

She nodded. "It's true. I was there when he fought the Demon. This mark was the Demon's last attack, in order to pit your kind against his cause. The Demons want us fighting each other, but there is a true enemy out there."

Her voice was soft, soothing, and compelling. The boy shook his head as if at a temptress. "I will not buy these lies. I see the mark. Eae warned you to stay out of it. I saw the aftermath of you killing that wolf. Despite their kind being an abomination, murder is not tolerable."

"People are murdered all the time and I've never heard of your kind getting involved." Too late, I realized that I hadn't argued the most important accusation.

"You see," he smiled. "You don't deny killing the wolf."

I groaned. "No, I didn't deny it. Because it's crazy. I arrived *after* he was killed, hoping to prevent it from happening. My best friend is a werewolf. But someone of your ilk pitted a whole pack of vengeful werewolves after me when I only showed up to help, so I'm more concerned with where your people come into the picture and why they have a hard-on for me. "

He smiled. "Well, our part is simple enough." There was no warning whatsoever. He lunged at me. Othello let off a few shots, pinging the blade out of the Nephilim's hands. He didn't miss a beat, and instead physically latched onto me with his hands, and threw me.

Like, *really* threw me.

I grunted with each impact as I sailed through what I counted as three glass-walled dividers before landing on a cushioned couch and knocking it over. "Huzzah!" I managed to cheer through the throbbing ache in my ribs, jumping to my feet, glad that the couch had somewhat broken my fall. Then I saw a blindingly white light whipping towards my face with a supersonic whine. I dropped like a sack of potatoes, not wanting to waste any more magic than necessary by deflecting whatever the Heaven it was. A freaking crucifix boomerang whizzed by overhead, spitting off electric currents of power as it tore through several hanging chandeliers, sending them to the ground in explosions of crystal and glass. The weapon crackled with lightning at each strike, seeming to deflect the sparks of electricity, before sailing back towards the Nephilim who caught it with ease. The energy danced over his frame as his glare pinned me to the couch.

Othello was nowhere to be found. Had he killed her?

The Nephilim strode over to the sword and picked it up off the ground. It was dented and bent in a wavy line from Othello's well-placed bullets. He knelt his head and began to mutter a prayer. His words filled the room, and a ring of liquid golden power began to build around his feet. After a few seconds, it began to rise, circling his body, and I began to feel a little uneasy at what it might mean. A shard of crystal from the chandelier fell towards his head, but when it came remotely near the golden light it disintegrated to powder, and I suddenly realized I might have met my match. Heavenly armor of some sort would make my attacks useless.

If this was a Nephilim... what could an Angel do?

I shivered at the thought, but readied myself for war. The ring rose to his head level, shrunk, and became a perfect halo of raw force around his head. I watched in disbelief as the blade suddenly reformed to perfection.

I grumbled. Heavenly armor *and* an unbreakable sword? That wasn't fair at all. The Nephilim took a single step, raised the sword high, and then with a roar of power he slammed it into the ground like it was Excalibur. The golden halo around his head fled through his body and into the sword, causing a low thrum like a tuning fork, and a blast of energy suddenly rang out in every direction, demolishing or knocking down every piece of furniture or bookshelf in its immediate proximity. Then the entire building began to tremble, louder and faster, with each passing second. Pictures and books from the surviving shelves and wall mounts began to rattle, dancing into a free fall to the floor, and the lights began to erratically flicker on and off. The espresso machine kicked on and began flinging coffee beans all over the place. A jagged crack suddenly split the wall behind me, and brick and mortar began collapsing into the room as the building groaned tiredly, giving up. The walls were coming down. Was this fucker crazy? He was going to kill us all!

I Shadow Walked without thinking, appearing right behind him. I noticed the only adornment on his back was a second sheath with a feather sticking out. Without thinking, I snatched it up and Shadow Walked back in front of him...

Where his fist was immediately introduced to my face. It broke my nose with a most indelicate *crack* of cartilage and my vision exploded in a sea of stars. I flew backwards into a bookshelf hard enough for it to shatter and rain its contents down upon me. One struck me in the already broken nose and I almost squealed like I had been electrocuted. I heard his steps approaching and frantically, blindly, began trying to dig my way out of the pile of buckram and paper. Then I heard a loud click amongst the falling debris. "Don't move. I don't want to hurt you, but I will. Even if it damns me for eternity. You are about to kill one of the only good guys left in this city."

Othello's voice was like an Angel singing a hymn. I hurriedly fell out of the pile of books to see a strange scene. Othello was holding her pistol to the back of the Nephilim's head, and the boy was letting her. Couldn't he magic his way out of that?

"You would damn your soul for him?"

"Yes." She didn't even hesitate, which surprised even me. "You're making a big mistake."

"Othello," I warned. "Step a few feet away from him please. It's not safe. He's a zealot."

"As much as I hate to admit it, she's as safe as a babe from me. She is righteous... to a degree," he added, sounding frustrated.

Othello blinked at him. "What? To a *degree*? Well... I guess I'll take it."

I frowned at him. "What do you mean?"

"She is only doing as she believes is right, and I have no command to punish her. I swear on Heaven." He sheathed his sword faster than anyone could move, and then dropped his hands to his sides. "I cannot harm her."

I blinked. "Huh. Imagine that. Glad you could be here, Othello," I muttered.

"Just doing my job," she answered quickly.

The Nephilim's face suddenly fell. "My Grace!" He was staring at the feather in my hand and took an aggressive step forward before halting at Othello's warning. His face fell, but he continued to stare frantically at the feather I had stolen.

"Grace?" I asked, looking down at it.

"A feather from my father's wings. It was entrusted to me. It gives me additional strength to fight Hell." He looked entirely different from before. More like a child fearful of his father's wrath when he discovered the family car missing on a Friday night.

I turned it over in my fingers. It was silver, and big, but it didn't look like anything that special. Just a gilded feather you might find at a high-end jewelry shop. "This belongs to an Angel?" I asked doubtfully.

He nodded anxiously. Another crack that seemed to come from the foundation interrupted my thoughts. The building rumbled ominously. "Why doesn't your father just come down here himself and take care of the Demons?"

"He can't. If the Angels act, the Fallen can act, and then the Riders will destroy us all. Eternally."

"*Jesus*! Talk about overkill," Othello whispered, sounding shaken.

"No, not him. The Riders." He looked genuinely confused. Othello blinked.

I sighed. "So why is this feather so important?"

"It's not just a *feather*. It's my father's *Grace*. It grants him the power of Heaven. My temporary possession of it grants me extra power to battle Hell. If that feather breaks it would kill my father."

I subconsciously made sure I was holding it with both hands. "Well that's reckless. Why would you carry it around so openly?"

"Only extreme power could destroy it. And even the Demons wouldn't risk it. It would be the same as killing an Angel directly."

"You mean that it would call the Riders?" I asked in astonishment.

He nodded. "Please, give me back the Grace. I'll inform my father of your words. Perhaps it will change Eae's mind." He didn't sound like he believed it.

"Eae is your father?" I asked curiously.

"Yes. He commands the Flight of Nephilim on my task force."

I wanted to give it back, latching onto the hope that his father, Eae, would realize we were on the same side and get off my back. Really. What if I somehow managed to break it and called the Riders? But I needed to teach these guys a lesson, let them know that I wasn't to be trifled with. After all, if they were scared to attack me in fear of harming the Grace, I wouldn't have to waste my diminishing power fighting them. "This isn't the playground, kid. You can lose your balls here." Othello frowned at me. I rolled my eyes. "You know what I mean." I turned back to the Nephilim. "You just tried to kill me. Without even telling me who you are!"

"I was told you were allied with the Demons. And you carry the... Greater Demon's mark." He seemed to dodge the Demon's name for some reason. No doubt to avoid his attention.

"I already explained the mark. Can we agree that I'm not the problem? The world is going nuts the last few days. Demons prowling around town in search of a project my parents worked on. Am I safe to assume that you won't attack me while I hold this?" I waved the feather. The Nephilim flinched, reaching out clawed fingers instinctively. "Swear it on this feather.

I can burn it with a thought. I am a wizard. You lie, pillow stuffing goes *poof.*"

The Nephilim looked visibly sickened, but nodded, clutching a fist to his heart symbolically. "Good. Let's get out of here. You caused quite a ruckus kicking down my door like that, and those police outside are bound to be on their way any second. Especially if the building collapses."

The man shook his head. "I runed them. They'll be asleep until morning."

"Oh. Well. Good. So... what do I have to do to show you guys I'm not on the dark side?"

"I'm not sure. End the threat, I guess." I blinked at him.

"You want me to cast a whole army of Demons back to Hell to prove I didn't bring them here? I've been fighting them, alongside you, ever since I discovered them. They directly threatened me. And branded me with this mark against my will."

He nodded stoically, seeming to slowly regain his confidence. "Yet your parents are the reason they have come. With them dead, it is now your issue. You cannot accept the gift of the Armory yet ignore the consequences of ownership. It's on you. Now, give me back the Grace."

His form visibly rippled with power. "Cool it, feathers. I'm not giving you anything until I understand the whole picture, and you promise that Eae and your brothers will also stay off my back."

The scent of burnt sulfur abruptly filled my nostrils, my only warning of a Demon's presence. Before I could react, a form suddenly materialized behind the Nephilim. "Sweet dreams, little Nephilim." The boy began to react, but without his Grace he was too slow. Inky black Demonic claws decapitated him right before my eyes, showering me in his half-holy blood, which I somehow had time to realize didn't look or feel any different than regular blood, which was slightly disappointing. Othello grabbed my shirt and yanked me backwards just as a second claw swiped at me, raking my torso. Her grab saved my chest from becoming sliced lunchmeat, but it still did a fair amount of damage, causing me to gasp in only near fatal pain. The Demon frowned at his misfortune. "Luckily, you have her to save your pathetic hide. Such a lovely hide. It will look splendid as a throw rug."

I ignored his threat, clutching the Grace against my lacerated chest, scared that I might touch something that was supposed to stay on my inside. Feathers covered his frame like a raven, and beady black eyes assessed me hungrily. He even sported a vibrant beak that was stained with blood from a recent meal. Or permanently stained from a life of feasting on blood. "You lied. There was no vampire. It was a trap to lure me into a confrontation with the Nephilim. Why? If he had killed me, how would you get your precious key?" I asked, confused.

The Demon blinked at me, a look of utter confusion painting his features for half a second. Then he shrugged it off and began to stalk closer, speaking very clearly out of his beak. "I grow tired of talking. I didn't spend eons in Hell to waste my parole on earth."

I had time to think, *Huh... he doesn't know about the Key,* before another party guest arrived.

The room abruptly pulsed with a bluish glow and every single window blew out as a vacuum of power filled the room. The scent of sulfur was obliterated in a blink, replaced with the smell of burnt gravel and frost. Oh, shit.

Eae, the Demon-thwarting Angel.

The bird-Demon's black eyes went wide as a sword pierced his heart from behind, a much-too-wide blade pointing in my direction through the feathers on the Demon's chest.

"Wait!" I began, then the sword gave a sickening twist, shattering the Demon's sternum, and the monster disintegrated to ash. As he fell, I saw the Angel from the bar, Eae, standing behind him, crackling with power. He gave one contemptuous flick of his sword, disbursing the Demon blood onto my floor where it sizzled.

"You killed my son, stole my Grace, and allowed it to be fractured." He was quivering with fury, his voice a series of rasps, totally unlike our first talk. "If it breaks entirely, Armageddon will officially ignite, which you no doubt desire. I finally see the truth. Now that your Demon is dead, there is no one here to save you." The Angel spoke through ground teeth. I glanced down at the feather in my hand, which also gave me a great view of my wounded chest from the Demon's claws. The feather was indeed broken, the two halves connected by only a thin thread of cartilage.

"*My* Demon? I had nothing to do with him. When will you people get the hint? I was having a peaceful chat with your son before the Demon attacked us and cut your stupid feather! I was trying to keep it safe! He had information I could have used. Information that could have guided me to the summoner! The *real* problem starter. What the hell is wrong with you guys?"

I didn't even see him move. I merely felt a fist strike me in the stomach like a moving truck, and I was suddenly slammed into the wooden staircase on the other side of the building. I heard Othello scream, but I was too shaken to get my bearings. The Angel was suddenly towering over me, wings snapping out with a whoosh of air, quadrupling his size. "I don't believe you. Jonathan was no novice. No Demon could have killed him so easily. You killed him after he let his guard down." I began to stammer an argument, but the look in his eyes stalled me. I knew that look. The look of someone with nothing to lose. When a rage so dark and overpowering controlled your every thought. The kind of look one got after their family had been murdered. I had lived with that look for a few months now.

"No one kills one of my sons, or causes them to be killed without retribution. I have skirted the line by striking you, but since Armageddon is practically imminent, I hold no long-term responsibility for my actions. Just know this. If that Grace breaks entirely, my brethren will hunt you down. If it doesn't, my sons will. Regardless, your death will be slow and painful for your sins. Heaven will not assist you, and will now actively seek your demise. I will not forget this." The last was a whisper that rang with such a deadly finality that I actually kept my mouth shut.

The building gave an ominous crack, and Eae was abruptly gone. Othello sprinted over to me only a second after the Angel had disappeared, looking angry that he had already left. "Nate! Are you okay?"

"I just got my ass smited. What do you think?" I wheezed.

"I think it's smote, but I wasn't much of a bible school kind of girl. I will say that I bet no one in history has been struck by a Demon and then less than a minute later been smote by a freaking Angel." She glanced down at my wound, eyes growing concerned. "Shit." She averted her gaze to my face and I saw her eyes widen at my broken nose. "Um. You look like a badass?" she offered encouragingly.

I managed to feebly throw a brick at her. She dodged it. Then she pulled me to my feet, causing me to hiss in pain. My torso was lacerated, bleeding freely, and I had an Angelic fist shape indented into my stomach. "I think he bruised my stomach. The actual organ." It took me a few moments to gather my breath, and Othello continued to dab at my wounds with a shirt from the bag I had packed. I winced when her hands gripped my ribs.

"Sorry." Her eyes dampened with fear at the number of wounds painting my body.

"Yeah, those bookshelves were sturdy. And the glass-walled dividers. I don't think any ribs are broken though. To be safe, I should probably take some aspirin. Not Extra Strength though. No need to take risks." The store groaned again, more alarmingly, and the stairs leading to my loft suddenly collapsed with a crash, filling the room with dust and debris. Othello began to cough lightly through the haze. I heard another deep crack that sent more dust into the air. I needed to call this one in. The building might collapse any minute. I grabbed a new shirt and Othello helped me put it on, wrapping up another clean tee into a makeshift bandage to wrap over my wounds. Several small fires dotted the floor, burning through my priceless inventory.

I sighed as she finished, grunting in pain when she pulled the knot tight. "Let's go." We exited the same door from earlier and headed towards her car. Gavin's car was nowhere to be seen. Othello merely scowled at that.

A low, vibrating hum suddenly split the night, a keening wail.

A Horn of War. I glanced up and spotted Eae on a nearby rooftop, glaring at us.

At me, specifically.

His voice boomed through the night. "The wizard has proven his crimes, consorting with Demons to kill Jonathan, your brother, who attempted to trust him. He has broken my grace, but not destroyed it, no doubt to use me as his pawn. Which will not happen. I would rather die in *His* name. Let Armageddon be on the wizard's shoulders. Permission to decimate at will." With a giant flap of his wings, he was off, and I heard hundreds of answering horns fill the night. I shivered. Armageddon? I hadn't broken the feather, it was the damned Demon! I would do whatever it took to keep that feather safe. My life, and the world, now literally depended on it.

We raced to the car and jumped in, eager to be away from the answering calls of the dozens of Nephilim. Othello started the car and we took off in a squeal of tires. After we turned the corner, I heard an earth-shattering *thump* behind me, and then a crash like the earth had cracked open. Othello swerved, shouting as the car was shoved ahead on screeching tires. Several fire hydrants exploded beside us, showering the street with fountains of cold water that quickly began to turn to ice. I turned to look behind, fearing some sort of Angelic attack, but saw only a black cloud of smoke rising from my shop. My shoulders sagged. "First my money's frozen, then I'm arrested, then framed a murderer, and then my shop is blown to smithereens by a gaggle of geese. Someone is going to pay for this." Othello nodded. The thing was, I didn't really have anyone to take out my pain on. The Demon was dead, the Nephilim, Jonathan, was dead, and I was on Heaven's Most Wanted list. My parole officer, Gavin, had abandoned me when I needed him the most, and the only one I had on my side was Othello, a Regular.

"Let's head to the apartment. I feel like resting my eyes. Not sleeping, but resting my eyelids. Either that or we need to find some caffeine to pour directly into my eyeballs. One hundred percent caffeine. Not that diluted coffee swill. The real stuff."

Othello sniffed beside me and I could tell she was crying. I didn't have anything to say to her, though. I just wanted it all to be over with. I leaned back in my seat and closed my eyes.

I grew silent as we drove to the apartment. The facts.

This was all about the Demons and their summoner. He had brought a Greater Demon up from Hell in order to kill my parents and take the Armory. As if that hadn't been enough, he had either summoned more Demons for back up or the Greater Demon had brought a gang of his friends up for company – some of which were privy to details on the Armory, and some that weren't. Which was curious. Maybe they thought a little additional chaos would help. It sure hadn't hurt their cause. I was beginning to think that this summoner was either supremely powerful, extremely clever, or that there was more than one summoner... I shivered at that.

The Angel, Eae, had warned me to back off in the bar. And then the first Demon had commanded me to give up the Armory shortly after. Something had happened to bring both parties out into the open, but I didn't know what that could have been. It had been months since the break in, but now everyone was suddenly moving like they were on a time frame. I had since pissed off both Biblical parties and was now actively being hunted or framed by both.

Othello had turned out to be quite the sidekick. Still, things were about to get a whole hell of a lot worse, and I was running out of juice. And I was still a fugitive from the police, meaning I couldn't even tap into my money or assets.

Then there was the greedy Academy, who considered it a simple to-do item for me to banish all the Demons without my magic, extorting me in a moment of drunken stupor to curse me into giving them the Armory. No matter what I chose to do I was going to piss off someone I really probably shouldn't be pissing off.

I leaned my head back into the worn headrest, barely surviving the dull throbbing agony that was my face. I would need to set my nose before I went to sleep. I could taste the fresh blood draining into the back of my throat, and my chest felt hot from the deep cuts of the Demon's claws. My entire torso felt like a giant bruise, and I was getting kind of sleepy, enjoying the heat blasting from the vents as Othello continued to drive in silence, taking the turns carefully so as not lose control of the car on the snowy streets.

I fueled my pain into anger. It wasn't hard. I had plenty of each already. I decided that I would find that Greater Demon again and ask him a few pointed questions. It felt good to finally have a direction for my anger. I was in a race to kill the Greater Demon before my power failed me entirely. Or before the Nephilim hunters found me. Perhaps I could get the Demon's attention by killing one of his brothers. It had worked last time.

Othello murmured softly and I realized that I had been dozing lightly. I agreed with her. We opted to go get sleep rather than pouring caffeine into my eyes.

Probably a good choice.

CHAPTER 25

*R*adio commercials from the car stereo droned on in the
background as we drove through town. A beam of sunlight
abruptly struck my eyeball like a spear, causing me to wince, which caused
my broken nose to flare with pain. I hissed instinctively. Even my pain was
causing me pain. I felt Othello glance at me, fighting a smile. "We still
haven't found the murdered vampire." I grumbled to her as she made a right
turn. "Let's swing by Temple Industries while we wait for news of the
murder since we struck out twice last night. I don't feel like running all
around town to be framed for yet another death I'm trying to prevent. I
don't see the Demons passing up an opportunity to kill when their boss
gave them free rein to do so." She nodded in agreement, navigating towards
my company. We had gone straight to sleep after the chaos at Plato's Cave,
and woken up late. My ribs ached from the fight last night, and my face was
a landscape of tenderness. Resetting my nose had felt less good than me
sticking my fingers in a live electrical outlet.

I shook off my injuries. They weren't going to get better any time soon.
Which meant that I needed to quit whining about them. In fact, I was
almost certain that they would increase exponentially before this was all
said and done.

Which wasn't too motivating.

Nothing to do about it, though, so I searched inwardly for a plan. I wanted to speak with Hope again so I could maybe get a second opinion on what the hell was going on. The spirit seemed to know quite a bit, and she had caused us to waste our last visit when she showed me the vision of Achilles' hollow vengeance, which I still didn't understand. I wasn't acting like him.

Was I?

I was doing the right thing. I angrily stepped out of the imaginary psychiatrist chair in my mind. Later.

Perhaps Hope would know if the summoner and his Demons were hunting for something specific. And she had called me a Maker. I hadn't had much time to think about that, and still didn't know what it meant, but it sounded like something I should know. After all, my parents had made me into one. With all the fighting and running around, I had apparently bottled that one away deep inside my mind. I didn't know how to feel about it – angry, curious, frustrated? Apparently, I was an experiment. One of the feared items from the Armory. Should I lock myself away? Did it even matter now that my power was practically gone?

The commercials on the radio ceased and the news returned. I turned it up and listened acutely as we drove. It was all about the random attacks in town. The Mayor was even considering declaring Martial Law until *Mardi Gras* was over. *"Detective Kosage allegedly came out of the closet at a big affair downtown, complete with a float and music. A real boon to the LGBT movement,"* the reporter declared, managing to sound both amused and politically correct at the same time. I chuckled, shooting a smile at Othello as I shook my head. She grinned absently. Silver lining. *"Master Temple is still at large after his apparent kidnapping from the Police station where he had been detained for questioning regarding the attacks from a few months ago. He was only a person of interest, but now he's been kidnapped. This happened while a large contingent of officers was absent in support of their fellow officer coming out of the closet. The resulting lack of security will no doubt be investigated shortly."* The radio grew silent for a moment. *"Newsflash. Apparently, Master Temple's arcane bookstore, Plato's Cave, was destroyed in an explosion last night. And, wait, a ransom has been declared on Master Temple! Imagine that. Who could afford to ransom one of the richest men in the country? One-hundred-million dollars from Temple Industries CEO, Ashley Belmont. No word from her at present, as it appears she is on vacation. Too bad for Master Temple."*

The artifact Hope had given me began to vibrate in my pocket, and I groaned. When it vibrated on its own it meant a Demon was practically on top of us. "I haven't even had my coffee yet!" I grumbled, scanning our surroundings anxiously.

"What are you whining about now?" Othello asked, seeming distracted by a swarm of activity at a nearby warehouse. We were between the city proper and Temple Industries. The area was occupied by numerous warehouses, reminding me of the area where Gunnar and I had fought the gargoyles and the silver dragon a few months ago. I began to pull out the map, not noticing any impending attack in our immediate proximity. Before I could situate myself, Othello slammed on the brakes. "Nate…" Her tone and the flash of pain from my tightening seat belt against my wounded chest made me look up with wide eyes. She was pointing at the same warehouse she had been studying. I leaned back as far as possible, breathing hard as I tried to loosen the seat belt. I spotted a gaggle of parents hanging outside the warehouse, drinking a hot liquid of some kind from Styrofoam cups. The flash of pain beginning to subside, I began to turn back to the map when I saw the vilest of evil scramble out of the building. Followed by another, and another of the beasts, each moving very swiftly. The kind of evil that cannot be vanquished. These creatures had mind powers to an exponential degree.

"*Must not give in…*" I whispered with great determination, clutching my seat tightly.

Othello turned to me. "They're just Girl Scouts. They must be building a float."

I nodded soberly. Girl Scouts were anathema to every grown man in existence who innocently decided to answer the front door in his sweats and a dirty undershirt after a long day of work, only to discover a pig-tailed, buck-toothed princess who so sweetly asked if you would like to buy some cookies. See, they knew when to catch you at your weakest moment, for they were tiny, vicious predators. You had just started a diet, but that didn't matter. Their power was too strong for you to survive.

The Girl Scout had arrived to steal your soul.

Your dignity.

And you were going to pay her to do it.

You couldn't find your wallet fast enough, even if you had to cancel your cable bill the next month to pay for it.

If that wasn't mind control, I didn't know what was. "*Will not give them my money."* I whispered in a strained voice. *"Thin mints are poisoned with mind magic..."* I continued, reaching for my wallet dramatically.

Othello slapped my hand, rolling her eyes. "Stop it."

"Right. This just validates my hypothesis that Girl Scouts wield Demonic power. The talisman goes off as soon as they're near. And look at all their servants. Like big dumb cows, unaware of the possessed little beasts' power."

Othello arched a brow at me. "Their parents?"

I nodded, folding my arms. "If you want to call them that." She rolled her eyes, turning back to the building. It seemed like there really were people inside building a float, judging by the several groups of adult minions standing outside. Sure, the parents *looked* happy, but being a wizard, I could see through the dark mind magic controlling them. Either they were building a float or we had found their secret lair, the place with the mind control ingredients that was added to their cookies.

Othello began to speak, her tone alarmed. "Why are they running—"

As if in answer to her question, the side of the building instantly exploded in a shower of aged brick, a balloon of fire belching out the side like a giant forge fire. Luckily, none of the mindless thralls had been standing on that side. Then the screaming began. Girl Scouts began pouring out the front doors like someone had kicked an anthill. Alleged fathers and mothers began scooping up their masters like football players before racing towards their cars. It was rather amazing how fast they vacated. Several of the girls looked sooty and terrified, but I didn't see any injuries. Filthy little liars, with their lying lies.

Another blast shook the building, and a freaking box of cookies the size of a minivan flew out the open wall, wafers of burning Thin Mints rolling into the street, leaving trails of fire in their wake, before the giant box of cookies crashed into the street a dozen feet away from us. Shit. The girl scouts *had* been making a float for the *Mardi Gras* parade. Smoke filled the street as I heard dozens of cars turning over and peeling out of the parking lot, leaving us alone for the most part.

A Demon like a giant, winged, hairy spider exited the building on scuttling feet, looking disappointed that no bystanders remained. Then the creature's eight eyes locked onto our car. I instantly climbed out, and Othello put the car in park, killing the engine as she followed suit. The building crumpled on one side, another wave of bricks falling into the street as more clouds of dust cloyed the air.

I heard Othello cock her pistol, glancing around for any remaining parents or children, but we were all alone. I smiled. That was a plus.

The Demon launched into the air, and landed before us with a great sweep of his wings, buffeting my coat. I held up a hand to shield myself from the smoke and debris, and then lowered my arm to appraise the Demon. He was huge, and his eight arachnid legs sported dozens of pointy protrusions that sunk into the asphalt as if it were grass. My gaze wandered down and I blinked.

"You're a chick!"

Her massive love pillows were out on display for all the world to see, hanging freely under her body. I reached into my pocket eagerly, latched onto something, and then tossed it at her feet, clapping with approval. The leftover beads from my travels atop the stolen police horse, Xavier, the night at the bar settled near her two of her legs, and both her and Othello's eyes moved from the beads to my face with hot glares of disapproval. They didn't notice the additional item I had snatched out of my pocket.

Which was the point.

"I don't desire trinkets. I was let out to play. My lucky day that you happened by, wizard. Any last words before I drink your blood?" The Demon asked with a sneer through dozens of clicking fangs. It reminded me of the Lord of the Rings.

"Shouldn't you be trying to find a way into the Armory or hurting one of my friends? Not that I'm complaining. This makes my work simpler. I can just kill you here instead of chasing you all over town." I lifted my palm, a ring of blue fire resting there threateningly. I wasn't going to waste time playing nice. I didn't have time for it. Or the patience. I needed to end this threat now. Before the Demon caused more harm.

The Demon blinked at me. "I know nothing of this Armory, but I really do have other things I would rather be killing... or is it doing? I get confused with your language. It's really much simpler just to kill everything rather than talking about it. More fun. More natural. Well, if you're done talking, I'll just finish up here and then move on to the slaughtering." It reared up on four legs, the other four clicking in the air, ready to pounce on us.

"You're lying! What do you want from the Armory? Who brought you here?"

My ring of blue fire pulsed in tune with my anger as I took an aggressive step forward. I was ready to decimate the entire block if necessary. There was no way this was a coincidence. The Greater Demon had to have planted this Demon. While the Demon was distracted by my accusation, I adjusted the throwing knife I had taken from my pocket when I had snatched up the beads. A throwing knife that had been dipped in blessed water. I flicked my wrist and released the blade. It sunk into the Demon's breast, right above the large dark nipple, with a burst of blue flame as holy water met Hellish flesh. The Demon yowled like a drowned cat, which made me smile. I then prepared a beam of white-hot flame to cast at her, knowing the dagger wouldn't be enough. Perhaps overkill, but I wasn't about to waste time trading punches. I didn't have the power for a drawn-out fight.

Then I felt a surge of power behind me, someone gathering a whole lot of magic.

A wizard.

A look of surprise replaced the pain in the Demon's multifaceted eyes, and I saw a dull reflection of a blazing inferno of black flame racing towards her. I unleashed my power and dove to the side as my second jet of black fire tore through the street, melting the asphalt beneath it.

The two spells touched for a split second, and then the ground exploded around the Demon, casting my body into a nearby building. My head struck a rearview mirror on the way, which didn't feel great, causing a flurry of stars to fill my vision, but the whiplash prevented my skull from also striking the brick wall. Between the twinkling blossoms of light, I saw that the twin fires had struck the Demon square in the chest at the same time, causing her to disappear instantly with a wail of anguish, leaving a crater of earth where the two bars of fire had not mixed together well. I touched the back of my head and winced. My fingers were bloody.

Gavin's voice filled the silence. "I'm not sure what you just did, but when our beams of power touched, it was quite efficient."

"I guess we just crossed swords." Othello laughed aloud at my innuendo, knowing my immaturity, but Gavin didn't seem to understand. I sighed.

"Regardless, she's been banished back to Hell."

"What are you doing here? I had things under control." I grouched, scrambling to my feet.

"You asked me to assist, and now you complain. Which one is it?" Gavin rolled his eyes.

"Boys," Othello warned, very matronly.

"Ring a bell or something. I almost offed you!" I snapped, stumbling slightly as my vision wavered.

"Your power is almost gone, and you look like you've been on a week-long bender, or the losing end of a car accident. Perhaps both. I doubt you almost 'offed' me."

I fumed. He was right, of course. "Where did you disappear to last night? We really could have used your help. Did the big bad Angel scare little old Gavin, fierce Justice of the Academy?"

Gavin scowled back. "Too much heat. I'm not supposed to be involved at all. Especially not to *aid* you. Toeing off against Heaven is a pretty good way to get fired. Jafar wouldn't see that as a good thing. Let alone, God."

"Pansy," I muttered, walking back towards the car. He and Othello followed. "Why did she lie about the Armory?" I asked, speaking more to myself.

Gavin, apparently, deemed himself important enough to answer my question.

"It must have been lying for some reason. Then again, maybe they aren't all here for the Armory. Maybe some were released to up the chaos factor and keep you distracted. Anyway, you're welcome."

"*Ordo ab chao...*" I muttered to myself.

Gavin grunted his agreement. "*Order from chaos.* Seems appropriate."

As much as I hated to admit it, he had come to the same conclusion as I had. And he had just solved a problem for me. Hopefully, his aid would let me conserve my magic for a bit longer. I guess I kind of trusted him. He didn't have to help. He could have let me battle the Demon and drain my power further before helping.

But he hadn't.

I turned to Othello. She looked both concerned with my presently injured state, and as if she didn't quite trust the Justice before me. I couldn't blame her. Othello wasn't the trusting type, and his people had put me in this position in the first place. She had even advised me to kill them all. Not trusting *or* forgiving.

I opened my mouth to speak, but instead collapsed to my knees, my vision tunneling to a single point on the asphalt as I threw up noisily.

Othello was at my side, rubbing my back with shaky fingers, no doubt scared for me. "Huh. Maybe I have a concussion," I mumbled, looking at the impressive display of regurgitated food and coffee.

"We need to get you to a doctor. This could be bad. No offense, but you've kind of gotten your ass kicked for a few days in a row now," she advised. Gavin laughed at that, but quieted under Othello's glare.

I shook my head slowly, careful not to throw up again. "Ain't nobody got time for that. We have somewhere to be," I said guardedly. Gavin rolled his eyes, but Othello sighed in resignation.

The sound of sirens began to wail in the distance, heading our way. The parents must have called the explosion in. I wasn't about to sit around and attempt to explain what had really happened, so I decided it was time to rabbit. I was fairly confident in the ability of Regulars to apply a totally logical, but incorrect, explanation for the explosion. Despite what some might have actually seen. No one wanted to admit they saw a Demon blow up the evil Girl Scout headquarters. The scorched ring in the pavement from a nearby Thin Mint tugged at my attention. Who knew what was in Thin Mints anyway. Perhaps it really was flammable. Or it was a gateway to another dimension.

The seventh circle of Hell, perhaps.

I was also allegedly kidnapped, and couldn't afford to be discovered wandering the streets with a concussion and a palette of fresh bruises. I motioned for Othello to start the car. She shook her head in resignation. Gavin threw up two fingers as if to say *Deuces*.

I flipped him the bird over my shoulder.

He chuckled, and then disappeared with a loud *crack*, Shadow Walking to wherever he spent his time when not tailing me. Maybe he hung out with the Girl Scouts.

CHAPTER 26

$\mathcal{T}$he massive oaken door to the Armory opened on now familiar creaky hinges. We stepped inside, welcoming the exotic warmth of the place.

Hope's pleasant voice called from the balcony. "Your power is almost gone, my host." Othello gasped, not realizing how rapidly I had been burning through my reserves, and apparently not having taken Gavin's earlier words to heart. She must have thought he had been lying.

I waved Othello's concern away, nodding in resignation to Hope. It was bound to happen sooner or later. Othello knew the stakes I was playing for. "Yes."

"You have many gifts at your disposal that could... even the score. But know that the path you are on is a dangerous one. Before seeking out revenge, dig two graves. Yet you still wish to proceed." Although it hadn't been a question, I nodded. "Even after I have shown you what unchecked rage can do? I fear what happened to the brave Achilles may repeat itself through you." I didn't respond. She studied me thoughtfully, tapping her lip. "Like your *Mardi Gras* festival, there is magic in masks...." she finally continued cryptically.

"Not many choices, and fortune cookie answers don't help," I grumbled.

"Oh, I wouldn't be so sure of that." Seeing that I still didn't understand her implication, she continued. "If you are unwilling to arm yourself with your new arsenal, then death seems the only solution available. Yet, there are many ways to die. To die heroically is honorable. And despite what you may think, death is not always eternal... seeking death has been a favorite repast of many young heroes."

I shivered at that. I wasn't eager to die armed with nothing but a hope for what came next. I also didn't want to die without seeing Indie again. I might not get that option, though. I sensed Othello watching me brood, so shrugged my shoulders. Despite the temptation, I declined Hope's offer. "It would be too dangerous. I don't know what I would be unleashing. The things in here are dangerous. They were put here for a reason."

She smiled, leaning forward, debating like a knowledgeable professor. "Need I remind you that you are now one of those... *things.* Now *you* could be considered dangerous."

I nodded wearily. "Yes. Without my magic, I'm downright terrifying. Speaking of that, what exactly is this Maker ability? Is it separate from my magic? Part of it? If my magic disappears, do I lose this new ability?"

Hope shrugged sadly. "I truly do not know."

I sighed, studying my little playboy Jiminy Cricket, and thinking about what I should do next. Hope met my gaze, refusing to blink, seeming to appreciate my scrutiny for some reason. A new thought struck me. I realized that if I failed, she was stuck here... forever. Since my blood was the Key, she would no longer have a means of escape. She truly wanted to help me, but if I couldn't figure this out, she would be locked up here for eternity. After everything she had done to help me, she was going to be stuck in this Armory. If I died, she would have no way of escaping. I made a decision I hoped I wouldn't regret. But then again, if I failed, the world would be facing Armageddon anyway. What harm could little old Hope cause? "If I die, you're free to go. That is all I can promise you right now, Hope." She continued to meet my gaze for what seemed like an eternity, and then shed a single tear as she bowed her head, overwhelmed with gratitude.

After a few moments, and a few sniffles, she spoke. "But you must meet death for your salvation, Master. It is the only way. Sadly, your death will grant me something I desire more than anything in this world, but know that it will be a bitter achievement. I do not wish you harm, my host, but it is the only way for you to win if you do not arm yourself. Just know that merely dying will not save you. You must meet death at the right time and in the right circumstances," she added sadly, a metaphorical iceberg of deeper meaning in her answer. I didn't know what that iceberg entailed, but I could see it behind her eyes.

So, I laughed.

I couldn't help it. The situation was so utterly ridiculous, I could think of nothing else to do. I knew Othello was growing more concerned by the moment, fearing long-term effects of my concussion, and that only made me laugh harder. I was facing my death. What did I care about a concussion? My laughter subsided after a few minutes and I wiped my eyes, careful not to touch my broken nose. I walked over to the railing and stared out at the harsh landscape stretching as far as the eye could see. I saw no signs of human habitation anywhere. I was alone. I pondered my life. All of it.

My friends. I hoped they were enjoying their vacations. I imagined Ashley's face when Gunnar proposed, and my tears of laughter turned to hot tears of happiness. And regret. I had hoped I would get to be Gunnar's Best Man. Not that I was really Best Man material, but I was confident I had earned it by default. By saving our lives from a silver dragon, at least. Also, I had introduced them. Despite all the chaos of the dragon war, I had inadvertently brought two people together, and they were about to commit to a lifetime together.

Because of me.

I thought of Tory and all the amazing sights she must be seeing with Misha and Raego. Being allowed to enter the home of the Dragon Nation was no small gift. What would it be like? How would she be received? It must have been an amazing experience for her. And she was doing it with the woman she loved. I smiled. I had hooked them up, too. In the middle of the dragon war.

I was a regular Cupid. My smile stretched wider as I imagined myself in boxers covered in hearts, wielding a tiny bow. It was so ridiculous that my smile stretched into a guffaw of laughter. What would Indie say if she saw me dressed like that? She would be beside herself with giggles. Her gorgeous dimples piercing her cheeks as her dazzling white teeth shone beneath her full red lips, just perfect for kissing.

Indie.

I had also managed to find love.

During one of the worst moments of my life.

She was my everything. The source of my strength. She had nursed me back to health after the fight with Alaric. She had encouraged me by giving me the strength to continue fighting when I was broken. She had accepted my demons, my past romances, my obvious flaws, my night terrors, and rather than run screaming, she had stuck it out. Not only that, but she had given me an ultimatum to remove my protective walls or lose her. She didn't want to *run*, she wanted to get *closer*. When everyone else fled, she darted into the thick of things. She was like one of those World War Nurses, diving into the chaos of battle in order to save a single life. She had also taken care of my friends. My shop. My life. She was a *fixer*. Wherever she went, restoration and order seemed to follow. Like her own special kind of magic.

And I would never get to see her again. I dropped my gaze, seriously considering my options. Accept weapons that had been locked away for a very important reason, potentially unleashing dangers that could threaten more innocent lives. Just so I could selfishly get more time with Indie and my friends. But how many would suffer for my decision? And perhaps the thing I took ended up changing me into a monster. I could end up squaring off with Gunnar. If the weapon changed me for the worst, my best friend's fangs and claws would be there to stop me. It was just who he was. I expected nothing else from him. Hell, I would do the same thing.

Or I could die, and let the world continue on as it was.

With a slow movement, I lifted my head and made my decision, suddenly feeling much better. My humor even began to return as I faced Othello and Hope, who were both watching me with curiosity and concern. I smiled softly to them, nodding my head to banish their concern.

"You have come to a conclusion," Hope said.

I nodded. "Quite literally, I'm afraid. I will not take any of the weapons."

Hope's head sagged, and Othello began to cry. "But you will *die*," she sobbed.

I shrugged. "Yes. And apparently, I'm not even allowed to die on my own *terms*. But why should I be given *that* option?" I continued in sarcastic amusement, realizing that the confidence of my decision had eliminated my fear of dying. I felt proud of myself. I would die honorably. "My death will *also* serve a greater good."

I turned to Hope with a smile, easing the pain on her stunningly beautiful face. She nodded with studious respect, like a scientist encountering a creature they've never seen before. But I still had questions for her. If I had to die, I wanted to make sure I took out as many of the bad guys as possible first. But one person above all others.

The summoner.

Before I could formulate a question, my lips moved of their own volition. "Well, I guess I'm finished here." Othello nodded without argument. We left quickly, having other very important things to do. I barely noticed any of our surroundings as we strode through the hallway and back to the large door that stood open before us. We exited hurriedly, stepping back into Temple Industries. Othello was still sobbing softly.

The door closed behind us before we had even realized the spell had forced us to leave. I had been too preoccupied with Hope's news about me dying at the right place and the right time to notice the spell. As the door sealed behind us, I groaned. "God—"

Othello coughed. "Let's hold off on cursing his name. Didn't pan out well last time."

I bit my tongue, nodding begrudgingly.

"So, you gave up." She looked both sad and disappointed at the same time.

I felt a wolfish smile split my face. "Oh, no. *Definitely* not. I've just accepted a very likely outcome. But I won't be going down without one hell of a fight. I'm going to cause such a ruckus dying that Death himself will shake my hand and send me back with a farewell party to get rid of me." Othello's face began to split into a hungry grin. "And I'm going to take as many sons of bitches with me as possible. Angels. Demons. Or Academy wizards. Everyone's on my naughty list. The Boatman is going to have a *very* busy day soon," I growled. She laughed, and I patted her arm reassuringly.

We began to wander towards the exit in silence, and ran into absolutely no one.

Which was odd. People were always working at my company, even on weekends. As the cold air hit me in the face on our way out of an employee side entrance, we realized why.

Helicopters filled the sky, and people were *everywhere*. Sound filled my ears after our peacefully quiet sojourn inside both the Armory and the building. My employees filled the parking lot in droves, some in lab-coats, others in suits. Then there were the cops. It was like the *Mardi Gras* parade was in my parking lot. I instantly hunched lower, hoping to disguise everything about my person, wondering if I should use any of my power to create a disguise so I wasn't caught. Were they here for *me*? Of course they were. Othello's eyes darted back and forth like a feral cat, making sure we hadn't been spotted. But we were relatively alone by the building. It didn't seem that the cops were organizing a raid or anything. In fact, they seemed to be barricading the front doors to the building in an attempt to keep people out, not in... like it was a crime scene. They simply hadn't gotten to our door yet. Or, they had missed it.

My tension at being caught slowly dissipated, my curiosity taking over as I edged closer to the tape, doing my best to remain inconspicuous. It wasn't difficult, thanks to the horde of bodies filling the parking lot.

Then I saw it. And smelled it. Burnt flesh. To me it was obvious, but to everyone else it just looked like a particularly violent hate crime. A vampire was staked to a light pole near the entrance to Temple Industries. I could see the fangs from where I stood, as well as the wooden stake through her heart. And she was smoking lightly. Vampires and sunlight went together as well as dogs and stray cats. One of the cops must have hosed her down at some point, because a puddle of watered down blood pooled at the base of the pole. An artsy, painted card seemed to be pinned underneath the stake. With the size and look of it from this distance, I could only assume it was a Tarot card. Several sets of speakers belted out newscasts, cameras whirling eagerly as each reporter fought to be first to drop the news.

"Another *Mardi Gras* prank, and at Temple Industries, of all places..." A voice boomed on a megaphone, heavy with enunciation on the location. The voice continued on, describing the scene for the world to hear, as well as rehashing my kidnapping and my bookstore being destroyed, her words heavy with curious implication in all the right places. Each call of my name felt like a hammer blow from Thor, the God of Thunder. I groaned, suddenly nervous about my proximity to so many people at such a high-profile event. I motioned Othello to quickly sneak back to our car as nonchalantly as possible. I couldn't be seen here. I saw Greta talking to a reporter and hoped she kept her sighting of me quiet. Why couldn't things ever be easy?

CHAPTER 27

I decided that a meeting with Asterion, the Minotaur, was in order. I literally had no one else to turn to, and the Greek legend was privy to a lot of juicy and arcane information in the magical community. Othello seemed eager to meet the legend in the flesh. I wasn't. I typically didn't receive favorable information when chatting with the 'born again' monster of Greek tragedies.

You see, the Minotaur had recently become a card-carrying Buddhist.

He was obsessed with it. Like all 'saved' members of any flavor of religion.

But hey, At least it was a peaceful choice. He spouted off about Karma, and *blah, blah, blah* a lot, but he wasn't murdering and devouring innocents inside a labyrinth anymore. So, he had that going for him.

As soon as we left Othello's car and entered the pasture proper, I could sense tension in the air. I loosened my shoulders, prepping for a scrap. One never knew, and it wasn't fun to be attacked when your muscles were cold. I felt marginally better after Othello had doctored up my wounds again. None looked infected, but several were concerning. The gash on the back of my head was just a deep scratch. Head wounds always bled fast and hard, but both of us had been nervous about that one. Especially after giving me what I was sure had been a mild concussion. My face felt worse, but as long as I didn't move it too much it was manageable. We continued on, heading more or less to the center of the field where I had first cow-tipped the Minotaur a few months ago... and then dueled him a few days afterwards in exchange for the book on dragons.

We hadn't really dueled *here*. We had instead been teleported to The Dueling Grounds, a place between worlds. I wasn't sure if it was a place one could accidentally walk into, or if Asterion had booked it from the supernatural time-share community. Either way, I wouldn't be pleased if I found myself there, now. I had enough on my plate.

A set of gleaming horns materialized out of nowhere, the only part of the creature visible. I instinctively shoved Othello into the grass and rolled away just as the ivory spears pierced the air where I had been standing. I heard grunts of disappointment from a heavy set of lungs, and clumps of grass and dirt flew into the air as it thundered past me. Then the horns and the hoof prints were gone again, leaving only a heavy silence behind.

"Calm down, you psychopath! Bad Buddhist!" I yelled, eyes darting about wildly. "It's me! Nate Temple!" I held up my hands in surrender, not daring to waste my magic, making sure Othello was out of the danger zone.

The Minotaur's form slowly coalesced into visibility. He towered over us, a full two feet taller or more, and heavily corded with muscle. A set of Buddhist prayer beads hung from an impressive set of hairy pectoral muscles. It was like he had been formed out of pure testosterone. "Ye' can't be Master Temple. He's a wizard, and ye' barely have a drip of magic about you."

"I cow-tipped you a few months ago. Then I beat you in a duel," I said with a dry smile, more confident that we weren't about to be suddenly skewered. Othello's ears seemed to be falling off her head in amazement as she climbed to her feet. Here I was, almost gored by a monster, and she was admiring him like a groupie. Luckily for her, she hadn't fallen into a cow patty. Would have served her right.

Asterion stiffened, then his shoulders bunched up arrogantly. He smirked at Othello. "Not how I remember it," he told her. "He beat me in a childish game. But he did earn my respect in the duel." Then he turned to me. "Gods be damned. Why are you practically without magic? Last time we met, you had too much and couldn't contain it all. Now you have almost none? Can't you find a middle ground like other wizards? Zen is the answer. Balance—" I cut him off with a rude gesture.

"Later. I don't want to have to kill you out of frustration."

"You wouldn't want that kind of Karma," he stated matter-of-factly.

See? I told you he did that. *Karma, karma, karma. Blah, blah, blah.*

I sighed in resignation. "Karma will just have to stand in line. I'm pretty sure God himself has damned me." Asterion's brow furrowed curiously. He remained silent, sensing my impatience. "I have questions for you. As you can see, I'm at the end of my rope. Oh, this is Othello. A great cyber warrior." The Minotaur appraised her with a newfound respect. Othello's eyes widened. She was blushing for crying out loud. "Groupie," I muttered.

She shot a brief scowl my way in answer. "Warrior, eh?" Asterion asked, studying her from head to toe.

"World famous," I elaborated.

The Minotaur smiled. "Honored to meet you, warrior. No disrespect, but I wouldn't have guessed it. Welcome to my domain. Now, why don't you start at the beginning, Temple?"

So, I told him. Everything. He would need all the details if he was going to help me. His eyes widened as I continued, shaking his massive head in disbelief. "So, to sum it up. If I do as the Academy commands, the Demons will obliterate me and kill more innocent supernatural citizens in the process. If I do as the Demons want, Heaven and the Academy will obliterate me. If I do as the Angels want, I'll never get revenge on my parents' murderer, the Greater Demon, Sir Dreadsalot. And the Demons or the Academy will still obliterate me. In summary, I will be obliterated. Unless I find the right time, place, and method to die, in which case I will somehow apparently have a chance to survive this whole mess, which makes no sense. I don't understand how dying grants me a chance at survival, let alone winning."

"Where did you hear such a ridiculous thing?" Asterion blurted.

"From Hope. In the Armory. She's some kind of memory construct or librarian. She's the one who told me that I'm a Maker." The Minotaur stiffened at the phrase, taking a cautious step away from me. Huh. I continued. "That my parents experimented on me. That's why I was juiced up on power last time we met. Apparently, you've heard of one before. That's good, because I haven't. Explain it to me, because no one else seems able or willing to do so."

"But your power is almost gone..." I nodded. The Minotaur grew a thoughtful expression, causing me to arch a brow with the obvious question to elaborate. "A Maker is limited only by his own creativity. His imagination is his palette. Magic is nothing compared to it. Used to be more common than a wizard, but *respected.*" He emphasized the last word. "They've designed things for the most dangerous of creatures. Like a supernatural blacksmith, in crude terms. More respected than the vermin who carry the wizard title these days…"

I blinked as Othello burst out laughing. "Ha. Ha. So, how do I use it?"

Asterion shrugged. "Never met one, personally. Regardless, I wouldn't begin to know how to teach you to use it. I don't even know if it's possible without magic. Even though a Maker is something more than a wizard, I've never heard of a Maker *not* being a wizard. I think they *created* wizards."

Of course it wasn't that easy, I chided myself. I chose a different topic. "Angels and Demons are involved. I thought that was … illegal or something."

Asterion smiled wickedly. "Seen any Heavenly glows? Wings saving the day? Gateways to Hell?" I shook my head in obvious frustration, having already told him the recent events. "They're using pawns. Demons, not the Fallen; Nephilim, not Angels, would be my guess."

"Well, that's not entirely true… I think I hurt an Angel pretty bad last night. Or they think I hurt him. It was really the Demon attacking me that almost shattered his Grace. I was holding it at the time. He told me that if his Grace were destroyed that I would kick off Armageddon. Then he called the Nephilim after me." I patted my pocket, where I had stowed the Grace in an unused pen case.

Asterion flinched, scanning the skies, as if searching for Angels, motioning for me to keep the Grace away from him. "A Demon could not destroy a Grace. They could harm it, but not destroy it. Remember, cat's paws. That would break the Covenants."

"The Covenants that keeps everyone in line? The Covenants that everyone seems to be ignoring lately?" Asterion nodded. I shrugged. "Well, the Angel didn't see it that way. He attacked me, thinking I was with the Demons and that I had killed his son, a Nephilim boy named Jonathan."

Asterion froze. "Wait a moment. An Angel *struck* you? Are you telling me that you just kicked off Armageddon?"

I frowned. "I don't think so. Possibly. I'm not sure."

"Funny, because if the Angels think you killed one of their Nephilim, and severely injured one of their brethren, then the first domino has been knocked over, and Armageddon is here. *Now.*" I stared back, unable to speak for a few moments. "But it's not. Everything seems the same as yesterday." He said, considering the situation. "I would appreciate it if you protected that Grace. Strenuously." He warned with a meaningful gaze.

"Sure, but it's spilled milk at this point. Why wouldn't the big guy stop them?"

"He can't. He'll let the Riders sort it out if anyone crosses the line."

"The Riders," I growled. "You mean—"

"Yes. The Horsemen. Of the Apocalypse. They're black ops at the moment, not unlike your own unruly band of misfits, but when they make an appearance, I guarantee you the world will notice. They know how to make an entrance... or is it example?" He furrowed a caterpillar unibrow. "I guess either works."

"Are the Riders good or bad?"

Asterion pondered that, tapping a meaty thumb on his massive, runed nose ring. I winced. It looked painful. "Neither. Both. Who knows? Only one way to find out. The eternal way."

"Mention of the Riders keeps popping up, but I don't know much about them."

"Well, to wax poetic for a moment, there are four of them, obviously. Death, War, Famine, and Pestilence. Their ultimate job is to cast their powers onto the world, destroying life in vast swaths if the Covenants are ever broken. Until that time, they are considered judges. They keep a tight rein on both sides, Heaven and Hell. Whoever kicks off Armageddon loses a significant amount of potential power, which would hurt in the upcoming War, so neither wants to be the one to ignite it. That's why they use cat's paws, in an effort to toe the line and hopefully cause the other side to break the Covenants first. But you're telling me that you almost kicked off Armageddon, which would mean that neither side loses power. Interesting. A paranoid person would not think that a coincidence..." he added.

"Wouldn't their very involvement signal the end of days?"

The Minotaur shook his shaggy head. "Not exactly. Like I said, they are judges. If either party – Angel or Demon – breaks the Covenants they are tried by the Horsemen. If a resolution can be attained, then the world goes on. If not, then... it doesn't. There haven't been many needs for their judgment, if you know what I mean... Both parties stay well clear of that line, neither one wanting to take the first shot that ends up kicking off Armageddon. There have been instances, less than a handful, when Armageddon *almost* happened, but from what I hear, the Riders found a peaceful resolution. I guess that has to be true or we would not be, well... *existing* right now. There are always times when Demons get close to the line, or Angels swoop in and save someone they shouldn't have, but so far, those occurrences have been judged, and deemed wanting. The Riders dealt out the punishment, and life went on."

The silence grew, Othello watching me curiously. Asterion finally spoke, facing the night pensively. "I'm more curious about this elusive little librarian sprite who seems to live in the Armory. Who is she?"

"I think she's magically bonded to the Armory, in an effort to guard the cache of dangerous powers hidden away."

Asterion suddenly turned back to face me, his face tight. "What did she say her name was?"

I frowned. "She didn't say. I just called her Hope. My parents nicknamed the room Pandora Protocol, so I gave her a moniker. *Hope,* for the last gift inside Pandora's Box."

"Oh, shit in Zeus' beard. You've got to be *kidding* me. As if you didn't have enough on your plate. You're telling me that you've been talking to—" Asterion suddenly stopped talking, mouth opening wordlessly in a fruitless attempt to finish his sentence. He looked as if he had just been struck in the forehead. Like he wasn't *able* to finish his sentence. He finally regained use of his mouth, but his words sounded scripted. "I am terribly sorry, but you must leave. Now."

Sensing my frustration, Othello stood. I knew that if Asterion couldn't even speak, I was out of luck. He wanted to tell me. But he couldn't. Of course not. Why would the lonely wizard discover the one thing he needed out of this meeting? Asterion looked torn, but waved a goodbye, and disappeared, head hanging low.

Apparently, Hope was more than I had initially thought. Someone dangerous for some reason.

And... I had just promised her freedom after my death.

At least I hadn't told Asterion that part. Judging by his reaction to her very *existence,* he might have had a heart attack at discovering she would soon be *free.* What had I done? It wasn't like I could rescind my offer. I had already been to the Armory today, so wouldn't be able to go back until tomorrow, which would be too late. Tomorrow was day three. My power would be gone, and possibly my ability to even enter the Armory. I didn't even know if I would be alive or have any power left to give up when the Academy arrived. I might not even be able to give them the Armory if I wanted to. We made our way back to the car and drove back to the apartment in brittle silence. It was late, and I had a lot to think about.

CHAPTER 28

*a*s we pulled up to the apartment, I spotted a lot of party revelers in the street. We weren't in a ritzy part of town, so the neighborhood was a little hectic with *Mardi Gras* in full swing. Not as bad as it would be tomorrow, but a lot of pre-gaming going on. Our drive back had been silent, Othello sensing my need for silence as I tried to determine my next course of action. She found a parking spot and we climbed out.

As we were walking back to the apartment, I noticed something out of place and snatched Othello's hand, halting her. A Girl Scout stood before us, tapping her foot impatiently, holding out a box of cookies as she watched us from beside a parked car. Then I saw that her eyes were red. And a blade was sticking out of her chest. The dagger looked slightly familiar. This kid was already dead. The Demon had possessed the corpse of a Girl Scout. Jesus.

"You've got to be *kidding* me. A Girl Scout? I *told* you they consorted with Demons!"

Othello smacked my arm with a glare. "I was a Girl Scout, Nate."

The Demon child was smiling at me with buckteeth. "Isn't it past your bedtime?" I asked. Her smile evaporated as she crossed her arms. "I'll give you one chance to answer honestly before I exorcise your ugly ass from that child, Demon. *Why. Are. You. Here?*"

Her girly voice was disarming, but her actual words had the opposite

225

effect. "Causing Chaos, of course. Death. Mayhem. It's what I do." She didn't mention the Armory at all. Which didn't make any sense. Was Gavin right? Were these Demons just pawns? A distraction?

"Your boss, Sir Dreadsalot, said he's here for a different reason. The Greater Demon's stink was all over my company. I know that's why you're really here. He told me so. Know anything about that or do I need to remind you what hanging in chains over the pits of Hell is like? It is past your curfew after all."

The Demon stomped her foot, and the asphalt crumbled to ash, the smell of sulfur permeating the street in a sickening wave. Well, she was juiced up. Not just a petty Demon, but something much more powerful. "You dare speak of the Great Lord and pretend to know what we have endured?! I already told you—" She bit her tongue suddenly, as if having said too much.

My arms pebbled. Wait... this was the same Demon from the warehouse earlier? I *knew* I had recognized the dagger. It was *mine*. I had cast it at her before Gavin had banished her. But... That meant Gavin hadn't banished her, or she had made the fastest return trip from Hell ever.

"Shall I show you just how weak you are, mortal? I can feel your power dripping away like the blood of a stuck pig. It pleases me... makes me thirsty. Let me show you what it feels like to exercise your baser instincts like we do. It's *fun*." Her eyes glittered with malevolent glee.

An orb of... dark nothingness in the shape of a giant Thin Mint slammed into my chest before I could react. I instantly realized that the Academy's curse had removed my innate ability to nullify a Demon's mind control. She wasn't able to possess me, but it was close enough.

Which was a tad alarming.

I sensed my well of ever-present rage building to a crescendo as the Demon fed it like gas over a flame. I wanted the Demons to burn. I wanted the Academy to burn. I wanted the Angels to burn. I wanted her boss, the summoner, to burn.

I wanted... the *world* to burn.

A nearby car had parked over the dividing line, taking up two spots. It suddenly exploded as I flung a boiling ball of fire at it, using my dwindling magic to ignite the fuel tank. The Demon chuckled, and Othello shouted in alarm. I scouted the street, searching for something else to destroy in order to sate my rage.

I blew off the side of a building with another ball of fire where flashing lights and loud music was bothering me. Some kind of house party. I was tired. How was I supposed to sleep with that racket next door? The music stopped instantly and I could hear screaming and shouting. All I could feel was *need*. *Sensation*. My baser instincts. The ones you have to constantly battle on a daily basis.

A small part of me, in the back of my mind, railed against the power of the Demon, furiously trying to escape, attempting to think my way out of my dilemma. This might not seem like a big deal, but when you have the power of a wizard, you can typically destroy anything that gets in your way. Regulars didn't have this kind of power. If a loud neighbor annoyed them, they would have to consider storming the house of partiers to silence the music by hand, no doubt igniting the wrath of the partiers, and starting a fight. They would have to call the cops about the illegally parked car and hope the police had nothing better to do.

But being a wizard? Those annoyances were somewhat... *easier* to solve.

Like just destroying them from a hundred feet away with balls of fire.

"See how pleasant impulsive instincts can be? No morality. No consequences. Just *desire*," the Girl Scout cooed, clutching her box of cookies and gingerly plucking one out to lick with an extremely long black tongue. That would haunt me forever. I just knew it.

I knew the only way to overwhelm the Demon's hold on me was to override my senses with a different emotion entirely, but I was fresh out of *nice* emotions. I had faced too much hardship lately, and I was full of anger and fury...

Like Achilles.

Othello was screaming something, which started to annoy me. I slowly turned to face her, ready to silence her, too. She was gripping my arm, shaking me, which was even *more* annoying. She saw the look in my eyes and paled. My brain threatened to shut down at the realization that I was about to murder a friend because she was bothering my destructive intentions, and that I couldn't stop myself from performing the deed. Then, she did something totally unexpected as I prepared to incinerate her forever.

She tackled me to the ground, briefly pressing her ample chest into my face. Then her tongue filled my mouth. My mind shattered.

I *needed* companionship, my baser instincts whispered to me. My brain, however, began to whisper a name. *Indie*. Over and over again.

The guilt made me begin to struggle, realizing this wasn't what I wanted, and that Othello was making me angry again. As if sensing my distraction, and that her ruse wasn't working, she ripped her freaking top off, and my hands instantly found her breasts in greedy handfuls. Then we began to make out.

Violently. Like we were possibly the last two people in existence. Mad Max style.

I lost all mental cognition for an indeterminable amount of time as passion fueled my veins. Memories of long nights and late mornings with Othello filled my mind. I could sense that Othello was enjoying her sacrifice. The Demon's frustrated hiss startled me out of my fantasy.

I heard cheering on the other side of the street and managed to dodge Othello's lips for a desperately-needed breath. Her starving lips found my earlobe instead, making my hands instinctively squeeze her rear end in a death grip, which she also didn't seem to mind, because she moaned encouragingly. I managed to spot the source of the chanting. The group from the building I had attacked was now in the street. Many were pointing at the building and crying, but a group of Frat boys were pointing at me and yelling enthusiastically. The Demon had disappeared, most likely fearing the attention of the mortals. It wasn't every day one saw a Girl Scout with a dagger protruding from her chest.

The group continued to hoot and holler me on, snapping pictures with their phones, and beads began pelting us like mortar shells. "Yeah! That is one hardcore make out session, white-collar man! Look at the car burning behind them. Tits like that would make me ignore a burning car too. Yeah! Ride her, man!" The words caused me to flinch for some reason, dousing my passion like a cold shower. I didn't know why, but the words scared the shit out of me, and without the Demon present, the mind control was gone. "Ride her!" A voice bellowed again.

I gently but forcefully pried Othello's arms from my neck. She was panting, and her eyes were slightly glazed over as if the Demon had been controlling her also. "Othello. Stop," I commanded. She managed to snap out of it with slow resignation, her eyes returning to normal. With a start at the crowd, she leaned back and pulled her shirt back over her head. It was torn, but she held it closed before her, looking embarrassed. I managed one last look at her glorious décolletage.

She began to stammer out a defense. "It was all I could think of. She kept talking about baser instincts, and I thought – I *hoped* – that I might be able to distract you with an altogether different instinct." She looked terribly guilty, but silently pleased at the same time. "I'm sorry."

I shook my head, climbing to my feet. "As guilty as I feel right now, I think you saved our lives." I told her softly. "I couldn't control myself." I didn't tell her what had my heart hammering out of my chest.

I had used up the last of my magic. I felt drained. Empty. Powerless. And I hadn't solved anything. The next time I saw the Academy I was going to castrate them. Individually. With a spoon. I had liked that way too much, which made me angrier. What the hell kind of boyfriend was I? Indie had been out of town for a few days and I had been *all over* Othello. Of course, I hadn't been able to control myself, and I *had* imagined it was Indie… hadn't I? I shook my head, storming off to the loft. Othello followed me in silence.

I tried to light a flame on my fingertips as I stormed away. All that happened was a searing pain stabbing my eyes. "Shit…" I gasped, grabbing the back of my head. Too late, I remembered my wound and flinched in pain all over again. I shook it off after a few steps, Othello watching me the entire way, but saying nothing. The words from the drunk kids still pressed on my mind, prodding for me to catch their relevance. Why had they caught my attention? "Ride her…" It must just be my guilt over Indie getting to me.

We entered the apartment, and collapsed into the same bed, each of us too tired to move. "Othello?"

"Yes?" she murmured tiredly.

"I'm in love with Indie. That won't change. I'm sorry about what happened, and I feel horrible. For both of you. I'm a crap guy."

I glanced at her, spotting a single tear as she nodded. "We had our time together, Pharos. Did you never wonder why I called you Pharos? Other than the magic reference about shedding light on darkness? A lighthouse does have a certain phallic reference, does it not?" She winked seductively, making me blush. I turned away, closing my eyes to escape the torment. Should I tell Indie? Should I keep it a secret? I had no idea. I opened my eyes long enough to text Indie and tell her I loved her. I set my phone on the table and closed my eyes again. My thoughts spiraled to nothing, not even caring what was going to happen tomorrow with my magic now gone.

My dreams were odd. Battles with Demons, being cast down to Hell, God judging me before all the citizens of Heaven. My parents were there, shaking their heads guiltily, as if ashamed to be related to me. In fact, I even had a dream about me sleeping next to Othello. In the dream, my phone rang. Othello answered it tiredly. "Mmmm? No, you don't have the wrong number. He's sleeping, love. We've had a long day and are both *reaaallly* tired. You know how exhausting he can be. Call back in the morning when we've woken up." She hung up.

I started, realizing it hadn't been a dream. Othello put my phone on her side of the bed, rolling over to go back to sleep. "Who was that?" I asked.

"Gunnar," she murmured tiredly.

"Oh, I'll call him later. Wait. I need to call Indie!" I reached for the phone, but Othello shoved it under the covers. I instinctively reached for it and realized Othello was gloriously naked. When had *that* happened? My breath returned to normal when I realized that I was still clothed. She arched a brow at me. My hands jumped back as if bitten. She grinned in amusement. "It's all yours," she teased. I scowled and she rolled her eyes. "Joking. It's late, Nate. She will no doubt be pissed at such a late call. She's probably spent all day at the hospital and you'll do her no favors by bothering her at such a stressful time."

I nodded in resignation. "Yeah, you're right. First thing in the morning, then." I rolled back to my side and passed out. I didn't even know what I would say to her when we spoke, but I needed to be on my game, which meant sleep was paramount.

Othello felt very warm beside me…

CHAPTER 29

I had woken up with my panties in a wad. The slow-motion replay of Othello and I making out in the street had repeated in my mind all night as I slept, filling me to the brim with guilt. After several hundred replays, I had fixated on the cheers from the frat guys on the sidelines. Listening to it again and again, feeling a punch of guilt to the gut with each repetition. *"Ride her. Ride her. Rideher. Rideher. Rider."* I had woken up with a start, the words filling my mind with a severe sensation of anxiety.

Rider.

Of *course!*

I slapped my forehead in frustration and almost shrieked out loud at the orchestra of pain it caused the rune branded there, and the resulting ripples of agony it caused my broken nose, alongside the pounding headache from the several cranial rebounds my head had taken lately.

I survived all of this in silence, careful not to wake Othello, because I'm courteous like that.

After regaining my sanity, I realized I was hungry. I couldn't remember the last time I had eaten. I had gotten used to my unique ability of not needing to eat as much as other wizards. We magical beings typically needed to maintain our nutrition pretty strictly, as it directly fueled our power. But thanks to my parents transferring their magic to me upon their deaths – or them granting the ability of a Maker into me – I hadn't needed to follow such a strict diet. But now that I was without magic entirely, I was *famished*. Seemed backwards to me, but I shrugged in resignation. Othello was still asleep, so I dressed quietly and went downstairs in search of some grub.

Today was day three, and my power was completely gone. I was, for all intents and purposes, a Regular. But other than a deep panic, I didn't feel any different. I mean, I had expected to maybe not sense as much as I usually did. As if I would suddenly enter a world that resembled a black and white television. But that wasn't the case. The world around me was more or less the same. *I* was the one who had changed. That made me feel marginally better, realizing that I wouldn't be facing the nostalgia of missing sensations every time I stepped outside from here on out. The world would keep on keeping on, more or less the same. I simply didn't have magic anymore. The world was still a beautiful, chaotic, little slice of craziness. I could live with that. Piles of snow lined the sidewalk, belying the fact that someone had shoveled the path since the most recent flurries. It was still icy, slushy, and dirty, but it was mostly clear.

I still had the feather in a pen case in my pocket. I pulled it out, contemplating what lay inside before pocketing it again. An idea came to me, but I let it age a bit as I walked down the street in silence. Hardly anyone else was outside at the moment, and I had the street to myself. Like those harmless little old senior citizens that woke up before sunrise to go for a walk. Which wasn't too far away from describing my weakened state. A few days ago, I had been a wizard. A billionaire. A celebrity. But now I was just a penniless fugitive without any allies or power. I was about as dangerous as a duckling. That sobered me. As if on cue, I saw an octogenarian round the corner before me. He sported a World War II Veteran baseball cap and moved with the aid of a walker, complete with tennis balls on the legs nearest his feet. Feeling a kindred spirit in the squat, little old man, I spoke. "Thank you for your service, sir," I offered, smiling politely as he neared.

He slammed one leg of the walker on my toe in annoyance at my taking up too much space, and then shuffled past me with a grunt and a curse. It hadn't hurt me, but I realized I was frozen stiff, staring after the man in disbelief. Maybe he was hard of hearing.

I shrugged it off and continued on, tapping my lips in thought as I walked, enjoying the crisp smell of fresh snow on the ground. With nothing else to do, and not eager to be looking over my shoulder for threats all day, I decided to speed things up. Flick the first domino, so to speak.

So, I decided to summon Eae. Why not? I was powerless. I might as well let them know they didn't need to destroy a city block to kill the harmless wizard. Even little old men weren't too terribly afraid of me at the moment. I wanted to save the Nephilim the trouble of hunting me down.

It began to snow big fat flakes of heavy precipitation, and I suddenly wished I would have checked the weather before leaving the apartment. How hard was it supposed to snow today? I shrugged. Did it really matter? My fight wasn't the type to get snowed out. Gathering my coat about my shoulders, I ducked into an alley for shelter and privacy.

Since I had no magic, I simply prayed over the broken feather in a darkened alley. It was a unique experience for me, not being particularly religious before now. Oh well, what was one more blasphemy? Finished, I attempted to walk into a delicious looking deli and promptly head-butted the solid wooden door. I crumpled to the ground, seeing stars, panting heavily from the numerous ripples of pain caused by my skull striking the door, reminding me of my too many head injuries and more than likely concussion. Maybe I shouldn't be outside unsupervised. I sat there, feeling sorry for myself, allowing the pain to fade away naturally before I stood up. The *closed* sign hanging on the door mocked me as I sat there like a vagrant. After a few seconds, I shambled to my feet and managed to put one foot in front of the other until I was more or less walking again. Luckily, no one else was on the street. I found another deli, and much more carefully, read the sign before trying to barge in. It was a health food shop. They specialized in sandwiches and smoothies. I wasn't particularly picky at this point. My stomach grumbled loudly.

After looking at the menu for a few minutes, I smiled. Then I ordered a pork sandwich, just to spite the Angel. I was fresh out of fucks to give.

The waiter came to my table a few minutes later with a steaming sandwich and I grinned. I lifted the sandwich to my maw and took a huge bite. The restaurant instantly grew silent. I looked up to see that everyone was frozen solid. I sighed, thinking about setting my sandwich down, then shook my head. I took another huge bite of blasphemous deliciousness as Eae entered the building, spotted me, and approached the table. "Thish ish delishus. Want shum?" I held out the sandwich to him. He slapped it out of my hand. Where it fell open into a messy pile on the table.

I scowled at him, chewing even slower, taking my time as I carefully reassembled the sandwich.

"Give me the Grace, wizard," he threatened. I finished building my sandwich in silence and looked up at him, unconcerned. His eyes abruptly widened and he took a step back in disbelief. Then his face slowly morphed into a predatory smile. "Wait. You're *powerless?* Praise the Lord. How foolish are you?" he asked, genuinely stunned. "Do you not realize what you have done? You have called your executioner directly to your door when you hold no weapon."

"Oh, I've got a weapon. Put your hand in my pocket and see for yourself." I smiled innocently. "But be careful. It bites." I was referring to the Grace, but I loved toying with him.

His glare was indignant, but I'd already accepted my fate. I sat there watching him in silence. "You slew my son, and then dare summon me with my fractured Grace? I will destroy you." He looked noticeably weakened to my eyes, as if the fractured Grace had hurt him. Badly. Either that or he had gone on a twenty-four-hour bender.

"No, you won't. You're not allowed." I reached over and picked up my sandwich, taking another bite. "And for the last time. I didn't slay Jonathan. The Demon you killed did that all by himself. Before he was killed, Jonathan said my partner, Othello, was honorable. He believed her, and wouldn't turn a weapon against her. Ask her if you think I'm a liar."

Eae fumed. "There is a reason we command the Nephilim. They are not without their... flaws. They are half-human after all. Just because he trusted your associate does not mean I will make the same mistake. I see the Rune on your forehead, after I specifically warned you to stay out of it. Remember, when the trumpet sounds your final hour, that you brought this on yourself."

I continued chewing my sandwich unconcernedly. He cocked his head, studying me for a secret ploy of some kind. "I will dispatch more Nephilim to hunt you down. If you survive, the Riders will sort you out," he finally added. I still didn't let any concern show, taking another bite. I chewed it slowly before swallowing, licking my lips in satisfaction.

"You sure you don't want some? It's quite excellent." Eae's weathered face purpled, the hidden wings tucked under his coat twitching in agitation. I shrugged. "Perhaps there's an alternative. The Demons want me to hand over something that is too dangerous for me to provide. You commanded me to back off the investigation. Then you attacked me, without knowing all the facts. After sending your little children after a full-fledged badass. That didn't turn out so well for them, did it? I didn't want to hurt anyone. Hell, I didn't think I could! The Demons won't let me back off. Your people won't let me solve the problem. My own people seem eager to kill me either way. As you noticed, they cursed me, taking my power, because they also want the Armory, and now I have no way to help *any* party. I'm in a tight spot."

Eae merely stared at me. "None of that is our concern. As you so wisely said, I can't get directly involved. So, follow your orders if you value your life."

"You see, Eae, I'm not too good at following orders. I get confused easily." He shook his head in displeasure, preparing to stand and end the conversation. "Just curious, since I'm pretty much screwed anyway, what is the end game? What could the summoner want so badly that he'd resort to summoning Demons to get it? *I'm* not even sure of the inventory of the place, so how the hell does anyone else know?" He didn't answer me. "Someone told me that the only way out of the curse is for me to meet my death at a specific time and place. I fail to see how death would help me remove my curse. Because, you know, the whole *death* part. Maybe my heart just needs to stop for a few seconds, and then be revived again?" I thought out loud.

Eae scowled down at me with judging eyes, seeming curious, but also like he was holding something back from me. "From what I understand of magic, something so simple wouldn't meet the requirements. Where does this talk of death removing the curse come from?"

I ignored that last question, fearing I had given up too much. "I'm being boxed in on all sides because of you and your fallen brothers, Eae. At least call off your dogs. I'm on my last legs here. Surely you don't fear me that much. Let me die swinging. Or help me to understand the bigger picture."

He bristled righteously. "I won't do that without proof of your innocence. At this point, I doubt even I could think of sufficient proof that you are innocent. My brothers are... upset with you." He smiled. "Oh, and speaking of my *dogs*... you were warned. Here come my nephews to destroy you and collect my Grace." Then he simply disappeared.

The windows suddenly blew inwards, and three human-shaped blurs pounced on me, tackling me into the counter of the restaurant. My head struck the bar, and a lance of pain sunk into my side before I could even complete my whiplash.

I was positive the blade had been dipped in molten lava beforehand. Warmed up especially for me. I could smell burnt flesh and fresh blood.

Then another one slammed into my leg.

Then my arm.

Each stab seemed hotter than the first, and each too fast for me to even scream, but the pain struck deep into my soul as if driven by a spiritual hammer. I was shocked at the raw violence of the attack, my impotence, and the potential life-threatening nature of the wounds. Three stab wounds to major appendages and organs in less than thirty seconds was downright psychopathic. Or was meant to send a message. Godfather style.

Heh. Puns.

I had never been powerless before. It was sobering. Scratch that. *Horrifying*. And my mind threatened to shatter, running away screaming to the depths of my psyche in order to avoid the scalding explosion of pain. My pocket was abruptly and neatly sliced open, and the pen case with Eae's Grace was extracted. One of the Nephilim kicked me where I had been stabbed, then spat on me for good measure. I could barely even keep my eyes open, panting in staggering bouts of agony.

When I managed to open my eyes, they were gone.

I took a few minutes to press my shirt into the wounds on my side and arm, hoping to slow the blood flow. I clumsily untied my belt and tied a makeshift tourniquet. I almost screamed when I pulled it tight, my entire leg throbbing. After a few moments, I was able to slow my breathing and look down. It hadn't struck an artery. I sighed in relief.

They had beaten me, stabbed me, robbed me, and left me for dead in a health food deli. And these were the *good* guys. But I refused to die in a sandwich shop. No matter how good their pork was. I managed to climb to all fours, and began crawling towards the door. My injured leg more or less dragged uselessly behind me, and I had a brief vision of me pretending to be a zombie. I was careful not to bump into anything, fearful of how pleasant it would feel. The occupants of the room were still frozen so that I was the only somewhat mobile creature in a world of statues. It was probably for the best. I didn't know how the hell I would manage to get out of here if anyone had seen the attack, or worse, if they had realized who I was. The notorious Nate Temple. The Archangel. The local billionaire playboy. The alleged *wizard*. The man wanted by the FBI, who had reportedly been kidnapped for a ransom the likes St. Louis had never seen before. If only they could see the quivering mass of shame that was the true Nate Temple, now. I was thankful that they couldn't see my pitiful state. I almost made it to the door before a thought struck me. I slowly turned around and began crawling back to the table, realizing I had left a long bloody smear in my wake. Like a zombie slug.

I reached into a back pocket, pulled out my wallet, and left a twenty-dollar bill on the table. I had snagged it from Othello's purse before leaving the apartment. It was the only cash I had to my name. The waiter had been nice, and he would probably have a lot of explaining to do after this. What with the store in shambles, the windows shattered, and a trail of blood crisscrossing the floor. Maybe Karma would remember my act.

As I exited the building, I realized that the street was still empty, but more snow had fallen while I had been inside, which would make my trip back even more difficult that it was already going to be. I couldn't imagine crawling that far. I would simply give up halfway and lie down, only to be trampled by the grumpy old war veteran when he returned. I leaned against the doorframe and slowly pulled myself to my feet, placing all my weight on my one good leg. After a few agonizing moments of leaning back against the door, breathing heavily, and expecting another gang of Nephilim to come finish me off, I decided to begin moving. I took off my coat and held it in a clenched fist at my side and began to shuffle slowly back to the apartment. At least I had gotten a few bites out of the sandwich before getting my ass officially smited.

I was careful to scuff up my trail behind me with my coat dragging behind me, as I would have left a quite obvious bloody smear all the way back to the apartment otherwise. After a few minutes of painstakingly concealing my tracks, I heard the first screams from the deli as time returned to normal. Eae's spell had lifted, and any second a gang of Regulars would be fleeing the deli in terror. I rounded the corner and stumbled along as fast as possible. I needed to get gone.

To where, I had no idea. But I wasn't about to go to jail.

CHAPTER 30

*O*thello ignored the tears streaming down her face as she used a medical kit left behind by her crew of shady mercenaries to doctor me up. Her hands were shaking as she suppressed sobs of concern, rage, and fear. "You just went to grab some food! Why didn't you wake me up? How the hell does a hit-squad of Nephilim find you in a deli?"

"I'm just lucky, I guess." I mumbled, trying to ignore the pain from her stitches. Her eyes weighed me. But she knew me too well.

"What did you do?"

I fidgeted. She poked me with the needle, a murderous gleam in her eyes. "Ow! What the hell? I'm injured!"

"Start talking. I can make this take a long time, each stitch could take a full twenty seconds if I really wanted to be careful." She poked me with the needle again.

"Fine! Fine! I summoned the Angel, Eae."

"*What?*" she roared, jumping to her feet, storming back into the kitchen and waving her hands around like a crazy person before finally rounding on me again. "Why in the *hell* would you do that?"

I sagged back into the couch, glad that she hadn't pricked me again. "I figured it was worth a shot. We need help. Answers. Regardless, it didn't pan out. He called his Nephilim on me. They beat me, stabbed me, and then took the Grace back. I'm not sure if that means they are out of the picture or not, but with my luck, probably not."

She came back over and resumed her stitching, more gently this time. "These look like they were partly cauterized." She said, studying the wound.

"Yeah. Felt like it, too. Not pleasant. Old Testament brutality with a hint of the New Testament love."

"But they're still bleeding. It would have been better if they had been completely cauterized."

I shivered. "I see what you're saying, but it hurt plenty enough without adding an extra two-hundred-degrees to what already felt like lava." She grunted noncommittally as she worked. I continued to talk, needing a sounding board. "I guess our next option is to see if Gavin will help us out. He doesn't seem like he's one hundred percent in cahoots with the Academy. Either that or summon Sir Dreadsalot to make a deal."

"I don't trust Gavin," Othello said instantly. I arched a brow, barely flinching as she poked me again to sew up my leg.

"You trust a Demon more than Gavin?" I asked in disbelief. The fire in her eyes made me back down. "Well, to be fair, I don't trust *anybody*." Her eyes twinkled angrily. "Except you. But it's not about trust anymore. We need *help*. I'm running on fumes," I lied. I couldn't tell her that I was helpless. Yet. "We have to stop this. I don't have a choice. It started out with me trying to find my parents' murderer, but now that I've entered the game, I can only leave by death. Hell, I can only *win* through my death, apparently," I growled.

Her eyes were sad, torn. "Still. Gavin's hiding something."

"Everyone is hiding something," I snapped. "At least he's helped us out a few times. Kind of. Like with that Demon yesterday." Before I could continue, Othello interrupted me.

"You mean the Demon that reappeared to attack us and turn you into a psychopath shortly after he supposedly banished it?"

I nodded. "I know. I'm as curious about that as you. Probably more. But it *is* possible that the summoner called the Girl Scout back from Hell to attack us again outside the apartment."

Othello rolled her eyes. "Sure, with your dagger still in her heart. She had a hard-on for you, Nate. I don't think the Fallen Angels would send her back up to earth with a major injury. It seems like our Gavin might not be such a White Hat..." she whispered the last words, looking curiously introspective for some reason. "This looks bad, Nate." She gestured at the wounds. "You need to get these checked out. By a professional."

"No time. Just doctor me up as best you can. I'm supposed to die anyway. Why not go out with a story like this? Would look good on my tombstone." Othello stood up, a storm of emotions crossing her face in the blink of an eye – guilt, sadness, anger, remorse, and determination. I gripped her hand reassuringly, which only seemed to make her feel worse.

"It wasn't supposed to be like this. I was supposed to come *save* you," she sobbed softly, seeming to break down. I patted her shoulder comfortingly in understanding.

"You did good, kid. Not your fault we're up against the heaviest of hitters."

She seemed to regain her composure after a few moments. "Well, I'm not giving up, even if you are. Rest. Contemplate how much of an idiot you are for trusting Gavin. I'm heading to Temple Industries with your Demon-sensing artifact. See if I can spot any of the foul bastards. Maybe find your new buddy, Gavin, lurking around so I can kill him. Slowly."

I halted her with a hand on the arm before she could storm out the door. I gave her one last request. Her cool eyes assessed me thoughtfully, but she nodded with a final sad smile, seeming reassured. She still looked torn, but resolute. "Oh, can you grab me the bottle of absinthe on the counter? I'm thirsty, and in need of some liquid courage." She rolled her eyes, but complied. I tipped an imaginary hat at her in gratitude as she handed me the bottle, and then she left. And I was alone.

The party of two had become one.

I sat on the couch, sipping straight from the bottle for a few minutes, contemplating my next move, trying to think of anything else I could do. "Ah, fuck it. Why not?" I looked at my watch and smiled. "But first, a nap. Might be my last chance." As if the words were a lullaby, I fell asleep.

CHAPTER 31

$\mathcal{I}$ woke up after my nap, and instantly realized that I had been asleep for five hours. More like a mild coma. I twisted my legs off the couch, and as they struck the floor I was reminded of the stab wound from the holy blade this morning. When Heaven had officially smited me. Stars sparkled across my vision from apparent dehydration as I gritted my teeth against the sharp throb in my thigh. The ensuing rush of endorphins then invited my other wounds to the party. Right. Long walks weren't in the cards for me today. Which could become a problem. Normally I would use my power to help me ignore my injuries, but having no magic to rely on introduced me to a whole new world of pain.

And it sucked.

I didn't know how people did it.

Since I didn't have anyone to help me, I called a cab to pick me up in an hour and take me to Soulard, where the festival and parade was taking place. It was as good a place as any, since the parties against me might be more careful around Regulars. It was a unique experience for me to plan a battle without my magic. I had to think differently, apply different tactics. I grunted as I slowly climbed to my feet and began to test my legs, walking back and forth across the living room. I really wished Mallory were in town. I could use the additional muscle to back me up. I still didn't know his full story, but he was a certified badass. Too bad he was on vacation too.

Now that I thought about it, it was kind of odd that all my friends were gone at the same time, leaving me all alone. I hadn't really thought about it until now. I wasn't typically the guy who made sure I had backup. I usually just went in on my own, or knew that a quick phone call could provide any kind of backup I might need. I had never really thought about making sure I always had a Plan B. I didn't typically make myself available for so much trouble on a daily basis, so hadn't ever considered it. Well, if I survived this, I'd have to change that. Having a plan for the future helped give me a bit of confidence, even though I was one hundred percent certain that this was my last hand. I mean, I had *nothing* up my sleeve.

I didn't even know which way was right anymore. Even *Heaven* was against me.

I shook my head and began to get ready for my last hoorah. A hot shower would be nice. I wanted to look good before I died. And I needed to redress my wounds, which might take a while without Othello to help. Thinking of Othello, I checked my phone, but didn't see any messages from her. Odd. I figured she would have at least checked up on me by now. I called her but it went straight to voicemail. Maybe her phone was dead. Oh well. I didn't have time to worry about it. I had slept longer than anticipated. I thought about texting her, but didn't know exactly what I could type. I wasn't entirely sure of my plan yet. So, I decided I would wait until she called me.

I turned on the shower and waited for it to get warm. And waited.

And waited.

It remained just a hair above freezing.

I turned it all the way to hot, hoping it just needed a boost. But it stubbornly remained frigid. "Give me a break!" I yelled into the empty apartment. A neighbor stomped on the floor above me in complaint. With no divine intervention warming the water for me, I resigned myself to taking a cold shower, which brought back the guilt over making out with Othello the night before. What the hell was I going to do about that? Indie would forgive me, right? But it had been the only way to stop me from destroying the neighborhood. It had been a smart move on Othello's part. But would Indie see it that way? Then I began to laugh. I couldn't help it. It was simply too ridiculous not to laugh about.

Here I was, about to die, no magic, no friends, a fugitive of the law…

And I was worrying about what my girlfriend would think.

Man, was I hopeless. Not that I didn't feel terrible, but it literally wouldn't matter by tomorrow morning. My wounds were that bad. Thinking of that, I glanced down. I was bleeding noticeably, and I knew beyond a shadow of a doubt that I was on borrowed time. At least I wasn't bleeding as badly as I had been before. I wondered how bad the wounds might have been if they hadn't been partly cauterized. Would I have even made it out of the deli? I was lucky that I had even woken from my nap. I really should have been in the hospital. That sobered me up. But I had no time for hospitals. I would see this through to the end. My parents deserved it.

Shaking my head and rubbing my arms to prevent frostbite, I finished washing as quickly as possible, eager to get out and put some dry clothes on. Highly motivated to maintain my core temperature, I jumped out of the shower in an effort to escape the icy water faster. Which wasn't a wise move, given my wounds. My injured leg touched first and I collapsed into the sink, shattering the cheap porcelain to the linoleum floor and snapping a pipe in half. Icy water instantly arced up into the air, splashing the room and my already frozen torso with more cold water. "Motherfucker!" I roared, stuffing my old clothes into the broken pipe in an effort to halt the spraying water. The neighbor upstairs began banging on the floor again. I wiped the water from my eyes, assessing the damage. The sink was destroyed, now a pile of cheap porcelain rubble, and my leg was bleeding freely thanks to my sudden acrobatics. Then my arm and side decided to join the bandwagon. My vision began to tunnel. I left the bathroom in a drunken crawl in order to find the medical kit and tie off the wounds before I bled out. Numb fingers and dwindling strength fought my inexperienced medical attention every step of the way, but I finally managed it. Once finished, I leaned back against the dirty couch, naked, panting heavily, and feeling very sorry for myself.

I couldn't even call Dean to help fix the bathroom. I was literally helpless without my friends. I growled to myself. "Pick yourself up, Nate. Don't be a little man-bitch. Roll your sleeves up. People are depending on you."

Feeling marginally better, I snatched up my bag and began digging through it for a fresh set of clothes. Apparently, I had left a can of shoe polish in the bag at some point in my life, because every single item inside the bag was coated with a heavy layer of the oily, black goo. I blinked in disbelief, shaking out the bag. "You've got to be kidding me," I whispered to myself. I spotted the bottle of absinthe on the floor by the couch and decided I deserved a drink. I gulped it for a good five seconds, the fire helping me wake up a bit. I coughed heavily at the pleasant burn, feeling my body warm up a bit as the liquor hit my bloodstream.

Having exactly no concern for my sartorial savvy any longer, I picked the least offensive clothing and began to dress myself. It was a pair of black sweatpants and a tee that I had picked up to sleep in. It had a single word on the front, *Touchdown*, and sported a cartoon image of a baseball player hitting a homerun. Indie had gotten it for me, mocking my lack of sports knowledge. I sighed, tugging it on – accepting the cosmic karma for making out with Othello. The back was liberally coated with shoe polish, but at least a coat would cover that up.

The cabbie honked outside and I growled. I didn't see my coat anywhere, but I also remembered that it was covered in blood anyway. I groaned with frustration. No time. I finished dressing in a rush, shoved my various knick-knacks in my pockets, and flipped off the bathroom for good measure. I snatched up the bottle of absinth and stormed out of the apartment, not even bothering to lock up behind me. The cabbie was waiting, and eyed me dubiously as he realized that the drunk, dirty, wet man limping towards him wasn't a homeless vagrant, but his fare. I couldn't blame him. I looked like I had just escaped *Fight Club*, I didn't have a coat, I was dressed like a dirty derelict, and I was clutching a bottle of liquor like my life depended on it. But it was *Mardi Gras*. Maybe he was used to it this time of year. "Soulard. Near a church if possible." I added as an afterthought, realizing with a sinking feeling that I was officially out of options, and that I would have to summon the Greater Demon, Sir Dreadsalot, after all.

My parents' murderer.

I leaned back into the headrest and closed my eyes.

This was it. My last hoorah. And I didn't even look cool.

I began guzzling the absinthe.

CHAPTER 32

*M*ardi Gras was in full swing as the cabbie stopped the car. We sat there in silence, the car idling. The cabbie finally turned to face me, announcing the cost of the ride, and holding out a hand for his money. I abruptly broke out in a sweat, realizing that I was broke and had no money to give him. I reached in my pocket instinctively and almost gasped in relief. I whipped out my hand to find a crumpled fifty-dollar bill. I could have cried. I hadn't even considered how I was going to pay for the fare, what with fighting to stay awake and not pass out from blood loss in the backseat. I handed him the whole thing, and muttered, "thanks," as I exited the vehicle. He stared back, stunned that his vagrant passenger had so much cash, and was willing to part with it.

I took a pull of the bottle of absinthe in my fist, swishing the liquid around my mouth, hoping to absorb the alcohol faster and alleviate some of my increasing aches. It wasn't helping too much, and I was feeling a bit tipsy. I decided to slow down. I hadn't eaten much after all, and I *was* severely injured. Not a good mix. But I knew the buzz was practically the only thing keeping me on my feet. Still, moderation.

I began to walk in order to maintain my body temperature. It was a little warmer today but still below freezing, and it looked like it might snow again soon. And I was only wearing a tee. I watched the parade for a few minutes, delaying the inevitable, and took a small sip from the bottle. An old church loomed ahead of me. They were serving hot cocoa at the door. That decided me. I shoved the large bottle in my sweatpants pocket and immediately felt a firm hand grasp my shoulder.

"No drinking out of glass bottles in public, sir. Even though it's *Mardi Gras…*" I turned to face him, probably faster than I should have. He had startled me though.

He lurched back, hand darting to his service piece. Great. A cop. At least he hadn't recog—

"Master Temple!" he shouted in disbelief.

I wanted to groan, but remained calm. I had been so close. All I had wanted to do was confront the Demon that had killed my parents so that I could die in peace. Or pieces, as was most likely the case. Then dumb luck had to intervene.

"Listen. I can explain," I began weakly.

"You were kidnapped! Are you under duress?" He abruptly scanned the crowd with cop eyes. People were beginning to notice. This wasn't good.

I shook my head. "No. I'm alone. I—"

"I think it's better for everyone if I placed you into my custody. We can sort everything out at the station. You look like death walking." He began to reach for his cuffs and my frustration spiked. That was it. He'd brought this on himself. I didn't want to hurt anyone, but I didn't have time for this. I called my magic to fix the problem.

And promptly collapsed to the icy street with a blazing migraine, barely able to breathe.

Oh. Yeah. I didn't have magic anymore.

The cop scooped me up in his beefy arms and began carrying me away, shouting into his radio for backup. I couldn't even raise my head to see where I was being taken. I tried to mumble an argument to him, but I was pretty sure it came out as "Mrghh mnnow." The world tilted back and forth crazily as if I had just stepped off a carnival ride. It was all I could do to not throw up on the cop. But throwing up straight absinthe would feel not good, so I stomached it like a man. People flashed by me, looks of concern and astonishment on their faces. This was it. I had hit a wall. No more magic, no friends, my wounds finally getting the best of me, and I was in police custody. I almost laughed at the fact that Detective Kosage wouldn't even have the chance to charge me.

Because, well… I would be dead by then.

My body was gently settled down onto an uncomfortable chair.

My vision steadied after a few minutes and I noticed two people staring at me with disbelief and concern. We were in a peaceful, warm room. The cop was nowhere to be found.

Apparently, he had brought me to the church.

Huh. That was convenient.

The two of them watched me for a beat, eyes flickering hesitantly from my bleeding wounds to my face, before moving closer. One was a Sister, and she was clutching a Styrofoam cup of hot cocoa. The other was the Father, and he was clutching his rosary, murmuring a soft prayer with his eyes now closed. I managed to signify with my eyes that I wanted me some hot cocoa. The Sister smiled and knelt next to me. I wasn't strong enough to hold it so she lifted it to my lips. "Careful, son. It's hot." Then the sugar hit my lips and I groaned in ecstasy, greedily drinking the entire cup. It didn't feel hot at all. But I was practically frozen by that point. My body began to shiver uncontrollably. From both the cold and my blood loss. I slowly touched the bandage on my leg and noticed that it was wet and sticky, leaking through my sweats. I hadn't done such a great job, after all. How long had I been slowly bleeding out?

The Sister slowly pulled the empty cup away, motioning for another Sister to replace it. The woman shuffled back to the front door with a nod. The saintly woman returned her warm brown eyes to me; pure concern and compassion filled her deep gaze. "Better?"

I nodded slowly. "Thanks," I rasped. "Where…" I was interrupted by a coughing fit.

"He's just outside. Waiting on the arrival of his partner." Her eyes slowly lowered to my obviously bleeding wounds. I noticed that I had a slight puddle beneath me. "Would you like to pray with me?" she asked softly.

I almost argued with her, but then had an idea.

"Do you think it would be a problem if I visit the confessional booth instead?" I pointedly glanced down at my wounds. "You know. A few things I would like to get off my chest before…"

I left the sentence open ended, hoping she would buy it.

Before she could answer, the Father stepped closer. "Of course, my son. I'll deal with the policeman if he has any issue. This is a House of God after all. The Big Man comes first, here." Then he was supporting my weight as he led me to the booth. He set me down inside and I managed to get my breathing back under control from the short trip. "Comfortable?" he asked.

"As good as. Considering…" I motioned to my leg.

His eyes tightened. "Everything will be well, my son. Do you need me to listen, or would you prefer privacy?" I was pretty sure confessions were a two-person job, but I appreciated his thought to ask my preference nonetheless. He wasn't sure how long I had left and wanted to grant the fugitive a bit of dignity.

My eyes grew a bit misty at his compassion, genuinely realizing that I was almost about to take my last breath. And no one was here to hold my hand. "I'd prefer the privacy if you don't mind." I whispered, my head sunk low so that the words were directed at my lap. He patted me gently on the uninjured thigh, and then hesitated as he felt the liquor bottle there. I looked up guiltily. He smiled softly, and then winked with an amused shake of the head. Then he left, gently closing the door behind him.

I sat there for a few moments, fully comprehending my situation. *These* two humans were the good guys. The Angels should take notes from them.

I knew I was on borrowed time so I shook my head softly. Did I feel bad for what I was about to do?

Yes.

I was about to make a deal with a Greater Demon in a House of God. After everything they had done for me in my time of need. And they had given me cocoa. I wondered what they would say if they knew their holy pals had done this to me in the first place.

But I could think of no other options available to me. The Angels had refused to help. Their Nephilim had – for all intents and purposes – killed me. Slowly. Just like Eae had told me they would. And my own people had tied my hands and pushed me into the ocean.

I delayed in calling the Demon for a few moments.

I deserved some *me* time.

So, I pondered my sins, feeling like this was the appropriate place to do so.

I had cheated on Indie. Sure, I hadn't known I was doing it, and I hadn't consciously chosen to do so, but the action was there. Intent didn't matter. I abhorred cheating. If someone was unhappy with their romantic situation, they should simply end it before seeking other opportunities. That didn't really apply to my situation, but still…

Now, I was one of the cheaters.

I wondered if Indie would have been able to forgive me, if I wasn't about to die, that was. I sighed sadly. The best thing that had ever happened to me, and I wouldn't even get to say goodbye. I hissed as I felt one of my wounds break open, reminding me of my limited time. I hadn't let Othello know, but I had known that the wounds were fatal, not merely superficial. I was literally dying. I was lucky that my nap earlier hadn't been permanent.

Then again, going out in my sleep would have probably been better than what I was about to experience. I pondered the upcoming battle, if you wanted to call it that. Without my magic, it was hopeless. Not a battle. An execution. I was making a last stand with no Ace in the Hole.

Merely for the sake of my pride.

I knew that I wouldn't have been able to live with myself, if I gave up now. Not that I had the option of living with myself afterwards anyway. Hell, I didn't even know if I would make it to the *fight*. I shook that thought off. I was freely choosing to enter the ring for a confrontation, where I was hopelessly outmatched. After all, I had proven that without my magic, I was a joke. I was no hero. Apparently, the only special things about me were my magic, my money, and my friends. Without them, I had been a wreck. Indie deserved better. My friends would be safer without me around to get them in trouble. The Academy was too ignorant to help, and even the almighty Angels were too proud to stand beside me. I had thought we were on the same side.

But I had been wrong.

With a sigh of regret, I pulled out the Tarot card the Demon had told me to use.

I prepared to light the card on fire with my magic, and was rewarded with another blinding headache and a deep warning tingle in my spine. I groaned, breathing hard. *Of course, idiot.* I didn't have my magic anymore. How dense was I? To be fair, it's easy to know that my magic was gone, but it's an altogether different concept to remember that the everyday actions I took using magic were no longer available to me. My subconscious was so used to doing things a certain way that it took an effort to remember those abilities no longer applied to me. I could only relate it to losing a hand. A phantom presence, where the amputee still felt like they had fingers and tried to use them to grab a glass of water, only to knock the glass from the table.

I looked down at the card with a scowl. The Thirteenth Major Arcana, as it was called. I guess I needed a lighter. Too bad I didn't smoke anymore or else I would have had one in my pocket.

That brought a grin to my face. It had been almost a week now, and over the last three days I hadn't even *thought* about smoking. Go, me!

… Just in time to die. I sobered up at that thought. Then I shrugged, whipping out the liquor bottle, and taking several deep pulls. Why not?

As I studied the image of the skeleton gripping a scythe on the card I was reminded of my own impending death. Several decapitated bodies surrounded the skeleton. The words *La Morte* were printed below the grisly image. Despite the somewhat obvious depiction, scholars and Tarot experts academically debated the card's meaning. Many thought that it didn't represent a *physical* death, but that it typically implied an *end* instead, possibly of a relationship or interest, and therefore implied an increased sense of self-awareness – not to be confused with self-consciousness or any kind of self-diminishment. Meaning that one should live every moment as if it were their last. *Memento Mori*, or *remember that one day you too shall die*. It was a reminder to make the most of what was given to you.

I pondered that in silence for a few breaths. It was comforting… in a way. Then a thought began to slowly emerge from the murky depths of my sluggish mind. I had never considered obtaining the card the Demon had told me to use. It was as if…

As if I had subconsciously known all along that I already carried one.

But I didn't typically carry around Tarot cards, so why hadn't I been concerned about finding one to use? I tried to remember where I had gotten the card. I noticed a stain on the corner and lifted it to my nose. I took a big whiff and smelled anise.

Specifically, Absinthe.

It was from… Hemingway. The card he had left me to call if I ever wanted another drinking partner. His words whispered in my ear. *I may be bored enough to assist you.*

An odd, creepy sensation began to squirm up my spine. No way.

Goddamn it. *Cat's paws.*

Having given up all other options, I felt my gaze intensify and begin to pulse with anger, a brief flicker of blue seeming to shade the world around me as my fury grew. I had been used. I had no magic left to me.

But the card burned to ashes in an instant.

Then I was Shadow Walked to the exact opposite of a church.

CHAPTER 33

*R*ather than sitting in the peaceful solitude of a confessional booth, I found myself suddenly gripped by the throat and held a few feet above the dirty floor of an empty biker bar. A pale, haunting skull was glaring at me, eyes afire with a green glow behind an authentic bone mask that was etched with ancient, powerful runes. His pale, bony hand clutched me by the jugular.

Not Hemingway.

Death.

One of the freaking Four Horsemen.

A *Rider.*

I gurgled between his fingers. "I'm here to see a man about a horse," I croaked.

The room was silent for a second, and then an all-too-familiar tone of laughter filled the room – Hemingway's laughter. "Took you long enough." He grinned, slowly releasing the pressure on my windpipe and lowering me to the ground, eyes twinkling behind the terrifying skeleton mask. "Bored yet? Ready for another nightcap?" He eyed my bottle, and then snatched it away happily. "Seems you've already started." I shook my head in bewilderment. He had released me, but hadn't taken a step back. I managed to remain standing on my own feet and stared at him. He seemed a lot...

bigger, more menacing than the last time we had shared drinks in *Achilles Heel*.

He took a swig of the liquor straight from the bottle and then leaned in closer, way too close for my taste. You shared a drink in a *Kill* and thought you knew a guy. He whispered to me, the sound like crackling leaves in the fall. "I'll grant you a gift. You may be the first mortal to view the world through my eyes in thousands of years. It will change your perception of the world, but it is a gift worth the cost. Remove my mask if you agree to my terms. You will receive the answers to your parents' deaths." I reached for his mask without considering the terms he hadn't yet stated. I was dead anyway, and would do anything for that information. Anything. My fingers brushed the cool bone skull mask and my mind fragmented into a million pieces as I pulled it away from his face.

I found myself floating in a room, as if underwater, and everything was tinted in a greenish hue. I was at Temple Industries. In a familiar storage room. But this room was now off limits. Even for storage. It was the room where my parents had been murdered. I saw my father valiantly fighting a Demon, neither of them moving, the battle taking place solely in their minds. My mother lie motionless behind him, but he fought as if to keep her alive. His forearm was bleeding from the self-inflicted cut he had caused to write me his last message. Then there was a brilliant flash, and it was over. Sir Dreadsalot left the room, looking furious. I saw Charon approach my parents and felt a single tear spill down my cheek. No one had called him. But he had still appeared. It made me glad that I had always paid respects to the Boatman. Maybe he had appeared *because* I always paid him respects. The odd part, though? For some reason, I understood why their deaths were necessary, in the cool mathematical precision of an equation.

Next, I found myself in a brilliantly white room. I squinted against the glare, assessing my surroundings cautiously. It was elegant, luxurious, and had a feel of royalty. *Where was I?* A couch sat to my right, mirrored by twin accent chairs to my left. The wooden floor stretched off into deeper sections of the house or building, but I was transfixed enough by what lay immediately before me. I didn't need to go exploring. A bookshelf was tucked against the far wall, loaded with elaborately designed spines of ancient books. A vase sat on a coffee table between the two chairs – stuffed with flowers – and paintings decorated the walls.

Except…

Everything was cocaine white. And when I say *everything*, I don't mean different things were each a slightly different shade of light colors. I *literally* mean that *everything* was exactly the same hue of brilliant white – the wooden floors, the painted walls, the vase, the bookshelf, the books, the furniture, the flowers, and even the *stems* of the flowers. They rested in what appeared to be milk rather than water.

I stood in a cocaine castle.

Even the paintings were white. When I stepped closer, I could see the ridges in the design, the painting emphasized with *texture* rather than *color*, and it was done so masterfully that I could actually see what the artist had intended just as well as if he had used colored paint.

I glanced down and saw that I was wearing a silver suit, Miami Vice style, with gray gator-skin dress loafers. My creepiness factor went up a few notches as I walked up to a window, placing my hand on the sill.

I stared through the glass to see that I was in a vast forest on the edge of a cliff that overlooked a milky white ocean. And, wait for it... everything outside was also white. The trees, the house, the sky, and the grass.

I lifted my hands from the sill and flinched in shock as my eyes caught the only color I had seen in this strange world. A gray stain rested where my hands had been. I almost had a fit of panic, fearing that the apparently obsessive compulsive owner of the building was about to come introduce himself and see that his perfectly pristine world had been tarnished by his gray-clad guest. I stared down at my hands, wondering why they had been dirty in the first place... and then I found myself just staring, and staring, and staring some more in utter confusion.

My hands were spotless.

I turned back to the windowsill, but the stain was still there. I furiously began rubbing it with my sleeve, but this only smeared the stain, as if my suit fabric was only exacerbating the problem, dirtier than even my hands had been. Realizing I was only making things worse, I hurriedly stepped away. My gaze flickered over the bookshelf and my eyes furrowed in thought. *Surely...*

I strode over to the bookshelf and grabbed the nearest spine, pulling it out, and leaving an alarming gray smudge. I opened the book anyway, hoping to see the familiar color of black font. But the pages were blank. Entirely. Well, everywhere but where my fingers touched. Those pages were stained gray with obvious fingerprints. I glanced at the cover only to see a raised title, *Through the Looking-Glass*. But it was also white. I could only read it because the letters had been raised above the surface of the paper.

Then I heard footsteps approaching. Big, heavy ones. I began to panic, shoving the book back in place, leaving another large gray stain. I frantically spun, wondering if I could hide my tracks, but it was too obvious in this place. Smudged boot prints also marred the wooden floor, and the approaching steps were only getting louder.

A glowing white form began to step around the corner of one of the hallways, but the world shattered like a priceless vase before I got a chance to see a face.

I abruptly came back to myself, panting. I latched onto the bar with shaky fingers, feeling sick to my stomach and dizzy – both from the visions and my beat-up body. The mask lay on the bar beside my hands, and Hemingway's familiar face was visible. Although now I knew it wasn't his real face. Hemingway. Death. I shook my head, the connection only making me feel worse. Death handed the bottle back to me. I chugged gratefully, scalding my throat, not even caring about what kind of germs I might be sharing with the Horseman by drinking out of the same bottle as someone older than the Bible. I was dead soon anyway. If this didn't merit a drink, I didn't know what did. "The effects are temporary, but know that what you saw is how I see the world. Past, future, and present."

"Where was that last place? The white room? And why was I—"

He held up a warning finger. "You were in a white room?" His voice was razor sharp.

I gulped cautiously at the look in his eyes, nodding once. "Yes."

"We'll discuss that later," he finally said under his breath, seeming nervous and... resigned. I watched him. What in the world could have terrified the Horseman of freaking Death?

I was briefly reminded of him mentioning something back in the bar where we had first met. *Between black and white is not a gray area, but a quicksilver, honey shade; a shiny, enticing, and altogether dividing line. If employed correctly...* "It sure looked to me like I was a big flashing, unappreciated gray line," I muttered.

"Silver. Not gray," Death corrected, apparently having heard me. I looked up at him sharply. He shrugged. "It's the color of the path you find yourself on. Silver for the path of walking the sword between black and white. Silver to remind you of the sword's edge you walk across. Because you must always fight tooth and claw to maintain the goddamned line." He was breathing heavily. But why the hell did he sound so angry about it?

Apparently, that wasn't for me to know. Yet. He composed himself, changing the topic. "Seeing the world through my eyes will change you. A storm is coming, Master Temple, and it has something to do with the little *box* your parents dared open. The world will need you in the days to come."

I couldn't help myself. I began to laugh. "I'm literally *dying*. I know fatal wounds well enough to know that I'm on borrowed time. I'm about to meet you on an *official* level. What could I possibly do to help? And for once, will someone please tell me what in blazes this has to do with the Armory?"

"You may have heard it by a different name." His smile turned wolfish, drawing out the moment. "Pandora's Box. Congratulations on being somewhat correct. Even though you didn't believe it. That was your father's point in naming it so obviously. Hide it in plain sight."

I blinked, too flabbergasted to speak for a few seconds. I took another longer pull of the liquor. "Well, if I'm still kicking around in a few hours, I'll deal with it. I'm out of juice, so I pretty much have zero chance of helping anyone, not even considering my fatal wounds. I'll let you deal with the Armory."

Death studied me, considering thoughts that – no doubt – only a Horseman could fathom, and then dropped a freaking bomb on me as I took another pull of the drink, no longer caring how drunk I became. "You have something of mine. I want it back."

I choked. "Um. What?"

"The bone artifact. In your pocket."

I reached inside and withdrew the bone Hope had given me to track Demons. The stone that had caused me to also hear millions of souls speaking into my ears when I commanded it to *Seek*. Death stiffened, staring at the bone with a look of such pain that I was suddenly concerned about my life's outcome over the next few *minutes*. I offered it to him.

He snatched it up. "This is all that remains of my son. Thank you. I thought it lost," he whispered. My hair tried to climb right off my head and run away screaming. His *son*? That was a bone from... but his next words saved me from responding. He had pocketed the bone and looked more or less the same as earlier. A nice older man. "The Greater Demon has your friend, the Regular girl. She's been working with the summoner from the start." My vision pulsed with a blue haze again, and before I knew what I was doing, I flung out my hand and slammed Hemingway over the bar in a blazing fit of rage. His body hammered into the mirrored wall of liquor bottles with a shattering crash.

I was heaving, shoulders hunched forward instinctively. "How *dare* you accuse the *only* person who has helped me during this clusterfuck," I snarled, instantly ready to burn the world to the foundations of Hell itself. Magic filled my veins, more power than I had ever wielded before, but... different.

Death climbed up from behind the bar and brushed his shoulders off, totally unharmed. He finally lifted his green eyed fiery gaze to me, as if to ask, *Really? You want to take on a Horseman?* He was grinning. The fury filling me began to wither and die as I considered his strength.

"With all due respect," I added sheepishly. "Sorry. It just sort of happened. My magic does that when—" I froze.

Wait a minute.

I didn't *have* any magic.

Then I remembered that I had lit the Tarot card on fire with... magic.

"I seem to be telling you this often, but *it took you long enough*," Death muttered with an amused smile. His form rippled below the chest and morphed into a fog of weeping souls that I was pretty sure made my ears bleed. I clapped my hands over them for protection. Then he walked *through* the wooden bar, appearing on my side as if it were an utterly normal means of locomotion. The keening wails halted as he solidified.

"So, you were saying something about being powerless?" Death answered, sipping a glass of absinthe. I hadn't seen him pour it.

I nodded, still trying to wrap my head around the subtle transformation that had allowed him to walk *through* the bar. And what had those sounds been? "How... did I do that? Is it the Maker thing?"

Death didn't answer my question. "What are you going to do about the Box?" he asked instead.

"Well, even though I somehow managed to use this new power, I don't really know how to do it again. And I'm still almost dead. I'm on borrowed time." I was silent for a few seconds, then, "And before I do anything for the world, I need to save a friend."

Death cocked his head. "You're more worried about your traitorous friend's life than the fate of the world?"

I thought about it for all of a second. "Do you have proof she betrayed me?"

"Would you believe me if I said *yes*? Or better yet, would it change your answer?"

I finally shook my head. "No. If she betrayed me, she must have had a good reason. I'm going after her. I need to talk to the Demon anyway. And the summoner. I've got a Blood Debt for what they've done."

Death nodded in approval. "Good for you. A man who stands by his oaths. I understand Blood Debts. If you recall, I fulfilled one myself." I frowned, not understanding. Then it hit me. The farmer's tale he had shared with me in the bar.

It was… *his* story.

I shivered, taking a quick pull of the liquor to mask my surprise. Hemingway continued, "I thought you would have picked up on that by now. The tale was my… *origin* story." He said with an amused smile. His face grew serious again. "Fulfilling Blood Debts… changes you. Revenge in itself can be a cataclysmic choice, but declaring it a *Blood Debt* applies *magic* to it, making it binding, permanently tying your soul to the act. But it's too late to call it anything else now. You've already declared it to an Angel. At the bar. Where we first met." I nodded, not sure what he was talking about with magical oaths. I had simply called it how I saw it. They killed my parents. I sought vengeance. Justice. So, a Blood Debt it was.

Death took another drink before speaking, "Just for the record, Othello had no choice. She was coerced into betraying you. The summoner kidnapped her nephew. Four-year-old boy. Blonde. Good looking. Might change the world someday. It's not his time… but that can always change." The way he spoke the last comment made an arctic chill run down my spine. Like an accountant talking ledgers. Harsh. Cold. Analytical. Precise. That was a tough way to live.

I felt marginally better that Othello hadn't betrayed me by choice. I had already dealt with betrayal once from Peter, and wasn't sure how long I could maintain my sanity if it happened again. I also found a calming swell of power building deep in my chest at the fact that the summoner had also threatened my friend, kidnapping her nephew.

The only person who had been there for me during this whole mess.

"Well, it's the only thing I know I can control, and it's my fault she's been taken. If the world is going to hell, I'm at least going to ease my conscience.

I need to save her." I thought for a minute. "Like I said, I'm on borrowed time, and I don't know how to reliably use my new power. So, I'm going to borrow your mask. You'll get it back. I swear on my pow... no, on my soul, I guess, which you'll have complete control over once I'm gone. Which is going to happen in the next few hours, regardless of what happens next. One last hoorah."

For some reason, it never crossed my mind to ask his permission.

This, apparently, offended him.

And I was reminded – quite severely – of where I stood on the totem pole of power.

Death spun faster than I could blink, and suddenly a wicked, ancient scythe drew a fine line of fire across my throat. Where the hell had it even *come* from? Death was wearing tailored slacks, for crying out loud. It took me all of a second to realize that I wasn't headless, but I was sure the whites of my eyes were blazing like floodlights. Death used his right palm to wipe my blood off the magnificent, gleaming, silver scythe – the weapon granted to him the night he had accepted his new job – and the blade disappeared with a puff of silver smoke. His other hand shifted into a glowing green set of bone claws and he slashed the palm that held my blood. He reached out his bloody right hand to me politely. I accepted the handshake.

And an implosion of blue and green light filled the bar, buffering us on a molecular level as my apparent blue *Maker* power joined with his green... *Horseman-y* power. But the force didn't affect anything in the bar, as if it were only a spiritual implosion. Which was super scary to think about. I knew we were somehow bound now. He didn't say a word about the strobe light show of our powers melding together. Kind of like how action movie heroes never turned around to watch the explosion, but instead continued walking away from it in slow motion.

After a minute, I pinched my arm. "Huh. That wasn't so bad." Death watched me with a raised brow. "I'm going to borrow your scythe," I said, since it had seemed to work for the mask. Maybe my charm was working overdrive to make up for my run of bad luck.

Death threw his hands up, and the room abruptly filled with a cold so deep that my joints ached, and then the scream of dying souls filled my ear canals, shaking my brain like a bowl of Jell-O. "Okay! Okay! Fine. No scythe! *Jeezus*, drama queen. A simple *No* would have sufficed." He smirked, and took another sip of his drink. "But I *am* going to borrow your keys. No more of that freaky death vibe. I get it, you're a badass. But a man needs a ride. I can't walk very well right now. And I refuse to show up in an Uber to my final battle."

Death smirked again, rubbing his chin. "Fine. Don't scratch him. He won't like it." He tossed me a set of small keys.

I caught them with a frown. "Well, *he* can just bite me, then." Death burst out laughing. I frowned harder for good measure, not catching the joke. I picked up the mask, mentally preparing for a scrap with... well, *someone*. I wasn't sure exactly who yet. Eae? Sir Dreadsalot? The summoner? I didn't rightly care.

I just wanted to hurt someone. Any port in a storm, right?

"Is there anything else you can do to help? I don't think you want a summoner traipsing around town either, and my power's unreliable. This bastard has caused enough damage already. Hell, my own people want to serve me up on a platter, and I haven't done a fraction of what *he* has."

Death shook his head. "Your own people do seem to hold you in high esteem. But I believe you have everything you need to accomplish your task. Piece of advice, I was never involved. Other than the bar where we met. You must have stolen my keys. And made a shiny new mask... *Maker*." He winked for some unknown reason. "I'll watch over your body while you're gone," he added. Then a door closed in my mind and I found myself standing outside below a streetlamp. *My body?* What the hell did *that* mean? Had I died? Or had the mask done something to my physical body? I pinched myself for good measure. I *felt* corporeal. Which should tell you something about me, that I was relieved to find my body still squishy and fleshy after meeting one of the *Four Horsemen*. Priorities. Mine were obviously screwed up. I didn't know exactly where I was, but I recognized the general area. I was near the church where the cop held me in custody. I wondered what he would make of it when they opened the confessional booth and I was nowhere to be found.

I wasn't exactly sure what I was supposed to be doing. My body was apparently in a strange biker bar, I had death's mask in my hand, and a Harley. It sounded like a bad action flick. I spotted the Harley and instantly felt a small surge of anticipation. It had been a while since I'd ridden a bike. I appraised the machine, admiring her almost glow-in-the-dark green hue with interest. Unique color. I wouldn't have guessed at it in a million years. To each his own, I guess. I started the engine, and heard a horse neigh loudly down the street. I glanced around nervously, ready to see a SWAT Team rappelling down the surrounding buildings, guns all pointed at little old me. But I was alone. No mounted patrol units, either. I was safe. The police were the last thing I needed. I'd been given a second chance. Time to make the most of it.

Memento Mori, indeed.

I put on Death's mask, and watched as the world morphed into a soothing green hue like I had put on night vision goggles. It was almost identical to the color of the bike, now that I thought about it. I turned to a previously-darkened patch between streetlights, and gasped. It really *was* night vision. I could see perfectly in all directions. Better than any night vision I had ever tested. I guess it made sense, thinking back on Hemingway's story of when he received the gifts in the first place. I shrugged with a smile plastered to my face beneath the mask, realizing that it fit perfectly. I could barely even tell it was there. And, now that I thought about it, nothing was holding it in place. I touched it curiously, but it merely stayed in place. I tugged it off, suddenly fearful that it might be stuck to me, but it pulled away easily. I put it back on and I felt it latch onto my face like a second skin. *Interesting…*

I began thinking about how to make something like it, and then burst out laughing as I realized what I was doing. I wouldn't have time to duplicate anything after tonight. This was my last run. Instead, I revved the engine, causing the unseen nearby horse to scream again in response. I smiled, imagining Kosage riding the beast as he scoured the city for me, and the horse bucking him off.

One could dream.

CHAPTER 34

I was getting closer to the crowds of humanity celebrating *Mardi Gras*. It was now evening, and the debauchery was in full swing. I couldn't count the number of times I had seen breasts of every size, shape, color, and age – and I didn't even have beads. They were everywhere. It was an adolescent's fantasy. All a boy had to do was simply walk the streets tonight and he would have a veritable buffet of visual stimuli to catalog for years. Revving the Harley helped clear the crowds when they got in my way. And watching breasts, *erm*, people jump back in surprised fright at the sudden sound pleased me.

Another perk of the night was that almost everyone was wearing Le Carnevale masks. This eased my primary concern, that I would be recognized prior to finding Sir Dreadsalot. I had already tried *calling* him with the Tarot card, but since Death had hijacked that phone call I wasn't sure if the Demon had ever heard it. As I was riding through a particularly dense crowd on the street – the sidewalks were at a standstill – my heart suddenly froze. Two Justices stood on a set of steps leading up to a building on the side of the street, eyes scanning the crowd like birds of prey. Maybe the fact that Gavin was my parole officer allowed only him to find me, because none of the other Justices seemed to be able to do so. Not yet, anyway.

In fact...

One glanced right over me, scanning the crowd eagerly. I shivered. Even this close, they didn't seem to be able to sense me. I carefully rode directly through the crowd, never attracting the Justices' attention. I wasn't the only bike in the crowd – there was even a unicycle wheeling around – but I was definitely the only *neon green* motorcycle. I let out a sigh of relief when I was a safe distance away. I had no idea what I would have done if they had attacked. I didn't know how to use the Maker ability effectively yet. It had just *happened*.

It was day three, and the Academy had shown up to collect their prize – like a schoolyard bully waiting to accept his lunch money from his smaller classmates at recess.

But they weren't getting their grubby hands on my Armory. Not on my watch. I *ate* bullies for *their* lunch money.

As long as I remained vertical long enough to stop them, that was.

Death's comment about Pandora's Box made me nervous, but I shut that line of thought down quickly. I didn't have time to think about that now. I had enough on my plate. Othello needed me. Right *now*. I had a fresh, steaming murder to deliver to the summoner, courtesy of your friendly neighborhood wiz... well, *Maker*, I guess. I grinned wide as another thought hit me. Not just a Maker, but also a temporary *Horseman*. Maybe I could just scare him to death by pretending to be a Rider.

All these thoughts flew through my mind as I frantically struggled to find a way to prevent any collateral damage. I glanced to the side, spotting a silver blur, assuming it was a Justice. But as my eyes focused, I realized that it was just a woman. Staring at me. *Really* staring. The silver glow had no doubt been caused by the streetlight shining down upon her.

I slowed down, glanced behind me to see if she was actually staring at someone behind me. But no one was there. I turned back and flinched. She was half the distance closer, despite the crowds and the impossible speed that such a movement would require. Then I noticed something odd.

She was floating. A foot off the ground, and the wind didn't seem to touch her. She also had no coat on. Then a creepy sensation came over me. She was a *spirit*. A ghost. A lost soul. And she was staring at her savior.

Death.

I waved guiltily. Not knowing what else to do, I spoke in a whisper, drawing on the power of Death's mask. "I'm only a temp-worker. Finish up any last-minute business you may have. The real reaper will help you tomorrow."

She could either read lips or had uncanny hearing for a dead lady. She smiled with a nod of acceptance, waved a frail hand, and faded away to nothingness. I realized that my shoulders were locked up with tension. I hoped I wasn't messing up some cosmic balance by making her wait. Or whether I even had the authority to choose to send her on her way to the afterlife or to allow her to stay behind for an extra day. I didn't want to mess anything up, so I figured erring on the side of caution was the safest bet. I would just tell any more wandering spirits that *business would resume as usual tomorrow. Our apologies for the delay – Management.* After all, Death hadn't given me a job description. Consequences would be his fault.

I continued on, but not before picking up a handful of discarded beads from the street, because, you know, *Mardi Gras.* When in Rome... it would help me to fit in better if I seemed to be enjoying the various flavors of ample bosom. I spotted another Justice a few minutes later, and although confident she wouldn't pick me out from the crowd, I grew anxious as I crept closer. Her silver mask resembled a laughing face, but she completely ignored the cheers and roars of the crowd. I crossed her line of sight with a wave of trepidation falling heavily on my shoulders. I was about to be made. Surely, they could at least *sense* me from this close. But as I passed, she looked right *through* me. I blinked in both relief and disbelief. How blind was she?

Then I thought about it. Death had said he would watch over my body. Was I not physically here? No, that wasn't true, because I had picked up those beads. Maybe they just couldn't sense me because of Death's mask. But then, shouldn't they have at least sensed a Rider of the Apocalypse among them? Then I thought about *that* a little bit. *I* hadn't ever noticed a Rider, or an Angel, in all my years of existence. Maybe they were immune from that sort of thing.

Interrupting my reverie, several young drunks stumbled up to the Justice and waggled beads in front of her to get her attention, noticing that she didn't have any beads. That was nice of them. They wanted to share. Poor girl. What kind of woman deserves to walk around on *Mardi Gras* without any beads? It just wouldn't be right.

She pointedly ignored them, still studiously scanning the street. I heard a loud bark of a voice and spotted another Justice not too far away. The woman obediently turned to him, body tense. The man motioned for her to participate. I could imagine the words. *"We must fit in. Do as they ask."* I grinned wider. Her head hung in resignation, and she quickly flipped up her top, displaying an impressive show, but just as quickly dropped it back down. The drunks seemed disappointed at the brief glimpse of heaven, but still fed the woman her beads so she wouldn't starve tonight. Very generous. I pelted her with my whole wad of beads. Neither of the Justices paid me any notice. This was awesome! One enemy out of the picture! Now, I didn't have to worry about any surprise visits from my own wizardly police force. The ones who had taken my power. I very seriously entertained teaching them a lesson, right here, right now. A breath later, I very responsibly chose not to do so. It was a tough choice. They deserved it. Well, Jafar did. The others were just doing their jobs, as Gavin had taught me. He actually hadn't been half bad after getting to know him a bit, and showing him the error of his ways.

I continued on, spotting several more souls hanging out, watching me expectantly. I motioned for them to come back later. They didn't seem too upset. Several of them nodded at me with gratitude, even bowing. It was enough to make a guy realize just whom he was impersonating.

Then I spotted an Angel on a rooftop. His Heavenly glare assessed the streets with disgust, but he was vigilant, eyes darting back and forth like a falcon, taking everything in like a gargoyle. Then his gaze met mine, and his jaw dropped in alarm. He began to lift a horn to his lips. I couldn't have that. With a thought, and the rapidly becoming familiar blue haze to my vision, I held up a hand and clenched my fist. The horn instantly crumbled to ashes. I opened my hand and imagined claws as I mocked grabbing a throat in front of me. I saw a large spirit hand grip the Angel by the throat and slam him to the ground. Not enough to hurt him, just shock him

"Fuck off, Feathers. I'm here on business that doesn't concern you," I muttered under my breath. The look of alarm on his face told me he had heard me just fine. As good as it felt to shut down an Angel with such ease, I didn't have time for petty vengeance against the pigeon. It seemed ironic that now that I had enough *power* to take revenge on all the parties against me, I had no *time* to do so. Specifically, *Othello* didn't have time for me to do so.

As if in answer to my blasphemous disrespect of the Angel, it began to rain. Fat, icy drops crashed down from the sky, drenching everyone. I was simply surprised that it wasn't snow. I found myself murmuring under my breath. "It's a good day to die. True rain washes the soul." The last sentence was something my father had always said at the first sign of rain.

Scanning my surroundings, I was surprised to see that the rain hadn't diminished the crowd in the slightest. But of course, the excessive amounts of alcohol in their veins convinced them that they were immortal and not already close to frostbite. They cheered with excitement instead. I rolled my eyes. The Angel had vanished, but I didn't hear any horns or other sounds of pursuit. Which made me feel better.

One perk from the rain was that it would make using magic almost impossible for the Justices. Cold rain was worse, as cold rain caused a sense of panic in your mind, and magic was all about mental clarity. But really, any type of rain would nullify magic to some extent. Running water was anathema to wizards. I wondered if it would affect my ability as a Maker. Then shrugged. I would just resort to the power of the freaking Horseman, Death, if that were the case. I was kind of nervous and anxious to test that out.

It was like test-driving a Ferrari. Of course, you *said* you wanted to drive it, but once you sat behind the wheel a sense of profound respect and fear often made you realize just how dangerous your desire could actually be. Did you *really* want to drive close to 200 miles an hour? Probably not. With only a strip of fabric holding back your body and a thin sheet of glass to protect your face? No thanks.

I sat there, revving the engine slightly, wondering where to go. I really had no game plan, having thought that burning the Tarot card would call the Greater Demon and I would die shortly after. The rumbling engine caused several mounted police officers' horses to rear back in alarm, but the cops themselves apparently couldn't see me either. Just the horses. They eyed me with wide, panicked eyes. Not me. The bike. That was weird. Surely, they weren't scared of a motorcycle. They must see them all the time, and the place wasn't exactly quiet. It wasn't like I had suddenly revved the engine on an empty street in the middle of the night. As my gaze swept past their hooves, I spotted something odd. Twin, quivering cords of energy trailed off into the night at ground level, piercing the crowds in different directions. One black, and one white. They glowed with untapped power.

Unlike Robert Frost, I chose the path *most* traveled, knowing it was easier for people to commit sin rather than adhere to righteousness. And I was Demon hunting after all. As I began to idle after the black cord of power I began to hum to myself. *Back in Black, I hit the sack...*

In my mind, I was nailing it, on key and everything. Even the voice was spot on.

I pumped my fist in the air and roared off into the night, chasing the cord of power. I cackled loudly into the rainy night, relishing the icy drops of rain striking the bone mask with little puffs of steam.

I bet I looked really cool right now. Even in sweats and my *Touchdown* tee.

CHAPTER 35

*T*had left the celebrations behind a while ago, and now found myself at the entrance of a gated scrap yard in a commercial district. The gate was wide open. Barely hesitating, I drove the Harley inside, following the black cord of pulsing energy to the center of the area, towers of salvage vehicles rising above me on either side, several stories high. I briefly remembered Greta one time saying something about salvaging my sinful soul and chuckled. If she only knew. I gently pressed the kickstand, and double-checked that the bike wasn't about to fall over if I climbed off. Then I sat there, studying my surroundings and the black cord of power thoughtfully. The pulsating cord led to a nearby tower of vehicles that was taller than the rest. More towers continued on in the distance, creating a giant-sized labyrinth built of the corpses of the once great auto industry. I rolled my gaze to scan the rest of my surroundings. Whomever I had followed must know I was here. The Harley wasn't exactly quiet, and I was just sitting there. I hoped I hadn't accidentally followed a completely different bad guy's icky slug trail, and that it indeed belonged to either the Demon or the summoner. I didn't even question what the cord was, assuming it had something to do with Death's mask. His vision of the world, as he called it. He had said it would affect me.

Weak floodlights attempted to illuminate the scrap yard, but it was still dark. Well, it would have been dark to anyone else. It was light enough for me, but dark enough to earn an ick factor of 10 for any *Regular* person's eyes.

A crackling, basso voice cooed from the darkness, making me upgrade the ick factor to a 12. "You don't call, you don't write, you don't make deals, and you don't burn the card. It's enough to hurt a Demon's feelings." The unseen Sir Dreadsalot launched from the top of the tower of broken vehicles and landed before me, back facing me. The knotted dreadlocks of broken teeth and bones even covered his back, making me decide that it truly was an armor of sorts. His mane of longer dreads hung low on his back, darker, thicker dreads than on the rest of his body. He was still missing an arm, and as he slowly turned to face me, I was pleased to see that the aftermath of the horrific steam burn I had thrown at his face during our first encounter still remained. Lifting his glowing red eyes to assess his prey, he instantly took a reflexive step back as he truly saw me for the first time. "No! You cannot be here. No laws have been broken, Rider."

I smiled, not speaking, but revved my engine a bit. The Demon jumped back as the piercing sound of a horse filled the night. I blinked. No way was a cop nearby. I turned to look and caught my reflection in one of the side mirrors of a crushed car.

And my heart stopped.

Where I stood was the most terrifying apparition I had ever seen.

A giant, shadowy cloaked figure with a wicked skull for a face stared back at me with eyes of green fire. And he was sitting atop a literal fiery-eyed, glowing green steed, not too unlike Grimm, my murderous pet unicorn. A distant cousin, maybe? I discarded that train of thought, assessing my reflection. I looked friggin' *Awesome*.

And now I knew for sure that the black cord led to the Demon.

"Why are you doing this?" I asked, not betraying my true identity, remaining atop the Harley. "Even *you* know the Covenants," I added, trying to sound pompous.

The Demon looked nervous. "We have broken no laws. I was summoned. My master required Temple's blood. His *lifeblood*, not just a vial from a wound, in order to gain access to something he desires. I merely obeyed my commands. I broke no laws, Rider. Call your brothers and question me if you must," he said the last in wary resignation.

I blinked. First off, when had they figured out my blood was the Key, and second of all, how had they gotten my blood in the first place? I mean, I had liberally gotten my ass beaten on an almost hourly basis over the last few days, but I didn't think any of the Demons were smart enough to – nor had I seen them – take the time to snatch up a sample of my blood.

That was wizardry 101. Never leave blood behind.

Only one person had been with me when I entered the Armory. And that's when I understood it all. *Of course...*

Othello.

She had also been a cat's paw. Death had tried to warn me. It was somewhat comforting to know that he hadn't been mistaken. Or lying. Othello was the only answer that made sense. She must have given them a sample of my blood from one of my various wounds.

To protect her innocent nephew.

Part of my heart broke. I wondered how they could have gotten to her nephew in the first place. Almost no one knew of our past relationship. And almost no one knew who she even *was*. Being a notorious cybercriminal kind of made that difficult.

I spoke in a clear, deep voice to the Demon. "The Armory."

The Demon nodded, looking anxious to depart. A *crack* split the night as another figure suddenly appeared beside the Demon. The summoner. The puppeteer. I felt my heart rate increase in anticipation of what I was about to do to him. The Demon flung out a claw in my direction. "This was not part of our bargain, *summoner*. Our pact is ended. You never mentioned the Riders. Our contract is through." The man nodded, not speaking, and the Demon sighed in relief, getting ready to vanish.

"Not so fast," I said. "You took something from me." The Demon blinked in confusion, then tilted his head curiously.

"I have only heard of your reputation, Rider. We have never crossed paths," he answered neutrally. Respectfully.

I smiled back, unsure whether he could see my pleasure or not. Oh well, this was solely for my enjoyment. I didn't necessarily need him to know how pleased I was. He would discover that indirectly in the next few minutes.

I somehow tapped into the mantle of Death. It was actually very easy to do, which made me nervous on a very distant level. I was too immersed in the rivers of power that were suddenly coursing through my soul. I wielded the power like I was born with it, and used it to give the Demon a gift.

I gave him empathy...

Sympathy...

And guilt.

Then I sent him deep inside the pits of his own immortal mind to relive his most personal losses, failures, and heartbreaks.

Over and over again for eternity.

And it *broke* him.

The sound that tore from his throat seemed to break the very fabric of reality. I smiled as he withered to dust. The summoner watched, eyes widening. I had a moment to wonder exactly how I knew how to use the power Death had lent to me. Was it something to do with me being a Maker? Similar to how I had learned to Shadow Walk? Since I had witnessed Death showing off a bit at the bar, perhaps? The summoner finally turned to me after toeing the ashes with a boot.

"Hello, Nate," a very familiar voice spoke from beneath the hood. My skin turned to ice.

"*Gavin*," I snarled. The Harley – Death's horse – roared all on its own this time. I jumped down to my feet and was surprised to see that my legs worked perfectly fine. In fact, I didn't feel *any* of my wounds. Which was good. They wouldn't slow me down as I faced off against the man behind my parents' murder. My Parole Officer from the Academy. The man who had been tasked with keeping innocent lives safe from me.

But *he* wasn't safe from *me*.

In fact, he was entirely *unsafe* from me.

This made me deliriously happy on a subconscious level.

"So, we come full circle. It's just you and me, chucklehead," I hissed excitedly as I killed the engine and pocketed the keys to the motorcycle, speaking with a voice that wasn't completely my own.

CHAPTER 36

G avin peeled back his hood and smiled. "Not entirely." He waved a hand and suddenly Othello was kneeling at his feet, tears streaming down her face. I didn't know how long she had been there, but she seemed relatively unharmed.

For now.

"It's good to see you again. Othello, here, was quite the assistant over the last few days, even though she didn't know who I was, or that she had met me several times as your parole officer. I do love using cat's paws. I got the whole idea from the Angels and Demons. Keeping your own hands clean while orchestrating everything. I rather enjoyed being the puppeteer. Not unlike how the Academy runs things." His gaze grew distant for a moment, a frown crossing his features. "But they've gotten full of themselves and have forgotten their true purpose. I'm here to remind them what that purpose is." Now, his gaze became feverish, as if imagining the chaos that he would rain down on the ancient ruling body of wizards. I couldn't whole-heartedly disagree with him. We did need a change. But maybe a nuclear reaction wasn't the best opening move. "We needn't be on opposite sides," he finally continued.

"I don't like the benefits package your side offers. Although I definitely agree that the Academy is a group of doddering old asshats, I think I'm happy where I am." I smiled brightly. "And where *you* are. It makes it easier to kill you. Now, stand still for a second. This will only take a moment." I took an aggressive step forward.

He held up a finger. "You do know it's an immediate death sentence for impersonating a Horseman. You can take off the costume any time now." I didn't move. He laughed. "Fine. If that's what you wish to wear to your funeral, so be it. I won't begrudge a man his fashion taste." He appraised me for a moment, and then a grin suddenly stretched from ear to ear, and he began to clap his hands in applause. "Oh, this is *delicious*. It seems the Academy's curse worked exactly as intended. You're powerless!" I remained silent. "You had to know that this was their plan all along." He chuckled, shaking his head. "Those fools. But don't concern yourself. I'll deal with them next. In your name, even, if you prefer. Seeing as you won't be around to watch them fall." His calculating eyes grew distant for a moment. "Now that I think about it, you would make an excellent martyr. A death for all other wizards to rally behind. And I will champion the injustice shown to you. Yes, I can see it now. It's neat. Tidy. Simple."

I growled, tasting bile in the back of my throat. He began to circle Othello, idly toying with her hair. "You being so weak does take the fun out of this part. Like robbing candy from a child. How did you possibly hope to fight me?" he asked, waiting for a response. Again, I remained silent. I could tell that he liked to hear himself talk, but I also sensed that deep down, my silence was bothering him. Silence was a powerful weapon when utilized correctly. "Tell you what, you give me what I want, and I'll let the girl and her nephew live. I have no need for them, anymore. It's not like you can stop me anyway. You're dying. A few hours, tops." He was right, of course, but I didn't know how he knew. After all, I appeared wound-free at the moment. Then I understood. Othello must have told him. Maybe she had pleaded my case? Telling Gavin that I was already dead. To leave me alone.

One could hope.

One could also hope that she hadn't told him about me being a Maker.

He continued speaking since I had yet to give him the satisfaction of a response. "Your impotence is astounding. No money, no friends, no magic. Tsk, tsk." He pointed at Othello. "Save their lives. At least you can do that. After all, it took so much work to turn everyone against you. A few files leaked to the cops, a few hints to Jafar at the Academy. You know, paperwork." He brushed his hands theatrically.

I decided to play along. It wasn't really that hard. I was exhausted, and

Othello was there. And I really didn't know how to reliably use any of my powers. One wrong move and Othello died.

My shoulders sagged as a new thought hit me, making me feel all sorts of guilty. It had been a rough couple of days, but that was no excuse. "Fine. You win. But allow me one thing," I finally said. He paused, considering, and then gave a slow, benevolent nod. "Let me make one phone call." His eyes flashed with suspicion. "Calm down. It's just my girlfriend. I haven't spoken with her for a few days. She's out of town."

"As are the rest of your friends," he said with a dark smile. I began to feel uneasy. "It made things so much easier knowing that I wouldn't have to deal with your friends assisting you. It was surprisingly easy to arrange for all of them to be out of town. You really should be more paranoid. Did you never think it odd that they all had occasions to be out of town at the exact same time?" He didn't even try to contain his laughter.

But... that meant a level of planning I could hardly conceive.

"You... sent my friends away from me?" I whispered, almost heaving with fury.

"Yes." His triumphant smile made me want to break something. "Free airline tickets for the werewolf and your other friends." He paused. "Well, to be honest, Indie was rather difficult. I thought the night terrors would be enough to send her running in horror. But they didn't work. They tossed in a wedge, sure, but since she didn't comply, I had to cause an... *accident* with her mother. It really was the only way." He said, shrugging.

"You son of a bitch!" I lunged forward instinctively, ready to destroy every shred of his soul.

He held up a single hand, and a razor thin line of fire suddenly pulsated to life a hair away from Othello's throat. She squirmed against the flash of heat. "Ah, ah, ah. One more step and she dies. Quite painfully, I would imagine."

I was quivering with anger as I slowly pulled the burner cell phone from my pocket. It didn't matter now. The facts hadn't changed. I was alone, and he would kill Othello if I didn't comply. I had to give him my lifeblood. Samples wouldn't work, so he needed all my blood. Voluntarily. I had assumed it would come to this, and that I was a dead man walking anyway. I had come here strictly to save Othello. This was the only option left to me. Time to be a man. But I would do it with all the dignity I could muster. He had me by the short hairs, so I did the only other thing that was left to me.

I called my girlfriend. To tell her that I loved her.

My gaze grew watery as I contemplated what I wanted to say to her. She was my everything. The one who had held my hand in the darkness. Helped me through the worst time of my life. Inspired me to be good. To forget the awful nightmares. The one who wouldn't let me be weak. My rock. My love. My life. I wanted to somehow tell her all of this. To thank her. To tell her I couldn't have survived without her. I wanted to hear her sweet, silken voice. I wanted to tell her I loved her. And I wanted to hear her say it back.

The call instantly went to voicemail.

I was totally unprepared as the device beeped in my ear. "Um, Indie. I was just... look, I don't really know how to say this on an answering machine," I said, struggling for words. "I wanted to hear your voice one last time. I'm in a tight spot and won't be able to see you again. Just know that —" The phone shattered beside my ear. I jumped back with a yell, pulling my fingers away to find fresh blood.

"I saved her from having to listen to the rest of your suicide note," Gavin said disgustedly. "Let her remember her infamous *Master Temple*, not the sorry excuse for a man you are now."

"If only I had my powers..." I cursed under my breath, my mind frantically trying to come up with a way out of this. I had no clue how to use the other powers, and couldn't risk indirectly killing Othello as a result. Gavin waved me off, looking bored. Othello very carefully lifted her red-rimmed eyes, trying not to brush the fiery death resting at her throat, and began to mouth a single word. I think it was *sorry...* But then she saw my appearance and flinched, eyes widening. That's right. She saw Death.

So, this was it. I wasn't really surprised, really, just frustrated that I hadn't been able to at least get a small taste of revenge, first. Oh well. Maybe I would get to see my parents again.

Nothing had really changed. I had already accepted my death earlier tonight.

If I'm not dead already, I thought to myself. After all, my body wasn't even here. It was with the Horseman at the bar.

Wait a minute...

I *was* the Horseman.

"Goodbye, Nate." And that was it. I didn't even have time to feel the pain or consider my latest revelation. A screaming ball of black flame struck me in the chest, and I immediately became one with the universe, little Nate-icles exploding out into the cosmos of existence at the speed of light.

CHAPTER 37

I floated in nothingness. I *was* nothingness. *So, this is what it's like to be a Buddhist,* I thought to myself, having a better appreciation for Asterion's frequent rambling about balance, Zen, and Karma. It was... well, boring.

I began to reevaluate my life, wondering if my current state of being might help shed some light on those age-old questions. Who was I? What had been the purpose of my life? Was it just supposed to end like this? Nothingness? I blinked.

Then blinked again, my heart rate suddenly increasing. Nothingness couldn't blink, and it sure as hell didn't have a pulse. I wasn't *nothingness*. For the first time, I visually concentrated on my dark surroundings, and almost fell out of the boat.

Because I was sitting at the front of a small, rickety, one-man canoe on a river of inky black water, floating through the darkest of nights *towards* nothingness.

Okay, this probably didn't bode well.

Craaaack! The darkness muffled the sound, almost as if it had happened underwater, but I still jumped like a little girl, rocking the boat slightly. It sounded like someone had just popped open a beer behind me. Here I was, being all one with the universe-y, and someone was cracking open a cold one? Did they have no respect?

I turned, and then flinched as I realized I wasn't alone in the boat. Charon sat behind me.

The Boatman.

He was extremely... *creepy* up close, making me reconsider the wisdom in being friendly with him in my past life. A darkly stained, burlap robe covered his frame and continued in a shadowy hood over his head. He pulled the hood back and I instinctively leaned further away in alarm, trying not to hiss like a frightened cat. His skin was the color of aged ivory, and parched like old leather. His lips were sewn shut with a decidedly unhygienic, thick, knotted leather cord, and his eyes were glittering ebony gems. His hands were entirely bone, no flesh, and they were slowly rising towards me...

To offer me a fresh can of beer.

Not knowing what else to do, I hesitantly accepted it. He nodded, and opened one for himself. *Craaaack!* He wasn't rowing. Apparently, he wanted to take a booze break between carting souls to the afterlife. He lifted his can to me in salute then dumped it over his sewn-up mouth, maybe succeeding in absorbing ten percent of the beer. It was... messy, liberally coating his chest in the frothy 'Merican drink of choice.

"Good run," he hissed in a rattlesnake on sandpaper voice, almost making me release control of my bowels in pure terror. His lips, after all, were sewn up tight. Then I realized that he had spoken entirely in my mind.

Once relatively composed, I chose to reply out loud, not sure how good I was at the whole telepathy thing. "Uh, yeah. I guess." I looked around. "So, this is it? Kind of dreary for Elysium." He didn't say anything. I quickly pressed on. "Because I'm 99% sure that's where you're supposed to be taking me. Not the other place. I hear it's hot down there, and I'm not a huge fan of anything above 110 degrees." I was babbling. He continued to watch me in silence.

"Should you be drinking on the job? Don't you think you've had enough?" I asked.

"Just satisfying my appetite," he said directly to my mind. Then, a sound like a dusty leather bag being beaten by a piece of driftwood emanated from his sewn-up lips, and I realized he was... chuckling. Even his laughter was frightening. I seriously considered jumping out of the boat to fend for myself in the current of never-ending woe. The River Styx, the River of Souls.

This was the guy I had been so friendly to? He was downright *terrifying*. "Who's going to tell me not to drink on the job? It's not like anyone else wants to do this. It... what's the word? Ah, yes. Sucks. But I do have job security." His voice of crumbling ashes pierced my mind. I wasn't sure how long my sanity would be able to take the sound of Charon's voice if he decided that he preferred to have a long, drawn out conversation with the wizard who had been so friendly with him in the past.

"I guess so. You *are* taking me to Elysium, or whatever you guys call it these days, right?" He shook his head. "I think I was pretty clear. I don't think I'm supposed to go to the other place."

Instead of answering, he poured the rest of his beer over his sewn-up mouth, and then picked up his paddle. Glowing green runes flared to life as soon as his skeletal hands touched it.

"Charon. Really. Listen. I'm not supposed to go there."

He hesitated, considering thoughts that only the Boatman to the World of the Dead could fathom, and then turned his nightmare gaze back to me. His ebony eyes glittered in the green glow of the runes on his paddle. Then he spoke, face screwed up as if trying to remember something. "I had twelve fucks as of this morning. Now I have a dozen fucks. How many fucks did I give today?"

I... blinked.

The Boatman was... making a joke? He was staring at me with what I thought was supposed to be eagerness, but instead looked ghoulish. So, I answered, understanding that he probably didn't get many chances to exercise his humor. "You gave zero fucks today, Charon."

He slapped his knees excitedly and his face bunched up in what I guessed was a smile, the knotted cords over his mouth pulling tight, which made me wince with imagined pain. His smile would have made hardened soldiers run screaming in horror. "And I'm not about to start giving fucks now," he added. Then he appraised me. "That was funny, was it not?" he asked me curiously. I was kind of getting used to his voice. The way someone gets used to nails on a chalkboard.

"Sure. Hilarious, Charon," I answered with a sigh of resignation.

Then he began rowing the boat, aiming for a sudden vertical split in the river before us, a beam of glowing green light.

"It's not up to you. Or me," he hissed compassionately.

I groaned, my temper rising. "You've got to be *kidding* me. You know how many enemies I have down there?" I snapped.

He shrugged, continuing to paddle towards the light.

So, I drank my beer. It tasted good. Really good. Perhaps it was because I knew it would be my last.

We didn't move very fast. I guessed Charon wasn't really in much of a hurry. After all, it wasn't like he cared about anyone else's time schedule. His fares were dead. They weren't necessarily in a hurry to get anywhere. Most were likely *not* in a hurry to get to their final destination.

I finished the beer as we entered the light. A faint tingling sensation coursed down my arms, and I mentally prepared myself for the worst thing imaginable. What would Hell be like? Was it individually tailored to each person? What was my worst nightmare? I had experienced a plethora of them over the past few months. What could be worse than those? But as the light washed over me, a familiar scene surrounded us.

The salvage yard.

I turned to look at Charon with a scowl. Was this my hell? To relive my death over and over again?

I turned away from the bastard, staring helplessly down at the familiar scene. Then I noticed something odd. My body was lying on the ground, dead.

Othello still kneeled where she had been. But Gavin was nowhere to be seen. Charon waved a hand and a metaphysical window appeared, showing me the entrance to the Armory at Temple Industries, where Gavin was liberally, and furiously, throwing a dark, viscous liquid against the door. My blood. Nothing happened. His scream of frustration was a soothing balm to my soul. Then, totally unexpectedly, the freaking door *exploded*. Gavin barely escaped in time as I watched my company implode like a nuke had went off in the lab. Huh. I hadn't seen *that* in the blueprints.

Gavin reappeared before Othello in the Salvage yard. He was not entirely unscathed, much to my satisfaction. His face was cut up in two places, bleeding freely, and his hands were covered in my blood. His clothes were singed from the explosion, and he faintly smoked in places from the embers that had nearly burned him alive. His hair also looked silly, like a toupee on a particularly windy day. No, not *like* a toupee, it *was* a toupee! Oh, that was rich.

Apparently, my Hell was not being able to make fun of him for it, which was abhorrently cruel in my opinion. Not even a chance for one wise crack. I sighed.

Gavin struck Othello across the face, screaming in rage. "The place was rigged to blow!" Then he began to torture her in earnest. Like a child plucking the wings off of a fly, and I suddenly knew that he was much worse than the Academy. He was of the school of thought that *Might was Right*. Just like Peter had been.

I was forced to watch Othello be beaten to death.

I slowly turned to Charon, sickened and enraged. "So, this is it, huh?" I accused. "You're leaving me here to watch her die? As punishment for my sins? What sins have I committed to deserve this?" I finally roared.

Charon calmly stared back at me. He was used to this, most likely. Then he spoke in my mind. "It was nice meeting you, Master Temple. Do better next time."

Without further ado, he flung a hand at my face, and reality... *collapsed*.

I came to, panting hoarsely, my fingers clutching gravel in tight fists. I squeezed the gravel tighter and a blue haze filled my vision as the gravel silently imploded into dust. Then nothingness.

What the...

I slowly looked up as I heard the sickening *thud* of fists striking flesh. Gavin was towering over Othello. "You lied to me! I will tear the skin from your nephew for this..." The rest was incoherent babble as I realized a very important thing.

I was back.

I began to hum to myself as I climbed to my feet, once again in perfect key.

Back in the saddle agaaaiiin...

CHAPTER 38

I climbed to my feet and called out Gavin's name. Softly. Gavin flinched, practically jumping in his skin as he turned to face me, a look of utter disbelief painting his features. It made me smile, but I realized I still wore Death's Mask, and wasn't sure if Gavin could see my pleasure or not. "You… can't be here. You're dead. I killed you. I used your blood on the door. The Armory is mine now. You wouldn't dare attack me."

"You didn't get into the Armory. I saw you fail."

He spluttered defensively, spittle flying from his lips. His knuckles were covered in Othello's blood. He went with his original threat, seeing that I had called his bluff about the Armory. "It's death to impersonate a Horseman! I'll call them and tell them what you've done! Nothing points to me. I made sure of it. It all points to you!"

I watched him squirm like a worm. It was immensely satisfying after thinking I had died and was going to Hell. This was almost like *Heaven* to me. Then *that* thought sunk in.

This wasn't… Heaven, *was it?*

I hoped this wasn't Heaven – granting me hallucinations of victory for eternity. Oh well. If it was, so be it. I was going to make the most of it. I spoke softly, with all the authority I could muster. "Who said anything about impersonating? I'm here to condemn you for your lack of proper toupee etiquette. It's downright embarrassing, like a hungover zombie squirrel took a nap on your dome."

Gavin's hands jumped to his hairpiece, straightening it instinctively before a scowl crossed his features. I smiled. *Yes! Toupee joke accomplished.* This really *was* Heaven. "You saw what I did to the Greater Demon. I think you've had this coming for quite a while, Gavin. Don't worry, I'll make sure it's slow enough for you to experience every moment of it. I want you to see the twinkle in my eyes that signifies my sublime satisfaction at every millisecond of your agony. But first, tell me why?"

He quivered with frustration, but it quickly turned to pleading his case. "The Academy is broken. They've forgotten their true purpose. It's all politics, now. Favors exchanged for more favors. Not true Justice." He sighed, his shoulders sagging. "I was going to reset the rulebook. Establish a new Academy with the power of the Armory at my back. Start fresh. Salt the earth. A New World Order of Wizards."

I let him finish, not entirely disagreeing with his cause, but utterly disagreeing with the means he had used to pursue it. I nodded once – both in appreciation of his answer and as an acknowledgment of hearing his last will and testimony. And, because I would literally never have another legitimate chance to say it, I quoted *The Princess Bride* as his farewell conveyance.

"My name is Inigo Montoya, you killed my father. Prepare to die." I had always wanted to say that, and... *damn* did it feel good. Especially with the accent.

Gavin jerked his head around in a panic, searching for any way out.

And his gaze settled on Othello.

He smiled. "Well, if I'm going to die, I'll do it with finesse. You killed my Demon, now I'll kill your concubine." Before I could even blink, he slit Othello's throat with a whisper of magic, too fast for me to even consider stopping him, being completely unused to my new powers. She hadn't even raised her head to look at me before she died.

Othello's soul slowly rose from her broken body. She stared down at it in pity, crying. Then her soul looked up and saw me. Her form quivered in fear as she realized she was about to meet Death in his official capacity.

I had seen my reflection. I didn't blame her.

I smiled compassionately, hoping she could see through my mask to the human emotion beneath. "It's me, Othello. It's okay. I forgive you. Come to me." I encouraged softly in my mind. She apparently heard me, her eyes widening. A tear fell to my cheek beneath the cold bone mask. She hadn't deserved to go through this. But she had done it all to save her nephew's life.

Othello was golden, folks. If you ever meet someone like her, never let her go.

And I wasn't about to let her go out like this.

Time for some fucking absolution.

She blubbered in a whispery voice, her soul drifting beside me like smoke on the breeze. "I didn't have a choice. He kidnapped my nephew. He threatened to hand him over to the Demons if I didn't help." I nodded sadly, patting her ethereal hand in forgiveness. Gavin watched me with a frown, no doubt wondering if I was hallucinating. Then his eyes widened in realization as he glanced at Othello's dead body beside him, and then back to the air in front of me. He couldn't see her, but had surmised that Othello's soul was still present. And that I could see her. Which meant that I might actually be Death in the flesh.

"Thanks for not telling him about me being a Maker," I whispered.

She nodded sadly. "It was the only thing I managed to keep back from him," she whispered back, heartbroken with shame.

I nodded, and then winked at her. I turned away from Othello's shattered soul and faced my tormenter. "You see, Gavin, one of the handy things about this mask is that I'm a temp-worker for Death. So, I get the final say on who lives and who dies." I hoped that was true. If not, I would beg Death to take me in Othello's place.

Knowing he was backed into a corner, Gavin began to prepare a nasty bit of magic to fling at me in retaliation, but I didn't know how to use my magic, and I wasn't sure how helpful the mask would be since I had already 'died' once. I simply reacted, not concerning myself with the numerous wizardly ways of defending myself. I didn't consider using magic.

Instead, like a teenager in a street fight, I used the only thing I had in my pockets. The keys to Death's motorcycle.

Now, you may not know this, but if you want to see some serious damage, throw a wad of keys at a milk carton. It *obliterates* the thing.

It's incredible.

I aimed the keys for Gavin's face, hoping to throw off his spell for a second or two so I could figure out how to use my new power to stop him.

But the damnedest thing happened.

Midair, I saw the cute little scythe keychain turn into a real scythe. *The real Scythe of Death – Horseman of the Apocalypse.* And that thing was both glorious, and horrifying as... well, *Hell.*

Heh.

Wails from a million trapped souls screeched through the night, causing Gavin's ears to instantly bleed, and the temperature dropped by about a hundred degrees. Just like I had experienced in the bar an hour ago. The scythe made a *whump-whump* sound like helicopter blades as it raced towards the summoner. Then it sliced right through his delicate little neck like a hot knife through butter, cleanly decapitating him. Gavin's body stood upright for a few seconds before finally toppling over. His head bounced, and Karma came full circle as his toupee fell off. His soul slowly rose up from the steaming carcass, a look of sheer surprise as he stared down at his body.

Then he turned to face me. Death's temp-worker.

And *this* temp-worker was a tad bit vengeful, not overly concerned about becoming employee of the month.

His soul began racing towards me in what I assumed was a spiritual attack. I held up a hand and he froze before me. He stared back, fearful and angry. "Speak. Tell me everything, shade." And, seemingly against his will, he did.

"I wanted power. Pandora. I needed her assistance to help me overthrow the Academy. She *gave* all the magical beings in our world their power in the first place. All the tricks we know, she came up with first. And we only know about them because she *told* us. But she is rumored to have found a pathway far past simple magic, and discovered an answer that is truly unfathomable." His eyes danced were feral with hunger as he spoke. Even though he knew he was dead, he *still* wanted into the Armory. To Pandora. To steal that little slip of a girl I had freed upon the world.

I would probably need to look into that later. But not now.

Right now, I had a dish to prepare.

Vengeance.

And I was about to serve it pure, raw, merciless, non-GMO, and *cold.*

I couldn't think of anything else I really cared to discover from him. The second his lips stopped moving, I decided to let his soul burn. Right there. In front of me. Out of pure spite. Because I wanted to watch. I was cold, and a fire sounded nice. I didn't know if any of this was strictly allowed or not, but who the hell was going to stop me? Death could clean up my mess later. Or punish me later.

Because at the moment, I only had attention for the task at hand, and I really wanted to make it memorable.

Which is why I made sure Gavin's consciousness remained, so he could watch *me* watching *his* agony.

I stoked the eternal flames hotter, enjoying the fact that he couldn't actually burn away. When I made it hotter, his suffering was more intense, but he couldn't actually burn away. He simply... *burned hotter.*

I don't need to tell you that he screamed. That was implied. Sometimes soundlessly. Mostly not. And he hit every note, every pitch, and every volume – from sobs, to cries, to shouts, to shrieks, you name it.

For curiosity's sake, I made it colder. And I watched with way too much enjoyment as spirit-cicles began to grow on his eyelashes, his soul quivering from the sub-zero inferno. All with a thought. After a time, I switched back to heat, since that produced more satisfying screams.

The sound of his ragged wails was like a Beethoven concerto to my ears.

After enjoying his torment for a few satisfying moments, I idly began to think about food. I don't know why that was my first thought, but I was downright ravenous. My vision suddenly pulsed blue, and two sticks with marshmallows appeared in my clenched fist. I glanced down in surprise. Then I looked at Othello's soul to notice her watching me with a sickened expression, like she wasn't sure what kind of person could enjoy something so harsh. I averted my gaze to avoid the judgment in her eyes.

Then I looked at her body resting in the pool of blood.

Why not?

Charon's boat interrupted my thoughts, appearing before us. I held up a hand, smiling at the drunken Boatman. "Dick move, Charon. You could have told me."

He shrugged. "Not in my job description." Othello's soul flickered as if trying to escape the repulsive sound of the Boatman's voice. Or the continuing screams.

I shook my head, smiling to myself. Then I turned to Othello. She looked as if guilt was eating her alive, and her voice had a similar tone. "I don't understand what's going on, but please make it quick, Nate. I never meant to hurt you. I just couldn't let my innocent nephew die for the

Armory. I thought I could do it all. Save him, protect you..." She trailed off, a spiritual tear splattering against her pale cheeks. "Don't let me suffer."

"Not today, kid."

She furrowed her eyebrows in confusion. I held up my hands, and the blue waves of power around them shifted to green. I sensed Charon and Othello both watching me, but I ignored them as I very ungracefully forced Othello's soul back into her body.

Charon grunted, impressed or disgusted, I didn't know.

After all, I didn't really have any idea how to use Death's power. I'm sure I could have been a little gentler, but I was forcing someone back to life! Surely, she could forgive me for giving her soul a few bumps and bruises along the way. Her spirit and her body melded together until only Othello's battered body remained. I waited, fearful I might have done something wrong. Then her body arced up with a spasm, and she gasped as if being given CPR after drowning.

"It's aliiiiiive," I cackled into the night. Charon rolled his eyes.

Othello panted, eyes wild as she turned from me to Charon, patting her legs and chest in profound disbelief. Her wounds were gone, but she still looked unsteady. Weakened. Then her gaze settled on me, and I almost felt like a hero from a storybook.

"Pharos..." she whispered softly, her word filled to bursting with emotion. It was all she needed to say. Then she slammed into me with a great big hug, and immediately began to cry. I let her, closing my eyes as I smiled.

After a long minute, I gently extricated myself, holding her shoulders and looking her in the eyes. "Bros," I said, and lifted a fist. She glanced down at it, then, with a twinkle in her eyes, she pounded it with her own delicate fist.

"Bros," she answered in a faint whisper. Something in her eyes let me know she understood me completely. We were friends. Nothing more. Nothing less. But what we had was solid, and would always be there. Dependable. Loyal. Unwavering.

Bros.

As a side note, *definitely* my hottest bro.

I gave her another big hug, enjoying the background music of Gavin's agonizing screams as his soul continued to roast. I stepped back and appraised Othello. She looked a mess, but her wounds were completely gone. Which was good. They hadn't looked promising. And I wasn't sure how fast I could have gotten her to the hospital. I realized another added benefit of her not needing immediate medical attention. It gave me just the time I needed.

I motioned for her and Charon to both sit down beside me on the gravel so that Gavin's soul twisted and shuddered immediately before us, writhing in the green flames. I set him on a slow spin for aesthetic reasons. And personal satisfaction. My friends complied, and we sat before Gavin's burning soul and roasted our marshmallows. "Want one, Charon?" I asked politely. He shook his head, pointing at his sewn-up lips. I hadn't really wanted to see him attempt to eat a marshmallow. Instead, he cracked another cold one from a fresh six-pack hanging at his rope belt. Othello blinked, then winced as he eagerly dumped it over his sewn-up lips. "Another minute and mine will be perfect," I said conversationally. "You see, it's about that perfect brown color. You can't let it catch fire, but you have to let it get close to burning…" Gavin's eyes watched me with pure agony as he continued to shriek – watching as his agony produced our delicious treats.

My marshmallow was profound. Probably the most perfect marshmallow I would ever taste. After some time, I quenched the green flame with a thought, and found myself rather enjoying the immediate sounds of Gavin's relieved whimpering. I turned to the Boatman, knowing that he typically took the entire body of supernaturals rather than just the soul. "Leave the body. I'll need it to clear my name… hopefully." Charon shrugged, and as he climbed to his feet, he gathered up the remains of Gavin's ragged soul with a flick of his hand. The once-dangerous summoner's soul was dragged across the ground behind the Boatman, too weak to float or stand, I guess. Charon forgot to help him climb in, so when he yanked his hand, Gavin head-butted the boat, hard. Charon wasn't looking at his passenger, and simply yanked his invisible leash again, banging Gavin's face back into the side of the boat.

Once. Twice. Three times. *Then* Charon grabbed him by the face with that skeletal hand, picked him up, and slammed him into the floor of his ride.

Charon waved at us one time as he departed. Much slower than he usually did. I heard another beer crack open as the boat slowed even further. Something unseen began striking Gavin from the front and the back, causing grunts and gasps of agony as his soul twitched to and fro, unable to anticipate the direction of the blows before they landed. I watched as the abuse continued. Then I began to laugh, putting an arm around Othello. She collapsed into my chest, sobbing all over again with exhaustion, apologizing, and generally leaking bodily fluids all over me, ruining my cool outfit with her blood, snot, and tears.

But it felt nice to hold her.

CHAPTER 39

I heard a horse stomp his hoof, neighing like a Demonic Clydesdale. I turned to see that it was only Death's – obviously not a Harley – horse. I appraised the beast thoughtfully, studying the same glowing green sheen to his coat as the bike had sported. Then I recalled Asterion's description of the Pale Rider. "I wonder if he knows Grimm?" I murmured out loud.

The horse fucking *answered* me, causing Othello to gasp and jump behind me.

"Ah, it has been eons since we slaughtered and grazed together. I thought you smelled familiar." Othello peered around my shoulder like a small child, eyes wide as she realized the horse had, in fact, spoken. He had a refined British Accent like a James Bond actor.

"Um… that was kind of a rhetorical question. So, you can talk."

The horse grunted. "As can you, Maker." He rolled his eyes.

"Do I just call you *pale horse?*"

"I am known as Gruff," he answered proudly. I dipped my head politely.

"Pleased to meet you, Gruff. This is Othello, and I'm Nate." The creature bowed his head in response. Othello's eyes were about to pop out at this point, and her fingernails were beginning to dig into my skin. I patted my pocket as an idea suddenly hit me. I found it and pulled it out. Othello blinked at the odd black feather with the red orb at the tip. "Grimm. Come to me," I called into the night.

A peal of black lightning responded, and my little death unicorn, courtesy of Asterion, appeared before us. He stamped a hoof, spotted Gruff, and trotted up to him, rubbing the side of his feathered head against Gruff's glowing green mane. Gruff made a surprised sound, but responded in kind. The two of them walked away from the humans, no doubt to catch up on lost time. I smiled, wondering if Grimm could also talk. I didn't hear any voices though. I pocketed my feather, glad I had snatched it up from Plato's Cave before it burned down.

"That was courteous of you," a familiar voice said.

Hemingway – Death – strode out from behind a pillar of salvaged vehicles, assessing the two horses with a thoughtful gaze. Othello sat down in the dirt behind me, legs finally giving out. Her wild eyes darted from Death to me, and back again with confusion. I wondered how she saw Hemingway. Was he a doppelganger of me at the moment or did she see the guy I had met at the bar?

"So," he nudged Gavin's detached head with an unsympathetic boot, turning the summoner's eyes the opposite direction. "You caused quite a stir. Who would have known that a little manling wizard child would almost start the End of Days? What have you been up to?" Death looked at me, weighing my soul.

"Whoops?"

He chuckled. "I don't think you made any friends today. I believe you won't be too long in the land of the living. Every Knight of Heaven will be after you now. Using Cat's Paws, of course. They won't be satisfied until your blood paves the streets. Did you at least have fun borrowing my... accessories?" he asked.

"Uh, the Scythe was a nice touch. Especially after you threw a bitch fit about me borrowing it." Death grunted.

"Bitch fit, eh?" My arms pebbled at his tone, but he finally shrugged. "Intentional. You'll see."

I frowned, unsure what he meant. "I met Charon. Real charmer. Might have an attitude problem, or a drinking problem. Or both. Kind of a dick, actually. He didn't tell me where I was going. This was the last thing I expected."

Death laughed. "That was kind of the point."

"You probably want this back…" I began to lift my hand to the mask, but Death held up a hand, stalling me.

"Did you know that our masks were created by the first Maker?" He threw in conversationally. "He was actually known as The Mask Maker after that. He made four… One for each Horseman. You are the first Maker in hundreds of years. I wonder what toys you might create if you live long enough. Perhaps a new mask?" he asked, tone heavy with implications. I merely stared back at him in surprise. "Your kind was hunted down quite excessively. Too powerful, what with the rise of the wizards." He watched me, grinning distantly. "Something to look forward to, perhaps."

"That's… nice," I finally stated. Now I was the most wanted man alive? I'd had enough of this. "Here, I've caused enough problems. Take this thing away before I do something even stupider than I already have." I began to take it off.

"Wait." His eyes quested the salvage yard. "We aren't alone. This is still Act Two…"

With a big sigh, I began to rub my hands together for a scrap. Othello cowered behind me. Couldn't I get a break?

CHAPTER 40

a rumble of thunder shook the ground, causing several of the towers of vehicles to groan.

Three men entered the clearing, two of them recognizable from the bar where I had first met Hemingway. One was the red-haired, scar-knuckled grouch who had been glaring at us. Another was the sickly, older gentleman I had saved from the Hail Mary knockout punch. The third was a stranger to me.

"Allow me to introduce my brothers, the Horsemen. War, Famine, and Pestilence. Brothers, Nate Temple. The... Rider of Hope?" he smiled in good fun. At least, I hoped this was just some kind of joke. "He already has a horse. Grimm." The other Horsemen turned to look at the two horses off to the side. And then they each burst out laughing. Rather than taking offense, I shook my head, chuckling nervously.

"No thanks. I would make a horrible Horseman."

"He also looks rather like you now, Brother. I wonder why that is?" The beefy, red-haired Horseman added, pointing at my mask. War, no doubt.

I began to pull it away from my face and saw Death shaking his head quickly. "Not yet. It still has one more part to play. Trust me." The other Horsemen shook their heads in amusement. What the fuck was he talking about? Hadn't I caused enough mayhem? I studied the legends more closely. Pestilence sported a mask on his belt that looked like it belonged on a

Renaissance Doctor, complete with the long beak for a nose and everything. It was a blood red color. Famine had an aged scarecrow mask dangling from his belt, having been made from what looked like a burlap sack. And dark, oily stains marred its surface. War sported a mask of laughing flame. Literally. The mouth moved as it made the motion of laughter. While burning. I shivered. And a Maker had *created* them for these four wraiths. Someone like me.

Before I could think about that too much, Heaven and Hell arrived amidst more peals of thunder and general ruckus. If this continued, the salvage yard wouldn't survive. Couldn't they simply walk? As if on cue, they congregated to separate sides and watched us.

Watched *me* in particular. They looked curious, glancing from me to the Riders to the two horses and murmuring amongst themselves. After all, thanks to Death's insistence, I still wore the mask.

Then the seven remaining Academy members arrived with their damning silver masks as the familiar *Crack* of Shadow Walking broke the silence. Jafar then saw that he wasn't alone. His eyes widened at the Riders, the horses, then further at the Bible Thumpers. He stumbled backwards, as if searching for a safe place to turn, and promptly tripped over Gavin's severed balding head. Othello groaned in disgust. He fell on his ass most ungracefully. His eyes finally settled on Gavin's face and he flinched. I burst out laughing.

Jafar's eyes rose to meet mine, pure fear filling his face. He was the only one without a mask. I briefly wondered what I looked like to the Academy.

"You cannot be here. It is not time to Ride, Horsemen! No Covenants were broken, were they?" His eyes darted nervously to the Angels. Then the Demons, searching for an answer. "I'm here for Nate Temple. He is to be arrested for crimes against the Academy," Jafar demanded.

I turned to Death, silently asking if it was time yet. He nodded back.

I took off the mask. The Academy members gasped. The Angels and Demons merely chuckled as if at a good joke.

After a brief flash of confusion, Jafar pointed an accusatory finger at me. "You have consorted with Demons. It's the only way you could have survived. The Academy will make an example of you for what you've done. I promise you that."

Gruff stamped a hoof, causing the earth to crack beneath him. Grimm was also there, staring hungrily, but he did it well. The wizards flinched at the implied threat. Death spoke into the silence. "On the contrary, wizards. He was the only one with the stones to stand against your arrogance. This was *your* responsibility, and you are lucky I don't make an example of *you*. I might yet. Your own soldier, Gavin, caused this. Such an arrogant name, *Justices*. The presumption." He shook his head in distaste. "Nate, here, has saved this city. Despite your interference."

Several dark shadows from the Demon side grumbled. I guessed they were Fallen Angels. A step above the pitiful Greater Demon I had battled. A single voice spoke up, a hissed warning like a snake had spoken. He still had nothing on Charon. "Aye. He has no relations with us, although I would like to extend a job offer to him..."

Jafar's eyes creased in rage, assessing me for some accusation that might stick. I turned to the Fallen Angels. "Lot of that going around lately," I muttered. "Thanks, but no thanks, weird shadowy guy."

His answering voice crackled with power. "Call me by my rightful title, *mortal*. Knight of Hell or Fallen, if you must. Do not show disrespect to a being such as myself. Continue at your own peril. Even with the mask, you dare not stand against our might."

I shook my head, showing my palms and the mask, placating. This only seemed to cause a stir among them, as if I was threatening them with the mask. "Okay, okay. Calm down."

"No one is about to calm down," Jafar turned an accusing glare to the gathered parties. "He wields the power of a Horseman. How can this be? Surely, this breaks the Covenants."

I cleared my throat, standing closer to Othello, who was still sitting on the ground, trying to avoid attention from our powerful audience. I wanted to be close in case anyone tried to take out his or her frustration on the only unprotected class here. "I borrowed it. Stole it, to be exact. Death had no idea. I used my Maker's ability. It was the only way I stood a chance, thanks to your curse. While you were lounging away at the Academy, sipping warm milk, I was fighting for my life and the lives of those innocents in my city. Without my birthright!" I roared. "Innocent people died while you schemed safely away in your ivory tower, hoping to get your hands on the Armory when all the cards fell. Everything could have been lost because of your arrogance!" I was heaving. My vision rippled with a blue haze, a warning that I was dangerously close to tapping into my new gift. War appraised me, nodding in approval.

The same Knight of Hell spoke up, still not offering a name. "Much to our regret, the mortal speaks the truth. It was almost in the summoner's grasp. We were all used here, Heaven and Hell both. But you Academy *Justices*, on the other hand, have no excuse. We of celestial origins were all forced to use cat's paws to fight here. Angels with their Nephilim, we with our Demons, and the mortal here decided to gain his own cat's paw. The Horseman."

Eae, on the Angel's side, chimed in. "And all without breaking any Covenants, apparently, despite our encouragement to leave well enough alone. He has saved this city from my brothers' children. We judged you wrongly, Maker. Although I am interested in how you duped the Horseman."

The Fallen Angels scowled from within the shadows, grunting affirmation that they too would like to hear the story. I wasn't about to share it, or the lie that I had stolen it and that Death had actually *assisted* me.

I shrugged my shoulders. "Maybe some other time…"

Jafar growled in defeat. "Fine. You have allies in high places, Temple. Who was this alleged summoner?"

I smiled. "You just missed him. Well, you tripped over his head, but other than that, you just missed him. We had a few marshmallows and then he hopped on a boat out of town. You remember him, right?"

Jafar blinked with doubtful eyes, briefly darting to the corpse at his feet. "You expect me to believe Gavin caused all of this?"

"Having witnessed firsthand your impressive ability to see the facts before you and still make a horrible mess of things, no. I don't." I watched him like a bug in a box, watched as his calculating eyes tried to go into damage control. Politics. Gavin had been right. He didn't care that they had a psychopath in their midst. He cared only about how to pass the buck. Lay the blame elsewhere, so that his reputation wouldn't be tarnished. "He seemed to have this crazy notion that the Academy was broken. Political animals, he called you. Did you, by chance, happen to start this whole mess, jumping into my life and cursing me, as a result of information he provided you? Incriminating evidence of some kind, perhaps?"

Jafar's mouth opened. Then closed. His scowl grew tight. Then he nodded. "What is this Maker appellation they mentioned?" He said instead. Several of his Justices shifted nervously from foot to foot. I wasn't sure if it was from Jafar's question, or my accusation.

296

"Not your concern," I muttered.

Jafar opened his mouth, but War cleared his throat, flexing his fists at his side in warning. Jafar quieted under the Horseman's gaze. War's mask hung at his belt, flames covering a roaring, gleeful face. How did it not burn his *clothes*? I shivered.

Eae spoke again. "As fascinating as this all is, I merely ask the Horsemen for my Grace to be restored as recompense for this... misunderstanding. And I recommend you also return what you have borrowed from the Rider," he added, turning to me.

I smiled. "Will do. As soon as our *guests* leave." I made a show of discreetly angling my head to indicate the Justices. "Courtesy must be extended to even the most unsavory types, after all." The Academy bristled.

"Watch your tone, Temple. You have no power. You are now a Regular. Give us the key or we will raze your home to the ground. The Armory belongs under our control."

I paused. They couldn't sense my power? Odd. It was coursing through my veins like my magic never had before. More violent, feral, and lethal. Hungry. The blue haze across my vision intensified. I liked it better than the odd green hue from Death's mask. I definitely needed to learn more about this. After all, it was my only power source now.

War took a step forward, a meaty, scarred finger cleaning out his ear. "I'm sorry, did you just demand access to the Armory? The one your fellow Justice almost ignited Armageddon for? After everything, you think you can just walk in here and take the candy? It belongs to the Maker, who is now safely out of your jurisdiction. He no longer wields the power of a wizard. He has..." He winked at me. "Transcended such petty claims."

I burst out laughing.

Jafar's hackles rose. "Petty?" he roared. The other Horsemen instantly grew more still, and power fairly crackled in the air. A warning. I almost wished I had a bag of popcorn. Jafar moderated his tone, sensing his impending demise. "Every wizard is commanded by the Acad—"

War spoke. "That's his point, impudent *child*. Listen, before I grow angry." His voice was raspy, and one hand rested casually on the mask at his side. "Thanks to you, he's no longer a wizard. He's a Maker. Without your curse, you would have had a Maker and wizard under your thumb. Now you have neither. You truly are fools."

Jafar bristled, but I held out an olive branch.

297

Kind of.

"I'll take you to the Armory for a quick view of what your insolence caused." I turned to the waiting crowd. "This will only take a moment." I offered Death his mask. He shook his head. "You wear it well, and it might keep them on their toes." He added the last under his breath with a smirk. I smiled, nodding back.

I Shadow Walked the Academy members to what remained of the Armory, and pointed at where the door once stood. It was different using my Maker power to Shadow Walk. More efficient even. It hadn't taken nearly so much power from me, and I had done it while lugging seven people with me. Jafar rounded on me in anger, unhappy at me taking them here without his permission. "How did you do that? I thought you had no magic?" He accused. I didn't answer, only adding to his anger I shrugged instead, turning to the wreckage before us.

The concrete around the door was charred in a black circle one hundred feet in diameter, and the building was destroyed for hundreds of yards, as if a bomb had gone off right where we stood. It still smelled. A light patina of snow had begun to fall here, somewhat dousing the flames. I heard sirens in the distance.

"Witness what you have wrought. This happened when I died." Technically it had happened after Gavin had thrown my blood at the door, but... semantics.

Jafar appraised me curiously. "Died?"

"Yes. I died."

Jafar cast a doubting gaze back at me, eyebrows furrowing like a caterpillar taking a nap. "Surely, you are exaggerating."

"No, I died. I can even get you a signed affidavit from Death confirming this. The ... ultimate alibi, if you will." I smirked.

"Death?" I nodded. "How are they *really* involved? I command you to tell me the truth."

I decided not to rise to the bait. "They weren't involved. He can merely confirm that I died. So, thanks to your curse stealing my power, I was unable to protect myself, died, and apparently lost control of the Armory. But you knew the curse was permanent, didn't you? You designed it that way." Jafar merely stared back. I thought I caught a flicker of concern at my knowledge of his ruse, but he hid it well. And it didn't matter anymore anyway. I was now a free agent, as War had stated. "I didn't even know for sure that the Armory was here until you pointed it out. But of course, thanks to you falling for Gavin's lies, you knew all about it."

Jafar grimaced. "And what of Gavin? Why would he do such a thing?"

"You know as much as I do. He knew about the Armory. Tried to get in. Killed me, but died in the process. Othello killed him before he could get in. She's the hero. I don't know what was in there, but it's your fault what happens next. If War wasn't clear enough for you, I'll restate it. I hereby resign. Immediately. You want the magical world to work together, yet you cursed me for not complying with your extortion scheme. Two members of our own caste were killed. My parents. You never helped. Like sniveling family members, you tried to come to the estate sale and take what you could. You wouldn't help solve the crime, but you wanted a share of the profits. Karma bit you in the ass. You not only lost your opportunity to work with me to keep the Armory safe, but you also allowed the door to be fucking blown off. Who knows what is now loose in the world because of your greed? I won't be a part of your club. And apparently, I'm a hot commodity. A Maker." I winked at him with amusement. "Now it's time for you to get the fuck out of my city." I sent out tendrils of my new power to latch onto each wizard nearby and yanked them all back to the salvage yard with a slightly rougher version of Shadow Walking than before. They weren't pleased, and apparently didn't feel me doing it ahead of time, judging by their squawks of surprise. I very unceremoniously dumped them onto the ground, which didn't make Jafar very happy.

Everyone else was waiting patiently for our return.

Jafar drew a freaking sword, taking an aggressive step toward me after he had composed himself. "You lost it all. You are hereby found guilty of unleashing a weapon of mass destruction upon the world. The sentence is immediate death."

I smiled, and then used my hungry Maker power to inch the sword closer to his face rather than mine, watching as his muscles rippled in protest. Everyone froze, listening to Jafar grunt in disbelief. "What power is this? It can only be Demon-craft!" he hissed. His minions extended hands towards me, and a single ball of white-hot flame abruptly screamed towards my face with a wailing shriek.

Before I could react, the fireball froze in midair as one of the Angels blocked it with a sizzling flash of blue light. Simultaneously, a sickening red bolt of lightning shot forth from the Demons' side of the yard, shattering the frozen flame into a muffled implosion of darkness, eating the flame in a puff of shadows. "Touch him and die, Academy. We may have use for him someday..." It was the Knight of Hell. I shivered. "He has done no Hellcraft. Or Angelcraft for that matter. Do you think him that reckless? A mortal to wield the power of God? In the presence of God's favored and disfavored children?" The Angel waved his hand around the room in agreement. The shadows of both sides hungrily watched the Academy, anticipating.

Jafar spoke with a quivering voice. I released my power and he sighed in relief. "How could we not sense anything if it's not from Heaven or Hell? It *must* be magic, but I sensed nothing."

Eae shook his head. "It is *old* magic. Not from Heaven or Hell. You cannot sense it because you do not have the imagination to comprehend what Master Temple wields. Perhaps it is because he truly is a Maker." His eyes grew pensive as he appraised little old me. "I must insist that you leave this place at once. Before your presence offends your betters. More than it already has. Take what Master Temple has so graciously offered you. Life. I dare say you are no match for his new power. Even without the aid of the Horsemen." Then he smiled, slowly counting the Justices. "Even with seven of you." They blinked at this in sheer disbelief, and then looked at me in an altogether new light. I shrugged innocently. As I dropped my hands to my sides, I felt Death's motorcycle keys resting in my pocket. I frowned. How the hell? But I didn't let any of my surprise show.

I grinned at Jafar, clutching the mask in my other hand. "The grown-ups have important things to discuss. Run along, now, children."

They disappeared instantly, but Jafar's eyes fairly smoldered with hatred. I knew it wasn't the last I would see of old Jafar.

Famine spoke up, clutching his scarecrow mask in a bony hand. "I'm famished. Let's eat."

War rolled his eyes. "It's *still* not as funny as you seem to think it is." Then, without my permission, I found my ass violently teleported to a strange dimension. Much less gracefully than Shadow Walking. It felt like we were momentarily ripped out of existence, making me think I had actually been attacked. Othello gripped my hand tightly as a brave new world opened around us.

CHAPTER 41

$\mathcal{I}$ found myself in a fiery courtroom of sorts, with volcanoes and glaciers in the distance to either side of us. The skies roiled hungrily. I instantly realized that we were the only mortals in a very immortal world. I managed to peel my eyes away from the scenery after a few moments, and with a start, I noticed that I stood before a chair, clutching the mask in a forgotten hand, all by myself.

As the accused would stand in a trial.

I saw War leading Othello off to the side, as if she was a... witness.

He left her there, and then approached a long ebony table with his brothers. It looked like aged bone. The Four Horsemen sat behind the table facing me like judges, and I abruptly felt all sorts of nervous. The Angels sat on the left, the blue glow from the towering glaciers behind them limning their now-visible true Angelic forms. Which was terrifying. They had chosen not to reveal those forms earlier. Now things were more... formal. It was blinding to look at them with their glowing white wings outspread – each pulsing with natural, but different, sources of power – whether it was fire, stone, ice, glass, jewel, ether, or water. They began neatly tucking them back behind their shoulders as they organized themselves efficiently – by rank, I guessed. I looked to the other side to see the Demons also flaunting their true forms, flickering geysers of lava spewing into the air behind them like acne from the surface of the planet. They were all uniquely different, some lizard-like, animalistic, and yet others representing the various elements on earth with a darker emphasis than the Angels' elemental power. And they appeared to be restless rather than orderly, their black wings fidgeting as they snarled at each other for better seats.

Death cleared his throat, so I turned to face him, but he was interrupted almost instantly. An IHOP waitress was suddenly there, pushing a cart of... pancakes towards the Horsemen. Her face was blank, devoid of any humanity. But she had the right apron.

She set a plate before each Rider, flinched when Famine thanked her, and then she disappeared. They began to chow down as if they were the parents at a family dinner, and the Angels and Demons were the children.

But what did that make Othello and I?

After a few bites, Death cleared his throat again.

"We are here to determine this young Maker's fate. Ultimately, it is up to me, but since there are... extenuating circumstances that could possibly ignite Armageddon, I called you, my Brothers to stand Watch with me." They nodded between mouthfuls, looking disinterested, as if this kind of thing happened all the time. "Now, since we went over most of this in the salvage yard, this is really just a formality. Begin, Eae."

Several Demons snarled to themselves as the name rang out, most likely past victims of his various Demon thwarting excursions throughout history. Eae stepped forward, and I got a fresh whiff of his being. Frost and burning gravel. Then he told his version of the story. It sounded pretty straightforward. It seemed none of the Angels knew how I had managed to survive, or how I had damaged Eae's Grace, but he and his brothers seemed to agree that it was because I was a Maker. At least that's what Eae told the Court. I was pretty sure that they just didn't want to admit to everyone that the Demon had been strong enough to do it. Save face and prevent any particularly motivated Demons from trying it in the future. Which was smart. But it was a lie. Here I was, listening to an Angel flat-out lie. If I weren't sitting as the accused I would have run away screaming. Political intrigue was apparently not limited to the mortal world. These pigeons could lie with the best of them. Then again, maybe Eae simply had a free pass to lie when convenient in order to thwart the Demons. I shrugged, cataloging the thought away deep in my mind for later scrutiny. Overall, the lie suited my purposes. It only added to my mystery. And I was still trying to come to grips with the fact that I was still breathing. It kind of messed with a guy when he prepared for his impending death only to find out that at the penultimate moment, it wasn't going to happen the way he thought. Or at all. But I was still on trial. Maybe *this* was the right time, place, and way Hope had warned me I needed to die. After Eae's story, there was silence as The Horsemen considered.

"Nothing further to add?" Death asked between mouthfuls. My stomach began to growl as I watched them eat. Eae shook his head.

Death glanced at his brothers and they gave varying nods of understanding between mouthfuls of pancakes. "We will allow your Grace to be restored. If we don't, then this would be the end of days. As much fun as that might sound, it is not yet time. Agreed, Brothers?" They nodded absently. I stared open-mouthed. This was ridiculous. They didn't even seem to *care*. Were these trials that common? My reverie was interrupted as Death continued. "Then I shall restore the Angel, just as I have brought Othello and Master Temple back from the grave." The brief warning glance he shot my way could have been measured in nanoseconds, as if to say, *don't say a word*. After all, *he* hadn't brought us back. *I* had done that. Death's mercurial gaze let me know that he was impressed, offended, and seriously, seriously didn't want Armageddon to start. Funny. You would think that he of all people would want Armageddon to set off with a bang. Death was the *source* of his power, because, you know, he was the friggin *Horseman* of Death. That many souls would make him and his Brothers amazingly strong.

He continued. "Since the Demons inadvertently started all of this, they do not get this boon." There were a few grumbles from the Demons, but they remained seated, having expected this outcome. Death flicked a hand at Eae. The Angel visibly shuddered, and then a ragged set of tiny, wilted wings snapped out from his back, reaching only a few feet to either side of him. He looked rough, no longer like a Calvin Klein model, as if he had just been found at six in the morning outside a Vegas strip club with no recollection of the last few hours. Or days. Several Demons chuckled lightly at the sight, but lucky for them, no Angels noticed. They were entirely transfixed on their brother.

Without warning, jagged bolts of lightning from both the nearby volcanoes and glaciers simultaneously hammered into the Angel with twin explosions of light. As the initial flare of light faded, I saw him again. He grunted. Once.

Holy crap.

He set his shoulders defiantly, withstanding the raging flood of crackling energy pouring into him in a continuous stream – fire and ice, the children of the unforgiving, merciless Mother Earth – and was slowly imbued with the powers that God had once created in seven days. The torrent continued unabated, the bolts of power only growing thicker, and thicker, wilder and wilder. Sets of eyes – inky obsidian from the Demons and galactic ice chips from the Angels – watched the spectacle with intense interest. Eae's wings slowly began to flesh out, sprouting gleaming, pristine feathers over rapidly growing corded muscle, until they stretched a good six feet to either side of him, quivering with sizzling elemental energy. With a crack that split one of the volcanoes down the middle, the cord of fiery power from over the Demons' heads simply ceased, and a single feather rose above Eae's head, gathering light from the remaining cord of power emanating from the glacier. Lava began spewing wildly into the air, a dust cloud filling the already dark skies. The feather began to glow as it slowly rotated on its axis, faster and faster, brighter and brighter with each passing second. A shockwave built around the feather and then screamed outward in a sonic boom that shook my hair. The glacier calved, sounding like the earth beneath me had suddenly split in two. The bolt of power disappeared, leaving a purple haze in my vision. I blinked several times to clear my sight.

Eae stood before us, a veritable mountain of muscle, much larger than when I had first met him, and his newly remade body would have made the famous Renaissance artists envious. His Grace had been restored.

"I declare the murder of the Demons, the Nephilim, and injury of the Angel even. Both were misunderstandings or misguided actions caused by the summoner, who I will deal with in my own way." The last was a dark promise that caused several pleased nods from the Angels, and hungry, thoughtful looks from the Demons. "It's not a crime that Master Temple successfully defended himself from several Demon attacks. And it is not his fault that he found a way back to the land of the living. It's mine." No one argued, as Death's judgment was the final word on the matter. After all, the Horsemen were the judge and jury of Armageddon, and I *had* been acting in self-defense, having done nothing wrong in the first place. I nodded in appreciation, but held up a hand.

Famine clapped excitedly, pointing at me. I blushed. Was he for real?

"I have a last request, if it's not already clear."

Death nodded.

"The little boy, Othello's nephew. He is to be released." I did my best to sound confident.

The Demons began to grumble unhappily, but Death held up a hand. "Agreed."

I nodded. Othello's knees almost gave out but she managed to maintain her feet, shooting me a smile of such happiness that I couldn't help smiling back. Famine leaned closer to her and offered her a sip of his orange juice with a friendly smile. She accepted, with wildly terrified eyes, as if fearful of refusing his offer. He beamed as she took the faintest of sips. I chuckled to myself, feeling my tension begin to drain away.

It was... *neat.*

Clean. Orderly.

The Angels couldn't be pissed, and neither could the few surviving Demons. They had only been on earth thanks to the Greater Demon and the summoner. Sir Dreadsalot and Gavin, and I had sent them both packing. Everything important concluded, the Angels and Demons left. Somehow. I didn't exactly dare to watch where they left to, not sure if directly catching a glimpse of Heaven or Hell would permanently destroy my brain.

Death held out a hand and I nodded in understanding. I handed him the motorcycle keys and his mask. As soon as they touched his hand, I collapsed in pure agony, as if every single one of my recent wounds had suddenly happened for the first time.

Simultaneously.

I was whimpering on the ground. The torture slowly began to recede, leaving behind only the lingering effects I had felt prior to the church. Which was enough all by itself to leave me as a quivering puddle of throbbing pain. Several eons later, the pain began to subside enough for me to move. Barely. I still hurt. Everywhere. But it was somewhat tolerable. Death was speaking to me as I felt Othello lift me back to my feet, supporting my weight completely. I survived it, but scowled at her for good measure. Then I turned to Death.

He watched me, speaking slowly. "You can either have your original power back or allow Othello to remain alive," He said. I felt Othello go rigid beside me.

It took me a few seconds to trust my throat with identifiable speech. I looked from him to Othello. I managed to answer with several pauses for breath amidst spasms of pain. "Not that this is my deciding factor, but... you think I want to get my magic back and be under the purview of the Academy... after all I said to them?" I grunted at a particularly nasty shiver, glad Othello still held me upright. "No thanks. Othello is the true hero. I consider it a win-win. No more asshats in charge of me, and she gets to keep on ticking." I was definitely a crock wizard, and didn't deserve my old power back. It would be a reminder, the grueling years it would take me to learn my new Maker ability – the cost of arrogance.

And failure.

I slowly began to feel more or less human, able to withstand my injuries on my own two feet. But Othello was shaking slightly with barely-contained cries, so I kept my arm wrapped around her, squeezing her shoulder for comfort.

War came down from the table, but Famine and Pestilence continued eating their pancakes. "If you are still alive at the End of Days, I vote that you become a Rider with us. It seems you already have a horse, Grimm, and he will fit in splendidly with Gruff. The grumpy bastard is intolerable." Death scowled back, but War merely smiled before continuing. "You will be the Rider of Hope, as that is your most cherished value." I began to nod in respectful appreciation for the offer, and the fact that he had considered Hope to be a cherished value of mine. Then he continued. "You will pillage and rape all Hope from the world." My nod froze instantly. *What?* I hoped that this was just idle talk, and that I wasn't actually being bound to such a career path.

"I'm not even a Christian," I finally stammered.

Respectfully.

"That doesn't matter, *Maker*. Ragnarok, Armageddon, etc. are all the same to us. Christians got most of the facts right, so we lean towards that title."

Famine spoke up from the table, seeming interested in our conversation for the first time in a while. "You think any of us are *Christian*? That would be a... what do you humans call it? Ah, yes. A *Conflict of interest*. We are all non-believers, judges, pious," he said, laughing. "Perhaps not *pious*, but cast-out. You will fit in *excellently*." The last statement was said as the Rider leaned forward with a lethal grin. Apparently, I had impressed the Horsemen.

"I'll… consider it," I answered softly. Othello's face was pale, but she kept her thoughts to herself.

"So be it. You're a good man, Nathin Temple. You can borrow my mask any time." I shuddered at the thought. "Now, your body *did* literally die, so you must rest while I finish the paperwork. This will not go easy on your friends. Your death is all over the news. Your body was found in a bar near Soulard." Death smiled sadly, waved a hand over my head, and I promptly blacked out to the sensation of my forehead catching on fire.

CHAPTER 42

I woke to the sensations of warm air gently caressing my eyelids, and soft conversation from several voices tickling my ears. Unsure of who was near me, I carefully cracked my crusty eyelids open. Someone must have superglued them together because it took me a mountain of effort.

I was in the Temple Mausoleum.

And my friends surrounded me. Gunnar comforted Ashley in a close hug several feet away, his eyes chips of cold stone, and Misha and Tory were holding hands, sobbing softly beside them. Othello stood off to the side, alone, staring up at the Temple family tree as if she knew she wasn't welcome in their grief. Then again, she knew I wasn't truly dead. Had she told them it was just a ruse? No, they wouldn't be so grief-stricken if she had.

Then I spotted Indie. She stood alone, staring blankly at nothing. I took a deep breath and sat up, causing a slight *creak* of flexing wood.

Indie stiffened at the sound, then slowly turned around. She saw me sitting up.

From inside a coffin.

She... blinked. I smiled back tiredly. Then she took a shuffled step backwards and gasped. Gunnar glanced over his shoulder and saw her staring at me. His forearms shifted to claws as he shoved Ashley away. Everyone turned to look at me, then, with varying degrees of horror and confusion on their faces. Rage immediately rolled over each face. Claws appeared from Misha's arms with a *snicker-snack*. Her eyes flared red, a feral gleam catching the soft light. Tory's hand shattered the table she was using for support as she suddenly clenched her fist. And Indie cocked a freaking pistol held in a shaking hand. Right, I probably needed to put them at their ease or something. Before they made me die for real. But I was still groggy.

"I'm not dead yet," I rasped in a Monty Python accent. Then I began coughing. My throat was bone dry.

Ashley and Tory passed out in unison, crumpling to the floor like wet laundry.

Indie just stared at me with glassy eyes – shock taking over. The gun clattered to the floor uselessly, causing me to flinch in case it went off. With my luck, I wouldn't have been surprised it if took out the leg of the coffin I rested in, sending me crashing to the ground where I would instantly be devoured by my best friends. No one else moved.

I began to feel guilty about putting them through this. No one spoke, adding to my guilt, but Gunnar was growling and sniffing the air hesitantly. Then he bent over Ashley, keeping one wary eye cast over his shoulder at me. "Uh. Did you get my message?" I asked Indie. She continued to stare blankly back at me. "I didn't do so hot on my communicating, did I? Also, it looks like you're unemployed, as Plato's Cave was smited while you were away..." I turned to Ashley, who had been violently shaken awake by Gunnar and was groggily getting to her feet. "Temple Industries has a big hole in it. Crater, to be exact. Not sure how much that is going to cost to fix, but we'll probably need to talk about it. Later. I'm kind of tired right now. And thirsty." Blinks answered me. "So, how were your vacations?"

Then Indie covered the distance between us like a ninja and pounced on top of me. She began poking, prodding, and kissing every square inch of my face. It felt glorious. I sighed, leaning back into my coffin on my palms, breathing in her scent.

"How?!" she demanded between angry kisses and hugs.

"It's a long story. I'm just—"

Pow!

She smacked the living daylights out of me with an open palm. Stars exploded across my vision. Othello burst out laughing as the stars ever so slowly began to fade away. I continued as if nothing had happened. "Glad you're alright. Is your mom okay?"

She stared back at me, heaving. "Yes. Mild concussion, but she's fine." Her next words were precise, clipped, and dripping with warning. "What the *hell* happened while we were gone? The whole city is abuzz with talk of murders, explosions, and attacks." She shook her head, focusing on the important question. "How are you *alive*? They found your body three days ago. This doesn't make any sense." She began to sob, unable to maintain her anger, let alone comprehend my revival.

Othello chimed in. "Oh, he just stole Death's mask!"

Indie's sobs silenced in a blink. She turned an icy gaze to Othello. "She finally decides to speak. Who might you be, mysterious stranger?" Her tone dripped venom, even more of a warning than she had used when speaking with me. "Your voice sounds vaguely familiar..." Indie's eyes were diamonds as they turned back to me. I realized that Indie knew exactly who she was, and that I was about to pay for it.

Unfortunately for me, I had been an open book on my past romances.

"She's a friend of mine. Othello, meet my friends. Friends, meet Othello. She helped me while you were out of town."

"And do you make a habit of sleeping with all of your friends?" Indie's voice was brittle.

Gunnar chimed in, still sporting his werewolf claws, as if unsure what to make of everything. "He tried once with me, but I was able to resist. Thank god."

"That was in the past. We were much younger then." Gunnar burst out laughing. "*Her*, not *you*, you damn dirty dog." I scowled at him, fighting a grin. I turned to Indie. "I didn't even know you back then," I said softly.

Indie's eyes were flame. "What about while I was in the hospital with my mother?" I blinked, and then Othello burst out laughing. I felt an icy shiver down my spine. Did she know about our make-out session? Me being a dirty cheater? I had completely forgotten about it, thinking I had been about to die.

Priorities.

"Um... what?" I answered politically instead.

"Don't you *what* me, Nathin Laurent Temple! She answered the phone when I called, and led me to believe..." She rounded on Othello.

Othello finally stopped laughing and held out a hand. "Relax. I swear. I don't poach. He wouldn't stop talking about you and it made me… jealous. But I understand now. What we had was in the past… where it will stay. He loves *you*. Not *me*. In fact, it was quite disgusting to be around him, what with all the *Indie this,* and *Indie that* commentary. I acted like an adolescent schoolgirl. And for that I apologize." Indie's metaphorical territorial fur flattened a bit at that.

Bros.

Othello was a true *Bro*.

I would have held up a fist, allowing the glorious bro-light of the bro-universe to imbue my arm with a bro-ish salute if I hadn't already been in enough hot water. But I knew Othello understood my glance and everything it entailed.

But then she ruined it. She began to babble on unnecessarily.

"Everything I told you on the phone was true. We were tired. We had just survived a big fight with things way out of *my* league. A Greater Demon. Girl Scouts. A pack of Werewolves. The Academy. We were sleeping in the same bed. I kept him safe while he was injured. That's all. I swear. I owe him my life. Literally. You wouldn't believe what he did while you were all gone. It was beyond impressive. Even to the Ange—" I interrupted quickly. This was getting out of control.

"Wait, *you* called? I thought that was Gunnar!" I practically shouted to overcome Othello's diarrhea of the mouth.

Gunnar shook his head and Indie nodded. Othello blushed, admitting her white lie from when I had caught her answering my phone that night. Right before she had hidden my phone under the covers. My face began to heat up at that memory, but luckily no one saw it. Indie spoke up. "And what about the FBI, or that… *Demon*? You said you were going to work on your communication!"

Gunnar cleared his throat, approaching my casket as he held up a clawed hand. "I think we should give him a minute. Maybe he can tell us all from the beginning." I nodded gratefully, staring at his claw pointedly. He smiled slightly, allowing it to shift back to normal. He still looked wary, as if not sure exactly what to make of all of this. After all, I had risen from the dead. Gunnar then literally lifted me out of the casket and set me on my feet. After stumbling on weak legs, he supported me over to a group of couches in a nearby alcove. Where a toasty fire was roaring. I fell down into the couch. Indie jealously, and very obviously, sat as close to me as possible. Othello sat in a chair in front of me, understanding Indie's territorial claim.

"It all began when a roaring drunk wizard," I pointed a thumb at my chest, "An Angel, and a Horseman of the Apocalypse walked into a bar..."

Their eyes widened and their jaws dropped further with each word, shaking their heads in disbelief and amazement as Othello backed up and clarified several points. Her version seemed to paint me as much more of a badass than my version did. Not how I saw it. I had been running from fire to fire with a leaky water bucket, trying to put out a raging inferno as someone else poured gasoline onto the flames.

I told them about the Academy stealing my powers, my parole officer, Gavin, working as a double agent and setting all my friends up to leave town. That elicited a dark growl from Gunnar, which was gently calmed by Ashley placing a soft hand on his knee. I told them how Gavin had even hurt Indie's mom when she wouldn't break up with me. Indie stiffened at that, a single tear spilling down her cheeks as she realized just how close to death her mother had been. I explained the source of my night terrors. The FBI arresting me. Othello busting me out. Gunnar grunted at that. Death, the Angels, the Demons, and of course, the Werewolves. Gunnar seemed particularly amused at mention of the wolves. Tory nodded with a grin, "He wasn't that tough. I slapped the shit out of him in the bar. Not even a challenge."

"I'd like to meet him." Gunnar said with a distant, menacing grin.

Indie was clutching my hand. "You make it sound so nonchalant, while Othello paints it as the scariest few days of her life."

A new, familiar voice spoke up from behind the couch. "Nate is too humble. He literally battled agents of Heaven and Hell after his own people stole his magic and tried to extort him to give up the Armory. And he *still* won. He's earned quite a reputation in certain circles."

Gunnar had jumped to his feet at the first word from the intruder's mouth, claws shifting entirely, and the threads on his clothes popping and snapping as his body began to mutate into partial wolf form. Everyone was glaring with lethal intent at the creature behind me. Misha sported red dragon claws and a hungry, eager smile. I held up a hand to calm everyone down, but was secretly proud of my friends. I didn't turn to look at him, speaking over my shoulder instead. "Shut up, Death. You're going to make me blush. Everyone, meet Death – the Horseman of the Apocalypse. A recent drinking buddy of mine, and generally a bad influence."

I then turned, gently applying pressure to Indie's hand in reassurance. She looked terrified. Everyone seemed to calm down a few notches as Death politely approached our gathering. "Don't worry. He's not on my list. His death was a ruse. Othello and I had to make it look legitimate." He waved a hand at our surroundings. Othello nodded guiltily, blushing slightly as Death smiled at her.

Hmm… *That* wasn't weird.

"My apologies for the discomfort this may have caused anyone." Indie grunted at the understatement. "This is merely a courtesy call. Checking up on my patient… and new friend." Death added the last with almost a questioning tone. I nodded, giving him a respectful nod.

The tension in the room slowly dissipated. But no one spoke, as if fearing what he or she was supposed to say or not say to such a feared legend. Death, with all the charm I had first seen in him from the guy at the bar, soothed everyone's concerns. Individually. He moved like a wraith from person to person, murmuring a private word or two to each of my friends. I don't know what was said, but he left each person as white as a ghost, yet also smiling at something only they knew. It was as if he had told them something that eased a hidden dam of emotions they had bottled up for years. As if he had given them peace of mind. The skin on my arms shivered as he approached Indie. She was close enough that I could hear. He also spent longer at her side than any of my other friends.

"As soon as I heard about Gavin's attack I rushed to your mother's side in the hospital in Colorado. She had been attacked by a Demon that he had sent. After seeing to her immediate safety, I decided that I needed to meet Nate, here. To judge his worth. To see what kind of enemy would push Gavin to cross such a line as attacking a peaceful, defenseless old woman. So, I went to the bar, Achilles Heel. I learned of his night terrors. His parents' murder. His bravery against the dragons. And much more that I'm sure he didn't realize he had shared. I have the gift of being able to draw out life stories from people. Then I was awed, as I watched him stand up to a very, *very* powerful bully. All because he found it necessary to find justice for his parents' murder. To fulfill a Blood Debt. He was a pillar of… righteousness, despite standing against a creature that hopelessly outmatched him. I wish I could have been half the man at his age… After that, I watched over your mother while she was in the hospital. Because Nate had impressed me… and *you* had impressed *him*. Be comforted in the fact that your mother will live to a ripe old age, dying of natural causes. In the distant future."

Then he stepped a polite distance back from all of us. I was dumbfounded. Indie's jaw was wide open. I touched her hand but she didn't respond, so I leaned closer. "I guess I'm as awesome as I think I am." Her eyes flashed towards me, as if just waking up. Then she leaned forward very aggressively and kissed me right on the mouth, wrapping her arms around me in a hug that hurt so bad it felt good. I patted her back as she rested her head on my shoulders, sobbing lightly, overwhelmed with joy at her mother's Guardian Angel – *erm – Horseman.*

Death cleared his throat. Everyone turned to face him, eyes filled with various flavors of appreciation and gratitude. "I hope that allayed any concerns you may have about me." Everyone nodded, so he continued. "As I just said, this is only a courtesy call. I received a request from a mutual friend." I squinted at Death, wondering what he was talking about. Then Charon appeared, nodding respectfully to me from his boat, drinking a beer. Luckily, he was keeping his face covered by his burlap hood. "He really thinks a lot of you," Death added.

"Well, I'd rather not meet him on official business any time soon. Again. Or you." I hoped Charon wasn't about to speak, or else all of my friends would find out what it was like to soil their pants. That voice was going to haunt my dreams. I just knew it.

Death nodded with a grin. "Agreed."

"How's Gruff?" I asked, curious about his horse.

"He's fine. He was… intrigued by you, and your connection to Grimm." Death arched a curious brow. "Is it merely a coincidence that…" he glanced to my friends, and then continued cryptically, "That you already have a horse to ride?" His emphasis on the last word made me shudder slightly, but I don't think anyone else understood his meaning. Except Othello, but her face was blank, giving nothing away. I was not going to become the Horseman of Hope. First off, it sounded cheesy. Second, it seemed like a horrible job to take Hope from the world at the End of Days. They had only been kidding with me, right? I shrugged, ignoring my friends' curious looks.

Death turned to my friends. "I have something to show all of you. Some people I would like to introduce you to." My shoulders tightened.

"That's probably not necessary—" I began nervously. My friends did *not* need to meet any of the other Horsemen.

Or Angels.

Or Demons.

"It was not a question," Death answered coolly, reminding me of my place.

Wow.

My friends nodded as one, intrigued. We climbed into Charon's boat, which seemed much larger than the first time I had ridden in it. I followed suit. "Just make sure you leave your hood up, Charon, and please don't speak. Your breath is literally fatal." He took another sip of his beer. I pointed at it frantically like a tattletale and looked at Death, who sat across from me. "You okay with our driver being drunk?" Death shrugged. Charon merely took another unconcerned drink as everyone climbed inside the boat. Then the world around us shifted between one blink of the eye and the next, and I found myself back on the River of Souls. My friends thought it really interesting. I merely felt tense.

Who wanted to meet my friends? Was this a trap of some kind? I mean, I really didn't know Death all that well. Was he kidnapping me and my friends? My unease began to build at an alarming rate as I thought of all the horrible things that might await us. After an indeterminable amount of time, my friends realized it was actually quite boring to float down the River of Souls. There were, after all, no sights. Just nothingness. Then a faint green haze abruptly appeared before our boat. I spotted towering statues on either side of the river, menacing creatures standing guard to what seemed like a large amphitheater.

They each depicted Cerberus, Hades' pet guard dog. The beast that both protected his realm and prevented a spiritual prison break. As I watched one of them, I was suddenly ninety-nine percent sure that it blinked. I flinched as I noticed a giant drop of drool fall to the river without a splash. My friends didn't notice, but Death shot me an amused smile.

As I turned back to strange sounds emanating from the amphitheater, I realized it was... *hopping*. Big band music blared from unseen speakers. And hundreds of people were dancing. I stared in curiosity as Charon rowed us up to an ornate pier. We came to a gentle stop and Death assisted the women out of the boat, but left Gunnar and I to fend for ourselves. He nodded respectfully at Othello, appraising her in a very hungry way. No way… She seemed to notice, blushing, but said nothing. I left *that* alone. It was none of my business.

Freak and let freak, I guess.

We entered what seemed like a banquet or dance hall. And I realized that it wasn't people dancing, but *souls*. And they were *everywhere*.

My mortal friends simply stared. The music quieted noticeably, but didn't stop, and the crowd of souls turned as one to watch the master of their domain and his guests enter the party. Talk about Red Carpet attention. Death cleared his throat. "I believe you said something to Othello about *not going down without one hell of a fight. That you were going to cause such a ruckus dying that Death himself will shake my hand and send me back with a farewell party to get rid of me.*" I felt myself shrinking in embarrassment as I stared into the Horseman's eternal eyes.

Then he extended his hand. "Well, here's your party, and here's my handshake… friend," he said with a smile. I relaxed, and slowly reached out to shake it with a guilty grin, acknowledging the quote and his offer of friendship. Then the souls surrounding us bowed respectfully, some pointing at me with interest, before they began to step to the side to make room for us. They made an empty path across the length of the room between them, and at the end I saw two souls in particular facing the opposite direction. The crowd hushed and the two figures slowly turned.

My heart shuddered and then stopped.

"Mom, Dad…" I whispered.

Death caught me before I collapsed. Indie grabbed me by the shoulders, helping Death support me.

My mom and dad approached, slowly at first, my father looking proud, and my mother full of love and… concern. Glowing tears trailed her cheeks. "My son…" she whispered. Then they were floating towards me in a dizzying blur. They abruptly halted before me and I heard Indie sobbing softly as she continued to hold me up. My legs were jelly.

My dad gripped me by the shoulder, despite being a spirit. "It worked!" He exclaimed. I blinked, and then understood that he must be referring to my Maker ability. I held up a palm, and a ball of blue flame filled my palm as my vision was transformed with the familiar blue haze. My eyes were misty as I stared back with a weak smile. My dad grinned like only a scientist could. "We are so *proud* of you, my son." He turned to the crowd of souls. "MY SON!" He roared, lifting his hands. The resulting applause was deafening, shouts of glee rattling my brain. My throat was raw. My mother latched onto me, hugging me tightly, and I broke down, tears falling freely. My flame died and I hugged her back. Desperately.

You see, I never thought I would ever get the chance to do this again. Like all stubborn youths, I had rebelled against them, pushing them out of my life to pursue my own dreams with Plato's Cave. But it hadn't necessarily needed to be a mutually exclusive pursuit. I could have, and *should* have, pursued both. But you never discovered things like that until it was too late.

The *pain.*

The *guilt.*

The *sadness.*

The *joy.*

It *broke* my resolve.

"I'm so sorry," I whispered. "I almost lost it all. I wasn't there to help you. My own friend, Peter, betrayed me to rob the Armory. I don't know if that was why the Demon killed you, or if you would have been spared without him breaking in, but it's all my fault. I couldn't keep it safe. The Pandora Protocol is broken, and... whom you had stored inside is now free. I failed."

My mother leaned back with a curious frown. I looked at my dad, who also seemed nonplussed. "The Pandora Protocol?"

I nodded guiltily.

Then he shrugged. "That's not really a big deal. She's been free before."

I blinked. "*What?*"

"The Armory was just a ruse for the Academy's benefit. We needed something to attract their ire so they wouldn't notice what we were *truly* working on. We also needed a way to free you from their clutches. Hence, the gift we gave you. The power of a Maker. Without the traditional magic, they hold no sway over you, now."

I stared, dumbfounded, unable to speak, despite my mouth opening and closing several times. "You mean to tell me that all this was for *nothing?* The Armory wasn't *important?*" I was huffing, sudden rage coursing through my veins. Everything had been for nothing. The death, Othello being killed, Indie's mom being hurt.

For *nothing.*

They watched me, abashed. "It was the only way. Dark times are coming, my son. You need to be out of their control. We fear what the Academy may do in the years to come. We gave you the tools to stand on your own two feet as an independent. The world will need you in the years to come. My Maker," my mother added with a loving smile. "Oh, how I wish I could see Jafar's face right now." Her eyes gleamed maliciously.

My anger began to fade as I remembered that I was with my parents again. *Really* with them. And that was all that truly mattered. "Yeah, he wasn't too pleased about my power surge, or the fact that I'm now a Maker and not a wizard." I pondered that. How had they known that my magic would disappear? After all, if I gained the Maker ability yet kept my magic wouldn't I still have been under their control?

My dad seemed to sense my question. "The reason your power spiked upon our deaths is that the Maker seed needed to feed on magic in order to survive. A very large amount of magic. It was the only way to birth the gift inside you. How long did it take for the power to dissipate?" he asked, again, like a scientist.

"It didn't dissipate. The Academy cursed me."

My dad blinked, and then... well, he burst out laughing, clapping and hooting as he did a little jig of joy.

"What's so funny? I almost *died!*"

My dad merely wrapped me in a bear hug. "They had no *idea!*" he roared into my ear. "Cursing you caused your magic to deplete that much faster, making you immensely more powerful as a Maker than anything we could have done. Oh, I would *love* to hear Jafar explain this to his boss. Not only did he curse you, but he made your gift infinitely more powerful than we ever could have. He literally gave you an adrenaline shot for your Maker power. The seed had to feed on the magic much faster and intensely in order to survive, which made it grow exponentially faster than it should have on its own. You are now something that has never before walked the earth. A Maker far more powerful than any who has ever existed." He clapped in sheer joy again, pushing me away to arms-length and then pulling me back in with several slaps on the back. My mother finally shooed him away.

I managed to reply. "Yeah. If I can figure out how to use it reliably," I muttered. My friends were staring at me as if they had never seen me before. Death merely looked interested. I was now more powerful than he had thought. Which could be utilized by any who knew how to manipulate me. I instantly wondered how much I could trust the Rider, and again, whether he had been serious about me becoming a fifth Horseman of the Apocalypse. My resume had just beefed up considerably.

"Don't worry, my son. We left instructions at Chateau Falco. Everything we could discover on Makers. That was our real secret. What I said to the security camera after our death. You did see the video footage, right?" I nodded. "Good. Also, the entrance to the Armory at Temple Industries was only a secondary entrance. Which is why there was a seventeen-minute window. The primary entrance at Chateau Falco has no such restrictions. You should find the Armory, more or less, as you left it."

I couldn't believe it. "This... really was all for nothing, then. Me trying to protect the Armory from the summoner and his Demons." They nodded, their excitement slowly fading.

I turned away in an attempt to hide my rage.

I almost lost it.

Right there.

But I was a restrained, wise, utterly in control wiz... no, *Maker*.

Instead, I took a few deep breaths to regain my composure.

I was alive. I had a woman who loved me. Everyone was safe. And I had learned a lot about myself. I wasn't just a wielder of ancient arcane power. I was something else entirely now. When I had been pushed up against a wall without backup, magic, or money, I had persevered. Even as a penniless Regular. I found solace in that.

I suddenly realized what the most important thing in the world was.

It was something I'd never thought I'd have the chance to do.

I turned back to my parents, grabbed Indie's hand, and walked up to my mother. I scrubbed a tear from my cheeks. "Mother, Father, this is Indie. She is... very dear to me." Indie's eyes filled with tears, and even Gunnar grunted with overflowing emotions.

Life wasn't all bad. It was actually pretty *good*.

CHAPTER 43

*W*e had left the Underworld, or Hell, or wherever we had been taken, after a whole lot of story-telling. Death had shared his origin story with my friends. The same one I had heard in the bar. My mother ignored all of this and instead fussed over Indie like only a mother-in-law could. Giving her advice on managing my temperament. I rolled my eyes at some of her tips, but curiously found myself listening as some of it was actually quite insightful. I would have to stay on my toes from now on. Indie was gathering quite a bit of useful knowledge. My father slapped Gunnar on the shoulder and hugged Ashley upon hearing of their engagement. He also recognized the stone on the ring. It had come from one of the diamond mines I owned. The girls had all fawned over Ashley's rock, causing Gunnar to swell with pride. My father had been very interested to meet Misha and Tory, even more so at their abilities. He had never met either flavor of supernatural before. They remembered Othello, and looked slightly nervous at her inclusion in my club, no doubt remembering our past romantic dalliances. But everyone seemed more or less accepting of that particular past, and had moved on to more important topics. To my relief, even Indie seemed less concerned about Othello than before. She even thanked Othello for watching my back when everyone else had been absent.

Death and Othello had walked off to the side, speaking to each other silently as the rest of us continued to talk to my parents. *Curiouser and curiouser.* Othello had a slight spring to her step after that, but I left it alone. She would tell me if she wanted to. I had enough on my plate without sticking my nose in that beehive. But I guess they did have the whole *shared life experiences* thing going for them after Othello had died and come back. It was practically like meeting the in-laws. Indie seemed downright encouraging.

Before we left, I pulled Death aside. "Can you do me a favor?" He grinned in anticipation of what I might ask, nodding. "I need you to deliver something to a werewolf for me. You still have it? Like I asked?"

Death began to laugh. "*That's* why you wanted me to preserve Gavin's head. You're one cold bastard." He chuckled with approval. "You're *perfect* for our club." He clapped me on the back.

I neither agreed with nor denied his statement. "I promised the wolf I would avenge his mate. Seems a fitting way to give him absolution, and Gavin deserves it," I added with a growl.

"I'll take care of it."

"Oh, and put a ribbon on it."

He rolled his eyes. "Okay. You're welcome back anytime," he offered with a grin. Then he left us to say our farewells to my parents and the other souls.

We had then retreated to Chateau Falco, and were now sipping drinks before a large fireplace. Dean and Mallory had returned from their trips and joined us, as well as Raego, at Misha's insistence, and Agent Jeffries at Gunnar's insistence. After the shock of my death had been proven false, things went splendidly. We had shared tales back and forth, and I was informed of the latest developments in my city. Apparently, I had been dead for a few days now. Kosage had been caught lying his ass off to get me arrested in the first place, pulling strings he really shouldn't have tried to pull. No doubt influenced by Gavin, but no one seemed to believe his story of a concerned citizen providing him information on my guilt. Especially since said citizen could not be found. Jeffries had apparently found proof that Kosage had bribed a judge to get the warrant for my arrest, as well as blackmailing a few of the FBI Agents. All that in addition to the blackmail footage Othello had left in the file at the police station with him in drag and BDSM gear had basically shut down his career.

Even though no one could explain how I had escaped my cell and been kidnapped, they had no proof of anything else, and I hadn't been spotted at any of the recent crimes.

Also, I was allegedly *dead*. I couldn't wait to reappear at an upcoming Gala with Indie on my arm like nothing had ever happened. Jeffries finished his story of Kosage's downfall with a grin. "Sound good, Temple?"

"Oh, if anyone tries to pull me back into any of this again you can bet your ass I will hire every lawyer in town to eviscerate him. I would destroy every lawman's career… Except you, Jeffries. You're the only honest one I've met. Agent Wilson wasn't too shabby either."

Jeffries grinned, "I spoke with him. They won't continue their inquiry, even after you announce your resurrection, if anyone could even call it that anyway. They even pardoned you and Gunnar for the dragon ordeal a few months ago. Gunnar has been reinstated if he wants to be. If not, he will receive honors befitting his retirement."

I grinned at Gunnar's resulting smile. "I also need Agent Wilson to call and formally apologize to Indie for what his Agents did. Hanging up on her. Not letting me get my phone call."

Jeffries winked. "Done."

"Also, it seems a patrol horse found his way onto my property. Could you arrange for Xavier to be quietly and anonymously returned to the police force? No one needs to know what happened, and I will look down upon any negative consequences his handler receives."

Jeffries nodded, chuckling to himself. Everyone left. Except Indie.

We made up for lost time.

And more.

She seemed exceptionally motivated to remind me what a catch she was. She thoroughly exhausted me. As I lay in my bed, Indie sleeping peacefully beside me, I felt a tug at my soul. Curious, I got up and wandered the mansion.

After a while, I realized I was being drawn to my father's old study. I sat down in the chair, and spotted the note that I had already read. It had been found on my desk when we came back. It was from Achilles. *Come back any time. I want to talk to you about something.* I shivered at that. Maybe later. I began fiddling with a pen, wondering about the odd sensation that had drawn me here, and its sudden disappearance. Was this the primary entrance to the Armory my father had spoken of? Somewhere in this room? It made sense.

As if in response, a soft voice abruptly invaded my thoughts, sounding defeated and weakened. *I've returned, my host. Freedom wasn't what I thought it would be. So much pain and suffering in the world, and I fear more is yet to come. You will need me in the upcoming years. I have foreseen great devastation, and you stand at the forefront of it all. Your parents and I await your presence in the Armory whenever you are ready. I have granted them temporary access thanks to the Horseman's... encouragement. You will need training in your gift. Only we can teach you to become The Maker.*

Then the voice trailed off. I shivered. My parents resided in the Armory with Hope? No, not Hope. Pandora. Death had *encouraged* Pandora to grant them access?

Then another thought hit me.

Pandora hadn't elaborated if I was at the forefront of the impending storm because I was *fighting* it...

Or *causing* it...

I wandered back to bed, very, very concerned about both my new powers and the role I would play in the days to come...

∿

ate Temple returns in **GRIMM** *– The Brothers Grimm – legendary supernatural assassins – have escaped their prison, and their first day in St. Louis could be Nate Temple's last... Turn the page for a sample...*

GRIMM (NATE TEMPLE #3)

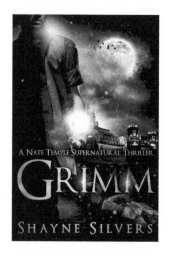

A lot can happen between *Now* and *Never*.

I once read that the phrase *it's now or never* was first coined to describe that moment that if one doesn't act upon right *now*, that they will never again get a second chance to do so. They would miss their one opportunity. Usually through their own fault, but sometimes that vindictive bitch named Karma could ninja flip out of a closet to give you a solid monkey fist to the stones.

You know…

Perhaps you had been facing a once in a lifetime opportunity – saying hello to the cute girl at the bar before anyone else; or maybe you had stood in silence for twenty seconds too long during your oral presentation in front of the classroom and desperately needed to formulate words that closely resembled anything intelligent.

Basically, you needed to do the thing *right freaking now*.

Carpe Diem.

Like me.

Right *now*, I was standing in the chilly sewers beneath the fine city of St. Louis in order to check off something on my to-do list. Something that was likely going to get my fancy new coat all smelly and icky in the process. Still, getting my coat smelly and icky was better than getting it bloody and hole-y. That's why I had brought backup. But the night was young. And I never counted my chickens before they hatched.

Especially when hunting vampires.

But I'll get to that in a minute.

Right *now*, I was getting ready to do something marginally dangerous, and even with accomplices to watch my back, I wasn't quite ready to strap on my big boy pants. I was stalling.

I was here – hopefully – to save some lives. The victims didn't have Batman coming down to save them, or even the fine police persons of St. Louis. None of those upstanding people knew anyone was in danger down here, or would have even believed the intel that had led me here: a Greek hero gossiping at the bar over a beer. And all those victims had for protection was one scraggly wizard, a disgraced werewolf FBI Agent, and a vanilla mortal to come save them.

Now was a brief period of time that was full of choices that would later result in more choices – harder ones – that would lead to penultimate consequences. The *now* part was pretty cut and dried for me. It was the consequences I was thinking about.

This whole mess had all started because of a favor I thought I owed Achilles.

Yes. *The* Achilles. The legendary Greek hero with – what some may call – anger issues.

And when one smashes up his place of business – allegedly – he could be known to display said anger issues by inflicting gratuitous amounts of pain upon the accused.

No thanks.

So, I wanted to make it up to him before the thought even crossed his mind. It wasn't like I could blame the Angel for fluttering into Achilles' bar and picking a fight with Death – one of the Horsemen of the Apocalypse – and I a few months back. Angels were Holy, above the law, beyond reproach, *blah, blah, blah ad nauseam.*

So. Rather than tattling on the pigeon, I had nervously waited months for the chance to earn his gratitude by doing him a solid.

Over drinks at his bar earlier tonight, Achilles had idly mentioned rumors about a vampire kidnapping young girls to bring them down to the sewers, after which they were never heard from again. The most recent disappearance was one of Achilles' own bartenders, and he feared the worst for her.

That was how I found myself in the sewer with my girlfriend and my childhood best friend on a perfectly cold November night. To possibly prevent my sad rear end from being dragged across St. Louis behind Achilles' chariot.

I glanced at my dismal surroundings. Maybe the vampire was just looking to Netflix and chill in his spacious tunnel home. I studied the slick, slimy walls with a look of disgust. No, not a home… a lair. Definitely a lair.

But this was par for the course in my experience. Find bad guy. Exterminate bad guy. Keep young pretty girls safe.

Or avenge them.

It's what we wizards did for a living. Well, most of us. The ones who didn't make millions of dollars per year on interest income from their daddy's technology company.

Ahem.

So maybe I was just doing it for the thrill. The challenge. Or maybe even to do the right thing. I grunted. *Who knows these things?* I asked myself with mild reproach. I shook my head before my inner Freud could psychoanalyze that too much further.

After the *now* comes the *never* part of the phrase. You know, the part where you won't be *here* anymore. The part where all of your family and loved ones have moved on and left you six feet under, while your soul is astral projected to the afterlife. Heaven. Hell. Atlantis. Nirvana. Or on a nice long boat ride with Charon – the chatty drunk, Greek Boatman – who ferried souls on their trip to Hades in his Underworld funhouse.

Been there, done that. It didn't stick.

The point is, you're *dead*, so the consequences of your actions won't be your problem anymore. They will be felt by others, or by no one at all, leaving you with the peace of mind that you did all that you could, that it was worth it. That you made your move. Kissed the girl. Muttered something vaguely English in your speech class.

But you know what's in the middle of *now* and *never*?

Life.

Or in my case, annoying questions that interrupted my well thought out inner philosophical monologue.

"Remind me why we are standing in the literal filth of St. Louis in the middle of November, rather than back at Chateau Falco tipping one back before a roaring fire. Or why I'm here instead of curling up with my fiancée looking at wedding magazines and drinking a glass of wine," Gunnar complained. He lifted his boot with a disgusting squelch, emitting a whole new level of foulness to the brittle air. The dingy environment only seemed to amplify the stunningly royal bearing of my Viking friend. His golden hair was tucked up in a golden man bun, and his beard was impressively thicker than usual, as he had been growing it out for his upcoming wedding. Or so he had told me. I had recently had a nightmare where we were wrestling over a Monopoly argument involving my rapid construction of hotels, and I discovered that he was actually growing the beard out in order to hide a secret guardian inside – a leprechaun-sized werewolf willing and able to defend his master's honor in the event his master lost the wrestling match.

In my dream, I had lost to the violent little bastard.

So far, Gunnar's sniffer hadn't located any vampire scent at all, so I was appointed navigator based upon my eidetic memory of the scant information Achilles had provided.

"Well, if we're speaking of the latter, you should thank me," I muttered.

Indie punched me in the arm, scowling. I shook it off with an idle grin, glad that she had accepted my jibe at surface level. After all, I had been reading over every damned wedding magazine ever printed these past few weeks, which seemed to make my mother deliriously happy.

Yes, even a mother who recently died still went bonkers mad at the topic of gowns and weddings. You just had to find a way to talk to her spirit. Which I had. And she had commanded me to use her engagement ring when I asked Indie to share my life.

Which was the other reason I was down here, and the biggest reason I was stalling.

I was distracted. Conflicted. The vampire part of the trip was secondary in my mind.

Which wasn't good.

But I couldn't seem to shake it. I was going to ask Indie to marry me!

My stomach made a little flip-flop motion at the thought. I shot her a discreet glance, but she was too busy fidgeting with her gear to notice. She was so goddamned beautiful that I found myself simply staring at her at times. Like now. Her long golden hair typically fell past her shoulders to frame her perfectly shaped curvaceous upper body, but tonight it was tied up in a pony-tail and sticking out the back of a Chicago Cubs baseball cap.

The St. Louis Cardinal in me growled territorially at that.

She was about my height, a hair under six-feet tall, with legs for days, and curves that most men would drool over. Her face was narrow with a thin nose and icy blue eyes like sun-kissed sapphires. I averted my eyes as she glanced up, seeming to notice my attention.

I pretended to scout our path as I mentally ran over my proposal plan. I had made reservations at *Vin de Set*, her favorite French restaurant. Two days from now. I had cleverly used the excuse that we were past due for our regular date night where we usually 'recalibrated' our relationship. We typically did this once or twice per month, but so far it had stretched into month two now without either of us bringing it up.

It might or might not have started as a result of Othello's visit to town a few months back when Indie had been out of town caring for her injured mother. Injured because of my enemies, we later found out. Either way, several events from that visit had created a bit of friction between us. Not because I had been unfaithful – not by *choice*, anyway – but because Othello had openly admitted her ongoing infatuation with me. One that she had secretly harbored since our brief romantic relationship in college several years back.

She had admitted this to Indie. In front of me. Without giving me any warning at all.

Which had required some deft maneuvering on my part, let me tell you.

The two were amicable now, but boy oh boy it had been interesting for a time.

My thoughts drifted back to my dinner plans as Gunnar began sniffing down one of the halls, hoping to catch a whiff of fanger, or Vampire. AKA *eau de corpse*. Indie was still fidgeting with her gear.

Before the dinner proposal, I wanted to see how she handled tonight, because, well, this was my *life*.

Hunting.

At least a big part of my life. And even though she had told me before that she could handle it, I needed to *know* that she could. There's a difference, folks. The proposal details were all set. The venue picked. Dinner dishes and wine already ordered. Her favorite dessert, strawberry short-cake, ordered from a local bakery.

Everything was set.

Well, *almost* everything... Which led me back to my *third* reason for jumping on tonight's opportunity.

Indie readjusted the contraption dominating her cranium, tightening one of the straps so that the headlamp mounted on top didn't jiggle around so much with each movement. Despite me being chock full of power, able to cast a ball of light to float beside us and illuminate the darkness, and Gunnar's near night vision thanks to his werewolf genes, a girl needed to accessorize to feel complete in this world. Practicality and logic be damned. And no man would ever get in the way of accessorizing.

Ever.

Indie looked grim at the unexplained dangers of tonight's extermination – seeing as how I hadn't yet explained it to either of them in depth – but was also conflictingly excited to be included in the boys' club. Even if she was completely mundane – as without magic as a boiled egg – it really didn't seem to bother her. Where Gunnar and I were at the opposite end of the spectrum. Dare I say that Gunnar and I were legen—

Wait for it...

Dary.

Indie and I had been binge-watching *How I Met Your Mother* lately. So, sue me.

I smiled to myself, which only made Gunnar's eyes tighten, as if it confirmed his sneaking suspicion that I was as mad as a hatter.

"We're all mad here," I whispered softly.

"What?" Indie asked, having successfully completed readjusting her straps.

I mumbled nothing in particular, putting my head back in the game.

"Alright, gang. We're hunting an Alucard named Dracula," I answered distractedly, focusing my ears towards the two tunnels that branched off ahead of us. One of them led to our target. The other led to more smelly things and my third reason for entering the sewers tonight.

"Are you drunk?" Gunnar asked, very seriously. Indie blinked, having not been around me for the past few hours and realizing that it could very possibly be a valid question.

"What? No. I'm not… I had one drink with Achilles, but…"

"You just keep staring off into the distance as if distracted. And you're not making any sense. It's… unsettling." He folded his arms.

"Yeah, sorry about that. Few other things on my mind."

He waited. And I realized what else was bothering him as I replayed our conversation in my head. "Oh. I see what you're getting at. I meant to say *a Dracula named Alucard.*" They stared at me, still not getting it. I rolled my eyes at Gunnar. "A vampire. The name *Alucard* is *Dracula* spelled backwards, you uneducated mutt," I turned to Indie, "and beautiful, intelligent lady."

Indie rolled her eyes. The silence grew before Gunnar finally let out a soft chuckle. "He seriously named himself *Alucard*? Does he have any idea how pretentious that is, or is it really his name?" He grinned hungrily. "I think I should ask him," he added, flexing his muscles. Or maybe he *hadn't* flexed. Regardless, his coat stretched along the seams of his arms and shoulders with a slight creaking sound.

"You're right. We should ask him. Word from Achilles is that he's kidnapped some girls. One of them was his. A bartender. I'm here to see if it's true. You two are here as witnesses. Especially you, Indie. No heroics. I'm serious. If he really is a vampire, stand back. Gunnar and I will handle it." She nodded her agreement, breath quickening slightly.

I consulted the mental map Achilles had shown me and took a left.

My posse followed me.

Which was good. A Posse is supposed to do that sort of thing. It messed up the cool factor when they didn't.

We continued on for fifteen minutes or so until I began to hear faint whimpers coming from what sounded like only a dozen feet away. Still, with echoes it could be a mile. Gunnar took a big whiff of the air and nodded at me one time, looking suddenly relieved. Apparently, his sniffer was back on track. Or the vampire's apparent concealment spell didn't work this close up.

"Not far now. A few hundred feet at most," he whispered. "Won't they be able to sense us?"

I shook my head, mentally checking our map. "No. I masked our scent." There were two bends before any kind of opening that could house what might be used as living quarters.

I rolled my shoulders and patted my hip reassuringly.

Magic was suave and all, but I hadn't really mastered my new abilities yet. A few months back during *Mardi Gras* when my friends had been out of town, Othello and I had had a run in with Heaven. And Hell. And my previous governing institution, the Academy – which ruled and dictated the laws of the wizard nation. They had thought I was working for the demons. Heaven thought so too. I hadn't been, of course. But everyone and their mother wanted to get their grubby hands on the secret project my father had gifted to me prior to his death. An Armory of the deadliest supernatural weapons in recorded history.

During the struggle, my own people had taken away my magic, permanently, but my father had given me something else along with the Armory. A new, strange power that had historically been placed higher on the food chain than even a wizard's magic. To be honest, even months later, I was still struggling to wrap my head around it.

So, having not mastered my new abilities as a Maker, I liked to be reassured by the hundred-pound gun at my hip. Not really a hundred pounds, but the SIG Sauer X-Five Gunnar had given me a while back was definitely reassuring, and right now it really did feel like a hundred pounds of confidence.

"Alright, gang. It's now or never."

I lifted my foot to take a step, and a silver ball of light – I somehow had the presence of mind to notice that it resembled a stunningly attractive, anatomically correct, naked *Barbie* doll – struck me in the dome, knocking me clear on my ass and into a puddle of nastiness. I quickly scrambled to my feet, shivering, ready to obliterate the creature. She hovered where my head had been, staring directly at me. It *was* a naked Barbie.

And I recognized her.

"She looks familiar..." Gunnar murmured to Indie, who was staring wide-eyed at the silver sprite.

"What *is* she?" Indie asked bluntly, cocking her head sideways as she assessed the creature. "She's beautiful."

"A sprite. A fairy. A very dangerous fairy. Looks can be deceiving," I warned, shaking the cold sewage off my coat.

The sprite smiled in approval at the warning, flashing needle-like teeth at Indie, who flinched back a step. "He's back, and he's coming to murder you and all your friends," the glowing sprite hissed darkly to me. "It's time."

Like I said, a lot can happen between *now* and *never*...

∼

*G*et the full book online!

MAKE A DIFFERENCE

Reviews are the most powerful tools in my arsenal when it comes to getting attention for my books. Much as I'd like to, I don't have the financial muscle of a New York publisher.

But I do have something much more powerful and effective than that, and it's something that those publishers would kill to get their hands on.

A committed and loyal bunch of readers.

Honest reviews of my books help bring them to the attention of other readers.

If you've enjoyed this book, I would be very grateful if you could spend just five minutes leaving a review (it can be as short as you like) on my book's Amazon page.

Thank you very much in advance.

ACKNOWLEDGMENTS

First, I would like to thank my beta-readers, TEAM TEMPLE, those individuals who spent hours of their time to read, and re-re-read Nate's story. Your dark, twisted, cunning sense of humor makes me feel right at home... I also couldn't have done this on time without Carol T's incredible editing services.

I would also like to thank you, the reader. I hope you enjoyed reading *BLOOD DEBTS* as much as I enjoyed writing it. 2 more Nate Temple Novels, 3 Nate Temple Novellas, and book 2 in my new bestselling Feathers and Fire urban fantasy series are coming in 2017...

And last, but definitely not least, I thank my wife, Lexy. Without your support, none of this would have been possible.

ABOUT SHAYNE

Shayne is a man of mystery and power, whose power is exceeded only by his mystery...

He currently writes the Amazon Bestselling Nate Temple Series, which features a foul-mouthed wizard from St. Louis. He rides a bloodthirsty unicorn, drinks with Achilles, and is pals with the Four Horsemen.

He also writes the Amazon Bestselling Feathers and Fire Series about a rookie spell-slinger named Callie Penrose who works for the Vatican in Kansas City. Her problem? Hell seems to know more about her past than she does.

Shayne holds two high-ranking black belts, and can be found writing in a coffee shop, cackling madly into his computer screen while pounding shots of espresso. He's hard at work on WILD SIDE - book 7 of the Nate Temple Series - coming September 2017, as well as RAGE - book 2 in the Feathers and Fire series for October 2017. **Connect with him online for all sorts of groovy goodies:**

Get Down with Shayne Online
www.shaynesilvers.com
info@shaynesilvers.com

ALSO BY SHAYNE SILVERS

NATE TEMPLE SUPERNATURAL THRILLER SERIES

OBSIDIAN SON

BLOOD DEBTS

FAIRY TALE - *FREE for joining my Readers Group*

GRIMM

SILVER TONGUE

BEAST MASTER

TINY GODS

WILD SIDE (#7) - *COMING SEPT. 1, 2017...*

FEATHERS AND FIRE SERIES

UNCHAINED - *Turn the page to read a sample chapter...*

RAGE (#2) - *COMING OCT. 10, 2017...*

UNCHAINED (FEATHERS AND FIRE #1)

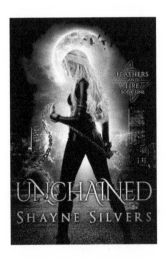

*T*he rain pelted my hair, plastering loose strands of it to my forehead as I panted, eyes darting from tree to tree, terrified of each shifting branch, splash of water, and whistle of wind slipping through the nightscape around us. But... I was somewhat *excited*, too.

Somewhat.

"Easy, girl. All will be well," the big man creeping just ahead of me, murmured.

"You said we were going to get ice cream!" I hissed at him, failing to compose myself, but careful to keep my voice low and my eyes alert. "I'm not ready for this!" I had been trained to fight, with my hands, with weapons, and with my magic. But I had never taken an active role in a hunt before. I'd always been the getaway driver for my mentor.

The man grunted, grey eyes scanning the trees as he slipped through the tall grass. "And did we not get ice cream before coming here? Because I think I see some in your hair."

"You know what I mean, Roland. You tricked me." I checked the tips of my loose hair, saw nothing, and scowled at his back.

"The Lord does not give us a greater burden than we can shoulder."

I muttered dark things under my breath, wiping the water from my eyes. Again. My new shirt was going to be ruined. Silk never fared well in the rain. My choice of shoes wasn't much better. Boots, yes, but distressed, *fashionable* boots. Not work boots designed for the rain and mud. Definitely not monster hunting boots for our evening excursion through one of Kansas City's wooded parks. I realized I was forcibly distracting myself, keeping my mind busy with mundane thoughts to avoid my very real anxiety. Because whenever I grew nervous, an imagined nightmare always—

A church looming before me. Rain pouring down. Night sky and a glowing moon overhead. I was all alone. Crying on the cold, stone steps, and infant in a cardboard box—

I forced the nightmare away, breathing heavily. "You know I hate it when you talk like that," I whispered to him, trying to regain my composure. I wasn't angry with him, but was growing increasingly uncomfortable with our situation after my brief flashback of fear.

"Doesn't mean it shouldn't be said," he said kindly. "I think we're close. Be alert. Remember your training. Banish your fears. I am here. And the Lord is here. He always is."

So, he had noticed my sudden anxiety. "Maybe I should just go back to the car. I know I've trained, but I really don't think—"

A shape of fur, fangs, and claws launched from the shadows towards me, cutting off my words as it snarled, thirsty for my blood.

And my nightmare slipped back into my thoughts like a veiled assassin, a wraith hoping to hold me still for the monster to eat. I froze, unable to move. Twin sticks of power abruptly erupted into being in my clenched fists, but my fear swamped me with that stupid nightmare, the sticks held at my side, useless to save me.

Right before the beast's claws reached me, it grunted as something batted it from the air, sending it flying sideways. It struck a tree with another grunt and an angry whine of pain.

I fell to my knees right into a puddle, arms shaking, breathing fast.

My sticks crackled in the rain like live cattle prods, except their entire length was the electrical section — at least to anyone other than me. I could hold them without pain.

Magic was a part of me, coursing through my veins whether I wanted it or not, and Roland had spent many years teaching me how to master it. But I had never been able to fully master the nightmare inside me, and in moments of fear, it always won, overriding my training.

The fact that I had resorted to weapons — like the ones he had trained me with — rather than a burst of flame, was startling. It was good in the fact that my body's reflexes knew enough to call up a defense even without my direct command, but bad in the fact that it was the worst form of defense for the situation presented. I could have very easily done as Roland did, and hurt it from a distance. But I hadn't. Because of my stupid block.

Roland placed a calloused palm on my shoulder, and I flinched. "Easy, see? I am here." But he did frown at my choice of weapons, the reprimand silent but loud in my mind. I let out a shaky breath, forcing my fear back down. It was all in my head, but still, it wasn't easy. Fear could be like that.

I focused on Roland's implied lesson. Close combat weapons — even magically-powered ones — were for last resorts. I averted my eyes in very real shame. I knew these things. He didn't even need to tell me them. But when that damned nightmare caught hold of me, all my training went out the window. It haunted me like a shadow, waiting for moments just like this, as if trying to kill me. A form of psychological suicide? But it was why I constantly refused to join Roland on his hunts. He knew about it. And although he was trying to help me overcome that fear, he never pressed too hard.

Rain continued to sizzle as it struck my batons. I didn't let them go, using them as a totem to build my confidence back up. I slowly lifted my eyes to nod at him as I climbed back to my feet.

That's when I saw the second set of eyes in the shadows, right before they flew out of the darkness towards Roland's back. I threw one of my batons and missed, but that pretty much let Roland know that an unfriendly was behind him. Either that or I had just failed to murder my mentor at point-blank range. He whirled to confront the monster, expecting another aerial assault as he unleashed a ball of fire that splashed over the tree at chest height, washing the trunk in blue flames. But this monster was tricky. It hadn't planned on tackling Roland, but had merely jumped out of the darkness to get closer, no doubt learning from its fallen comrade, who still lay unmoving against the tree behind me.

His coat shone like midnight clouds with hints of lightning flashing in the depths of thick, wiry fur. The coat of dew dotting his fur reflected the moonlight, giving him a faint sheen as if covered in fresh oil. He was tall, easily hip height at the shoulder, and barrel chested, his rump much leaner than the rest of his body. He — I assumed male from the long, thick mane around his neck — had a very long snout, much longer and wider than any werewolf I had ever seen. Amazingly, and beyond my control, I realized he was beautiful.

But most of the natural world's lethal hunters were beautiful.

He landed in a wet puddle a pace in front of Roland, juked to the right, and then to the left, racing past the big man, biting into his hamstrings on his way by.

A wash of anger rolled over me at seeing my mentor injured, dousing my fear, and I swung my baton down as hard as I could. It struck the beast in the rump as it tried to dart back to cover — a typical wolf tactic. My blow singed his hair and shattered bone. The creature collapsed into a puddle of mud with a yelp, instinctively snapping his jaws over his shoulder to bite whatever had hit him.

I let him. But mostly out of dumb luck as I heard Roland hiss in pain, falling to the ground.

The monster's jaws clamped around my baton, and there was an immediate explosion of teeth and blood that sent him flying several feet away into the tall brush, yipping, screaming, and staggering. Before he slipped out of sight, I noticed that his lower jaw was simply *gone*, from the contact of his saliva on my electrified magical batons. Then he managed to limp into the woods with more pitiful yowls, but I had no mind to chase him. Roland — that titan of a man, my mentor — was hurt. I could smell copper in the air, and knew we had to get out of here. Fast. Because we had anticipated only one of the monsters. But there had been two of them, and they hadn't been the run-of-the-mill werewolves we had been warned about. If there were two, perhaps there were more. And they were evidently the prehistoric cousin of any werewolf I had ever seen or read about.

Roland hissed again as he stared down at his leg, growling with both pain and anger. My eyes darted back to the first monster, wary of another attack. It *almost* looked like a werewolf, but bigger. Much bigger. He didn't move, but I saw he was breathing. He had a notch in his right ear and a jagged scar on his long snout. Part of me wanted to go over to him and torture him. Slowly. Use his pain to finally drown my nightmare, my fear. The fear that had caused Roland's injury. My lack of inner-strength had not only put me in danger, but had hurt my mentor, my friend.

I shivered, forcing the thought away. That was *cold*. Not me. Sure, I was no stranger to fighting, but that had always been in a ring. Practicing. Sparring. Never life or death.

But I suddenly realized something very dark about myself in the chill, rainy night. Although I was terrified, I felt a deep ocean of anger manifest inside me, wanting only to dispense justice as I saw fit. To use that rage to battle my own demons. As if feeding one would starve the other, reminding me of the Cherokee Indian Legend Roland had once told me.

An old Cherokee man was teaching his grandson about life. "A fight is going on inside me," he told the boy. "It is a terrible fight between two wolves. One is evil — he is anger, envy, sorrow, regret, greed, arrogance, self-pity, guilt, resentment, inferiority, lies, false pride, superiority, and ego." After a few moments to make sure he had the boy's undivided attention, he continued.

"The other wolf is good — he is joy, peace, love, hope, serenity, humility, kindness, benevolence, empathy, generosity, truth, compassion, and faith. The same fight is going on inside of you, boy, and inside of every other person, too."

The grandson thought about this for a few minutes before replying. "Which wolf will win?"

The old Cherokee man simply said, "The one you feed, boy. The one you feed..."
And I felt like feeding one of my wolves today, by killing this one...

*G**et the full book TODAY! Book 2 releases late 2017...*

CPSIA information can be obtained
at www.ICGtesting.com
Printed in the USA
LVHW110956190519
618377LV00005B/45/P